Fairy Tale Road

CHOOSE YOUR HAPPILY EVER AFTER SERIES

CHRISTINA FARLEY

Published by Everbound Press

Library of Congress Control Number: 2025911440

www.ChristinaFarley.com

Cover: Books and Moods

ASIN: B0F4KYPH9L

ISBN (paperback): 979-8-9864624-9-3

To Janice Hardy, for believing in this book before a single word was written.

CHAPTER 1

Stay on the Path

I've always believed someday I'd get my happily ever after. But as I stare at the text from my boyfriend Hunter, I'm beginning to wonder if that's just in fairy tales.

> Hunter: The best lead on a house in Daytona popped up. Got to jump on this one. I'm going to miss your talk. Sorry!

Those words churn a swirl of emotions through me. Anger, sadness, loneliness. Or maybe it's just the fact that he never puts me first.

Don't get me wrong, Hunter has a lot of great qualities. Hard worker, responsible, and a smile that warms my heart.

But sometimes it feels like our relationship is built off what-ifs rather than a deep commitment. He's been working so hard to build a future for us by renovating and then flipping houses that he hasn't had time for me. Will that ever change? Because in the past few months I've started to feel like I'm always second in his life.

I text him back:

You promised you'd be here for this.

"Scarlett!" The stage assistant calls my name, bustling over to me with a mic. "Let's get you wired up. You're on next."

My attention snaps from my phone, and I allow her to clip the mic to the lapel of my pantsuit.

"Thanks for your help," I say, yanking my long red hair out of the way so the wire doesn't tangle in my curls.

"There. You're all set to go," she says as she pins on the battery pack at my waist. "Once Trevor is finished speaking, you'll walk out on the path to that big circle in the center of the stage. Your presentation will be on the screen behind you."

"You're the best." I force a bright smile.

"Oh! And to turn your mic on, push this button here." She points to it on the battery pack. "Red is off, green is good to go."

"Green means go. Got it."

"Good luck! We're so excited to have you as our keynote today."

She rushes off, leaving me to pace the backstage area while a knot forms in the pit of my stomach. *I need to calm down*, I tell myself as I sit on my stool. How can I speak to thousands of people when I'm feeling like this? In fact, I'm probably making a big thing out of nothing about Hunter.

Except a voice in the back of my mind warns me: *He never keeps his promises.*

No, it's probably just nerves. I mean, this is my first keynote. It still feels surreal to see my name splashed on the banners around the convention center. Scarlett Walker, successful marketer bringing innovative strategies to the world. I've been working so hard for this moment, and I can't let my relationship fears get in the way of my career. It sure hasn't stopped Hunter. He always chooses his career first.

"You're on in five minutes," one of the stagehands alerts me.

"Sounds good." I wipe the trickle of sweat beading on my forehead and rise off my stool just as a guy comes barreling around the corner with a large, fake evergreen tree. Hard plastic branches smack me in the face, and the full force of the tree collides against me. It knocks me sideways, sending me smashing against the wall.

"Watch where you're going!" I call to his back as he hurries away.

I rub my cheek where the branches scratched my face. Even my hip is a little sore. But right now, what really is hurting is my heart as I stare at Hunter's text. This isn't the first time he's bailed on me. He missed our one-year anniversary dinner because he had to meet with his contractor. I waited at the restaurant for thirty minutes before he remembered to call. He never showed up for my work party last week like he promised. And I still don't think he ever realized he forgot my birthday.

My phone buzzes, and I nearly drop it. It's Hunter.

"Hey," I say.

"Scar?" Hunter says. I cringe. How many times have I asked him not to call me Scar? "How did your little talk go?"

All my composure scatters at his choice of words. It's as if a container of marbles that I've kept the lid tightly on for the last year popped open and burst out in a chaos of bouncing balls. I don't know which one to catch first.

"*Little* talk?" I ask. "This is not a *little* talk. It's a keynote to one of the most prestigious marketing conferences in the country."

"You're right," he says with an annoyed sigh. "I shouldn't

have said little. It's a big deal. I know."

"No, you don't know," I whisper into the phone as I turn to face the wall. A few backstage workers glance in my direction. "Because if you understood how important this was to me, if you cared or loved me, you'd be here in this audience. You wouldn't have promised to come and then not shown up."

"I'm literally driving all the way to Daytona Beach to build a future for us."

"But are you building *our* future? Or are you building *your* future? It's always about your house hunting. Your fixer-upper. Your sale. When is our relationship going to be about us?"

Someone taps me on the shoulder, but I wave them off. My emotions are gushing out like storm waves. For the last year of our relationship, I've been bottling them up, keeping them firmly behind a solid wall. But that wall just crumbled. The dam is broken, and the flood of emotions rushes through.

"You're one to talk," Hunter snaps. "You and your five-year plan. You're so goal-driven that you can't deter from your career path. You work, eat, work some more, and then go to bed because you're too worn out to be spontaneous. Would it kill you to have some fun?"

"I can have fun. I can deter from the path and be spontaneous."

He laughs as if I've just said the funniest joke ever. "Scarlett. We both know that you're not changing."

More tapping on my shoulder. The stage assistant waves her hand in a slicing motion over her throat.

Crap. It's time for me to speak.

"Do you love me, Hunter?" I press. "If you had to choose me or your house hunting, which would you choose?"

"Why do I have to choose? Where is this all coming from?"

Panic builds in my chest. "Listen," I say. "I've got to go and do my *little* talk. Don't bother calling back, because it's over between us. Now you won't have to worry about choosing me over your houses. We're done."

I hang up. The assistant is saying something to me, but there's a buzzing in my ears and the backstage swims just a little. I'm so upset. So mad.

But mostly heartbroken.

I thought he loved me. I thought we had a chance to make it as a couple. I march out onto the stage. Bright lights beam down on me, but all I can think about are Hunter's words.

Why do I have to choose?

Anger fuels my gait as I stride out onto the stage in my high heels. I follow the giant stickers that spell out "Success" created to symbolize the conference name: The Path to Success.

The audience fills every seat in the auditorium, thousands of eyes focused on me. As I step into the circle area at the center of the stage, a strange thought hits me.

No one is clapping.

In fact, the faces of the audience are filled with a mix of shock and concern. Which is odd. I glance down at my black suit, wondering if there's a rip in my pants or a button missing on my shirt. But everything seems intact. I plant a smile on my face and go to push the button on my battery pack only to discover it's...already green.

Dread pools in my chest, heavy as stone. I turn to the wings where the stage assistant is biting her nails.

"How long has this been on?" I hiss at her, covering the mic.

"During your whole talk with um...Hunter?" she squeaks out.

Crap, crap, crap! This is bad. Like destroy-your-career and ruin-your-credibility bad. My fair skin is probably as red as my hair right now because the entire audience just heard me break up with my boyfriend.

I turn and face the sea of faces. *Fix this!* I scream to myself. I can't let my career flush down the toilet because of a battery pack.

"Well," I laugh, a bit wobbly, "we've all been there when our vision doesn't match our client's and they break up with us, right?"

The audience chuckles, and the tension in the air releases. I take a deep breath and focus on my presentation, somehow salvaging the talk. But as I point out how to make it in marketing, all I can think about are Hunter's words about how he couldn't choose me over his career. How he sees me as boring and predictable.

Even when pushed, he couldn't say he loved me. It's time for me to move on and start making positive choices for my life. Except deep down I wonder if there's truth to his words.

Maybe I need to break off the course I've set up for myself. Try something new.

Somehow I manage to get through my speech, wave happily at the standing-ovation audience, and stumble off the stage. It's a bad idea, but I torturously check my phone to see if Hunter texted. No word from my now-ex, but I did get one from my sister, Bella.

> Have you ever felt like you got lost in the woods and were hunted by a wolf, eyeing you like a walking snack? Yeah, same. Call me…or send up a flare. Just kidding, but seriously, call me.

I blink. Wolves? Lost in the woods? What is she even talking about? Something is wrong.

CHAPTER 2

Have a Magical Day!

I stare at Bella's message, completely rattled. I need to call her, but not here. I'm desperate to escape all the eyes and even the kind words. My world feels a little off-kilter and can't seem to get grounded as I head down the red-carpeted hallway of the conference center. Everything I've worked for and fought so hard to get suddenly feels meaningless. I'm second-guessing every choice I've made. I shake people's hands who stop to congratulate me and try to smile.

"Great speech, Scarlett," one of my coworkers says. "That five-year plan was solid."

"I don't know who Hunter is," some stranger stops to tell me. "But don't you worry. You didn't need him anyway."

My smile is wavering by the time I get to the lobby. There were some panels I wanted to attend, but right now I just want to go home to Grams and have her make me one of her creamy cups of hot chocolate. Plus, she always knows what to say.

Then I'll call Bella.

"Excuse me, Miss Walker," an elderly woman says, stepping

into my path. Her silver hair is twisted into a bun, and her simple blue dress looks almost medieval with the trimmed-lace edging. A basket dangles on the hook of her arm. "I wanted to congratulate you."

I try to offer a kind smile, but my lips aren't cooperating. I really need to escape the sympathetic faces and concerned looks. "Thank you." I try to sidestep around her, but she blocks my way.

"You entered the raffle for the gift baskets and won!" She beams, trying to give me the basket.

"I think you have me confused with someone else. I didn't enter a raffle."

"Are you sure?" She pulls out a ticket and shows me. My name is written on it.

I blink at my handwriting. "Well, I must have forgotten." Grudgingly I take the basket. "Thank you."

"You are most welcome." She smiles knowingly. "Have a magical day."

"You, too," I say as she disappears, thinking how today has been anything but magical.

I peek into the basket, hoping to find something Grams would like. Inside are three gift cards: Hunter's Homes, Fairy Tale Tours, and Cinematic Studios. They sparkle under the convention center's fluorescent lights. Someone must have thrown glitter into the baskets to make them seem extra special.

I pick up the Hunter's Homes card, glaring at it. *You've got to be kidding me.*

I roll my eyes. Hunter must have donated these to the convention. His way of being supportive, but really he was just schmoozing his own business. I toss it in the garbage and head for the exit.

"Great speech, sis," a distant voice calls to me.

I jerk to a halt and spin at the sound of my sister's voice. Bella is standing in the center of the lobby, clutching her suitcase. She looks completely out of place among the swarm of suits in her blue floral dress that brushes the top of her brown ankle boots. Her auburn hair has the same curls as mine, but today they're tangled and wild like a bird's nest.

She's a wildflower amidst a sea of gray and black suits.

"Bella?" I throw my arms around her tiny frame. She was always the petite one, and I was the stronger one who protected her. But as I hug her body, she feels thinner. Frailer. "What are you doing here? You're supposed to be in Germany!"

"I wanted to surprise you and watch your big presentation." She throws on a smile, but it doesn't reach her turquoise eyes. Worry ghosts up my spine. "I caught the last half and it was very...practical."

Something happened. She'd never have left her fairytale trip otherwise.

"I got your text. What's going on? I thought you were extending your tour with your hot tour guide."

"There's no hot tour guide. Only an asshole tour guide."

"Bella! What happened?"

"You love Hunter, right?" she continues. The desperation in her voice makes my stomach sour. "Like you know he'd never leave or hurt you. That he would be there for you no matter what. Right?"

My suit feels itchy and hot. "He hurt you, didn't he?" I ask softly.

"I just want to go home."

"Then home it is." I take her suitcase. "Also, thank you for coming to my presentation. You're the best sister I could ever hope for." I hook my free arm through hers. She clings to me, nodding with a faint smile like I'm her lifeline. "We'll have some hot chocolate and cake, and you can tell me all about your trip and that villain of a tour guide."

CHAPTER 3

Take Down the Big Bad Wolf

Grams's house is a tiny white cottage on the outskirts of Orlando. Our parents died in a car crash when I was four and Bella was three. Grams took us in, and she's been like our mom ever since. When I pull into the driveway, Bella's face crumbles and tears begin to stream down her face.

"You okay?" I ask quietly, reaching over and squeezing her hand.

She shakes her head and then pulls away from me. She darts out of the car, rushing down the front walk lined with flowers and barrels into the house. I frown and tap my fingers on the steering wheel, trying to make sense of everything. Whatever happened in Germany was not good. I'm going to get to the bottom of this.

I lug her suitcase out of the car, honestly glad for Bella and her distraction. The last thing I want to think about is Hunter. Besides, it will be a good excuse for me to be coming home early from the convention.

By the time I enter, Grams is already banging about in the

kitchen. She steps out to meet me, lines stretching across her forehead.

"Whatever happened?" Grams asks, tucking on her apron. "Why is Bella back from her trip so early? I tried to ask her but she just ran into her bedroom and locked the door."

Throughout our whole childhood, whenever either of us had what we called a 911, Grams would whip up something sweet to get us through it all. And today is no different. Just seeing her white curls framing her face and her determination to make everything right calms my racing heart.

"I'm not sure," I say, squeezing her cool hand. "But I do know this is the best place for her to be at when she's hurting."

"You got that right! Now go find out what's the matter with your sister while I whip up some of her favorite apple cake."

I park Bella's suitcase outside of her door and knock once and then three times. Our secret code we created before I can remember.

"I don't want to talk about it," Bella calls out.

"Okay." I lean against the door. "If you change your—"

The door flies open and I stumble, nearly falling over.

"He's the worst," she announces.

"Oh!" I lift my eyebrows. "Are we talking about the German asshole?"

"Language!" Grams calls from the kitchen.

"Yes!" Bella switches to a whisper. "Total douchbag."

"What happened? I thought he was the hot, sexy tour guide."

"He was!" She throws her hands up and storms out into the living room. "Until he wasn't."

"What did he do to you? Do I need to chop off his limbs or his favorite private part?"

Bella gives a strangled laugh. She starts pacing in front of the TV, wringing her hands. "It had been a fairy tale. That tour I took was so perfect, so amazing, and so romantic. How could I not fall in love?"

"You fell in love?" Grams calls through the kitchen passthrough. "During the tour? You were there less than two weeks! Sounds fishy."

"He seemed perfect," Bella continues. "Kind, generous, and everything a girl could want in a guy. Plus, he's drop-dead gorgeous." She digs out her phone. "Here, I have a picture of him."

She shows me a picture of the two of them. A guy with light-brown hair and a close-cut beard has his arms wrapped around her as she leans against his chest. So what if he might be poster-worthy with those piercing blue eyes and chiseled features? I hate him already.

"Any guy who tries to destroy my sister's heart is a beast," I announce. "Grams, tell me this dude isn't beastly."

Grams bustles out with two steaming cups of hot chocolate, piled high with marshmallows. She hands them to us and then peeks at the photo. Her eyebrows rise.

"He's definitely not good enough for my Bella." She throws me a worried look.

Yup. This is not good at all.

"So what exactly did this dickwad do to you?" I ask.

"I said no foul language!" Grams fists her hips. She's usually not so uptight, but I get it. Seeing our sweet, carefree Bella like this has got us all wound up like a spring.

"Sorry, Grams," I say.

"Well, we started spending a lot of time together." Bella twists her mug in her palms. Then he kissed me and said he loved me. I told him I loved him, too. And then..."

"And then?" Both Grams and I lean forward.

"One day he appeared at my cottage and said he didn't love me and couldn't be with me and it was all a lie! Then he left."

"The as—troturf!" I yell.

"What do you mean he left?" Grams asks, face burning red.

"He just took off. Left our whole tour group without a guide. We didn't know what to do or where to go next. We were completely stranded. Everyone was upset, but I didn't care. I just wanted to get out of the country as fast as I could."

While I want to fly directly to that country and rip this guy apart.

"Drink your hot chocolate," Grams orders Bella and then turns to me. "You need to deal with this guy."

"What's his name?" I ask.

"Karl," Bella says in a choking voice as if just saying his name pains her. "Karl Wolfe."

"Wolfe?" I snort. "His last name is Wolfe. Figures."

I set my hot chocolate down and march to the computer, logging in. "Don't you worry. I'm going to take care of this guy. I'm going to leave a scathing review of this company. What's the name of the company? I'll email the owner."

"Fairy Tale Tours."

"Wait a second. That name sounds familiar." I dart to the basket and pull out the gift card. It sparkles in my hand. Sure enough, it's the same tour company as the one Bella went to. Coincidental? Maybe, but I don't have time to worry about that. I toss it on the desk. Right now, my sister needs justice.

My fingers fly over the keyboard, anger punching at each key as I email my complaint. "Oh! And I'll file a sexual harassment report to the labor division in Germany."

But once I finished, I still feel incomplete. Anger churns inside me. How could this guy use and abuse my sister? He needs to pay. My mind flicks to Hunter and how he dismissed our one-year relationship so quickly. Are all men selfish pricks?

I scan the Fairy Tale Tours website. It's packed full of pictures of thick woods, castles, and spreads of German food. My marketing brain takes over.

"This company's website really could use a makeover," I mutter. "The jerk's website is as outdated as Karl's ideas on women. Plus, they've got zero branding, the flow of their site makes no sense, and their images are obviously twenty years old."

"Who cares about their website?" Grams settles on the couch and tucks a crying Bella against her. "Find a way to shut them down. If this man did this to our Bella, who will be his next victim? Probably does this on every tour."

My eyes widen in horror. "Maybe he's a serial heartbreaker. I bet Bella is just one of many woman whose life he's destroyed. He needs to be stopped." I drum my fingers on the table, and my eye flicks to the gift card. A plan forms in my mind. "What Mr. Wolfe needs is a play from his own playbook. He needs to feel what it's like to lose something you love."

My mind flashes to Hunter's and my conversation.

If you had to choose me or your house hunting, which would you choose?

Why do I have to choose?

But he went to Daytona, which meant he did choose. And it was his first love: his job.

"Based on what you've told me," I continue, "his first love is his tour company. Which means, we're going to take it down. Piece by piece."

"How are you going to do that?" Bella sniffs and takes the tissue Grams hands her and blows hard. "The company is all the way in Germany."

"I'm going to go on that tour and sabotage it from within. And maybe use their own money to do the deed." I spin back around and grab the gift card. Before I even stop to think about what I'm doing, I click BOOK NOW. "Now who's fun and spontaneous, Hunter?"

"What does Hunter have to do with this?" Bella asks.

"Hunter and I broke up today," I admit quickly. "There. I've booked a tour for next Monday using their own gift card. Now to book my flight."

Bella leaps off the couch. "Woah. No, no, no. You don't get to skid by like that and expect us to ignore what you just said. I've been expecting an engagement any day now. What do you mean you broke up, and why are you going to Germany? You have your job. You can't just leave!"

"Hunter is a jerk because he puts his own selfish needs first." *Ugh.* Why are tears pricking at my eyes? "But don't worry about me. What we are worrying about is you and making sure Hunter...I mean Mr. Wolfe pays for what he's done to you."

I plaster on a bright expression, but they are both frowning, clearly not happy with my diabolical plan. "Why are you looking at me like that? This is good. Going to Germany will be the perfect way to fix everything. I've got weeks of vacation time saved up anyway."

I tried to shove confidence in my words. Bella's eyes are laser-focused on mine, her mouth dipping into a frown.

"Forget about me and forget about the Germany jerk," she says "Let's talk about you and Hunter."

I open my mouth just as the doorbell rings. I let out a breath of relief that I can avoid all conversation about the breakup. "I'll get it!"

I open the door only to freeze. There, standing before me, is Hunter himself. His dark black hair and brown skin accent against a tight white polo shirt. A whiff of his musk-scented cologne wafts past me, and his large brown eyes are giving me the "puppy-dog, I'm-sorry" look.

"I'm here to make things right with you." He holds out a bouquet of red roses and a to-go bag from Chaloli's, my favorite restaurant. "Will you give me a chance to properly apologize?"

My mind whirls, confusion reigning supreme. What should I do?

Do I let him inside and listen to what he has to say?

Or move on and stop another selfish jerk from breaking more hearts?

Option A: If you think she should let Hunter inside and hear what he has to say, continue to Chapter 4.

Option B: If you think she should say goodbye to Hunter and go to Germany, skip to Chapter 6.

Giving Hunter a Chance

"Hunter," I say in confusion. "What are you doing here?"

"Hey." He gives me a sheepish look and holds out the roses. Reluctantly, I take them. "I came to apologize for everything. What you said got me thinking. You had some good points, and you know, I was being a real jerk. I turned the car around because I realized if I have to choose, I want to choose you."

"Wow." I step back in shock. I had not expected those words from him. Is it bad that I'm surprised? I can't remember a time he's ever apologized for anything. It always bothered me, but I figured it's his way of dealing with things. Hearing him say this is a step in the right direction. He's putting forth the effort to place me first. "I don't know what to say. I appreciate the apology though."

"Can I come in?"

I open the door wider, and he steps inside but pauses when Bella rounds up on him, her eyes darting from the items in his hands to his face.

"Hey, Bella," he says. "I thought you were in Germany."

"Why are you coming in loaded with gifts?" she growls. Mascara streaks down her face, and her hair is wild as a witch mid-curse. "You think you can just waltz in with a few pretty flowers and food and think that can make up for being an asshole?"

"No." He hangs his head. "I don't know what I was thinking. And I want to make this right."

"I've been thinking, too," I admit. "I'm not sure we're right for each other."

Hunter blanches. "Please, Scarlett. Our relationship might not be perfect, but couples fight. We can fight through this."

"I think us two sisters need to go have a talk." Bella grabs my hand and drags me into my room, shutting the door behind her and locking it. "I see what you're doing—trying to avoid making this be about you—but you're not getting away with it. What really happened? Why did you break up with Hunter?"

I heave in a sigh and sag into my soft, cream-colored chair where I like to curl up and read at night.

"I know it's petty," I say. "But I feel like with our relationship, we're a couple of convenience. Like we get together when we're both free. And it works because both of us have demanding jobs, so we don't demand much from each other."

"I thought that's what you liked about him. That he's successful and has goals."

"I do, and our relationship makes sense in my head and on paper. We both like hockey so we can watch our favorite matches together. We both eat healthy food, exercise at the same time of the day, and plan out our shopping lists one month in advance so we can shop at Costco and save money."

"So boring." Bella scrunches her nose. "I never understood that."

"I thought it worked. Except maybe it doesn't."

She squeezes her tiny frame into the chair beside me and wraps her arm around my body. It's something we've done ever since we were little girls. Maybe it's the fact that we lost our parents at a young age and we needed that bond. Whatever it is, my heartbeat slows into a steady rhythm having her close.

"I don't know if what I feel for Hunter is actually love," I say. "You know the butterflies and sparks people talk about? The shivers when the one you love touches you? I've never felt that. I just assumed it was a *me* thing. But what if it's a *Hunter and me* thing? Does that even make sense?"

"One hundred percent."

I'm about to tread into dangerous waters with Bella's fragile heart, but I have to ask. "Did you feel those things with that Wolfe guy?"

"Yeah," she whispers, and tears creep into the corners of her eyes. "I did. And I think it broke my heart."

I pass her a tissue as she starts crying harder. Crap. I shouldn't have mentioned it.

I squeeze her tighter. "I wish I could mend your heart. But maybe I can at least make things right if I go to Germany. Then you can put him behind you and move on with your life."

"You know you can't go to Germany." She rises and stands before me. "You have your job and your career. Aren't you up for some sort of promotion? What will they say when they find you left the country?"

She's right, except seeing her broken and destroyed by his despicable Wolfe guy reminds me I absolutely need to go to Germany. "Today the breakup showed me who truly is important in my life. I'm looking at one of those people right now. Besides, my boss can handle things while I'm gone."

The two of us finally exit the room. Grams is sitting on the couch watching Golden Girls.

"I confined the ex-boyfriend in the dining room," she mutters. "I couldn't decide if I should kick him out or take the food and then kick him out."

"Thanks, Grams," I say. "I think I need to talk this out with him."

I duck into the dining room to find Hunter has set the table with two place settings. The flowers adorn the center, and he's laid out the takeout in neat rows. He's lighting a candle when I walk into the room. His face is a mix of desperation and hope when he sees me.

"I am sorry, you know." He fiddles with the lighter. "I shouldn't have hesitated on the phone. I was just surprised. I didn't know where it was coming from."

"I suppose all the things that have been bothering me over the past few months just became too much. The times you didn't show up when you said you would, the broken promises, and not being there when I needed you. I realized this relationship we built wasn't enough for me. I need to be first in my partner's life."

He nods. "What can I do to fix this?"

I can't help but laugh. "Hunter, I'm not one of your houses that you can just fix up. If the bones aren't good, it's always going to have problems. Our bones aren't right for each other because we're always putting each other second."

"Please don't say that." His eyes are shiny, and he reaches for me.

His warm hands wrap around mine, bringing me back to all the moments we had with each other. The midnight brainstorming sessions for my marketing ideas. The Saturdays I'd help him knock down walls for his latest fixer-upper. The times we'd sit in the back of his pick-up truck after a long day working and just stare up at the stars.

He's always been my safety net. Except did I enter a relationship of convenience rather than love?

"Please." He pulls out a chair for me to sit in. "Let's just sit down and make a plan on how to get us back on track. I know together we can work on whatever problem we face. Oh!" He digs through his pocket, withdrawing a gift card. It's sparkly lemon-yellow. The same style as the one in my gift basket. "This is for you."

"A gift card?" I lift my eyebrows. "I saw you gave these out at the convention."

"But this one is special. It's worth whatever you desire. You tell me what you want from it, and I'll make it happen."

"Like a yacht?" I can't help tease. "Beach house?"

He grins. "Well, if that's what you want, but I was thinking more about us. I want to prove to you that I'm willing to work to rebuild our relationship."

I stare at the card, indecision pulling at me. Do I take his card, sit down, and try to rebuild our lives? Or put an end to this forever? And what better way to do that than to jump on a plane and go to Germany?

What should I do?

Option A: If you think she should take Hunter's gift card and sit down with him, continue to Chapter 5.

Option B: Forget Hunter! She should focus on stopping this horrible Mr. Wolfe and go to Germany. Skip to Chapter 6.

Hunter's Offer

"We've been through a lot together," I tell Hunter but don't take the gift card. I know it's just a piece of plastic, but somehow it feels like it means so much more. "And because of that, I'm willing to listen to what you have to say. You're right. A year-long relationship deserves more than just a curt goodbye."

He lets out a long breath of relief, and we both settle into our chairs. Hunter starts opening the to-go containers. Normally, the scent of Chaloli's would chase away my worries, but not tonight. Between the very public breakup on stage and hearing how Bella was treated on her tour, I'm not sure I can stomach food.

"Thank you for listening," he says. "When you broke up with me on the phone, I was shocked. Was it because something happened at the conference, or was it just because I didn't come?"

"Remember our one-year anniversary and you didn't show up?" He grimaces and I continue. "I felt so alone that night, but I told myself it was because you were building something for us. But then lately it has felt like you're always too busy for me, and I'm wondering if what we have is just a really good friendship."

"You are definitely much more than a friend to me." His dark brown eyes search mine. "What can I do to change your mind?"

"I feel like we haven't been prioritizing our relationship." I fidget with the paper napkin. "But maybe that's because deep down we never wanted that too."

"Remember when I said I was going to Daytona to check out a property?" He digs into his briefcase and pulls out a folder. "This is what I was going to see."

I rub my forehead. "This is what I'm talking about. It's always about you and your business."

"Not this time." He grins and flips open the folder. "I wanted it to be a surprise, but this is as good of a time as any. See this beat-up old house? It's falling apart and there's roof damage from the last hurricane but based on these photos it looks like it has potential."

Despite my annoyance, I take the bait and study the picture. He's right. The white walls of the cottage-style house are peeling and the roof sags dramatically on the right side, but the overall structure of the house seems intact. What catches my attention is the location.

My eyes widen. "Is this a beach-front property?"

"Yup. And look at the price." He points to the cost. I gasp.

"Why is it so cheap?"

"That's what I was going to find out when you called. You broke up with me, and I was so upset I just jumped in my car and started driving to the site. But halfway there I realized what was the point of pursuing this place if we weren't together?"

"It's a cute house." I flip through the images of the interior.

"It's going to take more work than your usual project, but I think you could make some good money flipping this one."

"Except I don't want to flip it." He takes my hand. "I want this one to be ours. This place could be our next step. We could buy it, remodel it together, and make it our dream home."

My eyes widen, and a flicker of hope sputters in my chest. "Our dream home?"

"Think about it. You could move out of Grams's house, but you'd still be close enough that you could swing by anytime. In fact, it's close enough, you could drive over and have lunch together. Or she could come visit us, and we could have picnics at the beach."

"She does love picnics."

"We always have fun when we remodel together. Just you, me, and a sledgehammer. We could remodel the bedroom and primary bath first. For, you know, after the long remodeling days. What do you think?"

My heart pounds at what he's offering. A life together in a beautiful new home sounds so great. It's stability and something to look forward to with Hunter. It's what we've always said we wanted, except is it really what *I* want? Or is this just the easy path that I've always taken?

"This is a sweet gesture, and before today I would've seriously considered it," I finally say, "but I can't say yes. Our breakup was traumatic and revealing, and I can't just forget it by thinking about a house on the beach."

"I thought this is what you wanted. A commitment from me. A life with us doing things together."

"I did." I pull my hand away and stare at the cold food. "But today showed me I need to figure out what I really want in a relationship. I'm going to Germany to fix a situation that happened to my sister. I think this time apart and my trip will help give me some clarity and maybe you, too. But get the beach house if you can. You'll make a killing on it."

His shoulders sag in defeat, but he nods slowly. "If you change your mind, I'll be here. I want to prove to you that I'm ready for the next step in our relationship. If I do get the house, I'll work on it, but I won't sell it. I'm still banking on us getting back together. You're everything I want and are worth waiting for. Have fun in Germany. I hope you fix whatever it is that needs fixing."

CHAPTER 6

The Big Bad Wolf

The next week is a whirlwind preparing for an overseas trip on the spur of the moment. Thankfully, my passport is still active after my last work trip to London. By the time I need to say goodbye to Grams and Bella, it feels like it's all happening too fast.

"You don't need to go to Germany to get back at this guy," Bella tells me as I roll my suitcase outside to the Uber waiting to take me to the airport. "I'm fine. Maybe it's best just to forget about the whole thing with Karl Wolfe and move on with my life."

Except Bella isn't fine. Since she's gotten back, I've watched her grow thinner and paler. Seeing my bright and beautiful sister wither away before me only sets my resolve to go after this horrible beast of a man. He will pay for what he's done.

"I should be back before the end of the two-week tour," I tell them. "If all goes well, I'll have his tour company shut down and out of business."

"Good. That man has no place running a tour company,

much less one called Fairy Tale Tours," Grams grumbles. "Who knows how many other women he did the same thing to."

She hands me a pouch. "I made lunch for you to eat. You know how terrible plane food can be. And I bought you this raincoat. I heard Germany can be cold and rainy this time of year."

I tuck the gifts against my chest, smiling at my two favorite people in the world.

"I'm going to miss you both," I tell them.

Bella throws her arms around me in a fierce hug. "Be careful while you're there."

"And watch out for that big bad wolf," Grams warns me as I hug her next. "Keep to your plan and don't fall for any of his devious schemes."

"Don't worry about me," I reassure them. "I've got my path all mapped out. I'll be fine."

A LIGHT BREEZE smelling of flowers kicks across my face as I step out of the taxi into the main downtown section of Hanau, Germany. I clutch my suitcase and take in the charming town, famous for being the childhood home of the Brothers Grimm.

It's quainter than I could've ever imagined. Timber-framed houses rise up on either side of me as I stroll down the cobblestone sidewalk where old-fashioned lanterns dot each street corner. Pink and white flowers spill out of window boxes while cyclists breeze past. It's like stepping into a fairy tale.

I'm instantly in love.

I pull out my phone and set my GPS to the town's central marketplace where the Fairy Tale Tours office is located. My hotel room is not far away, but I'm eager to get a lay of the land

and start planning out the demise of Mr. Wolfe and his precious company. I'll scout out the place first and then check into my hotel.

A quick peek inside my tote reassures me the printouts of the company details are still safe. I pull out the notes I jotted down on my flight of ways to take Mr. Wolfe down thoroughly and methodically.

How to Destroy the Big Bad Wolf

1. Start a protest in the middle of a tour stop.
2. Get us lost.
3. Hide and/or destroy important materials.
4. Tell tour guests outrageous lies. (White lies, of course!)
5. Slash the bus tires so we're stranded. (Bring extra snacks so the tourists won't get hungry.)

This is going to be glorious! I pull out a printed picture of Karl Wolfe just to make sure I get the right guy. I stare at it, nibbling on my bottom lip. Unfortunately, guilt slithers into my heart as I think about the chaos I'm about to ensue.

Is it bad that I want to take revenge on a man who destroyed my sister's heart by ruining him? Maybe. But standing up and fighting for your loved ones no matter what is totally a good thing to do.

Right?

Right.

I shove the list and picture back into my tote. A biting gust of wind whooshes down the street, and I'm glad for the jacket Grams gave me before I left. It's cherry red with large red buttons running down the center and ties to cinch it into a fitted waist show it was designed to be stylish and comfortable. Plus, it's got pockets and an adorable hood.

I tuck the hood over my head and take off down the street. As I trundle along, my stomach rumbles, reminding me I haven't eaten anything other than the sandwich Grams packed. Plus, after telling Hunter we needed time away from each other, I haven't slept or eaten well since.

There's a silent ache in my chest that has lingered since I left Hunter. His face turned white as snow when I'd been adamant about not getting back together. He hasn't tried calling or texting since, and it feels like I just lost my best friend.

Maybe I should call him. Tell him I'm okay?

No. Do not call. Stand firm. I've chosen this new path for my life and I need to see it through.

For Bella's sake.

When I booked this trip, all I could focus on was the anger at what this man did to my sweet sister. But the next morning when I looked at the trip's itinerary, I realized I'd need to take off for two weeks just in case. I thought Shirly, my boss, wouldn't approve it. Sure, she wasn't happy about my sudden two-week vacation request, but she said it wasn't such a bad idea.

"After that public breakup you had," she said, "you need to get away and go have some fun."

I grimace, still remembering her pitying expression. Note to self: never break up with someone in front of a live audience.

A quaint coffee shop called Eiscafe Dolce and Freddo catches my eye. I step under the red and white striped awning and order a coffee and streusel. I pass over the Euros needed and say, "Danke," reminding myself to learn more German phrases. The to-go cup feels blessedly warm in this Florida girl's palm as I take it from the barista. The streusel smells like a present of apples wrapped in cinnamon and caramelized butter.

I turn around, my hunger shoving me into warp speed when I barrel into a tall and very solid man. My coffee catapults from my hand, erupting into the air like a volcano, while my beloved streusel smacks soundly all over the stranger.

I scramble to catch something—anything!—but manage to drop my tote in the process.

"I'm so terribly sorry!" I exclaim, quickly grabbing some napkins and rubbing them across the man's chest—a very firm, muscular one at that. "I didn't see you—"

My words die on my tongue as I look up at his face.

Stormy gray eyes rain down on me, sucking all my air from within and leaving me breathless. A wayward brown curl has fallen across his forehead, and the scruff on his face gives him a rugged, wild look.

I'm taller than average, but his presence is all-consuming. The intensity in his gaze as he takes me in makes me feel as if he could swallow me whole. When his eyes leave mine and he assesses the damage to his charcoal-colored shirt, his thick eyebrows lift.

"Appears as if I've been attacked by Little Red Riding Hood," he says, his accent making the r's sound guttural. The sound travels deliciously all the way to my toes.

"Your shirt. I'm afraid it's ruined." Quickly, I rip out more napkins, but they're tiny, flimsy little squares that don't amount to much. I turn back to the man as he's flicking pastry and apple chunks off his shirt.

This is mortifying!

He chuckles. "I appreciate your assistance, but I can clean myself off."

My face burns, and I step away from him. Of course, he can clean himself off. Also, he smells way too good, like an intoxicating spice that makes it hard to think. Except as I study him more carefully, I decide there's something intensely compelling about him. No. Not compelling, familiar.

And that's when it hits me. He's the Wolfe!

He doesn't quite look like the picture I printed out of him. Probably because he shaved off that beard, but there's no doubt it's still him. The vile mastermind of the destruction of my sister's heart. Also, the very one who is starting to gather up all my tote's evil, wicked, and very incriminating contents from the floor, including my list, "How to Destroy the Big Bad Wolf."

NO!!!!!!

I choke out a gasp and rip the list off the floor just as his fingers are about to reach for it. Quickly, I fold it in half and tuck it safely into my jacket. *See? Pockets. So useful.*

Except, I also forgot about the very large and very damning picture of him that's also lying on the floor. He picks it up and stares at it for a moment.

This is bad. I need to fix the situation immediately or he's going to know that I'm here to hunt him down.

"Quite the picture." He passes it to me, eyes twinkling.

Think of something clever to say!

"I'm so embarrassed." I grab a pen out of my tote. "I'm going on your tour, and I was hoping you'd give me your autograph. Being so famous and all."

I giggle, hoping to sound like a lovesick fan, but I think it comes out more like a choking gurgle. Mr. Wolfe cocks an eyebrow, studying me warily as if he's not quite sure what to do. One of the articles I read online about him said he is incredibly wealthy and the heartthrob of the fairytale fanatics. Some even call him Prince Karl.

"I would be happy to," he says with a grin that shows off perfect white teeth.

He scribbles out a swooshing autograph and hands it back to me. Quickly, I gather up the rest of my tote items, stuffing them into the bag while he steps up to the counter to order. I'm ducking away when I hear him call out.

"Little Red!"

I stop in my tracks, grimacing. He probably recognized me as Bella's sister. Our hair and eye color might be different, but we both have that same straight nose and pale Irish skin.

Slowly, I turn back around to find him jogging up to me.

"You forgot this." He holds out a fresh coffee and an intact steaming streusel. "Can't have my fans go hungry."

Those thick lips of his tip up into a smile that reaches his eyes. My stomach flutters a little as I take the offered gift, but it's probably only because I'm hungry. It has nothing to do with his villainously dashing looks.

"Thanks," I say. "That's really sweet."

But I know your moves, Mister. And you're not going to trick me!

"I suppose I'll see you later then," he says. "During the tour?"

"Oh, yes." Now it's my turn to grin. "I can't wait."

To enact my plan of your downfall.

CHAPTER 7

He's So Cunning and Crafty

"I met him," I announce triumphantly on the phone to my sister. I breeze out of my hotel and head down the cobblestone sidewalk toward the Fairy Tale Tours office.

"Karl?" Bella's voice trembles a little, and I grimace. Maybe I shouldn't have mentioned him.

"Don't worry, he didn't recognize me. And you're right. He's absolutely awful." And sweet. *Ugh.* I roll my eyes, remembering how he got me a fresh coffee and streusel. It's no wonder my sister fell for the douchebag. He's a total con artist!

"He was nice to you, wasn't he." She says this like it's a statement.

"Okay, so he might have been nice, but don't worry, I wasn't fooled."

"Good, because that's his MO. He lures you in with his Prince Charming ways and *bam*! He becomes this horrid beast who rips out your heart and swallows it whole."

Man. The dude really did a number on my sweet sister. I hate that she's become this jaded person when it comes to love.

She's never had a long-term relationship where a guy has treated her well, and it worries me this jerkwad may have ruined her desire for finding love.

"Well, now it's time to lure the wolf in ourselves," I say, trying to keep upbeat as I stroll past a bakery, the scent of warm bread and cinnamon filling the air. "I've got a great plan of action on how to take him down and stop him from doing this to others. Plus, he owes you a proper apology. I think closure will help you move on."

"What exactly is in this plan?" Skepticism tinges her voice.

"Don't you worry about that." Because she would be horrified if she saw even one thing on my "Destroy the Big Bad Wolfe Plan." Bella is too sweet and good, unlike me who spent most of my school years in detention.

"You know that I love you," she says. "But the more I think about it, maybe it's better to just forget about the whole thing. Move on and forget, you know?"

This is the difference between the two of us. Once I get something in my head, nothing will deter me. I'm an arrow heading straight to the target, while my sister is more like a boat gently floating down the stream.

Also, no one hurts my sister. NO ONE!

"You leave the Big Bad Wolf to me." I pause to peer through the window of one of the shops packed full of cuckoo clocks and decorated steins. I wonder if we'll have time to shop during this tour. "What you need to focus on is getting yourself back on track with your own life. Have you started applying for librarian jobs?"

Since she had the Germany trip planned after graduating, she put off applying for work until she got back. Maybe if she could focus on that, it might be a good distraction.

"I did," she moans, "but so far, no one is hiring. I was thinking of waitressing until something opens up."

"What about applying at a bookstore? You'd be great at that."

"That's a good idea." Her voice brightens. "I just might do that. So how do you like Germany? Was your hotel nice?"

"I just checked in. It's this cute little Bavarian-style place that feels more like a home than a hotel. It's too bad I'll only be there for one night."

"Don't worry. Some of the stops are even better. There's even a stay at a castle."

"Really? No wonder you were having so much fun." She's silent on the phone, so I revert the conversation back to taking down the beast. "I'm about to go to the Fairy Tale Tours office to sign in and pick up my packet."

She sighs wistfully. "I remember when I first picked up my packet. It was so magical."

I groan, rubbing my head. This was a bad idea talking to my sister about the trip. "I just arrived. I'll call you later."

Sun-faded posters of castles, knights, and horse-drawn buggy rides plaster the outside windows of Fairy Tale Tours. The photos look like they were taken twenty years ago. This place sure could use a design overhaul.

I step inside to find an older woman with peppered hair checking people in. She's tall with sharp gray eyes that remind me of Karl Wolfe's. Could that be his mother?

While I wait, I wander about the lobby. Banners of forests, a tower, and a fountain are scattered about. A mural of a castle with the tour company's name stretches across one wall.

A set of plastic chairs, a tired-looking plant, and a coffee table cloister together in one corner. I drop into one of the hard chairs and pick up a brochure from the table. The front flap reads, "Live Your Happily Ever After." This is the problem. They're promising poor, innocent people a chance at romance and magic, which is completely unrealistic. Not to mention that Mr. Wolfe is going to improper lengths to complete the façade.

As if to confirm my fears, a woman probably a little younger than my age of twenty-eight breezes into the office. She's got this bright, hopeful look in her dark brown eyes as she takes in the images. A smile spreads across her features, and her olive skin seems to glow like she was sprinkled with pixie dust. Her straight black hair has pink highlights that bounce on her shoulders as she moves. Her gaze swivels to my corner, and her lips curve.

"Hello." She plops into the chair across from me. "Do you speak English?"

From her accent, it's obvious she's from the U.S. too.

"I do. I'm Scarlett from Florida."

"That's such a relief. I was so worried I'd be stuck on a tour where no one speaks English. I'm Lilac Song. From Chicago. Oh, my gosh. I'm just soooo excited for this tour. I've been saving my Christmas and birthday money for four years to be able to afford it. This is going to be an experience of a lifetime."

A heavy stone settles into the pit of my stomach. How can I ruin this tour's experience for the girl? Unless there's a way I can make sure the tour continues while still taking down Mr. Wolfe. This is going to be more complicated than I first thought.

"So you're a fairy tale fan?" I ask, hoping that's the only reason she's on this tour.

"A little." She nods, and then her eyes dart about. She leans in and in a whisper says, "But I have a friend who found her

Prince Charming while on this tour. She said it was completely magical. They got married last month, and I was a bridesmaid."

Warning bells clang in my head. No, blaring sirens. *This is bad. Very bad.* Karl Wolfe is going to smell this hopeful romantic a mile away and devour her. It's time to activate "How to Destroy the Big Bad Wolf Step Four: Tell tour guests outrageous lies." Except this time, it's actually the truth.

"I need to warn you about the tour guide, Mr. Wolfe," I say, leaning in closer.

Her eyes widen. "Warn me? Of what?"

"Yes," a deep voice says from behind me. "Please tell us what you must warn us about Mr. Wolfe."

I swivel in my chair and find the Wolfe himself towering over me, muscles rippling beneath a form-fitting shirt with the company's castle logo and his name—K. Wolfe—monogrammed on it. But those stormy eyes don't scare me or the thick dark eyebrows raised in intimidation.

"Eavesdropping now, too, Mr. Wolfe?" I say, unable to hide the smile teasing my lips.

His jaw clenches, and he digs his thumbs into his jean pockets. The two of us stare at each other for a moment. Sure, he has this roguish, wild look about him with golden-brown hair hanging over his forehead, but I don't care how hot he may look or how sweet he may have been at the bakery. I'm not going to fall for his antics.

His pressed lips tell me he wants to lash out, put me in my place. But he won't. Because I'm the guest, and he's the host.

Also, I'm right, and he knows it.

I spin around to face Lilac, victoriously putting my back to him.

"Anyway," I continue as if the wolf had never shown up. "Just be careful who you trust on this tour."

"Oh." Lilac nods sagely. "I will."

Good. If one positive thing comes from this tour, it will be that I make sure this sweet woman doesn't fall to the same fate as my sister.

From the corner of my eye, I spot Mr. Wolfe storming across the small office, his strides eating up the space in two bounds. He slips behind the counter and whispers something to the older lady who is handing an elderly couple a packet. Her eyes dart to mine, and a frown puckers across her forehead.

She nods once, lips pressing into a line. Then she refocuses on the couple, smile back in place as she wishes them goodbye.

"Guess this is my cue to sign up next," I tell Lilac.

As I pass by the elderly couple who just checked in, they nod to me, eyes shining like they're already having the time of their lives. The knot of nerves tangles tighter in my belly. Seeing all these tourists reminds me of the stakes at play. Now I'm glad I signed up for the tour under Grams's last name so there wouldn't be a connection that Bella and I are family.

"Good day," the lady greets me stiffly as I step up to the counter. I anticipated her to have a German accent, but it's British. Interesting. "I expect you're here for the interview."

I'm startled. "Interview?"

"Yes, with Mr. Wolfe." She leans forward like a big mother bear. "You don't have to be coy with me. My son saw you had the picture of Karl in your bag and notes about our company."

Oh...so this is Mrs. Wolfe, his mother. I hadn't realized it was a family business.

"I know all about what happened between my son and that girl," she continues in an even, professional tone. So, she admits it! "A real shame is what it is. But we are happy to do any interviews and be transparent. We wish for our guests to have assurance that they will have a flawless touring experience."

I have no clue what she's talking about. I'm about to tell her no, that I'm only here to sign up for the tour. But then a new thought strikes me. If he thinks I'm here for an interview, this would be the perfect opportunity to interrogate him.

But if I say yes, he might figure out I'm lying about my identity and all my scheming could be sabotaged.

What should I do?

Option A: If you think Scarlett should seize this opportunity and pretend to be a journalist, read Chapter 8.

Option B: If you think Scarlett shouldn't lie or jeopardize her plan to take down the Big Bad Wolf, skip to Chapter 9.

Option A

THE SILVER-TONGUED WOLF

"Yes." I straighten tall, swallowing my fear of getting caught. "That's why I'm here. For the interview."

"He's ready for you just through that door." She points to her right.

My hands start sweating as I step into the office. What am I doing? This is a very bad idea. If I get caught, they might decide not to let me on this tour. Whatever happens, I need to tread very carefully.

A quick sweep of the place gives me no deeper insight into this guy since it's just a large metal desk with a computer on it and a stack of notebooks. A few framed photos line the front of the desk. The wall behind him is filled with certificates and awards, framed magazine photos of Karl Wolf smiling his toothy-white smile, and even pictures with him alongside celebrities.

Unfortunately, I'm impressed by the accolades.

My marketing brain kicks in once again. It would be much more effective if they showcased these awards outside in the lobby. But then that would help the Wolfe, so I'll be keeping my suggestions to myself.

"Please, have a seat, Ms. Tate." Mr. Wolfe uses my fake name and waves to the chair across from his desk. "I appreciate you coming in and hearing our side of the...situation."

That flame of anger flares up, calling my sister the *situation*. I plop into the hard linoleum chair and dig into my purse. I pull out my pencil and notebook packed full of research and ideas of ways to bring this man to justice because if I was actually here for an interview, that's what a reporter would do.

"So tell me a little bit about your side of the story." I cross my legs and settle in for the juicy details.

He quickly averts his gaze and focuses on the paned window that overlooks a tiny flower garden.

"Fairy Tale Tours is a company that my father and mother built from scratch," he explains. He picks up one of the picture frames and hands it to me. It's a photo of a young man and a younger version of the lady at the counter. "This has always been their dream. To give everyone a taste of a fairy tale and to spark a little magic in everyday life."

"I see." My heart stirs at the sweet story, but I shove those feelings firmly away. I pass the frame back to him, trying to ignore how our fingers touched for a brief moment. "But how does this relate to the woman?"

"My father got sick, so everyone in the family had to step up and do their part. We had to be more than just an image in a magazine, we had to get to work."

"So you admit that you had to be more than," I pause to find the quote from Forbes magazine on my phone, "Germany's billionaire playboy."

He jerks to standing, face bright red. "That is a lie. There are no playboys in this family."

Oh, that hit a nerve. He's totally guilty! I keep my smile in check and draw swirls on my paper, pretending to take notes. Based on my research, Karl Wolfe is a successful self-made man and a highly sought-after bachelor, known to "have a girl waiting for him on every continent." An actual quote of his. Just reading about him made my stomach sour.

"If you are so wealthy," I continue, feeling bolder, "why bother with this tour company? And no offense, but the place is severely outdated. It's hard to believe your sentiments when this office could use some of your extra cash to give the place a makeover."

He clears his throat as if collecting himself and settles back into his chair. "I do take offense to that. The reason I bother is because I care about my father. As far as the extra cash, my father is a proud man. He would never take a penny from any of his children."

Okay, so this is not good. I'm starting to feel bad for this family. Or...he could be lying, and I'm falling for his tricks just like my sister.

"So, let's get back to the woman," I say, determined to not get derailed. "What happened with that situation?"

"Things got out of control. But I assure you that won't happen again."

"Got out of control?" My pencil snaps in my hand. "The poor girl was devastated. Her heart was broken!"

He jerks as if I slapped him, and his eyes darken to a midnight blue. "I didn't know that," he says softly. "Do you know this young lady?"

"I'm here purely for the interview," I say stiffly. I need to be careful and keep my cards close. I nearly blew it with my usual fiery temper. "Continue with your story."

"All I know," he rakes a hand through his hair, "was that

she left suddenly. We just got alerted that a sexual harassment report was filed a few days ago. We are drafting up a formal apology, but I'd be happy to apologize personally to her on behalf of the family and make things right."

Apologize on behalf of the family? What a prick! He can't even admit to his own wrongdoings! And when do apologies ever mend broken hearts? Still, I promised Bella I'd get one from him. Maybe my issue is that this feels too easy for the guy. I've been listening to her cry every day since she's gotten home, and here he is worried about the company's reputation.

"I'm sure an apology would be a good start," I grind out.

Regardless, this conversation solidifies this man truly needs to be knocked down and put in place. There's a rap on the door, and it opens, revealing Mrs. Wolfe and another man wearing a suit.

"Excuse the interruption," Mrs. Wolfe's eyes narrow on me, "but the man for the *interview* is here."

Uh-oh. I totally got caught. I close my notebook full of scribbles and stuff it along with my broken pencil into my purse. I rise from my seat, trying to keep my face from revealing that I'm scrambling for some sort of excuse.

"It's no trouble," I quickly say. "I'm finished with my own interview for the Sun Times. You know the newspaper where the *woman* is from."

Mr. Wolfe lets out a low groan and runs a palm over his face.

"Oh!" Mrs. Wolfe lifts her eyebrows and then gives her son a pointed look. "This is interesting."

"And now I'll continue with checking in for the tour," I say, smiling wickedly at the wolf. He's not the only one who has a few tricks up his sleeve. "I can't wait to see how you treat your guests so I can write up a full report of my experience afterward."

I march out of the room, head held high.

READER NOTE: You can jump ahead to Chapter 10 or you can continue and read Option B in Chapter 9 and see what would happen if she didn't pretend she was the reporter.

Option B

HIDING IN PLAIN SIGHT

"Oh, I'm not here for the interview," I tell Mrs. Wolfe. "I'm here to check in for the tour."

"Really?" She chuckles, shaking her head. "We must have gotten you confused with someone else. What's your name, dear?"

"Scarlett Wal... Tate. Scarlett Tate," I reaffirm, nearly messing up and giving her my correct name.

She scans her clipboard and checks me off. "There you are. You paid the deposit with a gift card. How would you like to pay the rest?"

"Credit." I pop open my wallet only to find the three gift cards tucked into the pockets, glittering like stardust. I blink. What are these doing here? I'm sure I threw Hunter's gift card away and used the Fairy Tale Tours one already.

"Is everything alright?" the lady asks.

I startle. "Yes. It's great. Everything is fabulous." I pull out the Fairy Tale Tours gift card. "Could you just check and see if there's a balance on this?"

"Not a problem." She slides it through her machine. "Looks like it paid for the remainder of the trip, so you're all set."

"Great. Thank you." I bite my lip, still feeling off-kilter, but then maybe this gift card was a complete tour package and I hadn't realized it. I'd been distressed that day over the breakup with Hunter. My eyes wander to the closed office door. "I'm curious. Who did you think I was?"

"It's nothing." She passes me a solid white folder. I can't help but think that not putting their logo on it is a missed marketing opportunity. But that's good! Another check mark toward business failure.

"It's that my husband is quite ill." She chokes up at this. "It's a bit much for him to talk to reporters, so we're all here chipping in until he feels better."

My heart twists at her words. "I'm sorry to hear that."

"There was this incident," she switches to a whisper, "and evidently, that's what the reporter wants details on."

I freeze, hanging onto her every word. "What sort of incident?"

"Don't you worry about it." She chuckles nervously. "You just focus on having fun during our tour. My son is running the company while he's in the hospital. I know you'll be in good hands. I'm Sharon, by the way."

"I'm looking forward to it, Sharon," I say, "but I'm so sorry about your husband. I hope he recovers quickly."

My eyes fall on a photo hanging on the wall behind her. It's a faded picture of the lady standing in front of me, but younger. She's beside another man, tall with a thick brown beard and sharp cheeks just like Karl Wolfe.

"Is that you and your husband?" I ask.

Her smile brightens. "That it is! It's a photo of us opening this tour company twenty years ago. Such a lovely and exciting time."

A pit forms in my stomach. I don't want to hear her answer, but I know I need to. "Are you saying this isn't your son's company? That's your husband's?"

"Yes, that's right. But my children help out from time to time if they can."

My head spins as I reconsider every plan I've made. "Well, the two of you look perfect together. I hope he recovers quickly."

"Thank you, dear. That is very kind of you. Now let's go over your instructions. Tomorrow morning, arrive at the Marketplatz at 8 a.m. in front of the statue of the Brothers Grimm where we'll do introductions. Make sure you bring everything you need for the trip because you'll be boarding the tour bus there and not returning until the end of the two weeks."

"Unless we get abandoned along the way," I mutter under my breath.

"If you look at your itinerary, you'll see your first stop is Steinau. You'll get to visit the Grimms' childhood home and participate in a fairytale treasure hunt. Each stop showcases a fairytale with activities or games."

A man in a suit carrying a briefcase slides up to the counter. "Excuse me. I'm here for the interview," he says.

My eyes pop out. So there really was a person coming. Now I'm glad I chose not to pretend to be this guy. I totally would've gotten caught!

"Brilliant," Sharon says briskly like she's executing a business deal. "Just head into the office to your right, and you'll find my son there waiting."

The man nods curtly, face grim, and strides into the office.

"That reporter looked intense." I try to hide my gleeful grin, hoping he'll expose Karl for his bad behavior. "But the truth must come out."

Her face drops at that, and her hand shakes a little as she checks my name off the list. "Yes, I suppose that is true. I hope you have a lovely time."

Guilt slams into me. I mean, it's not her fault that her son is a jerk, right? We all make our own choices in the end. "I'm sorry, I just meant..."

"It's fine." She pats my hand. "Don't worry about us. You just focus on having a magical time."

My head spins as I shuffle outside. Am I going about this all wrong? Is taking revenge on this guy really worth it? Maybe I should be helping Bella get back on her feet instead. I sit on a bench tucked under a sprawling oak, soaking in the enchanted atmosphere of this quaint town. I pull out my phone and text my sister.

Me: I'm thinking of coming back home.

Bella: You just arrived!

Me: I'm worried about you.

Bella: Don't. I'm great! Never better!

Me: Really?

Bella: Just enrolled at UCF.

Me: But you already have your master's degree in library sciences.

> Bella: You got me thinking. I decided to
> take some business classes.

I gawk at the text like she just told me she was abducted by aliens. My sister is taking business classes?

> Me: I can't believe I'm saying this, but I'm
> starting to feel bad for the Wolfe family. You
> know with his dad being sick and all.

> Bella: I didn't know about that. That's too
> bad. But be careful, sis. I learned the hard
> way everything Karl says is a lie.

My stomach twists, and I stare at her words.

> Bella: You should stay in Germany. When
> was the last time you had fun.

She has a point. Life has always been work, work, work. I can't remember my last vacation.

> Bella: Just don't let Karl ruin things for you.

The town bells toll in the distance, and the door to the bakery across the street opens as someone strolls out. It's Lilac. She spots me and hurries to my side.

"I decided to grab a treat while waiting to check in," she explains and opens the crisp brown paper bag, revealing two gingerbread cookies. "Try one. You'll never eat packaged gingerbread again."

The scent of cinnamon and ginger wafts around me as she passes me one.

"Thank you." I take a bite. An explosion of spice and warmth fills my mouth. "This is divine."

"We're going to have so much fun, aren't we?" she says.

"We absolutely are," I agree.

Because as much as I wish to go home, Bella's right. I'm already here in Germany, and there is still work to be done. Not just to make sure Karl Wolfe pays for what he did, but also for all the women like Lilac who deserve better than men like the Wolfe.

CHAPTER 10

The Journey Begins

Morning comes too quickly. I can't stop yawning as I stumble out of my hotel toward the Market-platz. My suitcase bumps on the cobblestone as I drag it behind me. This tour doesn't have us stay in each city for longer than a day or two since we'll be traveling along the famous Fairy Tale Road, visiting locations that inspired the Grimm fairy tales. I had originally planned for this trip to be only about revenge, but after talking to Bella yesterday, I've decided it can't hurt to have a little fun along the way.

Last night, I didn't sleep a wink. I spent way too much time reading up on all the articles I could find on Karl Wolfe. But the search only confused me more. The flashy Karl Wolfe I read about online doesn't seem anything like the kind and considerate Karl Wolfe in the office. All the pictures show him with slicked-back hair, a thick beard, and wearing expensive suits. In every picture, his smile is always a little mischievous and there's a slightly wicked glint in his eyes.

The man I met yesterday was wearing a simple gray shirt and jeans. Unlike the photos, his hair has a wild, tousled look like it's begging for me to run my hands through it, and he's got a five o'clock shadow like he couldn't care a wink about his looks. And his eyes were kind and honest and—

Crap. I'm totally obsessing over this dude. What is wrong with me? Either he's great at faking things or changed his whole demeanor to show he's learned something profound from the *incident.* But that doesn't change how he treated Bella.

I turn the corner only to spot him just ahead as if my overactive imagination conjured him up. He's standing beside the bronze statue of the Brothers Grimm, smiling and shaking hands with the elderly couple like he's super excited to see them. My feet falter.

I can't do this. Before I met him and his mother and knew about the dad, it seemed so simple. Destroy and conquer was the name of the game.

Now, things are complicated.

I'm losing my nerve.

But then Lilac bounces up to Mr. Wolfe, shaking his hand and staring up at him with doe eyes. My gaze narrows on their handshake. Is he holding her hand a little too long? Is he looking at her with those dreamy eyes of his, smiling sweetly down at her like she's his next meal?

Yes. Yes, he is.

That conniving asshole!

Suddenly, I feel invigorated. Revived. My mission is clear once again. I'm going to make sure these next two weeks are so miserable and he'll be so humiliated he'll never lead another tour again.

As I cross the street, I pass by a lady who looks exactly like the woman at the convention who handed me the raffle basket. She's even wearing that same lace-trimmed blue dress with a basket swaying from the hook of her arm. I stop in the middle of the street and spin on my heels for a double check, but she's vanished.

A car honks, startling me. I scramble out of the road and into the square. I must have imagined her, I think, rubbing my head. Probably jet lag.

A tour bus rolls up with Fairy Tale Tours splashed across the side of it. Thankfully, Mr. Wolfe leaves Lilac to direct the bus into a parking spot. A quick glance tells me most of our tour group is already here. There's the elderly couple I saw checking in, two women in their fifties, another younger couple, a few singles standing off to the side, and Lilac, who waves to me but calls out, "Be right back! Running to pee real quick!" Then I spot two guys about my age sauntering up to join the group.

One has dark brown skin and black hair closely shaven. He's dressed like he's headed for a business meeting in black slacks, a shiny silver-buckled belt, and a green button-down dress shirt. The other has lighter, bronzed skin, sculptured features, and dark curls covered by a baseball cap. He's wearing sunglasses even though it's a little cloudy, and his purple shirt and faded jeans hug a trim, fit frame.

"Hey!" I greet the two. "You here for the tour?"

"You got it," Nicely Dressed Guy says and throws out a hand to me. "I'm Axel Williams. Perfume entrepreneur from Dallas, Texas."

"Perfume? Interesting."

"Just launched my own company." He passes over his business card. "I can send you some free samples anytime you like."

"Thanks." I take the card, tucking it into my pocket, then turn to Sunglasses Dude. "You two together?"

"Naw." Axel chuckles. "We've been best buds since kindergarten, but then he got..."

"Busy," Sunglasses interrupts. "But recently I decided I needed a break from life. So I called up my oldest and most *trusted* friend. Said let's hang out for a bit."

He throws an arm around Axel, who beams like he's a kid whose parents just told him he was going to Disney World.

"I was scheduled to go on this fairy tale tour because I'm obsessed with all things Grimm," Axel explains. "I told him to come along. Since he wanted to escape life, I'm like what better place than a fairy tale?"

"So you're on this tour to learn about the Grimm Brothers?" I ask Axel who nods and shows me notes he's already started. "I suppose I'd always assumed the tour was about romance and finding love."

"Maybe for some," Sunglasses says, "but I've only been in this country for a day and I'm already feeling relaxed."

"And inspired," Axel adds, nodding to Sunglasses. "This morning over coffee, my bud here had this amazing idea. I could start a fairy tale perfume line."

"It's a good idea, isn't it?" Sunglasses asks me expectantly.

"It's brilliant." I cock my head and study this Sunglass Guy appreciatively. He may look like a disheveled mess, but he's got a clever mind. "In fact, I'm in marketing and my brain is already flying with ideas. Like one scent could be Enchanted Forest with pine, berries, and a hint of floral. Or Sleeping Beauty with lavender and vanilla. The possibilities are endless."

"Woot!" Sunglasses lifts his hand and the two fist pump. "See? What did I tell you?"

Axel beams and points to Sunglasses. "This guy. He's the best."

"And what was your name again?" I ask Sunglasses. He

never gave me his name, but there's something intriguing about him.

"Oh, right." He tugs on the brim of his hat. "Call me Rob."

A bell rings, drawing our attention to where Mr. Wolfe is standing on the edge of a fountain.

And so it all begins, I think.

"Welcome to Hanau and the beginning of your fairytale tour!" he greets us. Everyone cheers, and we all gather around him. "I thought meeting here at the foot of the Brothers Grimm statue would be a fitting beginning to our journey into the land of fairy tales. This bronze was built in 1896 and sits in front of Hanau Rathaus, which is our town hall. In a moment, we'll be jumping aboard what will be your carriage for this two-week tour along the famous Fairy Tale Road that runs through the heart of Germany."

He points to our tour bus, and everyone chuckles. One of the ladies snaps a selfie with the bus.

"Grab some photos of this statue," Mr. Wolfe continues, "and then we'll board the bus and head to Steinau an der Straße, the home to Jacob and Wilhelm Grimm when they were twelve and thirteen years old."

As soon as he's finished, everyone whips out their cameras and starts taking photos. The atmosphere of the town and the sweet-scented air soothe me, loosening the tightness in my shoulders. Maybe I really do need a vacation. I find Lilac, relieved to find her running to join us. I wave her over.

"Let's get a selfie together with the statue behind us," I offer.

"Great idea!"

Once we snap a photo, we roll our luggage to the bus and slip it inside.

"Did I miss anything while I was gone?" she asks as we climb up the bus stairs.

"Just that we're headed to the Grimm Brothers' childhood home," I say as we settle into the soft, plush seats.

"Isn't our tour guide hot?" She nods toward the aisle. "He told me he's got a very special fairytale game for us to play when we get there."

"I bet he did," I mutter as I follow her gaze to where Karl Wolfe is striding up and down the aisle, checking to make sure everyone is set. "You need to be careful with him. I heard he sleeps around with a different girl on every tour."

"Really? He seems too sweet for that."

"Just be careful, okay?"

"Relax! You look really stressed out." She digs through her bag and procures a stack of notecards. "The only thing you should be worried about is how we're going to win this first fairytale game. According to the schedule, it tests our knowledge of the Grimm tales. I brought flashcards to brush up on my fairytale trivia. You quiz me first."

I take the stack of flashcards as the bus roars to life and we begin our journey down the Fairy Tale Road. But as I quiz her on glass slippers and poisoned apples, my mind schemes ways to show everyone our tour guide isn't the desirable prince everyone thinks he is.

CHAPTER 11

To the Grimm Brothers' House We Go

Thirty minutes later, we're all tumbling off the bus. The spring air is crisp, and the sky above is velvet blue, hugging the ancient stone walls and medieval-style buildings surrounding us. I tug my red coat tighter around me to ward off the morning breeze and hurry over to where Mr. Wolfe is calling for us to gather around him.

He's sporting a faded pair of jeans and a dark blue button-down shirt that makes his eyes look more blue than gray today. When his gaze flicks to mine, his expression darkens into an intense look that makes me a little weak in the knees. Maybe it's the wild hair or the five o'clock shadow, but he's got the smoldering look down pat.

He's trying to intimidate me, I realize, but I won't let him. I'm sticking this tour out and keeping a sharp eye on him. So I lift my chin and eyebrows and smile. *I'm coming for you*, I think wickedly.

His eyes widen almost as if he heard my thoughts. He looks away quickly, scrubbing the back of his neck. Maybe the Big Bad Wolf isn't so scary after all.

"Welcome to Steinau an der Straße," he begins once everyone has gathered round. "This old medieval town was first mentioned in 1140. Over the centuries, it became a popular market town and important for trade and commerce. Our first destination will be the Brüder-Grimm-Haus, where the famous Brothers Grimm lived from 1791 to 1796. Each of you will be given a ticket, and then afterward, we're going to play a fairy-tale game where you'll be competing for an amazing prize."

Everyone ooh's and claps at the word *prize* and then we set off down the road as if the world is waiting for us.

"Isn't this so magical?" Lilac says as we trail after our guide. She tucks her hair into a clip that matches her sleeveless knee-length mint dress that hugs her figure. "I'm totally going to win. All my studying is going to pay off."

I grin, trying to reign in my own red curls against the wind. "While I, on the other hand, am realizing I didn't properly prepare for this trip by not bringing a hair tie."

We wander the charming historic street complete with quaint half-timbered buildings of distinctive white facades and dark wooden beams. Flowered boxes are tucked beneath windows, splashing color against the stone. Mr. Wolfe pauses outside a pastry shop. The scent of cinnamon and buttery pastry wafts through the air.

"While you are visiting my beautiful country," his voice booms out, "I insist you taste some of its most famous foods. So I've had the chef here prepare for each of you Franzbrötchen."

Smiling, he collects a large bag from the baker and passes each of us what looks like a cinnamon roll on a crisp napkin.

When he offers me one, I shake my head. "I ate breakfast already," I say, but really, I can't stand the thought of taking gifts from the man who caused my sister so much heartache.

A devious grin curls his lips up. "Too scared to try it, Red?"

"Who says I'm scared of the Big Bad Wolf?" I pluck it from his hand, my words causing him to chuckle.

I sink my teeth into its warm dough. The richness of flaky pastry along with the spice and sweetness of the cinnamon and sugar make me groan in delight. I lick my fingers and look up to find Mr. Wolfe is still here, watching me, an odd expression on his face. He clears his throat.

"I see it meets your expectations," he says in a strangled tone. Then he clips away, tossing the empty bag into the trash and clapping his hands, warning for us to follow him.

"Now I see why this tour is so popular," the elderly woman says. "How can I not give them five stars when they feed us delicious morsels like that?"

I frown, not liking her thoughts at all because she's right. Who can't love a guy who feeds us food like that? Everyone is too happy and having too much fun. Including myself, apparently, because there's a lightness to my step and the grind of my day job is starting to slip off my shoulders like sifting sand. My muscles are more relaxed than they've been since my college days.

We line up at the cream-colored manor with the traditional exposed wooden beams and cross-crossed designs encasing the tall windows. A lone tower rises up on one side of the house like a castle turret, while a smaller one is tucked into a corner of the building.

"This whole place is too adorable." Lilac lifts her vintage sunglasses to study the area before snapping a photo. "Admit it. Doesn't the top of the tower remind you of an ice cream cone?"

I nod. Unfortunately, this place is utterly enchanting. I

could see myself getting lost in the whole magic of this tour, which is very, very dangerous.

"Those two guys are pretty cute over there," Lilac says, pointing to Rob and Axel. "Do you think they're single?"

"Maybe? I didn't ask, but they seem nice." And maybe too much of a distraction from my mission.

"I'm going to find out," she says. "Scope out our prospects while on this trip."

She winks and I laugh as she takes off, leaving behind a trail of Chanel. Being on this tour makes you feel like you've left reality and entered a fairy tale. Now I understand why Bella fell so hard for Karl.

That thought alone yanks me firmly back to reality. My brain scours for a way to show these guests that their tour guide isn't so great after all. To the left on the other side of a low wall, the lawn has a full set up, including a large red throne, some statues, and a gingerbread house. Could that be where the game is taking place?

"Hello there," the wife of the elderly couple says, coming to my side. She's wearing a whimsical, loose-fitting purple shirt with capris. Her husband is sporting a flowered shirt and khaki pants complete with a straw hat, which he tips at me in greeting. "I'm Evelyn, and this is my husband, Gary. That red coat is such a lovely costume. I never thought of taking on a character while on the tour. Such a clever idea!"

"I'm Scarlett," I say. "The red jacket was a gift from my grams."

"How delightful!" Evelyn clasps her hands. "You even have a character name to go with your costume."

She's so pleased with her discovery that I don't have the heart to tell her she's wrong.

"Is this your first time in Germany?" I ask, deciding to switch the subject.

"We're from London, but we've been to Germany a time or two. This is our first time taking this tour, and we are quite pleased with it already. Mr. Wolfe is such a great guide, don't you think?"

"It's hard to know." I look down the line where he's passing out tickets to everyone. "Have you read the news about him? He tried to seduce one of the guests on the last tour."

The woman gasps. "No! This is dreadful."

"It is." I sigh dramatically. "Personally, I think he's trying to just bribe us with those pastries he handed out so the company doesn't fire him."

Suddenly, Karl's large frame is standing before us. He smiles kindly at the couple and passes them their tickets, but when he comes to me, his face takes on that scowl as he holds out my ticket.

"Thank you." I try to take it, but he holds it firmly despite my tug.

"I'm assuming as a reporter for the Sun Times," he says, pointedly, "that you'll be writing up a review on your trip."

"Indeed." I finally wrench the ticket free with a jerk. "And the verdict is still in the air whether or not the tour guide is going to start another scandal."

"If you're looking for sensational media," he half-growls, leaning in closer so only I can hear, "you've come to the wrong place."

The timber of his voice jolts down my spine, his closeness overpowering. The two of us stare each other down as if daring the other to be the first to break eye contact. A woman with curly bleach-blonde hair dressed in a sleek satin shirt and black pressed pants clatters to us in heels.

"There you are!" She hooks her arm through his, batting her eyelashes at him. She's probably thirty years his senior. "You're coming inside with us, right? You know so much about all this Grimm stuff. I'd rather have you explain it than some cold recording in my headset. You understand, right?"

I lift my eyebrows victoriously as if to say, *I told you so*. His brow knits and his gaze flicks to the woman.

"As much as I'd love to, Felicia," he says, extracting himself effortlessly from her clutches, "I need to make a few final touches to the game."

The game. That's right. A very devious and wicked idea springs to mind of the perfect sabotage, which would make the Big Bad Wolf look very bad indeed.

Also, it might put me in the Evil Queen category. But sometimes sacrifices must be made.

"I explicitly booked this tour because I heard the guides take time for the guests." Felicia's thick red lips pull into a pout. "Don't tell me this tour is going to be a disappointment."

I snort at her audacity but quickly cover my mouth, pretending to cough. I may have inadvertently found a partner in crime in my least likely source.

"It sounds like Mr. Wolfe is not the tour guide you were expecting," I say, capitalizing on Felicity's negativity. "It makes me wonder why we pay all this money if guests can just do this on their own."

"You may have a point." Felicity's lips thin.

Mr. Wolfe eyes me warily. "I won't be long," he tells Felicity with a tight smile. She practically melts into a puddle. "In fact, I'm sure it will only take a few moments for me to make sure the game is ready. Go ahead and start your tour. I'll join up with you soon. I'm happy to guide you along."

"We'll want to join, too," Evelyn says, and her husband bobs his head happily. "If that's alright?"

"Even better," he replies.

He glances my way with a lift of his brow and an expression that says, *Take that.* Then he strides away out to the lawn.

"Such a fine-looking specimen, don't you think?" Felicity says, pulling up her sunglasses to get a better look at him as he strolls away.

I find myself bristling at her words, which is silly because she is right after all. Plus, she might be a useful pawn in my plan. The doors to the entrance open, but while the other guests begin to shuffle inside, I linger, debating what to do.

Do I go inside and enjoy the tour of the Brothers Grimm house? After all, this is my vacation. The only vacation I've taken in five years.

Or do I follow the Wolfe and sabotage his little game, making him look the fool?

THIS IS the point where Scarlett's love life takes a turn. As you read, you'll see some possible paths she can take: Hunter, Wolf, or Movie Star. The chapter titles along with these notes at the bottom will guide you along your journey. Or read them all and experience every path!

Wolf Path: If you think Scarlett should sabotage his game, continue reading Chapter 12.

Movie Star Path: If you think Scarlett should just enjoy the tour, skip ahead to Chapter 13.

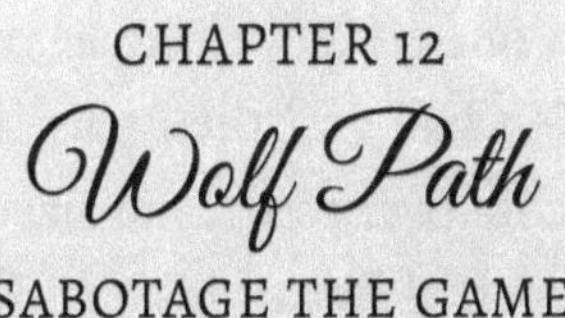Wolf Path

SABOTAGE THE GAME

Reader Note: This choice is when Scarlett sabotages the game.

THE LAST MEMBER of our tour group is stepping through the doorway. It's now or never. My eyes flicker to the garden area where Mr. Wolfe is walking around holding a stack of envelopes. My eyes narrow.

Game on, Mister. I'll show you what winning looks like.

I slip away from the entrance and duck behind the bushes, holding my breath. My red jacket probably looks like a beacon, so I'm going to need to be very careful where I stand. I set the phone to silent mode and push aside the branches to peek through the narrow gap.

The lawn almost looks enchanted with the collection of fairytale paraphernalia scattered about the lush greenery. A wishing well stands in the center, and cute cobblestone paths wind around flower gardens and statues of Snow White and Red Riding Hood. Tall oaks, birches, and hedges surround the area, giving a sense of privacy and a mood like it's from another place.

Mr. Wolfe tucks one envelope into a crevice on a statue of a frog holding a golden ball and then pats the frog's head playfully. Next, he marches over to the kid-sized gingerbread house with those long, powerful legs of his. His frame is so large that it's hard for him to squeeze through the tiny door, but he manages by crouching and twisting his body inside.

A giggle escapes me, and I clamp my hand over my mouth. There's something incredibly endearing about him putting the game together as if he truly loves his job. Like he's a dad on Christmas morning stuffing stockings. I assumed he was this tough, gruff guy, but maybe I was wrong. My heart twists as he wrestles an envelope into Cinderella's slipper.

I frown. *What am I thinking?* I push away from the bush, annoyed with the fact I'd not just been enjoying that gorgeous body of his, but I was actually starting to feel for the guy.

Unbelievable.

"Who are we spying on?" a deep voice whispers behind me.

I spin around to find Rob standing there, a sly grin on his face. My whole body stiffens rigid as a board. There's no doubt that guilt is splashed all over my face.

"Hey," I say, trying to speak softly. "I'm just...enjoying the garden area. Why are you out here and not on the tour?"

He shrugs, and I wish he'd take those glasses off so I can get a better read on him. "Had to take some calls. Or at least I should take some calls. But you looked far more fun than my phone."

"Oh?" I hitch an eyebrow. "I'm going to take that as a compliment."

"As you should."

A flutter stirs in my chest. Maybe it's his smile or perhaps how his focus is completely riveted on me. Hunter was always so busy, always on the move, always keeping close tabs on the alerts for new homes that I never really felt seen. But this Rob guy...he's here in the moment looking only at me.

Movement in the garden yanks my attention back to our tour guide. Quickly, I peek through the bushes again to see Mr. Wolfe striding away toward the house. Rob squeezes in and joins me in my mischievous game.

"Ah," Rob whispers. "So we're spying on our tour guide. Why is that?"

Caught red-handed. I might as well come clean. "Because he's evil, and I'm here to take revenge."

"Really? Now this is exciting. Why exactly are we taking revenge?"

"Because he was awful to my sister, and now he must pay."

He rubs his jaw. "When you put it like that, I feel like I must help in this endeavor."

"You can't say anything." I point a finger at him. "Promise?"

His mouth quirks. "Promise."

The moment Mr. Wolfe enters the manor, I step away from the bushes and run toward the little green frog statue on the ground, Rob trailing after me. My hands shake as I pull out the first envelope and peek inside to find a note and a bunch of letter E's. I'm a little nervous. Okay, so a lot nervous. After all, I've never sabotaged anything in my life or cheated once on a test. I don't even break the speed limit!

"It's some sort of riddle or clue," I say, and read it aloud to Rob. "I'm a tiny creature who's quite small, but I helped a princess, after all. Who am I?"

He stares at the frog. "A frog?"

"Yes. That's it." I tap the envelope against my leg as I study the lawn. "It looks like he's put these all over the garden. Every envelope has a riddle and a bunch of letters."

"Perhaps you solve the riddle and then use the letter for something else?"

I rise to my feet, scanning the area as my evil plan unfolds. "If I mix up the numbers with different clues, it will make the game confusing."

"And why would we do this?"

"Because the tour guests need to see the Wolfe is not the Prince Charming they think he is."

"And that's a good thing?"

"Yes!" Determination pushes me into action, and I slip the riddle back into its envelope, then dart to the gingerbread house to switch the letters out of its envelope. "It's a very good thing."

"What exactly did he do to your sister?"

"He took advantage of her and broke her heart. So yeah, he's got to pay."

"Wow. I've got to admit I didn't peg him for that sort of guy. But you're right. He must pay. But won't this plan mess up the game for the others and not our tour guide?"

"They'll be fine." I check my watch. Time is ticking! "Unlike my sister."

A ring erupts through the quiet of the garden. Rob pulls out his phone and answers it.

"I told you I'm fine," he says and hurries away, but it's so quiet out here that his voice carries. "I need more time away. Yes. I'm just not ready. They can start without me."

There's a pause. I know it's rude to eavesdrop, but it's not my fault I've got good hearing.

"I know I signed the contract!" He must realize he practically yelled that part because he glances around. I revert my focus to the large throne in the middle of the green. "Tell them I'm sick. That I broke a leg. I don't care."

I'm stuffing the A's into the throne envelope when Rob returns, a frown pulling on his face.

"Everything okay?" I ask.

He stares at me for a moment and then at the envelope I'm shoving back into its hiding place on the throne. His frown morphs into a smile. A stunning, beautiful smile I could drown in. One that might make me forget about Hunter and that obnoxious Wolfe.

"Yeah, everything is great now." "I was going to actually ask how I could be your partner of mischief in this grand scheme of yours."

I laugh. Finally, someone understands me! I reach out and touch his arm. "Thank you. That means a lot."

A commotion to our right drags my attention from Rob. Three men stride into the area wearing traditional German outfits with brown sleeveless shirts over breeches. They each hold a different instrument: an accordion, bagpipe, and teardrop-shaped guitar.

But what is highly concerning is that the trio is being led by none other than our tour guide.

"Uh, oh," Rob says.

It wouldn't look so bad if I didn't have a clue in my hands.

"Quick! Hide!" I dive for the nearest thicket of bushes.

Branches scrape my face and tug at my hair. Something snags on my jacket, forcing me to hunker down and wait. I'm not quite sure where Rob went. Can't blame him for not choosing this hiding spot. It's not exactly on my list of comfortable hangout places.

The whine and trill of an accordion fills the air as one of the men starts warming up. It sounds beautiful.

Mr. Wolfe's voice cuts through the music. "Rob! You're missing out on the museum tour."

"Yes, well. Had a call to take so thought it was quietest out here."

"I am afraid my friends have interrupted your solitude. But if I'm correct, I saw you out here with Scarlett."

Damn it! Maybe if I can untangle myself from this branch, I can sneak back inside. I twist about, trying to free myself when the branches above me pull back.

Soft gray eyes look down at me and a breeze shivers across my face, bringing with it the scent of spice and smoldering firewood that warns me it's the Wolfe. As I peer up at him, his broad shoulders and wide chest should look imposing. Menacing. After all, he's my arch-enemy, even if he doesn't know that yet.

But instead, there's a twinkle in his eyes and the corner of his mouth is quirked up. His thick arms look inviting, and suddenly I just want to step closer to him. Drink in his smell and feel his presence.

I blink and shake my head. What is wrong with me? Those are horrible, terrible, ridiculous thoughts! Guilt and horror burn my face.

"Well, Little Red," Mr. Wolfe says. "This is unexpected. What are you doing in the bushes?"

I clear my throat and try to muster as much dignity as possible. Which, let's be honest, is nearly impossible. "I seem to be stuck."

"Let me see if I can help."

He pulls back the bush further as if it's just a bunch of tiny twigs rather than angry, stubborn branches. Then he reaches down and takes my hand to help me escape the bed of thorns, but the moment his hand touches mine, a spark races up and down my skin, warming my entire body in the cool spring air.

He pulls me up as if I weigh nothing. Once I've extricated myself, I brush off the leaves and twigs from my body. A piece of paper flutters to the ground at my feet.

One of his clues.

Nothing like being caught red-handed. Both of our eyes land on it at the same time. His eyes lift to find mine.

"Oh! That's why I was in the bush." I swallow down the truth that's dying to escape and form a bitter lie. "One of the clues blew into the bushes. I went to get it."

His palm runs across the scruff on his jaw as if he's considering my words. I'm momentarily distracted, wondering what it would be like to run my fingers across his face.

"Miss Tate," he says, using my fake name. He searches my face carefully before plucking a leaf from my hair. My breath catches at how tender his action is. I can't help but be disappointed that he's using my formal name. But wait, that's good. He's evil, and it's important to remember this. "I am glad you found this clue. The tour guests would be disappointed if they couldn't play the game."

He reaches his long arms and snatches up the paper easily, striding away with those powerful legs of his that seem to eat up space and time. Suddenly the air feels too cold, as if he took all the sunshine and its warmth with him. I curl my jacket closer around my body and hurry to join the others from the tour who are now entering the grove.

I shake away the guilt that's desperate to take over my choice because it's time for the games to begin and for the wolf to become my prey.

Movie Star Path: Curious what would've happened if Scarlett took the tour instead? Read Chapter 13.

Wolf Path: If you wish to continue where Scarlett sabotages the game, jump ahead to Chapter 15.

CHAPTER 13
Movie Star Path
TAKE THE TOUR

Reader Note: *This choice is when Scarlett takes the tour and doesn't sabotage the game.*

As much as I'd love to sabotage the game, I just can't do it. I've always been a rule follower, and the thought of ruining the game for everyone else seems too evil, even for this girl acting under the pretense of being the Evil Queen.

So I pass over my ticket to the attendant and step into the manor that once served as home to the Brothers Grimm. The scent of old wood mixed with fresh paint drapes over me, and since it's warmer in here, I unbutton my coat and push back the hood.

Lilac is up ahead laughing with Axel, the perfume guy. As much as I'd like to hang out with her, I'm glad she's with him and not becoming the wolf's next victim. I break off from the others since we're free to wander about. Most of the rooms have been converted to more of a museum-style look with walls illustrating different fairy tales and printed words spilling across the surface.

I cross into the restored kitchen, its floor made up of brown square tiles. Thick wood beams crisscross the white stucco walls. I can almost imagine Jacob and Wilhelm as little boys stealing hot, baked sweets from one of these counters and hoping the cooks wouldn't notice.

My phone rings, and I pull it out. It's Hunter. Why is he calling? My heartbeat kicks up, in part from nerves and part because talking to him scares me. It reminds me of what I had, and I'm still not sure if that was good enough.

It rings and rings, and still, I stare at his name, unable to bring myself to answer. Mercifully, the ringing stops, and I tuck my phone back into my pocket. The room spins a little, and suddenly it's hard to breathe. I need fresh air. Somehow, my shaky legs carry me outside through a side door. A breeze smelling of fresh cut grass wafts across my face, and I sag onto a nearby bench.

I know I made the right decision with Hunter, but it's still hard.

"I need more time," a voice says from just the other side of the tree. "Come on. You know they can start without me."

I sit up, feeling a little guilty that I'm eavesdropping, especially when the guy raises his voice and carries on about a contract. Sounds like things are not going well for him. The voice gets closer and then Rob steps out from behind the tree as if he is pacing. His dark eyes catch mine, and he stops talking. *Uh-oh.* He's going to think I was purposely listening to him.

"Listen," he says. "I've got to go."

He hangs up and pockets his phone. "How much did you overhear?" he asks, slipping back on his sunglasses. Which is too bad. His eyes are a rich chocolate shade and crinkle at the sides, giving him an endearing look.

I shrug. "Something about contracts?"

He closes the distance between us and plops beside me on the bench, sighing as he sprawls out like he just ran a marathon. The spicy scent of expensive perfume mixes with the fresh grass. It must be one of Axel's scents. It's nice.

"Everything okay?" I finally ask.

"My life is...complicated, and there are things I should deal with but..."

"Don't want to." I nod. "I get that completely."

"You do?"

"I broke up with my boyfriend of a year just before I left." I hold up my phone. "Unlike you, I couldn't even deal with answering the call."

"Intense."

"Yeah. I said I was taking this tour to help my sister, but really, I think I just needed an excuse to run away."

He swivels on the bench so he's facing me. "That is exactly how I feel. Well, except for the sister part."

He smiles at me, and it's so beautifully intense—like it's meant for only me—that I find myself blushing. Yikes, I need to be careful with this one. He's a charmer.

"So tell me," he says, "how does coming on this trip help your sister?"

"Karl Wolfe broke my sister's heart so I came to take revenge."

"Woah!" He tugs down on his baseball hat as if my words nearly blew it off. "I'm sorry to hear that happened to your sister. But your actions? That is dedication. True love. You care about your sister a lot to do this."

"I'd do anything for her."

"But I'm super curious. Exactly how are you planning on enacting this revenge?"

I dig through my bag and pull out my plan for the demise of the Big Bad Wolf. I've slowly been adding ideas to it since I arrived in Germany. "I was going to sabotage the game, but then I worried it would ruin the fun for everyone else, so that got nixed. I'm failing my mission so far."

He takes the list from me, and as he does, his hand brushes mine. Was that a tingle shooting up or static electricity?

"This list is a bit scary." He glances my way, but I can't read his expression with those damn aviator glasses in the way.

"I know." I sigh. "I'm the Evil Queen. Or at least I want to be."

"I think it's a noble list." He hands it back.

"You do?"

"It shows your passion and the depth of your love for your sister. That's not something I've come across in a long time."

"Thank you." I hang my head because suddenly I'm blushing and also a little teary-eyed. It's like someone finally sees me for who I am. Other than Bella, no one has ever done that before.

"I want to help with this sabotage-the-wolf business. We can be co-conspirators because two is always better than one, right?"

Seriously? He's going to help me out? I think of all the times I assisted Hunter, but he never offered it in return. It was always about him and his houses and his work.

"You sure?" I ask. "It sounds like you have your own stuff to worry about based on your phone call."

"You said you needed a distraction, and so do I. Letting me be your assistant helps me, too. It's a win-win."

"Perfect." A smile tugs on my lips. "I've always wanted a partner in crime."

I hold out my hand and he shakes it. Someone clears their throat, and we both look up to find the villainous wolf whose ruin we had just been discussing.

"Why are you two not inside on the tour?" he asks. A storm brews in his eyes, and his face is a lightning storm, ready to strike.

Crap. How much did he overhear?

Movie Star Path: If you want to continue with Scarlett not sabotaging the game, read on to Chapter 14.

Wolf Path: If you want to see how the sabotaged game turns out, skip to Chapter 15.

CHAPTER 14

Movie Star Path

THE FAIRY TALE GAME

Reader Note: *This choice is the continuation of when Scarlett takes the tour and doesn't sabotage the game.*

"We were just enjoying this beautiful day here in Germany," I tell the Big Bad Wolf from where I'm sitting on the bench beside Rob. "Even you can't deny that today is perfect."

His fists clench, but then he takes a long breath like he's trying to exercise self-control. "I'm glad you're having a good time. Speaking of which, I'm headed over to the garden to meet up with the band. Would you like to join me and meet them?"

"A band?" I ask.

"Why not?" Rob says.

"Nothing but the best for my clients," he tells us as we take the path to the garden. "I must admit they're friends of mine. We went to school together for a few years so they do this as a favor for me. Not to say they don't like to have a live audience."

"They do it for free?" I ask.

"They would, but I pay them."

Suddenly, Rob stops as three large guys strut onto the lawn wearing traditional German clothes of tanned sleeveless tunics over breeches. They each have an instrument: a bagpipe, an accordion, and a teardrop-shaped guitar.

"I don't know about this," Rob mutters.

"Don't worry," Mr. Wolfe says. "They don't know."

"Know what?" I ask.

Both Rob and our tour guide ignore me as the trio cheers upon seeing us.

"Jaxon!" the large one with a ponytail yells, clutching the bagpipe. He's as tall as Mr. Wolfe but larger all around. "It has been too long, my man."

They give our tour guide a hug. There's a smattering of German and English being used, so it's hard for me to follow the conversation. Finally, our guide turns to Rob and me and introduces the two of us.

"Jaxon will not disappoint you on this tour," Max, the bagpipe guy, says. "His company is the best around."

"Why do you keep calling him Jaxon?" I cross my arms and lift my eyebrows as I focus on my evil tour guide. "I thought your name was Karl."

The three musicians burst out laughing.

"What did I say?" I search their faces while the Wolfe shakes his head sadly.

"Karl is my twin brother," he explains. "People get us mixed up a lot since we're identical. I like to believe I'm the better twin."

"What?" Shock ripples through me, my mind unable to process this information.

This makes his friends laugh harder, but Max nods, slapping his hand on Jaxon's shoulder. "It is true," he says in his deep voice. "He's the better one. Maybe not the prettiest though."

"Or richest," Guitar Guy adds, which makes them start laughing all over again.

The three take off to warm up and Rob excuses himself to answer another call, leaving Jaxon glaring and me frowning.

"All this time I thought you were Karl." I rub my forehead, still processing this information. What does this mean? How can I enact my revenge now? It's completely pointless.

"Are you disappointed?" Jaxon asks. "A lot of girls come on this tour to try to hook up with my brother."

"What?" I spit out like I just tasted something bad. "No! I would never be interested in you...I mean him."

I mean, he's totally hot, but I'd never consider dating someone who broke my sister's heart. But now that I realize he isn't that jerk, it's all a bit confusing. Unless he's in cahoots with him. They are brothers, after all.

His eyes crinkle sadly as if he had been hoping I might be interested in him. "Right. Well, you two have fun playing the game."

He strides over to a table in the center of the lawn just as the rest of our group tumbles out of the manor, having finished their tour. Lilac runs to join us with Axel at her side.

"There you are," she says breathlessly, cheeks flushed. Her eyes are bright, making her look like a sunflower facing the sun. "They had this adorable puppet show inside. Axel and I were looking everywhere for you two. We thought you'd appreciate it."

"I wanted to get some fresh air," I say.

"Everything alright, man?" Axel asks as Rob rejoins us. He shrugs and looks away.

I wish I could see Rob's eyes under his sunglasses so I could get a better idea of how he's feeling, but something is obviously bothering him. Probably something to do with that call he just had. Our guide blows a whistle and waves us to join him.

"For this game, you'll search the area for envelopes in teams of two," Jaxon explains. It's still hard to think of him not being Karl, the destroyer of my sister's heart. "Inside the envelope is a riddle and a letter. Once you've collected all six, come back to this table. You'll solve the riddle and match its answer to the letter. It will reveal a word that's a clue to our next destination. The winning team wins a spa session at our next stop."

A cheer erupts from the group.

"Go ahead and pick your teams," Jaxon continues.

I face Lilac, but she's bouncing beside Axel, smiling up at him.

"Guess my best bud ditched me for someone prettier." Rob tugs on the bill of his red baseball hat. "Want to be partners?"

There's something endearing about Rob and his hat, and despite the sunglasses, I can see the vulnerability on his face. Is he worried I'll say no?

"There's no one else I'd rather be teamed up with," I say, reaching out and touching his arm. Sure, I'm only touching his sleeve, but there's something intimate about this moment like I'm breaking a barrier between us.

Rob leans closer. "I feel the same way," he says in a low voice meant only for me.

My breath catches, and I peer up into his face, wondering what it is about this guy that captivates me so much. The whistle blows and everyone on the tour bolts into a run, jerking me back to the moment.

Rob's mouth quirks. "Guess that's our cue to start searching for clues."

I nod, pointing to the gingerbread house. "You check there while I look by the frog."

We race to action. I snatch one of the envelopes stacked by the frog. As I dart across the lawn toward Rob, I don't see Axel until it's too late. His large body slams into mine, sending me flying through the air, directly toward Rob.

Rob tries to catch me, but I bounce off him, and the two of us crash to the ground. My head hits a rock. The world goes black.

Option 1: Want to read the Wolf Path version? Go back to Chapter 12 and then read Chapter 15.

Option 2: Want to skip the Wolf Path? Jump ahead to Chapter 16.

Wolf Path

THE WOLF UNMASKED

Reader Note: *This choice is the continuation of when Scarlett decides to sabotage the game.*

"WELCOME to your first fairytale game of our tour!" Mr. Wolfe announces. Everyone cheers and claps.

Now as I look around at the hopeful, eager faces, my grand idea of sabotaging the game doesn't sound like such a good plan after all.

In fact, I'm beginning to think it was a terrible idea.

I shake my head. No, this will be good. Once the game is a disaster, I'll make sure that everyone puts in a bad review for Mr. Wolfe. That will solve the problem.

Mr. Wolfe explains the rules. "You'll be working in teams of two to hunt about the lawn and gather up riddles. Each riddle has a number. Read the clues and grab their letters. Bring them to the table here where you'll take one of these cards." He lifts a card up. "Place your letters beside the answer to the riddle on the card. Here's a hint. The letters form a clue to our next stop on the Fairy Tale Road tour."

There's a rush of oohs among the tour group.

"The first team to fill up their cards with the correct letters," Mr. Wolf continues, "wins a spa treatment tonight at our next destination."

The group cheers again, and a sinking sensation hits me as everyone hurries to pick a partner. I'm too distracted with my guilt to notice who is choosing who.

I stride to the table where the cards are ready for the teams to fill in the letters. Fairy tales are listed vertically while a space is beside them for a letter to go.

Cinderella ____
The Frog King ____
Snow White ____
Sleeping Beauty ____
Rapunzel ____
Little Red Riding Hood ____

Yup. My meddling will completely mess this whole event up. It's going to make Mr. Wolfe look like an idiot. But it will also ruin the fun for everyone.

"Hey," one of the guys on the tour says as he comes up to me. I'm trying to remember his name. Troy maybe? He's got dark brown hair, closely cut, somehow making his ears stick out and clean-shaven face. "You're Scarlett, right?"

"Uh...yeah."

"Cool. Lilac might have mentioned your name." He chuckles lightly. "I'm Trey. I was wondering if you—"

"Scarlett," Rob calls to me and hurries over. "Do you want to be partners? I was going to be Axel's but he chose beauty over brains. His loss."

He points to where Axel is talking to a blushing Lilac.

"Really?" I say. "Because Lilac was studying flashcards on the bus ride over, so I'm thinking he chose beauty *and* brains."

Rob presses his hand to his heart and throws his head back dramatically. "You speak the truth. Will you be my partner out of pity?"

I giggle at Rob's dramatics. "I suppose so."

"But I was going to ask her to be my partner," Trey says, whining.

"Maybe next time," I mumble vaguely, because my gaze has slid over to focus on Enemy #1 who is kindly helping Evelyn and Gary. Why does the wolf always look like he's being nice?

"Fine." Trey rubs his buzz cropped hair. "Next time then."

He wanders off, but my eyes narrow on our tour guide. I know what he's doing. This is all a game to the Big Bad Wolf. A long con. Since Axel is obviously catching Lilac's eye, Mr. Wolfe is working extra hard to show kindness in hopes of getting Lilac's attention.

Rob follows my gaze. "You think Jaxon knows we messed up his game?"

"You mean Karl?" I whisper conspiratorially. "I doubt it."

"Aaaannd he's coming this way."

Mr. Wolf marches over to me like he's on a mission. "I'm going to give everyone else a head start since you two already had a good look at the course. You don't mind, do you?"

Yup. He's upset. And he knows we did something. Except it doesn't make me as happy as I wish it did, and that just puts me in a bad mood. Right now, Bella is probably having a hard time getting out of bed. She's probably not eating enough and losing weight because of this jerk, while he's running about having a fabulous time, hunting down his next prey.

I glower at him.

"No, that's fine, *Karl*," I grind out. He's not going to win this round. "But I'm keeping a close eye on you."

Suddenly, the guests' voices quiet down and the music stops playing. I might have been a little too loud.

His mouth twists. "What did you call me?"

"Karl. And I know what you're up to."

"What am I up to? Wait a second." He holds up a hand. "You think I'm my twin brother, Karl?"

Confusion whirlwinds through me. "I...don't understand."

"Last I checked, my birth certificate says my name is Jaxon Wolfe." There's a flash of a dare in his eyes. "But perhaps you'd like to see it for yourself?"

I swallow, completely off-balance. I'm not sure how to process this information. He's not Karl Wolf. He's not the guy who broke Bella's heart. "No, it's fine. Forget I said anything." A quick glance tells me everyone is listening intently. I've managed to make a complete fool of myself. "Let's just have fun and play the game."

"Very good suggestion," Jaxon says. He steps onto a stool. "Everyone ready? On your marks, get set, go!"

He blows a whistle and the music bursts back to life. Everyone springs to action, racing about the gardens in hunt for the clues. Meanwhile, Rob and I stand there, waiting awkwardly.

"You two can go as well," Jaxon (who I still can't believe is *not* Karl) says. "I was just giving you both a hard time for running about with my clues."

"Thanks, man." Rob fist-bumps Jaxon. Then to me, he says, "I'll grab the letter from the gingerbread house."

"I'll get the one from the throne."

Rob takes off, but I'm rooted to the ground, eyeing Jaxon

and trying to read his face. "So you really have a twin?" I ask, my skepticism lingering.

"Since before birth." He shrugs and chuckles a deep, rich laugh that tumbles about in the air. It's especially mortifying that he's being so nice about this. I would be so much easier if he were a jerk and I could put him firmly in the villain box with a big fat label.

But nope. All my devious, diabolical plans for revenge come crashing down. I turn away, a million questions demanding my attention, but it's hard to focus on which one to address first. Between the music filling the air and the tour guests running about like lost chickens, it's hard to focus. Unless he's lying...

I spin about, searching for Rob. Across the lawn, he's squeezing out of the gingerbread house, waving a letter in his hand. He's trying so hard to win this game, even though he knows it won't make sense after our sabotage. He looks cute with his baseball hat skewed on his head and his glasses slipping down on his nose.

There's something wrong with his hair. It's almost like it's tipped sideways along with this hat. I shrug and hurry to him, except I don't see Axel running in his direction at the same time. The two of us collide, knocking me forward and right into Rob. We bounce off each other and both fall to the ground, my head slamming onto a rock.

Option 1: Want to read the Movie Star Path version? Go back and read Chapter 13 and 14.

Option 2: Want to find out what happens next? Continue to Chapter 16.

He Smells of Spice and All Things Nice

The whistle blows and the music falls silent. My vision swirls a little, and I'm slightly stunned as I lay still, trying to orientate myself. The sun seems too bright. A face looms over me, blocking out the light. A large hand pushes the hair out of my eyes. Fingers brush gently against my skin, shooting tingles down my spine, all the way to my toes.

"Scarlett." Jaxon says my name, full of worry. "Are you well?"

I grunt and try to sit up.

"Easy there." Strong arms support my back. *Jaxon's arms.* "Perhaps take a moment before you get up."

I gaze into those wolf-gray eyes. He smells of spice and all things nice, which just shows I must have a concussion. I hope that tingling thing isn't a sign something is wrong with me from the fall.

Lilac rushes to my other side, her eyes wide. "Oh, Scarlett! Should we call the ambulance?"

"No, I'm fine." I sit up, rubbing my head. "Just a minor bump."

"I'm calling the medics." Jaxon pulls out his phone. "You hit the ground pretty hard. Everyone, give these two some space."

As he talks to the someone on the emergency line, the tour guests back up a little, quieter than usual. Felicia is whispering with her two friends, eyeing Rob, while Evelyn is wringing her hands, and her husband, Gary, pats her shoulder. Trey is holding Rob's baseball hat, and...I squint, Rob's hair?

"Why are you holding Rob's hair?" I ask.

"Glad you're okay, Scarlett," Trey says. "But the real question is why is Robby Ricci here on our tour?"

Lilac gasps at Trey's proclamation, and I whip my gaze to Rob, who is sitting on the ground across from me. His hat, and apparently what must be a wig, are missing from his head. Instead, he's got short black hair, and without the sunglasses, I can see those familiar chocolatey-brown eyes that I've seen in so many movies.

It's that beautiful face that has endeared hearts across the globe. I don't know how I missed it. Trey is right. This is the famous, blockbuster movie star Robby Ricci. Or at least someone who looks the spitting image of him.

Sure, he's not dressed in his usual attire of tight shirts that stretch over his muscular arms or the skinny jeans that wears in Levi commercials showing off his cute ass. Between the baggy clothes, sunglasses, wig, and hat, it makes sense I missed the connection.

My mouth dries up. I've been sneaking around, hanging out with a movie star all this time? I think back to the conversation he had on the phone. He'd been asking for more time. Could he have been talking to his manager?

"Is it true?" I ask. "Are you really Robby Ricci?"

"Who cares about me?" he deftly avoids the question. "You're my concern now. You fell hard. You sure you're okay?"

"I'm good," I say, but when I go to stand up, I start swaying. Rob leaps to my side, holding my arm to give me support. "I just needed a minute for someone to turn off the sun."

His eyes narrow with worry. "Here. Put these on." He passes me his sunglasses. "This will help with the brightness."

"Trey is right. He really does look like Robby Ricci!" Felicity announces and holds up her phone for everyone to see.

The group starts talking at once.

"Listen, everyone," Rob calls out, holding up his hands. "You're right. It's true. I am Robby Ricci."

There's a mix of gasps and "I knew it" among our tour guests. I feel like I've entered another reality. How ironic that I had been accusing Jaxon of faking his personality but really it was Rob pretending to be someone else. Maybe if I'd taken time to consider the people around me rather than just assuming everything, this whole situation wouldn't be so full of surprises.

"I knew there was something fishy about this guy!" Trey announces. "He's here pretending to be one of us, but he's really a spoiled, rich movie star."

"Hey!" Axel snatches Rob's hat and wig from Trey, glaring at him. "Leave my friend alone. He's been through a lot. He was just trying to have some fun like the rest of the world."

"I didn't want to hurt anyone, nor was I trying to be fishy," Rob says. "Things have been tense at work lately, and I needed an escape. I called Axel to tell him what I'd been going through, and he suggested I come with him on this tour."

"You poor thing." Evelyn pats Rob on the shoulder. "I can't imagine how stressful your job must be."

"Don't you worry." Felicia slips to Rob's other side and winks. "Your little secret is safe with me."

Rob smiles uneasily at Felicia. I resist rolling my eyes because I'm sure it would hurt right now. She didn't give him the time of day before, but now that she knows who he is, she's all over him. Meanwhile, Jaxon strides back to us, concern stretching at his face.

"An ambulance should be here any minute," he says. "I'd like them to take a look at both of you."

"I'm fine," Rob says. "But I don't know about Scarlett. She looks like she's seeing more stars than just me."

A few people chuckle.

"I'll be okay," I say. "I'm going to sit this game out."

"Do you need me to get you something?" Lilac asks. "Water? Aspirin?"

"I'm fine." I settle onto a stone bench by what looks like Snow White's wishing well.

Thankfully, everyone's attention quickly refocuses back to our resident movie star. Some guests start asking for his autograph while others ask if they can take his picture.

"Everyone listen up," Jaxon calls over the excitement. "When Robby signed up for this tour, we agreed to keep his identity a secret so he could enjoy the full fairytale experience just like the rest of you. So I need to ask for you give him some privacy. Can you all do that?"

Everyone nods, but Trey mutters something under his breath. Felicity lifts up her phone, pretending to take a selfie but from her angle, it's clear that Rob is right behind her. Jaxon steps in between her and Rob.

"Sorry," Jaxon says. "No photos of the other participants on this tour without their permission. No exceptions."

"I was just taking a selfie," Felicity huffs.

"Then you'll need to make sure Rob isn't in your selfies when you take them," Jaxon says patiently.

The ambulance arrives, and the medics check out both Rob and me. He's fine, of course. No surprise there with all those muscles.

"You, though, may have a concussion," the medic tells me. "Someone should keep an eye on you for the next twenty-four hours."

"I can help her," Rob says at the same time as Jaxon says, "I can do that."

The medic glances between the two of them and smiles knowingly at me. "Looks like you're in good hands then. I could have them check in on you a few times tonight," she adds with a wink.

My cheeks flush. "Thank you for your help," I say, my eyes darting between the two guys. "I'll be fine. It's just a bump."

Once the ambulance leaves, Jaxon gathers the group around while I sit back down on the bench.

"Let's get back to the game," Jaxon tells the other guests, "and have some fairytale fun."

The group cheers. He blows the whistle and the tour guests burst back into action, racing about the area grabbing clues.

Rob sits beside me. "Without my partner, I think I'll sit out, too." He fidgets with his wig. "At least we gave them something to talk about at dinner tonight."

"We or you? I still can't believe you're really Robby Ricci. Like you're the guy who won last year's Oscar for best actor?"

He grimaces. "Does that bother you?"

"And starred in the blockbuster, *The Titan Warlords*?"

"I promise I don't really chop people's heads off when I get angry."

"Well, that's a relief!" I laugh and then regret it as the world spins. I grimace and rub my forehead. "It does seem strange having you here. Sitting on this bench with me."

"I'm just a regular guy."

A regular guy who's like a multi-millionaire and has been on the cover of People's magazine.

"Can I still call you Rob?"

"Absolutely. It's actually the name my family and friends call me." He runs a hand through his short, dark hair, reminding me of the way his character in *Battle of the Royals* acted where he played a fierce—and quite sexy—knight. "Please don't be mad at me. I wanted to tell you the truth; it just didn't seem like the right time, you know?"

"No need to apologize. We just met, after all. Who knows? I could be some crazy stalker who's wanted to marry you since I first laid eyes on you as a child star."

He cocks his head and scoots away an inch. "That does sound a little creepy." He grins and scoots back next to me, so close I can feel his warmth. "The truth is, it's more than that. When we were hanging out, I had a lot fun. I didn't want to ruin things by throwing in this whole I'm-a-movie-star thing into the mix."

Now it's my turn to laugh. "So knocking me out seemed like a better idea?"

"Yeah, sorry about that. I felt like we had a connection today. I know this sounds weird, but hanging out and talking to you felt real. Maybe it's because I knew you didn't know who I really was." He chuckles. "Now I'm the one who sounds like the creepy stalker."

"I get what you're saying. You're used to people wanting to hang out with you only because you're famous, not just because you're *you*."

"Exactly! Do you think now that you know who I really am you'll still want to hang out together during the tour?"

It hurts to think right now, but does that mean he wants me to be a friend or that he wants something more? I mean, we did have a connection. The way he looked at me made me feel all fluttery inside. I press the ice pack the medic gave me to my head, needing it more than ever.

My eyes drift to Jaxon, standing tall in the center of the chaos of tourists. Who is he really? And why did I feel tingles in my toes when his fingers brushed against my skin? I need to get answers and find out what happened between his brother and my sister. Could Jaxon have been a part of that?

Or maybe I should just forget about revenge and have a holiday fling.

With a MOVIE STAR!

The Wolf Path: If you think Scarlett should explore these feelings she's having for Jaxon and follow up with what his brother did to her sister, read on to Chapter 17.

The Movie Star Path: If you think Scarlett should explore this connection she has with Rob, skip ahead to Chapter 19.

Wolf Path

CONFRONTING THE WOLF

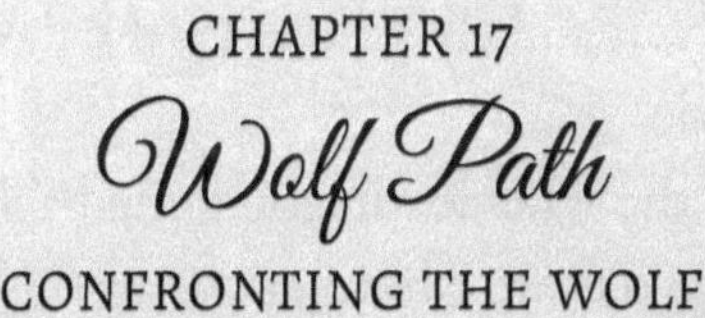

Reader Note: *You have chosen to have Scarlett to investigate things with Jaxon Wolfe.*

I'M NOT sure if the tingles from Jaxon's touch were from hitting my head or if it's a sign I'm attracted to him, but I do know I need answers.

I told Rob I would love to be his friend, but I didn't want to hog his time with Axel. A flash of disappointment fell over his face. It's then I knew he really had been hinting at something more than just friendship. He nodded and seemed to understand, and we've been sitting in awkward silence ever since.

It's not that I don't care for Rob or that there couldn't be something between us, but the reality is Rob is a superstar. He lives in a completely different world than me. There's no way things could work for either of us outside of this tour. I've seen him in magazines with beautiful models and glitzy movie stars.

I'm the practical girl in the business suit, not the glam girl in the sheer dress.

Sure, I wouldn't mind slipping on a gorgeous gown, but how long would our relationship last? Celebrities are known to get bored quickly. It's likely I'd just be the flavor of the month and then cast aside.

Jaxon blows the whistle, dragging me back to reality. "The winners of the spa day are Evelyn and Gary!"

Rob and I rejoin the group gathered around Jaxon and give Evelyn and Gary a round of applause.

"Go ahead and tell the group the word you were able to unscramble," Jaxon says to the couple.

"It says forest," Evelyn replies.

"That's right." Jaxon nods, shoving back the wayward swoop of hair that likes to tumble over his eyes. "Our next stop is Alsfeld by the Schwalm River, which is the setting for Little Red Riding Hood's adventures." He looks at me, and his lips quirk when he says *Little Red,* causing my face to burn. "We'll be visiting the Alsfeld Fairy Tale House, staying the night in town, and then participating in another game tomorrow. I hope you'll find Alsfeld as enchanting as I think it is."

Then he tells us to break for a quick lunch on our own before returning to the bus at 2 p.m. I join the others in congratulating Evelyn and Gary before we all head off on our own.

"That game was so much fun," Lilac tells me as we leave the garden. "It's everything I'd hoped it would be. But how are you feeling? You hit your head pretty hard."

"Appears as if I'll live. The ice pack helped."

"And maybe hanging out with Robby Ricci." Lilac waggles her eyebrows.

I laugh. "We're just friends. There's nothing going on

between us. But you and Axel did pretty well together as a team. I thought you two were going to win it there."

"We were close. It's just that some of the clues didn't quite match up."

"You should've told that to Mr. Wolfe." I frown, feeling bad it hadn't worked for her. Thankfully everyone still had fun.

Lilac gives me an odd look. "Why do you keep calling him Mr. Wolfe? He's not that much older than us."

I shrug, but my skin feels itchy all over. "I guess I thought he was Karl, his brother, and now it's hard to get this new picture of him in my mind."

Axel and Rob stroll up beside us. Rob wig, hat, and sunglasses are back on. I wonder what it must be like for him to never really live life out in the open, always hiding his true self.

"Hey, partner." Axel beams at Lilac. "We rocked it back there. Just a little unlucky with those clues. But tomorrow, we're totally going to win the next game."

Lilac soaks up his smile like he's the sun and she's a flower. "I wonder what we'll be doing," she muses. "Maybe we could study together on the bus ride. I have heaps of fairytale trivia we could review."

"Sounds awesome," Axel says. "I'd be up for it."

"Awesome?" Rob snorts. "This I've got to see. Axel Williams flashcarding fairy tales."

"Laugh now," Axel warns, "but wait until tomorrow when we decimate you."

"Ohhhh!" Rob rubs his hands. "Challenge accepted."

We arrive at a cute little bistro with faded bricks and an arched wooden doorway. Lilac suggests we eat inside, but my eye catches Jaxon entering a pub on the other side of the road. As fun as it would be to hang out with these three, I need answers about his brother's treatment of my sister.

"I have to talk to Jaxon about a couple of things," I tell them. "But I'll see you on the bus."

"If you change your mind," Lilac says, "you know where to find us."

Rob opens his mouth as if to say something, but when I give the group a little wave as I back away, he closes his mouth.

My feet hurry across the uneven cobblestone street, but when I reach for the handle of the thick wooden door, I pause. What do I ask him?

I pull out my phone and text Bella.

Our tour guide isn't Karl! Apparently Karl has a twin brother named Jaxon and it's him.

I tap my phone impatiently, hoping she'll answer, but she doesn't.

Sucking a deep breath, I yank open the door and march inside, my hair billowing behind me. But the moment I cross the threshold, I jerk to a stop. Jaxon is here, but he's not alone. He's sitting in a booth with the three other musicians. They're all drinking beer and laughing like they're having a great time.

Now is obviously not the time to confront him about his evil twin brother or ask him if he too is a mastermind of villainy. I'm about to spin on my heels and vanish before I look like a complete fool, but Max, the bagpipe guy, glances my way before I can duck outside.

If only I were a real Evil Queen and had magical powers to poof me away in a cloud of smoke.

"Ah, look who we have!" Max exclaims in a thick German accent. "The Little Red Riding Hood."

I back up, but Jaxon's storm gray eyes pin me to the floor. Damn his wolf powers!

"So we do." Jaxon smirks, making one eyebrow lift. "You need to see the paper, don't you?"

His accent is more German than British with his friends. I frown and step closer to their table. "What paper?"

"My birth certificate."

I shrug. "I suppose I wouldn't mind. Evidence is always helpful."

"Listen, I know you and Rob tried to muck up my game." He digs into his pocket and pulls out his wallet. "But it all worked out in the end, yes? And I don't have my birth certificate, but here's a photo of Karl and me, and here's my driver's license."

He slaps both on the edge of the thick wood table. I take the bait and edge closer to peek down and study the photo. Sure enough, there are two guys similar in look, except one is obviously Jaxon with the wild hair and scruff on his chin as if he didn't have time to shave. While Jaxon is more rugged and built, Karl is leaner and more sophisticated with slicked-back hair and a neatly trimmed beard.

Max says something in German and everyone at the table laughs. My eyes jerk up to the group. Are they laughing at me?

"Don't mind them," Jaxon grumbles. "They love to tell me I'm the ugly twin, but then I remind them that I'm the better friend."

"This is true." Max nods. "And less of an arschloch."

The group laughs again, and I can't stop the smile teasing my lips. There's something about these guys that I like. Maybe it's the easy way about them or how they seem to be genuine. Where I work, I'm always trying to hide my true self, never letting anyone see my weaknesses. I have to stay strong to keep up my professional image and deliver results. Because marketing is so competitive, it's like we're all trying to outperform the other. Revealing weaknesses only gives my coworkers a competitive advantage to undermine me. It's how I've gotten promotion after promotion.

"Why don't you join us?" Jaxon offers. "Then you can tell me why you're so interested in my brother."

I bristle at his insinuation. The accordion player gets up and drags over a chair to the end of the booth, which I expect is for me. But then Max moves and plops his large frame into it, opening a place next to Jaxon.

"Sit," Fritz, the accordion player says, pointing to the empty spot.

Jaxon reddens and focuses on his beer while I twist my hands together, unsure if I should sit in enemy territory or not. He's given me solid proof he's not his brother. I could forget this whole situation with my sister and join Lilac, Axel, and...Rob.

Or I could stay and learn more about Jaxon. After all, what if he's a player just like his brother? Plus, I still need to follow through with making sure his brother sends a formal apology to my sister.

Except there's one teeny, tiny problem. His friends are completely wrong about him. Karl might be good-looking, but Jaxon is undeniably hot. And that could be very, very dangerous.

The Wolf Path: If you think Scarlett should stay and sit with Jaxon, continue reading in Chapter 18.

The Movie Star Path: If you think Scarlett should leave and go find Rob, skip ahead to Chapter 19.

CHAPTER 18

Wolf Path

MY, WHAT BIG TEETH YOU HAVE

Reader Note: *You have chosen to have Scarlett stay at the tavern (kneipe in German) with Jaxon.*

IT CAN'T BE that dangerous to sit next to the Wolfe for a little while, right? Besides, my stomach is growling. I really could use something to eat before we get on the bus. Might as well sit down. Think of it as multitasking. Answers and food.

I edge into the seat beside Jaxon, but his whole presence seems to fill every inch of the space. The smell of him makes me a little dizzy. No, it must be the fact I haven't eaten. Or maybe my concussion.

"I'm starved," I say. "What's good to eat here?"

"Everything," Accordion Guy says at the same time Max says, "Nothing."

"You must be starved." Jaxon grins down at me. My heart does this weird little flutter. I rub my chest to calm it down.

101

"After all that sneaking about and hiding my clues in the bushes."

I swallow down my guilt and quickly pick up a menu.

"I...uh." I stare at the words. Nothing is written in English.

"This is good, you know," Max tells me. "This man needs someone to keep him in line. Runs about like he can do whatever he wants. You are the first woman who's put him in his place."

Now would be a good time to admit why I'm here and explain my situation. Get some answers and maybe find a way to make things right. But as I peek over at Jaxon, his gray eyes catch hold of mine. There's no anger in them, only a mischievous twinkle.

"Hallo!" A voice to my left startles me, and I whip around to see a lady holding a notepad and pen. She rattles off a bunch of words in German.

I'm completely at a loss.

"The sauerbraten is good," Jaxon offers.

"The what?"

"It's a roast beef stew. She wants to know what you wish to eat."

"Okay, I'll have the sauerbraten," I say, butchering the pronunciation.

The others at the table chuckle, and Max says, "You must teach her some German, my friend."

"No need." Jaxon takes a sip of his beer. "She's just here for the two-week tour."

"That's right." I nod, firmly. "Two weeks of pure fairytale fun."

The guys around the table give each other looks. When my stew is deposited in front of me, she also brings me a stein of beer.

"I didn't order a beer," I point out.

"You are in Germany," Fritz says. "It is what it is."

"Well, when in Germany." I lift my stein. "Prost!"

They grin and hold up theirs, clanging them against mine. I sip, and the warm, bitter liquid slides down my throat all the way to my toes. Slightly relaxed, I dig into my stew. Thick chunks of meat and warm vegetables fill me up while the four guys chat in German.

"It is for the best that you leave for America soon," Max says, switching to English for me. "This man is pure trouble."

I perk up at this. Ammunition! "Tell me all about it."

Jaxon groans while the three launch into a story about how he secretly shaved all of his brother's hair off when Karl got drunk one night.

"Oh, that is evil," I agree, nodding happily.

"Ah!" Peter, the guitar guy, holds up his hands, eyes lit up. "Remember when he took that one group to the wrong castle and crashed the wedding?"

The three laugh hard, slapping the table while Jaxon leans back in the booth, arms crossed and a scowl on his face.

"I don't know why I bother hanging out with you three," he grumbles. "You are the worst friends."

"We are the worst," Max agrees, slamming his empty stein down. "Now, we must leave. We perform tonight, and it is a long drive."

"It was nice to meet you," I say as the three climb out of the booth. "Will I see you again?"

"Depends." Fritz takes my hand and kisses the top. "If Jaxon is not enough of a man for you, come find me."

Max smacks him on the head while Jaxon bats him backward with a, "Hey, watch it there."

"Tschüss," the three say goodbye to me and before I know it, I'm sitting alone with Jaxon.

I should be terrified to be sitting next to my enemy, but the warmth of the amber liquid, the thick stew, and the laughter has relaxed me. I lean back against the wooden headboard of the booth with a contented sigh. Jaxon, however, seems to tighten up like a corkscrew and shifts away.

"I like your friends," I say.

"You just like their terrible stories about me."

"This is true." He's staring at me with an odd expression. "What is it? Do I have stew on my face or sticks in my hair?"

Suddenly, he seems too close. Like if I were to lean in, my lips could brush against his. My mouth parts in shock at those thoughts, and I scoot toward the edge of the booth.

What am I doing? I came here to confront him about my sister, not daydream about kissing! I must have drank too much. Or maybe it's jetlag. My whole body is too relaxed and far too happy. I push myself out of the booth and slip to the opposite side, clasping my hands on the table in my most businesslike manner.

"It's time you know the truth," I begin.

His eyebrows lift. "Truth?"

"I'm actually on this tour because of my sister, Bella Walker." I blow out a long breath. *Here goes nothing.* "She's the woman that your brother messed around with and hurt. I'm not a reporter or a random American tourist. I'm Bella's sister, Scarlett Walker, and I came to get justice for my sister."

His eyes widen and he leans back, running a palm across his face. "Wow, alright. This is rather shocking. First of all, I'm terribly sorry for your sister and what happened. It was wrong of my brother to treat her that way."

"I'd like a formal apology from him."

"Consider it done. What would be the best way for your sister? A phone call? Letter?"

"A letter should suffice. She doesn't need to hear his voice ever again. He broke her heart, and I don't want her to have to deal with him more than necessary."

"Of course." Pain etches across his face. "I would never wish your sister to ever experience what she went through again. And just so you know, I would never have allowed it if I was aware."

"I appreciate that." I stare down at my hands, feeling a little deflated now that my reason for coming has been revealed. "Anyway, that's why I'm here. I came to seek justice for my sister."

"Is that why you sabotaged my game? You thought I was part of it?" A wry look flickers across his eyes.

I shrug. "I was angry. Thinking back, I know it was childish and I should've asked you first."

"No, I get it. Fighting for those we love makes us heroes and humans. When we love someone, passion and protectiveness have a way of taking over."

"Thank you for understanding." I stare at him, shocked by his words. There is great wisdom in them and I find myself respecting him.

"Is there anything else I can do? First off, I'd like to offer this trip complimentary to you. Or if you feel like you need to leave now that you've said your piece, we'll reimburse you for all your expenses."

"That won't be necessary. I actually won a gift card for your tour, which your company paid for."

"Strange, I don't remember us making gift cards." He shakes his head. "But if you feel like you need to leave the tour, I am happy to arrange for transportation."

I don't know what to think of Jaxon or his kind offers. Is he playing this role knowing that I could sue his ass off and completely decimate his family? Or does he really mean what he's saying?

"I'm actually having a good time, so I'm planning on staying for a while. Besides, I need to keep a close eye on you and make sure your brother follows up on his promise to apologize to my sister."

I say this in a teasing tone, but deep down, I mean every word.

"You can keep a close eye on me for as long as you wish." Then, as if realizing the implications of his words, his face reddens. "I mean, you are welcome to stay for the remainder of the trip. I will speak to my brother about this matter right away."

"I should go." I stand, trying to look everywhere other than at Jaxon, but somehow my eyes still track to him.

He's running a hand through his thick brown hair, ruffling it up even more. It takes a little effort for him to get his large frame out of the booth, but when he stands up beside me, heat ebbs off him onto me like a warm blanket. What would it be like to have those muscular arms wrapped around me and lean against his thick chest? I should run away, but for some reason, my legs are rooted in place.

He picks up my jacket that I forgot on the booth and wraps it around my shoulders. His fingers brush against the skin of my neck, and it's like I've been burned with fire. Terrifyingly hot and searingly delicious.

I back away, tucking my arms into my coat. "Thank you for listening," I babble. "I almost forgot it. I have money here somewhere." I dig into my purse.

"My treat," he says. "Besides, I already paid."

"You did?"

"We should go." His voice is thick. "Everyone will be waiting for us."

He holds the door open for me as the two of us leave the pub, then redirects me to turn right by touching the tip of my elbow when I'm disorientated by the brightness of the day. It's like we were on a date and now walking back into reality.

But we weren't. It was just lunch where I demanded justice for my sister. That's all.

Movie Star Path: Want to see what would've happened if she had told Rob she would like to hang out with him more on this trip? Go to Chapter 19.

Wolf Path: Want to continue and see how this relationship with Jaxon will turn out? Slip ahead to Chapter 20.

CHAPTER 19

Movie Star Path

LIGHTS, CAMERA, LUNCH!

Reader Note: *You've chosen for Scarlett to get to know Rob, the movie star, better.*

I STUDY ROB'S FACE—THAT sharp jaw, the long lashes, and eyes I could swim in for days—and consider his question. Do I want to hang out with him during the tour?

What am I saying? Who wouldn't? I mean the guy might be famous, but he's also proven to be fun. The real question is if he's thinking of me as a travel buddy or something more? I came on this tour to get justice for my sister, but now that I've realized Jaxon isn't Bella's beast of an ex, my priorities have shifted. I could continue this tour and enjoy my vacation. After all, when was the last time I had fun?

"I'd like that," I tell him. "But let's not knock each other out in the future."

"Oh, Scarlett." He shoots me this look that sends my heart

swooping on the loops of a rollercoaster. "Every time I look at you, I only think *you're* a knock-out."

He winks, and I roll my eyes, shoving my palm against his arm.

"The tabloids were right," I say. "You *are* a charmer."

"You wound me!" He dramatically presses a palm over his chest as if offended, but I've also gotten my answer. He's not looking at me just as a tour buddy, and I can't deny that I'm not opposed.

The whistle blows, dragging our attention back to Jaxon, who's announcing Evelyn and Gary as the winners of the game. We join the others just as Jaxon makes another announcement.

"You're going to love Alsfeld, our next tour stop," he tells the group. "It's the location where many believe the fairy tale of *The Little Red Hood* originated. We'll be staying the night and then tomorrow we'll visit the Alsfeld Fairy Tale House and play another fairytale-themed game. You've got some time to grab lunch. Meet up at the bus at 2 p.m."

After congratulating Evelyn and Gary, Lilac and Axel herd Rob and me out to the main road in search of food. The spring air is sweet, and if it weren't for the cars buzzing past, I can almost imagine I've been swept back to a time when knights dueled for honor and maidens tossed flowers to their favorite heroes.

"All that running around has me starved," Lilac says. "And I've found us a place that is highly rated."

"We were so close to winning!" Axel clenches his fists. "Tomorrow though, we're going to be victorious. Right, Lilac?"

"We've already made a plan of action." Lilac holds up a list she's created on her phone. Inwardly, I shrink, thinking back to my list on how to take down the Big Bad Wolf. I really need to rethink my own plan of action. "We're going to start studying right away on the bus."

"First you steal my competition partner and now my bus seat?" Rob leans his head back in agony. "I'm devastated!"

"Now that I know you're a professional liar," Lilac wags a finger at him, "your acting skills don't fool me."

"Not to worry." Rob gives Axel a pointed look. "I've already secured a better partner anyway, and the view is much better. Right, Scarlett?"

Rob throws his arm over my shoulder like we're best friends.

"It's your lucky day," I say wryly and shrug as if I couldn't care less, but my insides are squirming about like jellyfish on the loose. I mean, I'm hanging out with one of the most famous celebrities on the planet, which is beyond weird. When I text Bella she will never believe me.

The four of us have lunch at a cute bistro where I try schnitzel for the first time along with a pile of fries. Axel explains his plans for his perfume line, and I give him some marketing pointers to get him started. Once we finish, Axel and Lilac ditch us for a sensory shop down the street, leaving Rob and me to wander alone. There's an awkward silence for the first time between us, and I push my fists into my jacket pockets, desperately trying to think of something to say.

"Have you picked out your costume for the ball at the end of the tour?" I ask.

"Ball?" Rob frowns. "No one told me there would be a ball."

I spot a tourist shop with traditional Bavarian clothes and drag him inside.

"It's on the itinerary. Don't worry, I didn't pack anything

either. I was too busy trying to make a list of ways to destroy the Big Bad Wolf."

He chuckles. "Now that you know it's not him, are you planning on staying for the rest of the tour?"

"I'm considering it." I snatch a gray felt hat off the shelf and replace Rob's baseball hat with it. "Not a bad look." I tilt my head sideways as I assess him. "But then I suppose you could look good in anything."

"Are you saying I'm good-looking?" He grins mischievously while adjusting the hat.

My body zings like that smile jolted me with caffeine.

"You know you're handsome." I roll my eyes. "Didn't People magazine already announce that in some list that they made?"

"Who cares about People magazine? What matters is what Scarlett Walker thinks."

"Wait. I never told you my last name."

"I may have had my assistant look you up."

I cock an eyebrow, teasing. "Now who's the stalker?"

"Sorry." He looks away. "I had a few crazy exes. I fully admit that I'm paranoid."

"Well, just for that," I pluck a pair of dark brown lederhosen from the rack and push it into his arms, "you're going to wear this for the ball."

"Am I now?" He shoots me a wicked glance and goes to a rack lined with dirndls. He presses a green dress with golden ribbons against my body, assessing the result with lifted eyebrows. "This should work well with you as my partner."

"*If* I'm your partner. I still haven't decided if you pass the test yet."

"Oh!" he hoots. "She's playing hard to get. Okay, okay. Bring it on. I'll rise to the occasion."

My head spins a little. What is this game we're playing? It's starting to feel a little too flirtatious. Too fast. And definitely too dangerous. I shove aside my worries, telling myself that I'm making something of nothing. That's always been my problem in the past. I love to overanalyze and overthink everything. A handy skill for my job, but perhaps it's held me back in other areas.

We try on a few styles, and before we know it, we're laughing and taking selfies of ourselves in front of the mirror, mimicking the different poses for his various movies. His wig falls off twice, but it's the second time that gets one of the shoppers' attention.

"You look just like Robby Ricci," a young woman points out, rounding the clothes racks. She holds up her phone and shows us a picture of him on the red carpet. "The resemblance is striking."

"Really?" I scrunch up my nose and stare between the photo and Rob. "I'm not seeing it."

"I get it all the time." Rob's eyes glint playfully. "If only I were as hot as that guy."

I snort. "At least you're not as self-absorbed as him."

"There is that." He smirks, rubbing his chin as he studies me.

I quickly look away.

"How can you not see the resemblance?" the lady presses. Then her eyes narrow on his hair. "Is that a wig you're wearing?"

"My boyfriend is very sensitive about his hair." I tug Rob's arm through mine in a show of solidarity. "I'd appreciate it if you wouldn't make fun of him."

"You're his girlfriend?" the woman asks, and her eyes go wide.

Okay, so maybe we've gone a little too far with the joking. But it's hard with Rob. He's fun and everything is easy and simple with him. Here he is, one of the most famous men in the world and although I've only known him for a day, I feel more comfortable with him than I ever did with Hunter. Which is problematic on too many levels.

"Do you have a problem with my girlfriend?" Rob asks, tucking my arm close to his chest. I don't want him to let go.

"But Robby Ricci isn't dating anyone." The girl's blue eyes widen like she's just found a mine of gold.

"Sweetie," Rob says in a sugary voice, smiling at me like I really am his girlfriend. "I think we should leave."

The woman gasps. "It really is you!"

Quickly, we duck out of the shop before anyone else notices us. Once we step onto the street, Rob pulls me along until we're tucked away in a tiny beer garden. We peek around the corner to see if she's followed us, but she's nowhere in sight.

"That was quite the experience." I start laughing and his serious face relaxes.

"I'm glad you're cool with all that. Some of my exes weren't so great about the invasion of privacy."

A server comes to greet us and asks if we'd like to sit for a drink. Since we still have about twenty minutes before we're expected to get on the bus, we find a seat at a long wooden table under the shade of a chestnut tree and each order a drink and pretzels.

"So how many exes are you talking about here?" I ask, dipping my pretzel into the mustard ramekin.

He takes off his wig with a frown and scrapes a hand across the top of his head. "I know I shouldn't take this thing off, but since no one is paying attention to us and we're out of the way, we should be fine."

"Are you avoiding the question?"

"Guilty as charged." He winks at me and takes a long swig of his frothy, golden beer. "Ah. Nothing like German beer."

I decide to let it go. After all, we might have had a little fun today together, but we hardly know each other.

"So now that you've discovered our tour guide is the wrong Mr. Wolfe," he smoothly changes the subject, "what will you do with yourself for the rest of the trip?"

"I was considering heading back home, but I haven't quite decided if he truly is innocent. How do I know he's not just like his brother or covering for him? What Karl did to my sister was wrong and if this company allows sexual harassment, the public needs to know."

"I couldn't agree more, which is why I insist you stay for the remainder of the tour. Axel is great, but I'm afraid he's fallen victim to the lovely Lilac."

"They do seem quite smitten with each other."

"We must be vigilant during the rest of the tour. Remember, you've asked me to be your co-conspirator, and I don't plan on breaking my promise."

"Well, in that case, it sounds like I must continue."

"Excellent. We shall be champions of justice. Avengers for your sister."

"How can I say no to that?"

"Here's to swift justice, where our villains tremble and wrongs are made right!" He holds up his stein.

"I'll drink to that." I clink mine against his.

CHAPTER 20

Stepping into a Fairy Tale

When I get off the bus, it's like I'm stepping into a fairy tale. Alsfeld is a medieval village, complete with beautifully adorned, half-timbered houses that are intricately carved. The sun is setting over the eaves of the stiffly peaked roofs, casting golden light across the geometric patterns on the houses. Winding cobblestone streets meander out from the main road where we're parked as if tempting us to explore unknown paths.

I'm so enraptured I bump into Trey. Instead of moving out of the way, he flashes me a leering smile that makes me a little uneasy.

"Excuse me." I back away. "Didn't see you there."

"I'm not sorry." He winks. "You can bump into me any time."

As if sensing my unease, Lilac appears at my side and hooks her arm through me, pulling me off to the side. "That guy gives me the creeps. It's like he's staring at us all the time."

"And here I'd been worried about our tour guide being the

creepy one," I say. "He reminds me of Gaston from Disney's *Beauty and the Beast.*"

She shudders. "Our tour guide isn't that bad, is he?" She nods at Jaxon as he gets off the bus and escorts the elderly couple to a taxi. He hands them an envelope, which must be their voucher for their spa day.

"He has been surprising."

"Along with you and Rob who seem to be hitting it off." She gives me a knowingly look.

My face burns. "He seems nice."

She snorts and rolls her eyes as Jaxon rejoins our group.

"Alright, everyone," he says in a loud enough voice to capture everyone's attention. "Feel free to grab dinner on your own or stroll about the town for the rest of the evening. First thing tomorrow, we'll meet up at the Märchenhaus Alsfeld, or in English, Alsfeld Fairy Tale House. Until then, gute nacht."

Jaxon heads off to talk to the bus driver while Rob has stepped aside to take another phone call. I grab my suitcase from beneath the bus and join the others in trundling into the Mainzir Tor Inn. Once I've checked in, I part ways with Lilac, promising to meet up later for dinner. My room is simple but quaint with a wooden ceiling, a single bed with a clean white bedspread, and a pine cabinet to store my suitcase. I slip off my shoes and sag onto the bed, eager to finally get some rest after the long day.

It's when I pull out my phone, I frown at a stream of messages from my boss. Plus a missed call. *Odd.*

> Sheryl: Hello, Scarlett. I know you're on vacation, but can you give me a call?

> Sheryl: The sooner the better.

And then there is a missed call from Hunter as well. My heart skips, but I'm not sure if it's in a good way or bad. Am I really ready to talk to him yet? No, definitely not. So I call my boss instead.

She answers on the first ring. "Scarlett, is that you?"

"Hey. What's up?" I lean back against the headboard of the bed.

"We have an emergency here. Google has changed their entire algorithm and half of our marketing ads aren't translating correctly to the customers."

I jerk up, now standing. "What? This is bad."

"I've got five clients on my back about their drop in sales, and I suspect more will jump in line soon once they start seeing their products tank."

"I'm sorry, but what do you want me to do? I don't have my computer or access to the internet like I do back home."

"How soon can you be back in the office?"

"Sheryl, I'm in Germany."

"I know." She sighs heavily. "And you deserve time away. But no one can do the job or problem-solve issues like you can. I'm sure you're having the time of your life, but if you could come back right away, I will offer you a bonus."

I bite my lip, not believing I'm even going to ask this, but I say, "How much?"

"Fifteen thousand."

I sag onto my bed, my head swimming at that number. "Are you serious?"

"It's a big number, but if we don't get our shit together over here, I'm going to lose everything. Crap. I just got an email from Tella Communications saying they're pulling us as their marketing firm. I need you, and I need you now."

Then she launches off a slew of new issues that just popped

up along with a line of curse words that would make Grams's toes shrivel.

"I know this is bad," I interrupt her panic-streak, "but there must be someone else who can help you."

"Who?" she throws back at me. "Give me one damn name that could do half of your job."

My mind comes up blank. "What about Larson? He's good with numbers."

"Larson?" She snorts. "He can't troubleshoot big issues for the life of him."

"That's valid. What about Kelsey?"

"Twenty thousand," Sherly shoots back. "Get on the first plane tomorrow and come directly to the office. Plus I'll give you the senior director title you've been asking for."

I blink. She's throwing out titles and money like candy at a parade. It's everything I've ever wanted from my job. It's everything I've been dreaming and working toward for years.

So why am I balking?

"I'll think about it." I rub my forehead. "I'll give you an answer in the morning."

"My offer for the bonus and new title expires at 6 a.m."

"Try to stay calm," I tell her. "And ask Gary to run the analytics on the ads still serving correctly."

"We need you here," she says. "Don't let us down."

She hangs up on me. I collapse onto the bed, burrowing my head in the pillow. Twenty thousand dollars in cash is a lot of money. It would give me that boost to get ahead. Besides, it's not like I'm helping my sister anymore now that I know the guy who ruined her life isn't actually the tour guide. After learning the truth about Jaxon, my plans of revenge feel pointless.

My mind flickers to Hunter and the house at the beach.

This would give us a huge fund for renovations. It could be a great way to start our lives together.

But do I really want that life with Hunter?

A knock on the door interrupts my thoughts. I slide out of bed and peek out into the hall. Rob is standing there, leaning against the old wooden doorframe. Even with the strange hair, he looks like he just stepped out of a magazine commercial with his tight black pants and form-fitting, button-down white shirt that shows off a tanned complexion. His wig is tilted a little off-centered, but it gives him an endearing look.

"Hey, you." His smile widens. "Axel ditched me to have dinner with a prettier partner. But I'm positively starved. Perhaps you'd be willing to escort a poor, hungry soul to dinner?"

I fidget with my phone. Do I forget about Hunter and go out to dinner with Rob? Or do I tell Rob I have things I need to deal with and to go to dinner without me?

Or maybe do a little wolf hunting and find out the truth about him.

Hunter Path: Yes! Scarlett should call Hunter and hear what he has to say. He deserves a chance. Read Chapter 21.

Movie Star Path: Forget Hunter! Live a little and go out on an almost-date with a Movie Star! Go to Chapter 22.

Wolf Path: Tell Scarlett not to call Hunter and send her back on the Wolf Path by jumping ahead and reading Chapter 24.

CHAPTER 21

Hunter Path

CALLING HUNTER

Reader Note: *You choose to have Scarlett call Hunter back.*

THE DEBATE TO call Hunter swings back and forth like a pendulum in my mind. If I call him back, I'm reopening the door to our relationship. Do I really want that? I lean against the headboard, staring at my tiny hotel room in Alsfeld, Germany. Sitting here on this hard bed, I suddenly feel alone. I'm in a foreign country with complete strangers. It would be nice to talk to someone I care about.

I press Hunter's name to make the call.

"Scarlett?" Hunter's voice tumbles through space to me. I hate to admit it, but my heart warms hearing his voice. "Thank you for calling me back."

"Hey. How are you?"

"Terrible." His voice is laced with agony. "Life just isn't the same without you. I've been trying to work and go about my day, but all I can think about is you."

My heart flutters. It actually flutters! When has it ever done that while we've been dating? Is it because I've finally truly fallen in love with this guy or am I just deprived?

"I've missed you, too." I pick off a speck of dirt from the bedspread.

"Really? You have no idea how much that means to me. That gives me hope it isn't all over between us. I've been thinking about everything you said, and you're right. I have been taking you for granted. I haven't been working on growing our relationship. I need to water the plant."

I grin. "I'm a plant now?"

"Water the flower," he amends, chuckling. "You're a flower, and I've been an idiot to not appreciate you. You know, not stopping and smelling the roses sort of thing."

"That's a weird analogy for our situation, but I'll go with it."

"When you get back from Germany, I want to show you I mean what I say. If you're willing to give me a second chance."

I trace the thread lines on the blanket. "I'm thinking about coming back early."

He gasps. "Really?"

"There's an emergency at work, and my boss offered me twenty thousand dollars if I leave Germany tomorrow to help put out her fires."

"Must be a pretty major fire."

"It is. Do you think I should go back?"

There's a pause of silence. "I'd love it if you came back tomorrow and I had the chance to see you, but you need to do what's best for you. I've been thinking a lot lately. This past year, I've been putting my career first and you second. I want to put you first from now on. You need to do what is best for you and not put me or my feelings into the equation."

My heart thaws at his words. He really has come around! Maybe the time apart, even if it's only been a few days, has been good. We just needed a wake-up call to get our relationship back on track.

"If," I say, "and I mean *if we* get back together, I'd want to first put some ground rules in place."

"What kind of ground rules?"

"We set aside one day each week where we go out on a date. It doesn't have to be expensive, but we do something fun together."

"I'd love to do that."

"And we commit this time. None of this dating because it's convenient. We are there for each other when we need each other."

"I agree. I love you, Scarlett, and I can't wait to start proving that to you."

I want to believe him. Want to believe that whatever this is between us is true love.

"Okay," I say. "I'm going to do it."

"You're coming home?"

"Yup." I sit up in determination. "I'm going to book the first flight back to Florida. Would you be able to pick me up and take me to work or should I get an Uber?"

"I'll be there with bells on. Just send me your flight details. We'll get you to work and you can save the day for your boss."

"Thanks, Hunter. Okay, so I guess I'll see you tomorrow then?"

"I can't believe this. You've just made my whole world complete."

We hang up, and I search for the first flight out on my

phone. There's one available at 6 a.m. My finger hovers over the *Book Now* button. Am I really going to do this? It means I'll have to head out before I see anyone on the tour, but I'll leave a note for Lilac and Jaxon. After all, this is an opportunity I can't say no to.

I book it, and then I text Sherly, my boss.

> Me: Great news! I just booked my flight back to Florida. I'll be at the office by 2 p.m.

> Sherly: You made the right choice.

> Me: Send me the data you've got so far. I'll review what I can on my phone.

My mind flickers to the guy who I had been desperate to make miserable, but all I can think about are those gray eyes staring intently at me and what it might feel like if those strong arms of his wrapped around my body. I swallow, and for a moment my determination wavers. Was there a spark between us or had that all been my pent-up anger toward the man I thought hurt my sister?

And then there's Rob. Sure, he's a movie star, but that doesn't mean that we don't have a chance. We had a connection. Should I just throw out that possibility?

Maybe running off is a bad idea. I have thirty minutes to cancel my flight before it's non-refundable. Somehow, I feel like this decision could literally change the course of my life. I just hope I'm making the right choice.

Hunter's Path: If you think Scarlett made the right choice and should go back to Florida, skip ahead to Chapter 48.

Movie Star Path: If you think Scarlett should not go home and instead spend more time with Rob, continue to Chapter 22.

Wolf Path: If you think Scarlett should not go back to Florida and instead explore her connection with Jaxon, jump ahead to Chapter 24.

CHAPTER 22

Movie Star Path

FAME AND FORKS

R *eader Note: You chose for Scarlett to go out to dinner with Rob, the movie star.*

How can I resist that charming face of Rob's? Besides, I don't have to make a decision right this second. I have time, and according to my stomach, it's time for food.

"We can't have you wilting away from hunger, now can we?" I say. "Let me change real quick. Something more appropriate for escorting a poor, hungry soul to dinner."

"Take your time. But not too long or I may waste away before you return."

The second I close the door, I hurry and toss open my suitcase. My heart patters against my ribcage as I rummage through my clothes, scouring for something suitable for a dinner date with a hot movie star. Except there's one problem. I don't own anything cute or fun, and even if I did, I certainly wouldn't have packed it for my revenge trip.

125

Maybe Hunter was right. Maybe I'm not such a fun person. This must be fixed.

But as I squeeze into the only dress I brought, a smile plays on my lips. Look at me now! I can be fun and spontaneous. Take that, Hunter! I run my fingers through my long red hair, and my eyes land on my "How to Destroy the Big Bad Wolf" list peeking out of my satchel. My plan to sabotage the game fell through since I hung out with Rob instead, and my white lies didn't really land home, especially now that I know Jaxon isn't Karl.

But seeing it reminds me once again of my purpose in coming on this trip. To get justice for my sister. I snatch up the list and tuck it into the pocket of my red coat. Rob promised to be my co-conspirator. Maybe he'll have some ideas on how to help me make things right for Bella.

When I leave my room, I find Rob on the phone at the end of the hall, his back to me. I start heading toward him when his next words stop me short.

"What if I want out?" Rob asks. "I can't stand to breathe the same air as her."

Who's he talking about? A girlfriend? I frown, trying to remember from my online search if he's dating anyone. But then he could also be talking about a co-worker or even his makeup artist.

"I *know*." Rob sighs, but then he turns slightly and his eyes spot me. "Listen. Got to go. Yup. I know. I owe you."

He pockets his phone and hurries to me.

"You didn't have to hang up on my account," I say as we head down the narrow stairwell of the old inn. The air smells like grilled meat and fried potatoes from the inn's dining area. My stomach growls as I spy Evelyn and Gary at a table as well as Felicity and her friends. If she sees us, she'll be all over Rob.

"It was a boring conversation anyway," he says, touching my back lightly and directing me toward the front door. "Let's head outside and find a restaurant where we won't be hanging out with people from our tour."

Heat creeps up my spine where his palm presses against me as if my dress is paper thin. Rob reaches for the door just as Jaxon enters. Our tour guide practically fills the whole doorway due to his size, or maybe it just feels that way because he has this commanding presence that demands a room to expand just to fit him.

Those piercing gray eyes flicker between Rob and me and then land solidly on where Rob's hand is located on the small of my back.

"Headed to dinner?" Jaxon asks gruffly.

"Any place you recommend that's off the beaten path?" Rob asks.

"The Ristorante Pizzeria Da Franco is quite good," Jaxon says, "if not a bit pricey. Do you need me to take you there?"

"Naw. GPS can escort us." Rob pulls out his phone and taps on the screen.

"Before we go," I say, "I'd like a moment to speak to Jaxon in private."

Rob's eyebrows rise. "Of course."

Rob steps aside while I edge to the corner of the hall for privacy. Jaxon follows me, but now that it's just the two of us, his presence is all-consuming. I can't keep my eyes off how his muscles bulge beneath his shirt. The scent of him drifts over me like a wolf hunting for its prey. Suddenly, I feel cornered, and yet, I don't want to escape.

Get a grip, Scarlett!

I stiffen and reach into my pocket where my list on how to

destroy him is safely tucked away, empowering me. I will not be lured in by his mysterious charm.

"I need to come clean," I announce. Those thick eyebrows lift. "My name is Scarlett Walker, and I'm the sister of Bella Walker, whom your brother seduced and then ditched, leaving her broken-hearted. The real reason I'm here is to get a formal apology from your brother."

There. I said it. I wait for the elation of victory from the surprise, but Jaxon's face is unreadable.

"I wondered why you had my picture in your bag that day in the café," he says.

I'd forgotten about that. I'd been so busy rubbing my hands on his chest—I mean wiping off the streusel—that I'd forgotten about my papers that he'd picked off the floor. Damn it!

"So I'll be expecting that apology from your brother tomorrow," I say, determined to keep the upper hand.

"I'll do what I can, but it seems like you may be heading down the same road with our movie star. Be careful with him," Jaxon half-growls. Then his eyes slide to my forehead where my bruise blooms purple. His eyes soften into heather gray. "But how are you feeling? I've been thinking about you." He clears his throat. "Thinking about your health, that is."

Instinctively, my hand reaches up to the bump. He's caught me off guard again. He's too nice. Too perfect. How am I supposed to despise him when he's the perfect gentleman and always looking out for me?

"I'm fine." I lick my lips, and his gaze flicks to stare at them. My face burns. I need to get out of here. Escape. Quickly.

Thankfully, Rob slips to my side. "Ready to go?"

"Yes," I say, breathing out with relief. I hook my arm through his. "I'm positively starved."

Jaxon's eyes darken, but Rob whisks me away before the Wolfe decides to attack.

~

ALSFELD IS A FAIRY TALE, embodying all the charm and character of a traditional medieval town. Rob and I stroll down the stone-paved street under the glow of the street lamps and stars pinpricking through the night. Half-timbered houses squeeze together along the road, and I can almost imagine I'm lost in a storybook. Finally, we spill into the central market-place lined with quaint cafés and taverns. The white-timbered buildings glow as if infused with magic even though I know it's only the lantern light.

We peek through paned-glass windows, debating which restaurant to eat at while the clock in the tower above chimes seven times. A musician plays guitar, filling the air with music.

"The restaurant Jaxon recommended is further down the road," Rob says, "but the atmosphere here is quite nice, don't you think? How about we pick one of these? Otherwise, I might collapse and you'd be forced to carry me."

I laugh. "Now that would be a sight."

We stroll up to a restaurant with white lights strung across the potted plants and candle-lit tables scattered outside.

"We'll sit outside," Rob tells the host after we're asked if we'd like to sit inside or out. "The view is too beautiful not to enjoy."

He says this, but he's looking straight at me as if I'm the beauty he's talking about. My heart clatters about. Only my rib cage keeps it securely locked in place.

Once we're seated, the host hands us menus in English, promising our server will arrive shortly. I glance about, wondering if anyone will notice Rob, but the guests are too busy eating and chatting, completely obvious to the block-buster star in their midst. Even our server looks bored as she takes our order, convincing me we're safe from discovery.

"It appears as if your disguise is working well," I note after we ordered our food.

"I admit I don't usually sit out in the open like this, but sometimes it's nice to live a little."

"Living on the wild side."

"Speaking of wild," he says, sipping from his drink. "Your talk with Jaxon looked a little heated."

I gulp. *In more ways than one.* "I demanded his brother write an apology letter to my sister. He agreed to make it happen."

"Good for you." Rob leans back, lounging his lithe body. "I'm glad you stuck up for your sister. So what else are you planning for justice against your sister's villain?"

I pull out my "How to Destroy the Big Bad Wolf" list. "Don't laugh, but here are my ideas. Except now that Jaxon's going to get him to apologize, maybe I need to let it go."

"Slash the bus tires?" Rob reads off. A devious smile spreads across his face. "Aren't you a little vixen?"

"I need to cross that one off." I go to take the list from him, but he holds it out of my reach. "Now that I know the tour guests, I couldn't do that to them."

"But you did note that you would bring snacks." He rubs his chin, thoughtfully. "The question is, what sort of snacks?"

I toss my straw wrapper at him. "You're no help. Now give me back my list unless you have something worthy to add."

"You absolutely must continue with your plan. An apology is too easy. Anyone can apologize. It's meaningless without concrete and serious action."

"You have a point."

"I always have a point. The key is to make Karl pay. Literally." He hands me my list. "Jaxon and I chatted a bit before the tour. I'm paying extra for my privacy, and during the conversation, it became apparent that Karl has the means to afford the very best of lawyers in case something should go foul. Since Karl evidently funds the tour's operations, I'd suggest that you consider ways to make Fairy Tale Road pay extra as often as possible. AKA, Karl."

"What a devious mind you have," I tease.

He leans forward and takes my hand. His finger runs across the surface of my palm, sending tingles up my veins.

"This has been fun, you and I," he says softly. "And I'm not saying that just to say it. You're not like the other women in my life."

"Thank you...I think."

"Believe me, it was meant as a compliment."

"I don't keep up with the tabloids, but are you dating someone?" Okay, so I totally Googled him on the bus.

"Naw," he scoffs. "Reporters make up all sorts of stories to sell magazines. But as far as exes, I've had too many for my taste. In fact, two years ago, I vowed never to date again."

"Wow." I sit straighter at that. "That is quite the statement. It must have been really bad."

He releases me. Instantly, I miss the warmth of his hands.

"I just finished shooting *The Titan Warlords*." His forehead wrinkles as he gazes across the square as if recalling a bad dream. "I came home to find an empty house and a note from Tia saying she took my stuff instead of suing me for neglect."

"Ouch."

"I didn't really care about the furniture or even my weapon collection. I'd started that collection with the money from my first TV commercial, so it was sentimental but not the end of the world. It was the fact that she threw a certain, *special* box in the trash. Wrote me a note specifically telling me which dumpster she tossed it in. When I went to look, it was full of ashes."

"She burned your stuff. Wow."

"It was a calculated, targeted attack because she knew it would affect me emotionally. I couldn't forgive her for that. Couldn't forgive myself for giving her access to my life like that."

His eyes darken, and his jaw tightens as he looks away.

I reach over and touch his hand. "I'm so sorry."

He shrugs as if he's tossing the pain behind him, and that mischievous grin is back. "But who am I to complain, right? I'm famous and rich, all is good in the world."

"Somehow I get the feeling you don't mean that."

Our meal arrives, and we spend the next hour finishing our food and chatting.

"I can't remember laughing and enjoying myself like this," I pause, my mind flicking through my memories, "maybe ever?"

"Ever?" Rob gasps. "That is no way to live."

"Crazy, right?" I shake my head. My phone pings, pulling my gaze from Rob's. "My sister texted. Finally. I've been trying to keep her updated on all things concerning the Big Bad Wolf."

Bella: Is this real life?

I frown and quickly text back. *What's wrong? Is everything okay?*

Bella: Why didn't you tell me?

Me: I talked to Karl's brother, and he's going to give you an apology letter.

Bella: Who cares about Snarl Karl? I'm talking about you and your movie star!

The beast has a new name.

Me: Snarl Karl?

Bella: Do not deviate. MOVIE STAR!

Me: How did you know about Rob?

Bella: It's true! OMG. OMG!

Next, she sends over a picture and a link. I gasp, my eyes popping out of my head.

"What's wrong?" Rob asks. "Everything okay?"

I look up at him and swallow. "No. Not at all."

CHAPTER 23

Movie Star Path

CAUGHT IN THE ACT

I cringe as I drag my eyes from the phone and look over at Rob.

"You're not going to like this," I say.

"Like what?" Rob's eyes crinkle with worry.

My hand shakes a little as I pass him my phone. He stares at the photos and his jaw ticks. He's angry. Or maybe embarrassed. After all, hanging out with me can't be good for his image, and these pictures make it look like we're together.

Me putting the felt hat on his head.

Him holding up the dress to my body.

The worst one is where I've got my arm wrapped possessively around his.

"I'm sorry," I finally break the silence. "I shouldn't have touched you like that. I was just trying to help. Obviously pretending to be your girlfriend was the stupidest idea ever."

"Where were these photos posted?" he asks tightly.

I stiffen at his cold tone and click on the link. "*Celebrity Unchecked*. And they did a pretty big write-up of it." I grimace and start reading it out loud. "In a shocking turn of events,

Hollywood heartthrob, Robby Ricci, reportedly ditched the set of his highly anticipated film, *Shadow Hunter*, to tour Europe with this mysterious beauty! Sources close to the star reveal that Ricci's girlfriend, Tianna Ulci, was utterly devastated upon hearing news of the fling."

Rob swears while I pause to say, "Tianna as in your ex, Tia? I thought you two broke up."

"We did. She's determined to keep screwing me over." He slaps a hand over his eyes. "Is there anything else?"

I continue, "While studio execs scramble to explain the unexpected hiatus, fans wonder if this real-life romance will inspire his next blockbuster role or if it's merely a fleeting affair. Stay tuned as we uncover more of Robby Ricci's clandestine antics."

"Clandestine antics?" he sputters. "Are you serious?"

I set my phone down and we stare at it in silence. My brain whirls trying to process everything I read.

"The shopkeeper must have taken those photos." I close my eyes, hating how that moment has now been ruined.

"Yeah," Rob says dully. He digs through his jacket pocket and turns on his phone, glaring at it before slamming it on the table. "Great. Just great."

I want to grab him, shake him. Beg him to explain what's really happening and what it means for us. Except, what alternate reality have I let myself slip into? I'm just a nobody girl who's too tall and definitely not model-thin unlike his stunning girlfriend who isn't just Tia, but Tianna Ulci, drop-dead gorgeous with long black hair and a body she's not afraid to show off.

"Let me get this straight," I say. "According to this article, you're supposed to be filming a movie and Tianna Ulci is your girlfriend. The very famous Tianna Ulci?"

"First of all," Rob rubs his forehead, "don't for one second be sorry or think this is your fault. This is *my* fault. I wasn't careful enough, and yes, I was the jerk who left my film shoot because I was so stressed out. It was completely selfish that I got you involved in this mess. I'm so sorry. There are no words I can offer to tell you how awful I feel about this."

He rises, glancing around furtively. "I should leave you. Who knows who else might be taking photos of us right now."

"Don't be ridiculous." I leap to my feet. "I don't care about those photos. What I want to know is the truth about Tianna."

He nods for me to follow him, and we take off at a brisk pace down the street.

"Tianna and I broke up two years ago," he explains. "But my co-star for *Shadow Hunter*, Liv Salter, got in a car wreck and broke her back. Poor thing has been bedridden for a month."

"That's terrible."

"The studio hired Tianna as Liv's replacement, but they never told me because they knew our history and worried how I might react. They weren't wrong to worry. When Tianna arrived on set last week, I lost my mind. The producers thought it would amp up the ratings by having us together because we had such great chemistry—we don't by the way—which is why they wouldn't listen to me when I told them I wouldn't work with her. Said I needed to be professional."

"That's terrible! How can you be professional after what she did to you?"

"I can't work with Tianna." He shakes his head, his steps quickening with anger. "I won't do it. I told them I'd rather quit. I called up Axel—he's always been my rock—and he offered to have me join him on this tour. I literally walked off set and only told my manager where I was going."

"Can you do that? Didn't you sign some sort of contract?"

"According to my manager, the studio could, and likely will, sue me. I could lose everything. All my savings, my reputation, my entire career."

I stop him in his tracks and pull him to face me. "I had no idea you were going through all of this."

"No one does except Axel...and now you." He leans his head back and groans. "I feel so out of control, and I hate it. My manager talked to the executives, and they've agreed to give me a week to figure out what I want to do. They're currently shooting every shot that I'm not in because every day we delay is money. But now you see my predicament and how you've become another victim of Tianna's. I know she lied to the press about us."

"Don't worry about me." I take his hands in mine. "I don't care what the paparazzi say, or what they call me, or even what Tianna thinks about me. And you don't need to apologize for something someone else did to us. I'm in the middle of trying to figure out what I want to do with my life, too. So I understand on a much smaller scale what you're going through."

"Thank you." His face becomes serious. "That means a lot to me. You've heard enough of my drama, what are you dealing with?"

"It's nothing."

"Nope. You don't get to do that. Whatever you're going through is just as important. Besides, I wouldn't mind a distraction."

I explain to him what happened with Hunter along with the possible bonus and new title my boss offered me earlier tonight. He doesn't interrupt but listens to what I have to say. Ironically, just talking about it all makes it feel like a weight has been lifted off my shoulders. We reach my room all too soon.

"I guess this is goodnight then." I fiddle with my key.

"Ironically, and despite Tianna's best intentions, it was a good night," Rob says, and then that twinkle flashes in his eyes once again. "Maybe tomorrow you'll sit with me on the bus?"

"What are we in, fourth grade?" I joke, lightly hitting him on the arm.

"We're definitely not in fourth grade. In fact, if you need me to stay the night and keep an eye on that concussion for you, I'm willing to sacrifice my time."

He winks, and I roll my eyes. "I'll call if I need anything."

"You do that," he says and saunters off.

I sigh and slip back into my room. It feels too empty and too quiet. I'm tempted to call Rob back, but nope, that would be a very bad idea. So instead I ring my sister, Bella, who has called me four times while Rob and I were talking.

"I've been dying here," Bella says as she answers the phone. "Dying! What is happening? Are you really hanging out with Robby Ricci, you mysterious beauty, you."

I chuckle as I kick off my shoes and shrug out of my coat. "I don't know why *Celebrity Unchecked* called me that."

"Because you are! Now tell me everything. Oh! And Grams is here. My screaming woke her up. I'm putting you on speaker."

"Hey, Grams," I say. "I'm sorry we woke you."

"Fiddlesticks!" she says. "This is far more interesting than any of my *Golden Girls* Chapters. Are you really dating a celebrity?"

I launch into an explanation of everything that has happened so far. "So we're not dating, but maybe tonight you could call our dinner excursion a date."

"Sounds like you went on a date with him this afternoon, too," Bella says.

"I don't know," Grams wavers. "Aren't those movie stars known to be cheaters? Fame can be a tricky thing."

"You're right, Grams." I nibble on my finger. "I might be his holiday fling to help him get over his ex."

"Of course, I'm right!" she trills. "About time you two realize that."

"Grams thinks you should forget about the Germany trip and come home," Bella says.

"Those Wolfe men have been nothing but trouble to you two girls," Grams says.

"Not until I insure you get that apology letter from Karl," I say.

"I thought we agreed to never say that K word again," Bella grumbles and my heart sinks as realization sinks in. She hasn't gotten over him, has she? I thought she'd moved on, but it's apparent he still has a grip on her heart.

"Wretched man!" Grams agrees.

"Don't worry, sis," I say. "I'm not going to leave until the beast pays and regrets ever having crossed paths with you."

I'd let Jaxon weasel his way into making me think an apology would be enough. But it's not, and Rob nailed it. I need to find a way to break Karl's heart as much as he's broken my sisters, and thanks to Rob, I've got a few ideas I can add to my list.

CHAPTER 24

Little Red Riding Hood

Fresh morning air blows across my face as I step outside my hotel into what feels like a fairy tale. The cute German houses with their geometric brown frames against the white stucco gleam cheerful in the morning light. Flowers spilling out of the window boxes brighten the day with their reds and yellows.

Last night, I almost booked a flight back home. I was so close. After all, my boss offered me twenty thousand dollars. I even called Hunter back, and he nearly talked me into giving him a second chance.

But work will always be waiting for me and Hunter might be telling me all the right words, but my heart wants more.

I take in the view around me, deciding I made the right decision.

Besides, the more I think about it, the more I realize an apology from Karl isn't going to be enough to soothe Bella's heart. Based on a little research last night, I read an article where Karl said he's the one paying the bills to this Fairy Tale Road company. Which means if they have to pay extra, it's really Karl. It's time to take things to the next level and stop messing around.

"Scarlett!" Lilac calls my name as she breezes through the doors of the hotel. She's wearing a chic blouse the color of the sky and gray high-waisted trousers. Her sleek hair is pulled back into a ponytail, a modern Audrey Hepburn. "Good morning. Or as the Germans say, guten morgen."

"A guten morgen to you as well. What do you think we'll be doing for our fairytale game?"

"Since this town is considered where the story of *Little Red Riding Hood* originated, I'm thinking that might be our clue."

We head toward the Alfred Fairy Tale House where we're supposed to meet the group.

"You and Axel have a nice time at dinner last night?" I ask.

"He's so funny. He was telling me this story of when he was a kid he made a gingerbread house to be a superhero house instead. Isn't that adorable?"

"He seems like a nice guy, but we just met these people. You never know who they really are until you get to know them."

Trust me, my sister fell into that trap.

"I suppose, but this girl can have a little fun while on vacation. And Axel is definitely fun. So dreamy with those dark eyes."

"Take Rob for example," I carry on. "All this time we thought he was just a regular guy but turns out he's a movie star! Perfect example."

"I heard my name in the same sentence with *perfect example*," Rob says from behind us.

Lilac and I stop in our tracks, eyes widening, and slowly turn to find Rob and Axel walking behind us. "That's a good sign, right?"

"How much did you hear?" Lilac looks like she swallowed a mouthful of flies.

"Enough to know you were talking about us." Axel rubs the top of his head sheepishly.

"You were eavesdropping!" I cross my arms.

"For the record," Rob pulls the bill down a little on his hat, "I am a normal guy just like anyone else. Being a movie star is just my job. This is exactly why I did this whole disguise. I wanted to escape all the judgment and expectations."

"You're right, and you deserve that," I admit. "From now on, we'll pretend you're not some famous star. So why don't you tell us what you *really* do?"

I say this last part with a wink, and he chuckles. The four of us continue walking while Rob spins a tale for us about how he works at a convenience store and sells more lottery tickets than hot dogs.

When we step into the Alfred Fairy Tale House, my eyes drift across our tour group and the plethora of fairytale para-phernalia, searching for Jaxon. I spot him across the room, listening to Trey yell. Which is good, right? An unhappy customer will often leave a bad review.

Jaxon's gaze shifts to look over Trey's shoulder, almost as if he senses my presence. Our eyes lock. My heart kicks up a beat, and my whole body feels flushed like I'm standing on a hot Florida beach in July. He turns to Trey and says something, which makes Trey's face redden even more.

The two part ways, and I dart over to Trey.

"Wow," I say as sympathetically as I can. "Looks like things got heated between you and Jaxon."

"The asshole says he can't help me with my room situation. What kind of customer service is that?"

"The worst of kinds. I wish you'd known before you

booked this trip how poor Fairy Tale Road's customer service was." Then I add deviously, "Like if you'd read a *review* about it."

"He said he can't control what the hotel does."

Which is likely true, but telling him that does me no service. "I'm so sorry you're dealing with that. But if *you* were ever to leave a review, it could help potential tourists."

He rolls his neck with annoyance but then his eyes land on me as if suddenly realizing I was there. I take that back. As if he suddenly realized my breasts were there.

"One look at you makes this whole tour worthwhile." A creepy smile slithers across his face, and I shudder in disgust. Why I ever thought this guy could be helpful in my cause is beyond me.

I spin around before he can make some more lewd comments and find Jaxon a few steps away. A lump forms in my stomach. Did he overhear what I said? Quickly, I slip in beside Lilac as Jaxon steps up to the front of the room between a life-size doll of Little Red Riding Hood holding a basket and a table full of brochures.

"Good morning, friends," he calls out in his rich, booming voice. "I hope you had a restful sleep. Today for our tour, we will be heading out into the forest that inspired the tale of *The Little Red Riding Hood*."

Lilac squeaks beside me, her ponytail whipping behind her head. "I knew it!"

"Take some time to tour this lovely Alsfeld Fairy Tale House and then check out this rack where we've got Little Red Riding Hood themed clothes for you to wear for our next competition. Grab an outfit, change in the fitting rooms, and then in thirty minutes we'll head to the competition site."

About half of the group leaves to tour the house while the

other half rushes to the rack of clothes and starts picking out outfits. Axel holds up a set of pants with suspenders while Rob pulls on a vest jacket and replaces his baseball hat with a feathered green felt one.

"You look like an elf," I tease Rob.

"It's a good thing." He pushes on his sunglasses and poses as if he's at a photo shoot. "Because I'm about to make all your dreams come true."

I roll my eyes. "I think you're getting fairy godmothers and elves mixed up."

"Damn fairy tales." He shakes his head. "Too confusing."

Lilac and I pick out dresses with close-fitting bodices and full skirts. It takes some time to squeeze into the dress, and by the time I lace up the ribbons on the front of the bodice, my chest seems to almost spill out of the material. A glance at the mirror in the changing room shows my dress was created specifically to highlight the breasts, because man, they looked pretty damn good. Too bad it's hard to breathe like this.

I step out of the changing room to find Lilac fidgeting with her sleeves, a frown pulling at her face.

"I've always wanted to wear a dirndl," she says. "But who would've thought they would be so constricting?"

"Let's hope this competition doesn't have us running through the woods while being chased by a wolf," I joke.

Lilac's eyes pop wide. "Maybe I should change into lederhosen. I don't want anything to come in the way of winning this time."

"Trust me." I smile as I think about the secret plan I plotted last night. "Nothing is going to stop you from winning."

"Now you, my Lady Lilac," Axel says, his eyes drinking her

in like she was a feast for the eyes, "look stunning in that getup."

"It's called a dirndl," she explains, but her frown has vanished and she's looking quite pleased with herself. *Good.* She deserves a guy who treats her well. "I'm dressed as a commoner, not royalty, but thank you."

From across the room, Rob heads my way, but Jaxon steps into my path.

"You're a natural, Little Red Riding Hood," he says. His eyes catch on my breasts and he clears his throat. Well, now I know the Big Bad Wolf's kryptonite. "All you need now is a red cloak and a basket."

He snags a cherry-red cape from the closet and settles it over my shoulders. He barely touches my skin, but it sends a wave of heat through me.

"So I'm to be Little Red Riding Hood?" I ask.

"If you wish." His eyes darken. "What do you think of Germany so far?"

"It's lovely. I keep thinking how much this place looks like Disney World only to realize Disney looks like this."

"This is very true." He chuckles, and I soak in his deep, rich voice. "I also wanted you to know that I wasn't able to get hold of my brother yet, but I'm working on it."

I snap out of whatever trance he's put me in. Do not fraternize with the enemy! "I hope you're not avoiding the situation with my sister and taking it seriously."

"You can be sure I'm taking this *very* seriously." He steps back. "Again, I'm very sorry for what your sister went through. I wish you two could've done this trip together. But then maybe not. If I went on a tour with my brother, we'd kill each other."

"You two don't get along?"

"For a while no, but then he was there for me during a tough time I went through. Now, we're close as thieves."

So he admits he's conspiring with his brother. "Are you two alike?"

"Identical twins, but we couldn't be further apart in personality. I've always been the quieter one, but my brother got into an argument with my dad years ago and left to run his own company. Can't blame him. He's become incredibly successful and has made his millions. In the end, he's been a big help to the family."

Millions. Jaxon's words confirm what I've read about Karl online. Here my sister is struggling to make ends meet while the jerk blows through money and girls like candy. It only makes me even more enraged.

My phone pings. I check it and frown.

"Is everything alright?" he asks.

"It's my boss." I sigh. "She's desperate for me to return back to Florida. So desperate that she's willing to pay me twenty thousand dollars to leave my vacation and fix her problem. Am I crazy for not leaving? I mean that's a lot of money."

"She must really value you. That's not a bad thing."

"Huh." I stare at her text. "She said, 'I understand. Have fun, but never leave me again. Just kidding. Not really.' Now I feel guilty. Maybe I should go home."

"She sounds like a great boss, if not a little pushy. Ultimately, she's just your boss, not your forever person. Life has taught me that jobs come and go. And my brother taught me money can't make you happy."

The words *forever person* tumble around in my mind. What would it be like to find the person you would spend the rest of your life with? My chest aches for that.

"Those are wise words."

"If you need to go. I can arrange a ride to the airport for you. It's no trouble. That said, you'll miss out on all the fun we'll be having during this tour."

Why does Jaxon have to always be such a good guy? He's supposed to be the Big Bad Wolf and this kindness is really starting to get under my skin. Unfortunately, in the best way possible.

I fiddle with my phone. There's no doubt I feel something between us. But does he feel that, too? And is risking my career for some flutters in my chest really worth it?

He says he's nothing like his brother, but they're more genetically alike than not. What if he's playing me just like Karl played Bella? Am I falling for this wolf's trap just like my sister did?

Hunter's Path: There's still time for Scarlett to catch her plane back to Florida! If you think she should leave, jump ahead to Chapter 48.

Movie Star and Wolf Path: If you think she's made the right choice, keep reading to find out what happens on the Fairy Tale Tour.

CHAPTER 25

Into the Woods

Ancient oaks drape over us as Jaxon leads our tour group of sixteen guests on a hike deeper and deeper into the thicketed forest. The air smells of moss and musky leaves. About half of us dressed up for the occasion so we look like a ragtag group of medieval villagers and clueless tourists. Felicity and her two friends didn't bother with the costumes, but Evelyn and Gary are both decked out in the traditional garb complete with a handkerchief, apron, and suspenders. They could be Hans and Gretel's grandparents.

By the time we trundle into an open clearing, some look like they might pass out and Trey finally stops complaining about how hot it is. A soft breeze blows across the field, smelling of heather and fresh leaves. A bunch of tree stumps are scattered around with an ax head dug into each one. Beside each stump are logs of wood.

"What is this dreadful place?" Felicity asks. "All those axes. It's like something from a horror movie."

"My guess is we're going to be chopping wood," Rob says.

"Now who's wishing they had chosen a career as a woodcutter rather than a convenience store worker?" I elbow him, and he laughs.

"Are we pretending to be Jack in the Beanstalk?" Lilac asks.

Jaxon beams. "You know your fairy tales, but today you're all going to pretend you're the hunter in *Little Red Riding Hood*."

My heart sinks at the name Hunter. He called again this morning, and I ignored it. At some point, I'm going to need to tell him we don't have a chance.

"We're not going to kill the wolf like in the original fairy tale," Jaxon continues.

"If only life was so simple," I mutter.

"In this game," Jaxon says, "you'll team up with a partner. The team who chops the most wood and carries their chopped wood to their platform at the other end of the field wins."

There's a murmur among the group and Lilac says, "What if we don't know how to chop wood?"

"Seems like the competition is skewed toward men." I cross my arms.

"Really?" Jaxon's eyebrows rise. "I'll have you know that my mum is the best woodcutter in our family."

"That's impressive especially considering—" I was going to say the size of your arms, but I'm not going to give him the satisfaction I recognized how muscular he is. "Considering she's quite a bit older than you."

"Age is only a number." Jaxon grins, showing off white teeth. "Wouldn't you concur, Gary and Evelyn?"

The two whole heartedly agree.

"What is the prize?" Felicity asks.

"The winner gets a horse-drawn carriage ride to the ruins of a beautiful medieval castle," Jaxon says. "There they'll have a romantic champagne picnic lunch."

Everyone cheers and claps while Lilac gasps, her eyes darting to Axel. My heart twists seeing the two of them. If anyone should win this game it has to be them. Lilac wants this so badly. My mind calculates how I can manage to sabotage this game and yet still make sure Lilac wins.

"Go ahead and pick your partners," Jaxon says. "Then stand by one of the tree stumps to begin."

Felicity slides between Rob and me and bats her eyelashes at him. "Will you be my teammate?" she asks.

"Sorry," Rob says, "Scarlett already agreed to be my teammate, right Scarlett?"

He pulls off his glasses and pleads with those gorgeous eyes of his that have girls across the planet swooning. It works because, honestly, who can say no to that?

"Yes," I say. "I've already claimed him. In fact, he's my partner for the rest of the tour."

"Is that so?" Rob flashes me a fascinated look while Felicity tosses visible daggers at me with her eyes.

"That's not fair," she huffs. "You can't be his partner for the entire tour."

"Sorry." I sigh dramatically. "He's taken."

"Is this true?" she asks Rob.

He shrugs as if he can't help it. "You heard her. Scarlett gets what she wants."

Felicity storms away to join her friends while Rob and I grin at each other.

"Whew," Rob says. "That was close. You're my hero for rescuing me there."

"Don't be silly. You could've rocked the competition with Felicity. In fact, you could still change your mind."

"Not in this lifetime. I'm sticking with you."

As we move to stand to go to our tree stump, I realize Jaxon is right beside us. My face burns. He probably heard the whole conversation with Felicity.

Does he think Rob and I are really a thing? But why should I care? It's not like I want to be with Jaxon. His brother broke my sister's heart. He's the enemy.

We pair up into teams, and I study the competition. Axel might be great with perfumes, but he doesn't really seem like a guy who would win a wood chopping competition. Plus, Lilac is about the size of the log they're supposed to chop up. Trey is flexing his arms, showing off massive muscles to the other teams while his partner, Natisha, bites her nails, eyeing the ax like it might be a murder weapon.

Whatever happens, I won't let Trey win this. The creep doesn't deserve it. Besides, if he wins, he might forget to leave that bad review.

"Alright," Jaxon calls out. "Grab your axes."

I take hold of mine. The surface feels cold compared to the warmth of the day. It's firm and solid in my palms.

"When I say go," Jaxon explains, "you have fifteen minutes to get as much chopped wood as you possibly can to your platform. Any questions?"

My nerves zing around me as I prep my body.

Jaxon holds up his arms. "Ready. Set—"

"Wait!" Felicity screams, waving her hands. "This game is totally rigged."

Jaxon drops his hands and gives her an incredulous look. "What do you mean?"

"Don't you see? Every team here except two have men in them. There's no chance we can win."

"It's how we've always done this competition."

"Well, I say it's a completely unfair advantage. I propose we draw for partners."

Unfortunately, her friends and the two college girls glance over at Rob and chime in their agreement with Felicity.

"I think they're all hoping to compete with a movie star," I mutter to Rob.

"I know I sound like a conceited prick when I say this," Rob says, "but I think you're right."

"Gary and I are happy to split up if you need us to," Evelyn says. "We just want to have fun."

"Let's vote," Felicity says. "All in favor of drawing for partners, raise your hands."

Everyone raises their hands except for Axel, Rob, Lilac, and me.

"It appears as if we have a majority," Jaxon says diplomatically, "and ultimately this is your tour. I want you to have the best touring experience."

Felicity orchestrates the drawing by having each of us write our names on a piece of paper. Once all the names are placed into Gary's felt hat, she hands it over to Jaxon to read off.

One by one, teams are created. Axel gets paired with Natisha, one of the college girls, much to Lilac's disappointment, but ironically, I get paired with Rob, to the horror of Felicity and her friends.

"Our last pairing is Trey and Lilac," Jaxon says.

Lilac sucks in a shocked cry of distress. "Are you serious?"

My heart dives. *No! This isn't fair.* Trey will totally ruin the whole experience for her.

"Come to Papa!" Trey says, rubbing his hands. "Don't worry, little Lilac. I'm going to win this for us, and we're going to go on an amazing fairytale date together."

I can't let Trey be Lilac's partner. It's just not right. I debate what to do. I could volunteer to take her place. Trey is annoying, but he's nothing I can't handle. Or maybe I'm over-reacting. After all, she is an adult. She can take care of herself.

Wolf Path: If you think Scarlett should switch places with Lilac, read Chapter 26-28.

Movie Star Path: If you think Scarlett should not get involved and keep Rob as her partner, skip ahead to Chapter 29.

Wolf Path
AN AX TO GRIND

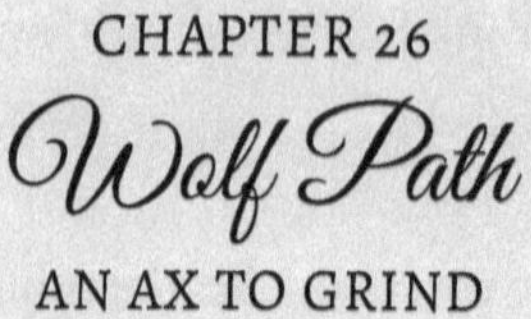

Reader Note: You choose the Wolf Path, which has Scarlett switching places with Lilac for the game. Trigger warning: A character makes inappropriate advances in this scene. Feel free to skip ahead to Chapter 27.

I TURN TO ROB. "As much as I'd love to be your partner, I can't let this whole experience be ruined for Lilac. She's been saving up for this trip, and I want to make sure she has the best time."

"I'm disappointed we won't be partners but also impressed," Rob says. "You're a good friend."

I take off toward Lilac just as she says, "I'd rather sit this game out."

"Or, we can switch places," I offer. "You team up with Rob, and I'll be Trey's partner."

Lilac shakes her head. "I can't let you do that."

"I want you to enjoy this trip. I mean, how long have you been practicing for these games?"

"Still…"

"Rob says he'd be happy to have you as his teammate."

"What if I don't want Scarlett as my partner?" Trey says. "Don't I get a say in this?"

"No," Lilac and I both say simultaneously.

I lean close to Lilac and whisper, "Wouldn't it be fun to go home and tell your friends you competed with Robby Ricci? I mean, how can you say no to that?"

"You sure?" Lilac wavers.

"Absolutely."

"Okay, then I'll switch. Thanks. I owe you one." Lilac squeezes my hands and then jogs over to where Rob waits.

"I think we're all set now," I tell Jaxon.

His eyebrows lift, and his gaze darkens, flickering between Trey and me. Does Jaxon think I *want* to be with Trey? I bite my lip. Unless he overheard what I told Trey at the Alsfeld Fairy Tale House.

"Wait a moment," Felicity says. "Don't we have a say in this?"

"The choice is Scarlett's," Jaxon says as if he thinks I made the wrong decision.

"Didn't know you felt so strongly about me to ditch a movie star," Trey says as I come to stand with him. "But trust me, you won't be disappointed."

"Too late for that," I mutter. I want to tell him I'm only on his team to keep his grubby hands off Lilac. Jaxon blows his whistle, calling our attention to him.

"On, your marks," Jaxon starts up again, "get set, go!"

I'm in no mood to compete, but Trey is taking this task so seriously I worry we might actually win this thing. His accuracy is annoyingly impressive like he's secretly a wood-chopping

Olympian. He sets each log precisely on the stump and splits each one with a smooth crack.

"Where did you learn to chop wood like that?" I ask.

"Impressive, isn't it?"

"If you're into that kind of thing." The last thing this guy needs is someone feeding that hungry ego.

"I grew up on a farm." He winks at me. "But let's keep it a secret between us."

This guy grew up on a farm? I'd never have guessed with those dress pants, tight designer shirt, and shiny black shoes. *You've got to be kidding me.* At his rate, we'll win in no time. I stand beside him, biting my lip as I assess the other teams. Rob managed to split one log of wood and Lilac is running with it to the platform. Axel looks like he's succeeded in getting his ax's head stuck in the wood. Felicity is too busy complaining about breaking her nail to actually do anything useful.

The only couple who has a chance at beating us is Evelyn and Gary. Gary is splitting the wood at an impressive rate while Evelyn is already carrying a handful to their crate. If I can figure out how to slow Trey down, they could beat us. I study his movements and where his feet are placed.

"There's an extra ax here." He points to the second one next to the stump. "I could teach you how to use it."

"I'm good. A little thirsty though." I pick up my water bottle, pretending to take a swig. I take a few steps and purposely trip and fall, dumping all the water in my bottle into a pool at his feet.

"Watch where you're going," Trey says. "You got the ground all muddy. My shoes are going to be ruined."

I stand and shrug. "Guess I'm clumsy."

"I know what you're up to." He smirks. "You can't keep your eyes off me, right?"

I groan. *He's impossible.* "I'm going to carry this log to our platform," I say.

I load up my arms and start trudging slowly to our platform. But when I arrive, it already has a few logs on it. I dump my armful onto the platform and frown in confusion. Did someone else put their logs on our platform by mistake?

Jaxon steps to my side. "Everything okay?"

"I think someone accidentally put their logs on our platform." I point to our pile, which is significantly greater than anyone else's.

"Are you sure?" Jaxon's eyes sweep across the groups' platforms.

Gary and Evelyn's platform has no logs on it, but I was sure she had a handful finished.

I cross my arms. "I refuse to win unfairly."

"Based on the speed of your partner, I think it's obvious you're going to win," Jaxon says. "I've got to admit, I was surprised you ditched Rob for Trey. I don't really see you two as a couple."

"Trey and I as a couple?" I snort. "Only in his dreams."

As if saying his name has conjured him out of the air, Trey races up to join us, arms stacked with wood. "Only one more round left, and we're picnicking, baby!"

"Yay," I say dryly. "All my dreams have come true."

"Maybe you should be careful what you dream for," Jaxon says with no sympathy whatsoever before striding away.

I scowl at his hard, muscular back. See? His true self just came out. Anger boils up inside of me and I start gathering up logs. If I can put these on another group's platform, that should help get rid of them.

But then Evelyn hurries over to me, a load in her arms. She beams kindly at me.

"Scarlett," she says. "That was so sweet of you to offer Lilac to hang out with Rob. Gary and I were impressed with your act of kindness. No one else would've done that."

"It wasn't a big deal."

"We're going to help you win this competition."

"Oh, no. Please don't."

"Think of us like your fairy godparents. You showed us kindness in action, and we insist you feel the kindness back." Her gaze darts to where Jaxon is standing, eyeing us with those wolf eyes of his. "Oh, he's looking. I can't give these to you. But that's fine. Looks like Trey is nearly done."

"So it appears," I say morbidly as he chops up the last log.

"You know, we won the last competition, but helping you out for this one has been far more fun. Good luck!"

She takes off, and guilt slides through me. If she knew I didn't want to go on this trip with Trey, it would ruin her whole day, too. Why does everything have to be so complicated? Trey is back once again, pouring the final load of logs on our platform. I stare grimly at the pile while Trey hoots and dances around our platform like a witch performing a ritual.

"We won!" he exclaims.

"Yup." I sigh. "We sure did."

I remind myself if I hadn't volunteered, Lilac would definitely be in my place. Besides, Trey might be annoying, but how bad can he be? Visiting castle ruins and drinking champagne might be just what I need to relax a little. Plus, seeing Gary and Evelyn grinning mischievously like little fairies spreading magic does make it worthwhile.

Jaxon blows the whistle and announces us the winners. Trey's shirt is still wet from sweating and my dress has bits of wood still clinging to it. The group claps politely as Jaxon escorts us over to a barn where a large brown horse and carriage are set up for us. It looks like one of those old-fashioned buggies with two wheels. The air smells like hay and horses.

I step up to the horse and pet its soft mane.

"Everything all set?" Jaxon asks the attendant.

"That we are," the man agrees with a proud smile.

"Brilliant," Jaxon says, but there's a slight pucker on his forehead as he assesses Trey and me. He peeks into the back of the carriage and then nods as if everything meets his approval. "The picnic basket is in the back. It's a simple drive. Just go straight down the road, and you'll dead-end into the ruins. They're quite stunning so make sure you get photos, too. You have my phone number from the tour packet in case you need anything."

"We have to drive the carriage?" I ask. "Isn't that dangerous?"

"Naw," Trey says. "We'll be fine."

"Here." Jaxon hands me a card. It sparkles like it's been dipped in glitter. "My number is on the back. Don't worry. The horses know the route, and they've done this hundreds of times."

"This looks just like the gift card I used to book the tour with," I say, taking it.

"My mum ordered too many," he explains. "Since the company's number is on it, I use the ones not loaded with cash as business cards."

"That's a strange business tactic," I say and input his number into my phone. If I could have one day with this company, I bet I could totally transform their business. But then that would be against everything I'm here for.

"Alright." Jaxon claps his hands. "You're all set then. Mr. Thompson will give you directions on how to drive the buggy."

But Jaxon doesn't leave right away. He shifts on his feet, eyeing me. "You sure you're alright?"

"What do you mean?" I lift my eyebrows.

"Going this alone with Trey."

"Sure she is," Trey says. "She's the one who asked to be my partner, remember?"

I don't understand Jaxon Wolfe. One moment he's lecturing me about my choice in what I should dream of and now he seems worried about me with Trey. *Who are you really?*

"We'll be fine," I say and then with a sassy grin, I add, "Unless you wish to join us?"

I'm teasing of course, but a tiny part of me wouldn't mind if he did come. He's a whole lot more fun than Troublesome Trey.

"I wish I could," Jaxon says, "but someone has to take the guests back to the bus. Once you're finished, Mr. Thompson will drive you back to town. Have a lovely time."

He spins on his heels and strides out of the barn, eating up the ground with his powerful legs.

"Step into the buggy," Mr. Thompson begins his instructions, and we clamber onto the long seat. "It's pretty simple. Hold the reins like so. Pull back to stop and flick gently to have her go."

"Sounds easy enough." Trey takes the reins. "We had horses at my family's farm."

"Ah!" Mr. Thompson's eyes light up. "Then you will have no problems."

"What's the horse's name?" I ask.

"Betty." Mr. Thompson backs away from the carriage. "She's the sweetest thing and calm even in a rainstorm. You'll be just fine."

"Heeya." Trey flicks the reins like he's an expert cowboy.

Betty plods out of the barn, down the lane, and onto the dirt road at a nice, even pace. Large oaks canopy above us, their leaves shifting in the cool breeze. The road curves and follows a deep river through a narrow valley. The land slopes up on either side, secluding us in this magical slice of Germany. It's a romantic trip, and it pains me to think I'm here beside Trey. Thankfully, we ride in silence. I need to be grateful Trey is keeping to himself. Maybe this trip won't be so terrible after all.

"So you wanted to be my partner, huh?" Trey breaks the silence.

"More like I didn't want Lilac to be your partner," I rectify.

"I knew you were my type the moment I saw you. You've got the right curves in all the right places." He nods knowingly at my chest, and my lips dip into a frown.

"I think you misread the situation. I'm not interested in you, and I don't appreciate you looking at me in that way."

"But how can a guy not look at you?" He skims a finger along the edge of the ruffle bordering my cleavage. "Such plump—"

I whack his hand back. "How dare you!" Fire rages through my veins. "Do not touch me, or I'll break your finger off! And here I was just starting to think this trip might not be that bad."

"What are you talking about? I saw how you were eyeing me while I was chopping that wood. That look of hunger in your eyes was there. Don't deny it."

"I most certainly will deny it! Stop this buggy this instant."

"What?" He chuckles. "But we're almost there. I can see the ruins just ahead. I promise I won't touch you again."

I glower at him and then pull out my phone.

"What are you doing?" Trey asks.

"I'm texting Jaxon," I snap.

Me: Help!

I push send. Then add,

Trey is making inappropriate advances

"That's not necessary." He moves to snatch my phone. I push send and hold it out of his reach. "Give me the phone."

"Stop the carriage."

"You don't tell me what to do."

"You need to keep your hands to yourself."

He shifts in the seat and grabs my hands. I clench my phone tightly and elbow him in the neck with my other arm. It's then he turns and uses all that brute strength he showed off earlier to physically rip the phone from my hands.

I may not be the strongest of women or the fittest, but I've got fight in me. Grams used to call me Spitfire when I was a kid. I rear back and kick my leg, shoving it at his stomach.

"You don't tell me what to do," Trey growls, grabbing my arm.

The horse tosses its head, but Mr. Thompson was right. She's a calm little angel.

Fear curdles through me. *Think, Scarlett! Find a way out of this.* I reach through the gap between the seat and dig into the basket until my hand wraps around a cool bottle. The champagne. Squirming to get the right angle, I heft up the bottle and smash it on his head. He cries out from the impact, flailing his arms. Desperately, I squirm away, falling into a heap on the floor of the buggy, my skirts billowing out around me.

The horse rears up on its hind legs, finally spooked.

"Whoa! Stay still," Trey yells at Betty, yanking back on the reins. "Damn horse."

The horse rears up again, neighing in agitation. She twists her body in a sharp turn and takes off in a full canter. The carriage is not designed for such a move, as the whole buggy lifts off the ground. We're rolling on one wheel out of control like a banshee set on fire. The world tilts and jerks.

The carriage hits a bump. Instantly, Trey and I are tossed out like sacks of potatoes. My body is airborne for what feels like an eternity. I claw at nothingness, screaming. Then I drop into the river with a giant splash. Icy-cold water engulfs me. My skirts tangle around my legs. I cry out in shock, but the river swallows scream.

CHAPTER 27

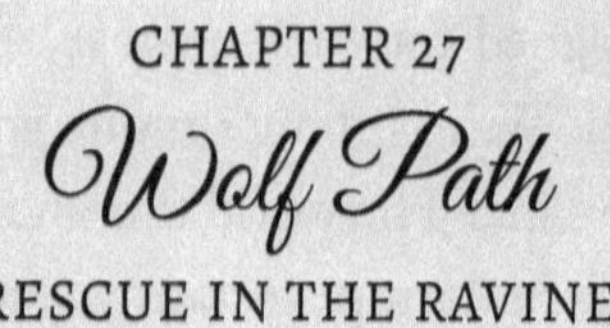

RESCUE IN THE RAVINE

Reader Note: *You are reading the Wolf Path where Scarlett decides to take Lilac's place in the competition.*

MY HEAD PUSHES above the surface of the river. I gasp for air, sputtering and coughing. Water coats my eyelashes, and the world blurs with panic. The current has pulled me deeper out and farther downstream. I tread water, but my sneakers are weighing me down.

Trey spews out a long string of curses from where he's lying in the shallow section of the river. He didn't fall as far into the water as I did. But I'm too busy trying to keep my head above the surface to worry about him. A thud of what sounds like horse hooves pounds the air. A man riding a horse comes racing around the corner. Hope surges inside of me.

"Help!" I yell. "Over here."

But my voice is gravel rough and weak. Gritting my teeth, I begin my attempt to swim.

"Scarlett!" a deep voice calls out.

I search for the voice. It's Jaxon, leaping off his horse. Every stroke is a battle. He sprints down the river bank and splashes through the water to meet me.

"Jaxon," I croak, trying to hold back the tears as he pulls me into the shallow water. "You came."

He sweeps me off my feet like I'm feather-light and cradles me in his arms. Eyes gray as storm clouds stare down at me.

"Are you alright?" he asks.

I nod, my emotions flailing around inside of me. I'm a kite caught in a windstorm, and I don't know if I should cry or smile. But mostly, I just want to bury my head against Jaxon's warmth.

So I do. He's firm and strong. I close my eyes and drink in his scent of spice and pinewood. He came for me when I asked for help. He's here when I need him. How could I ever have thought he was the Big Bad Wolf?

He lowers me to the ground, and yet I cling to him, fear still lingering. This time I allow it to sharpen my focus.

"Trey." I swallow. "Where is he?"

Jaxon's gaze flicks upstream, darkening. "He's sitting on the river bank. Still alive, but he's holding his ankle. Maybe injured, so I don't think he'll go anywhere."

Jaxon eases his arms away from me. He rips off his jacket and wraps it gently around my shoulders. His large hands push the strands of hair out of my eyes. He looks me over as if he's searching for any wounds.

"The real question is, did he hurt you?"

"Thankfully no."

"You're safe now." His mouth flattens into a harsh line. "I won't let him harm you again."

He pulls out his phone and says something in German before hanging up.

"Who were you calling?" I ask.

"The police. They will be here shortly to arrest Trey. No one on my tour should ever feel unsafe. I'm sorry this happened, Scarlett. I shouldn't have let you be alone with the arschloch."

"It's not your fault. I volunteered to go. I didn't think things would get out of control. Thank you for coming." I lick my lips, not believing my next words. "You saved me."

I tell him everything that happened, relaying the events as best as I can.

"Sounds to me as if you saved yourself." He glances over at Trey, and his fists clench. "I hope the police arrive before I do something I might regret."

"I'm afraid Mr. Thompson's horse and carriage might not be in the best of shape though."

"Don't worry about it. I'll call him and take care of every-thing." He rises to his feet and talks to Mr. Thompson on the phone, once again switching easily to German.

"Hello!" Trey calls out to us and rises to his feet, hobbling our way. "I need help, too. I think I broke my ankle on these damn rocks."

"Good," Jaxon mutters under his breath. Then to me, "Are you able to stand and walk or should I carry you?"

I rise to my feet but sway. He dives and catches me, his strong arms keeping me from falling. My body shudders. I can't stop shaking.

"I don't know what's wrong with me," I say.

"You should sit for a moment longer, but I want to get you out of those wet clothes. You're shivering. The river is cold this time of year."

"I promise I'm not normally like this. I've never been knocked out before or thrown into the river."

Pain etches across his face. "This is all my fault. I'm going to make it up to you."

"Hey!" Trey moves closer, surprisingly fast for his apparent injury. "I said I needed help, too. Where's our carriage? You promised a fairytale experience, and this is what we get? You better fix this situation or I'm going to give you the shittiest review you've ever seen."

"Brilliant," Jaxon half-growls, striding up to Trey. "Then be sure to add this to the write-up."

Jaxon punches Trey in the jaw. The guy flies backward, landing with a thud on the river bank.

"Dude!" Trey's hand goes to his jaw, rubbing it. "What was that for?"

"For treating Scarlett with disrespect. I never want to see you near her ever again. Do you understand?"

"You punched me! I'm gonna sue the hell out of you. And press charges."

"Press charges for what? I didn't see a thing," I say coldly, daring him to challenge me.

"But look at my face!" he yells and points to his bloody lip. "How do you explain this?"

"You did fall out of the carriage after you tried to assault me, so that can cause a lot of damage. I guess you hit your face on a rock."

Trey looks at both of us and then sits down, muttering under his breath.

Jaxon rolls his shoulders as if to release the anger. He turns back to me, and the tension in his jaw softens. "Is there anything else I can do to help you?" he asks.

"No," I exhale with relief, "I'm just glad you came."

I've been totally and utterly wrong about Jaxon. Seeing him standing up for me is thrilling and scary all mixed into one. I have no idea what to do with these feelings or what they mean.

CHAPTER 28

Wolf Path

COCOA AND WISHES

Reader Note: *You are reading the Wolf Path where Scarlett decides to take Lilac's place in the competition.*

THE POLICE ARRIVE, and after I give them my statement, they handcuff a very angry and annoyed Trey, who totters into the car.

"She said she was interested in me!" Trey yells. Then as they're pushing him into the car, he throws over his shoulder, "Tell them, Scarlett. Tell them the truth."

I glower back, stepping closer to Jaxon.

"You wish to ride with us?" the officer asks me. "Or I can call another car for you."

"You're welcome to ride with me," Jaxon offers, "but all I have is Roger here."

He nods to the horse, chomping blissfully on a patch of grass.

"I'll go back with Jaxon," I tell the officers, "but thank you for your help."

The police take off while Jaxon grabs the horse's reins and helps me into the saddle. Once I'm settled, he slips in behind me, wrapping thick arms around my body. My breath hitches but for completely different reasons than it did when Trey came after me. As we take off down the road the adrenaline rush from earlier seeps away, leaving every muscle in my body weary and aching. I allow my body to relax against Jaxon's, nestling into his large form. His quiet presence blankets me in peace.

"I'm going to take you to Mr. Thompson's house," Jaxon says. "It's just up the ways. We'll get you some dry clothes and food. Once you're settled, I can take you to our tour's next hotel."

"What about the group?" I jolt straight. His arms tighten around me as if to keep me from falling off the horse. "Are they okay?"

"I got your text as we were hiking. I told Gary to take everyone back to the bus and I called the driver. He's taking the group directly to our next hotel. Then I raced back and grabbed one of Mr. Thompson's horses. I got here as soon as I could."

"Thank you for coming," I say as we plod through the entrance of a farmyard. "I don't know what I would've done if you hadn't."

"Well, we at Fairy Tale Tours always provide top-shelf service for our guests," he says in his best commercial voice. "I couldn't live with myself if he had done anything worse to you."

The horse trots down the main road of the farm where open fields line either side. The afternoon sun glimmers across golden wheat fields. The drive leads us up to an old half-timbered farmhouse with a steep tiled roof. Carved artwork and flower boxes tumbling with geraniums add a bright touch to the home. A garden stretches out on one side with a large barn not far away on the other side.

"This place looks so quaint," I say. "It's like we stepped into one of the Grimm Brothers' tales."

"It is quite nice, isn't it?" Jaxon muses as he directs the horse to a post outside of the house. "I always find the German countryside a place of rest."

"You make it sound like you don't normally live here."

Jaxon slips off the horse, taking the warmth with him. But then he's reaching up to help me down. I hold out my arms and allow him to grab my waist. I plant my hands on his shoulders as he lowers me. My body brushes against his as my feet hit the ground. My heartbeat scatters around like butterflies set loose from a cage. We seem to be frozen, my hands resting on his broad shoulders and his palms gently tucked around my waist.

"Hallo, there!" a voice calls out.

We release each other like we've been burned. A woman stands in the doorway, a handkerchief covering graying hair. An apron stretches around her waist. She's wearing brown pants and a soft yellow shirt dotted with flowers. She smiles widely and waves to us.

"Come, come," she says with a thick accent. "My husband told me you were on your way."

"Thank you for opening your home to us," I say as I step through the doorway.

"My name is Clara," she says. "We have known Jaxon since he was a wee thing. But I must say, he's never brought a young lady over to our place."

"I'm Scarlett." I hold out my hand and she shakes it. "Jaxon rescued me from the crash. I hope your horse and carriage are okay."

"Asch. Never mind that. Old Betty brought the carriage back in one piece earlier." She leads us through a hallway and into the living room. Exposed wooden beams and plank wood floors give the place a rustic and cozy atmosphere. A large couch and chairs piled with plump pillows ring a large hearth. Tall windows lined with crème-colored curtains allow sunlight to stream through lighting up the room along with a metal ringed chandelier that hangs from the arched ceiling.

"This place is lovely," I say, taking it all in. "Thank you for having me."

"Oh, you are quite wet, yes?" Clara asks, eyeing my clothes. "Come. We must get you into something dry."

Once I've changed into a pair of soft brown pants, a flannel shirt, and thick socks, I pad out of the bathroom to the main living room area. Jaxon is kneeling by the hearth stoking a tiny flame. A faint smell of wood and kindling fills my nostrils.

"Feeling warmer now?" he asks, taking me in.

"Much warmer and much better," I agree and sink gratefully onto the couch.

He pushes the poker around, moving a chunk of wood closer to the flames and then tosses on some kindling. Flames spark and a fire bursts to life. He sets the poker aside and brushes off his hands. His eyes catch mine, and he frowns.

"Something wrong?" I ask.

"You still look cold." He picks up a blanket and tucks it around me. "Better?"

My words are swallowed up as I gaze up at him. Everything about him makes me uneasy and yet completely comfortable. He's too perfect, which makes him tempting. I try to remember all the things I hated about him and his family, but sitting here, warm from his fire and snuggled under the blanket he gave me, all those thoughts fly away.

I manage a nod as Clara bustles in with a tray of two steaming mugs, a plate piled with cheese, cold cuts, and sausages, and a basket of rye bread.

"Such a traumatic event you had," she says as she sets the tray on the coffee table before me. "Jaxon told me all about it. I am dreadfully sorry. I brought you hot chocolate and some food to boost your spirits. I must go milk the goats, but you should be fine here, yes?"

"This is wonderful." I smile. "Danke."

She leaves the room, and Jaxon and I both grab a mug. He settles on the couch beside me, and I sip my chocolate. It's rich and creamy, and its warmth slides into every chilled crevasse in my body.

"The hot chocolate here is like nothing I've ever had before. It almost makes me forget today."

Jaxon leans back and sighs. "It has been a day."

"You don't need to stick around here on my account," I say. "I know you have a whole group of other people who need you. I can take a taxi or maybe Mr. Thompson can take me."

"The group will be fine. I'm not worried." He studies my face. "That was kind of you to take Lilac's place. I feel bad you had to suffer for your act of kindness."

"It was the right thing to do." I slice off a chunk of cheese and flash him a sardonic smile. "Maybe next time, don't draw names."

"You're right." He rubs the scruff on his chin. "This is the first time I've led this tour, and it's clear I don't know what I'm doing."

"This is your first time? I'd never have known. You seem so

confident. You know your facts and exactly what to say and do."

"I helped my father for years when I was younger. That said, I've never been in charge. My brother and I have been trying to help him out. He had a heart attack two months ago."

"A heart attack?" Instinctively, my hand touches his. "I'm so sorry."

"He's doing well, but I appreciate your sentiments. My brother, Karl, had more flexibility than I did with his job so he helped out for a bit, but then he abruptly ditched the whole tour. Come to find out, it apparently had to do with your sister. I didn't want my parents to lose everything they'd built their lives for to fall apart. So I requested a temporary leave of absence from my job and flew in from London to help out this spring until my father is back up and running."

The pieces of who this family is and what they've been through are snapping into place.

"That must have been tough for you," I say. "What do you do? And why London?"

"I'm a manager of a furniture company." He shrugs and sips his drink. "Nothing special, but it pays the bills. My mum is from London and after I graduated university, I wanted to get out and spread my wings. London seemed to be the obvious choice."

"You are full of surprises."

"As are you."

I snort. "Me? Hardly."

"Honestly," he grins, eyes flashing knowingly, "I was surprised you showed up this morning to continue the tour."

"Why do you say that?"

"When you told me who you really were and why you were here, I didn't think you were actually going to take the tour."

Guilt burns my chest. "What your brother did really hurt Bella. I don't know if she'll ever be able to trust in a relationship so completely again. If we're being honest, I came here trying to make you and your family pay for what Karl did. Not only did I try to sabotage your game, I gave Trey the idea of the bad review."

"Ah, yes. I heard your inspiring speech."

I grimace, scrunching my nose. "I'm sorry. Thinking back, and especially after what happened today, my decisions seem so childish and trivial."

"You have passion. I see that in everything you do." He sets his mug on the coffee table and inches closer to me. "Perhaps your passion for your sister may have made you quick to judge me, but I can respect that. Just maybe don't mention bad reviews to the other guests."

I chuckle. "I can work with that."

"I'm going to make sure everything is settled between my brother and your sister. He's agreed to meet me tomorrow when we're in Kassel."

"That's great." I set my mug down. The fire crackles and pops in the hearth. "Because I talked to Bella on the phone last night, and I don't think she's over him yet."

His brow furrows. "If there is anything you think I can do to help, please let me know."

I lean closer to him. He responds by reaching across and lightly brushing a finger along my jaw. A thrill shoots through my chest, and I tuck myself in so close that his lips are a moment from mine.

His breath catches, and his stormy eyes widen. "What is this between us?"

"I don't know." My fingers clutch the edge of his button-down shirt like I'm holding on for life. My body aches for his touch. For those lips to press against mine. What is happening to me? Maybe it's the whole rescuer syndrome.

But I don't care. Because I want him.

He closes his eyes and groans as if being close to me is agonizing. "We shouldn't. I'm your tour guide. You're a guest. This is unprofessional of me."

He breaks away, rubbing a palm over his face.

"You're not the only one here at fault," I say. "But you're right. We should keep our relationship strictly in the friend zone. After all, I'll be going back to Florida in less than two weeks."

He rises to his feet, blinking against the fading light. "It's getting late. I'll call a taxi to take us to Kassel."

I nod because that's the right choice. The smart choice. Except, why does it feel so wrong?

The Wolf Path: Are you loving seeing how Scarlett's relationship develops with Jaxon? Keep on the Wolf Path and skip ahead to Chapter 31.

The Movie Star Path: Are you curious how things would've turned out if Scarlett hadn't traded places with Lilac? Then keep reading onto Chapter 29.

CHAPTER 29

Movie Star Path

COMPETITION CHAMPIONS

Reader Note: This is the path where you choose not to switch places with Lilac and stay and compete in the wood-chopping competition with Rob, the movie star.

"Are you ready to win this thing, Scarlett?" Rob asks, securing his wig.

"Whew. I'm so nervous." I wipe my brow dramatically. "I mean, the chance to win a romantic carriage ride to castle ruins? Too exciting."

"With a movie star, no less."

"Now you're just making me nervous."

"Really?" He cocks an eyebrow. "I make you nervous? Like I stir those little butterflies all around?"

"Shut up." I roll my eyes, laughing. But my face warms and the way his eyes are twinkling sends a burst of fireworks through my veins.

The whistle blows, pulling our attention to Jaxon standing on the other side of the tree stump chopping blocks. He's frowning at Rob and me as if having fun on a fairytale tour is strictly forbidden. What a grouch!

"On your marks," he calls out, "get set, go!"

The clearing erupts with the sound of chopping. Everyone is desperate to win their trip to the ruins. I pick up the ax. Its warm handle settles in my palm.

"How good are you at chopping wood?" I ask.

"I haven't the faintest idea." Rob grins slyly. "I suppose we're about to find out."

"I learned in middle school camp. I wasn't too bad. How about we take turns? I chop and then you have a go at it?"

"I see we have a competitor in our midst. Let's do this."

He's not wrong. I do love a good competition, especially when the stakes are high and it's a measurable goal. I set the log upright on the tree stump, heft up my ax, and drive it onto the log, splitting it.

"Look at you, an expert wood-chopping Little Red Riding Hood," Rob says appreciatively.

"It's not a perfect slice in half, but it's a start."

"And a perfectionist to boot."

Once I split my wood, Rob takes over. I hurry my armload to the platform where we're supposed to stack our finished product. A quick glance down the line tells me Gary and Evelyn are making good progress while Trey is a wood-hacking machine. His normally slicked-back hair has gone wild, and sweat has soaked through the armpits of his red shirt.

Lilac runs, carrying a full stack of wood, but trips and falls, spilling logs everywhere. Jaxon goes to check on her, calling out to see if she's okay. She laughs and shakes her head at the mess she created. Since she's fine, I race back to take over the wood chopping from Rob.

"How are we looking?" Rob asks.

"It's close." I snatch my ax. "We need to pick up the pace."

"Your word is my command." He looks up and takes off in a sprint.

I swing my ax onto the wood, remembering the swarm of emotions I felt during the very public breakup with Hunter. The wood splits with a crack. I heft up the ax again and again. There's something therapeutic about putting all my frustrations into a physical object. It's like I'm releasing all that pent-up anger and letting it go.

When I go to grab another log, I realize I've just split the last in our stack.

"Hurry!" Rob yells, running back to our chopping block. "Trey is about to win!"

The two of us scoop up the remainder of the hewn wood and take off toward our platform. Frantically, we toss the wood on top of our pile, but just as our last piece drops into place, Trey is shouting, "We won, we won!"

Jaxon blows the whistle and we all assess Trey's victory. Sweat drips from my brow and both Rob and I are panting heavily.

I hold up my palm in a high-five. "Good job, partner. We didn't win, but we worked well together."

He slaps my hand and then leans over, placing his hands on his knees. "I haven't gotten that much of a workout in ages."

Jaxon marches up to Trey's platform, studying his work, but then he goes out into the center of the field where Lilac tripped. He picks up a lone piece of firewood.

"You are close," Jaxon tells Trey, "but you missed a piece. The competition is still on. Is anyone else finished?"

"We are!" I lift on my toes and wave.

Jaxon jogs to us and assesses our station.

"We have our winners!" he announces.

Rob and I start jumping up and down like two little kids. He hugs me, but mid-hug it quickly gets weird as if we both realize we're definitely not just buddies. I swallow and duck my head so he can't see how his closeness affected me. The group gives us a half-hearted clap, except for Axel and Lilac, who hurry to congratulate us on our success.

"If you'll come with me," Jaxon interrupts our celebration, "I'll lead you to your carriage."

OUR CARRIAGE REMINDS me of those open buggies characters in Jane Austen movies ride through town. Rob offered to drive the carriage but warned me it's his first time.

As we leave the barn area, our tour group waves us off. Felicity snaps a "selfie" as we pass by, and Lilac yells, "Make sure you kiss him," which sends my mind heart faster than I'm sure our old horse could run.

I peek over at Rob to see if he heard Lilac, but his jaw is tight and eyes are on the road as he holds the reins. We enter the forest where a steep incline rises up on one side and a small river rushes along on the other.

"You look like a pro carriage driver," I tell him as our horse clips down the road.

"Horses terrify me," he grumbles. "I avoid them at all costs."

"Didn't you ride a horse in *Raiders of Nineveh*?"

"For a very brief moment. Most of those shots were courtesy of my stunt double."

"I had no idea." I frown. "If that's the case, are you sure you should be driving this carriage? What if the horse gets spooked and we tumble into the river and you get hurt?"

"Now who's being dramatic? Our horse Betty here looks about as stable and as fast as a rock. No one is tumbling into the river."

Speckles of sunlight filter through the leaves, scattering over us like glitter. The road curves, revealing vine-coated towers and thick stone walls, weathered and crumbling. Free-standing stone archways and roofless brick buildings are scattered around like they're not quite ready to give in to the elements.

A wide green lawn lies in front of the ruins with a picnic table and a few benches. Blue wildflowers dot the edges, making it a perfect location for a romantic outing. The only things that ruin the experience are my bark-smeared dress and my sweat-slicked skin.

"Looks like we've arrived." Rob pulls back on the reins.

"This place is so peaceful." I jump out of the carriage. "It's like time forgot it."

"And like the world forgot us. I can almost imagine I've escaped the pressures of Hollywood by entering a fairy tale."

Rob secures the horse to the hitching post while I pull out the picnic basket Jaxon gave us. I set it on the table and begin unpacking. Cheese, crackers, meats, and breads.

"The pressure of always being in the spotlight must be hard to deal with. I get stressed out over an ad campaign that doesn't perform to my projected expectations."

"Can't remember when I felt this relaxed, actually. The pressure is off. Right now I feel more like myself than I have in years."

He yanks off his wig and runs his hands through his dark hair. There's a softness to his features, and his shoulders aren't quite as stiff. My movements falter, watching him be so at ease. It's as if I'm really seeing him for the first time, and my pulse drums to a beat I've never felt before. I blink, desperate to keep myself grounded.

"That's wonderful. Sounds like this trip is what you needed. An escape into a fairy tale."

"Maybe." His eyes find mine. "Or maybe it's the people I'm with."

My hands freeze on the container of cheese I was opening. What is he saying? I search his face, but his expression is inscrutable.

I decide to change the subject by lifting out the picnic blanket. "Do you want to sit at the table or blanket?"

"Are you asking me if I want to be civilized at the table, or comfortable, and perhaps a little naughty, on the blanket?"

I press a hand to my hips. "Just because we picnic on a blanket doesn't mean we have to be naughty."

"You're absolutely right." He flashes me that mischievous grin I'm starting to fall in love with. "Let's picnic on the blanket, and if I fall asleep and start snoring you must promise to defend me against any attacking dragons."

I wave a fork at him. "Now you're just getting demanding."

I spread out the blanket and set the food onto it while he digs into the basket and plucks out the champagne bottle.

"I see Jaxon didn't skimp on this excursion," he says. "Shall we celebrate our success?"

I drop onto the blanket. "We shall."

He pops open the cork, and we cheer as mist erupts from its top. He sits beside me and generously pours the bubbly liquid into plastic flutes.

"To you, Little Red Riding Hood." He holds his glass to mine.

"And to our win," I add.

The champagne bubbles in my mouth, and I finally allow myself to settle into the magic of this place.

"Should we explore the ruins or eat?" I ask.

"Eat of course. After you made me run around like a chicken set on the loose so we could win this thing, I'm positively starved."

"It was a close race."

"And you were a taskmaster." He pops a grape into his mouth, and I look away before it seems like I'm goggling at his lips.

"Someone must keep you in line."

He passes me the bread, and I pile it with cheese and sausage. "So tell me about your life as a marketing manager," he says. "That's what you do, right?"

I tell him about my role and how hard I worked to get it. "The wild thing is last night my boss offered me a twenty-thousand-dollar bonus and a new title if I were to jump on a plane today to fix things for her at her company."

"Considering you're here, I take it you said no."

"It's literally my dream offer. She knew it, too."

"So why didn't you leave?"

"I told myself it was for Bella, and it is. But maybe it's more than that. When I broke up with Hunter, I realized I'd been on the wrong path. I was caught in this career that didn't allow me to live and breathe and love like I'm supposed to."

"What would this other hypothetical path look like for you?"

"I have no idea." I stare at the bubbles in my drink. "I've been so busy doing the thing that was supposed to make me happy that I never took the time to think about why I wasn't happy. Does that even make sense?"

"Utterly."

I draw in a deep breath, taking in the dark curls hanging over his eyes without the wig and those long eyelashes every woman on the planet would kill for. But what really hits me is the intense expression on his face, telling me he's completely invested in what I'm saying. With Hunter, he was always checking his phone, making sure he didn't lose a new listing that might be popping up.

"I want this trip to help me figure out what I really want," I finally admit.

"It sounds like both of us are at a crossroads." He lies on his side, running his finger along the edge of his glass. "We're both all grown up and yet desperately trying to figure out who we're truly meant to be. If you could go back to your high school days, what life would you dream up for yourself?"

"Now that's a thought." I press my lips together and stare at the ruins that echo from another time. "I think I'd like to be my own boss."

"Yes," he agrees slowly, "you'd be perfect running a company of your own. Put that taskmaster to work."

I chuckle. "I always have a million ideas in my head. It would be nice to set them into action the way I see they should be executed and in the timeframe I feel they should be completed."

"What's holding you back?" He stares at me as if my dreams are in my palm, ready to be thrown into action.

"Everything." I set down my drink. "Experience, support systems, and unfortunately cash to start up a business."

"What if none of that held you back? Would you do it?"

I consider his question, but it doesn't take long for me to know the truth. It's deep inside me, buried in the furthest corner of my heart because if I were to ever pull it out, it would leave me with the reminder that I have unfulfilled dreams and goals that could never be achieved.

"Yes," I whisper.

"Then let me help you." He shifts closer. "Let me help you make your dreams come true."

"I can't let you do that." I know this is breaking our boundary of friendship, but I reach out and take his hand. A spark flutters across my skin. "I know we've just met and we're supposed to be friends, but you mean too much to me to bring business into a relationship. Still, talking to you about this has been good. Scary. Terrifying to actually admit to dreams I didn't want to acknowledge, but necessary."

"You want to know what's terrifying? You." His voice whispers to my soul. "You are the unexpected. The not-supposed-to-exist. And yet, here you are."

His lips hover over mine. His eyes are dark, hungry. Hot liquid pools into my belly. If I lean in closer, our lips will collide. A part of me aches for his touch while another part knows this can't possibly be more than a holiday fling. Should I kiss him? What do I really want?

CHAPTER 30

Movie Star Path

PAPARAZZI PANDEMONIUM

Reader Note: You are still reading the Movie Star Path after the competition.

HIS LIPS ARE TANTALIZINGLY CLOSE, but I just can't do it. He's a movie star and likely a player. The guy probably has a girl waiting for him in every city on the planet. How much do I really know about the person he is? If he truly believes in what he's saying, then he can wait a few days for a kiss.

The question is, can I?

With a sigh, I pull away. "As incredibly tempting as you are, I think we should focus on getting to know each other better. I mean, I keep wondering if you're Jack of the Water World from *The Titan Warlords* or Tramon from *Raiders of Nineveh*."

"I can be whatever you wish me to be."

"I'm serious." I can't help but laugh. His expressions completely disarm me. "Let's explore these ruins before we run out of time."

"See? I was right about the taskmaster title." He rises to his feet, brushing crumbs off his hands.

I duck through the entrance and step into what must have been a courtyard. My mind wanders, thinking about what life might have been like without running water and electricity. Rob reluctantly joins me, complaining about leaving behind our delicious food to the forest critters. We explore the grounds, and I pick wildflowers along the way until I've gathered a brightly colored bouquet.

We spin a random tale about the two of us being the last humans on Earth (his idea) after an alien invasion (my idea) and how we're trying to survive in secret. As we roam through the ancient buildings, my defenses fall down. It feels like it's just the two of us, sharing silly tales and living in an imaginary world.

"First one to the tower wins!" I call over my shoulder and race through the ancient stone archway.

Steps twist up the circular staircase. My feet slap against cracked stones, and my skirts swish against my knees. Behind me, Rob is panting, trying to catch up. I'm breathless by the time I reach the top. The roof has long disappeared, giving way to an impressive view of the forest. Evergreens and oaks stretch out in every direction like a soft blanket. In the distance, the modern world pokes out of the tree line, threatening to disrupt this fantasy we're in.

"You cheated!" Rob gasps out the words, leaning over to catch his breath.

"According to my rules, I did not." I laugh, grateful for the cool breeze blowing across my face.

His phone rings, shattering the magic. He checks it and sighs. "I've got to answer this. It's my manager."

"Of course," I say.

"Curt, my man. Any updates on my co-star?" I expect him to run off and speak in private, but he puts it on speaker.

"Are you still on that damn fairytale tour?" Curt asks. "Get your ass back to Fiji pronto. Are you really willing to flush your career down the toilet for some red-haired chick? Don't lie to me. I saw the pictures."

Rob frowns darkly. "Never talk about her like that again."

"Okay, okay. Chill, will you? What do I need to do to get you back here?"

"Get rid of Tia. You know I can't work with her. She's despicable. I bet she agreed to do this film just so she could ruin my career."

"She doesn't have to," Curt says, clearly exasperated. "You've done that yourself."

"Good pep talk. And oh, by the way, you're fired." Rob hangs up and pockets his phone, peeking over at me. "Sorry about what he said about you. That was inexcusable."

"That was sweet of you to stand up for me, but you can't just fire him. He's right. I'm a nobody and definitely not worth losing your career over."

"You're not a nobody." His phone rings again, and he puts it on silent. "I want you to know that when it comes to you, I'm taking whatever this is between us very seriously."

"Fiji, huh? Maybe you should reconsider. I could put up with a lot for Fiji."

"But then there's Tiaster."

A grin tickles my lips. "Is that your nickname for Tianna Ulci?"

"That's the nice one." He smirks but reaches for me. "Let's not let her ruin this moment. Look at us. We're on top of the world."

The wind catches his hair, tempting me to push it from his

eyes. He tugs my hand, drawing me to him so my chest is pressed against his. His eyes drink me in like he hasn't touched water in days, and his fingers trail down my jawline and along the side of my neck to tug on the lace hemline of my bodice. My chest heaves in and out. His gaze slips to my mouth, and this time, I know I won't be able to stop him.

Those luscious lips swipe across mine, a whisper of a dare. I clutch the front of his shirt, my heart galloping. Then his mouth is on mine, and his hands cup my face. The wind gathers around us, whipping at my hair and the hem of my dress as if our kiss had stirred up the elements. A haze drifts over my thoughts. All I can think about is him and the gentle, perfect way his tongue explores my mouth. The way his palms run along my body as if every inch of me is perfect.

"I see them!" a voice calls out from the fog in my mind. "Up on the tower!"

Somehow I extricate myself from Rob's arms and blink back to the moment. More noise drags my attention over the edge. Rob swears under his breath.

"They found us," he mutters. "Kissing no less."

Sure enough, a group of people is standing below the tower, snapping photos of our picnic area, his discarded wig, and us on the tower. There is no doubt we gave them some great shots of our passionate kiss. My face burns.

Rob yanks me backward into the narrow stairwell, out of view. "I'm sorry, Scarlett. I don't know how they found us, but they did. We need to leave right away. We're going to go straight down these stairs, not talk to anyone, and get in the carriage. Got it?"

"Got it." But no, I don't get it. How did they find us, and why do they even care?

He slips on his sunglasses and gently takes my hand. We

hurry down the steps, only to be met with reporters holding out microphones and cameras.

"Is this your secret girlfriend?" one reporter asks.

Another jams her mic in my face. "What's your name?"

"How long have you two known each other?"

"How do you think Tianna will feel about your betrayal?"

Rob ignores the questions, marching us to the carriage. Thankfully, no one jumps onto the seat. One guy hurries to get footage from the front of the horse, but when Rob flicks the reins, he dives out of the way. Thankfully, the horse manages to get around one of the camera crew's trucks and then we take off at a fast trot.

"Is that the way it always is for you?" I ask.

"Yes." Sadness pulls at his lips. "Always."

The reality of what a life with Rob would be like hits me hard. The rush of passion has seeped away, leaving me cold and confused. Is this the life I want? To always be looking over my shoulder? To never have privacy?

To always feel inferior?

I don't know if I'm up for this sort of relationship.

Wolf Path: Are the Movie Star Path and paparazzi too stressful? Jump back on the Wolf Path and continue to Chapter 32.

Movie Star Path: Forget the wolf! You're totally invested in this relationship with the Movie Star. Skip ahead to Chapter 33.

Of course, you can always read every chapter 😊

CHAPTER 31

Wolf Path

WE ARE, OH, SO PROFESSIONAL

eader Note: You are continuing the Wolf Path—the day after Jaxon rescues Scarlett and they nearly kiss at the farmhouse.

I SIT on top of my suitcase and yank the zipper tightly around the perimeter, finally closing it shut. This is what happens when you don't take time to pack properly and just toss everything in. We're about to leave for another day touring the Fairy Tale Road, but I keep revisiting how Jaxon swooped me out of the river and into his arms—how those arms engulfed me like I was someone he needed to protect at all costs.

How close his lips had been to mine as we sat cuddled on the couch, the fire crackling from the hearth. An ache swirls through my belly. I would've kissed him if he hadn't stopped us. I definitely wanted to.

Obviously, he didn't.

My phone rings, yanking me back to reality just in time

191

before I started fantasizing what that kiss might have been like. I blink down at my phone. It's Sherly.

"Hello," I answer. "I've been meaning to call, but it's been a little busy."

"Busy flying back to Florida or eating bratwurst and drinking beer as you stare at old buildings?"

I could tell her I dressed up as Little Red Riding Hood and competed in a wood-chopping competition and won, but Sherly is a get-to-the-point, don't-waste-my-time sort of boss so I say, "One of the tour guests tried to grope me while we were taking a carriage and I fell into the river."

"What?" For once, she sounds truly horrified. "This is terrible. Scarlett, you need to leave that tour. I'll connect you with the best lawyer who'll sue their asses off."

I rise off my suitcase and give my hotel room one last look before I head out into the hallway to meet the others on the bus.

"I know you want me to come back," I say, "but I can't leave yet. Besides, Jaxon had the guy arrested."

"Who's Jaxon?" she asks warily.

"The tour guide."

The sexy—with eyes that drown you in a rainstorm and muscles hard as rock—tour guide.

"I don't care if you have a tour fling, and after your whole breakup with Hunter, you deserve it. But don't throw away your whole future for a crush."

"Who says I'm having a fling?" Damn it. My voice totally squeaked. "Listen, we're headed to Kassel today. When I get there, I'll find a café and do an initial write-up of possible solutions for you. That will at least give you a direction of which way to go."

"I suppose that could suffice. I'll be waiting for your email. Or you could come back and grab that promotion and bonus."

"I appreciate that."

I hang up and step up to the checkout counter, handing over my key. It's not the same woman that checked me in, but there's something very familiar about her. That silver hair pulled into a bun and sky-blue dress...

"We are so happy you came to stay," she says. "Please, pick out a gift from our gift basket as our way of showing our appreciation for choosing us."

"Thanks." I dig my hand into the basket and retrieve a sparkling gift card from Fairy Tale Tours. *Weird.* I shake my head as I stick it in my wallet. "Can't seem to escape these. They're giving away their gift cards everywhere."

"So it appears." She gives me an odd, knowing smile.

I wave goodbye and slip outside, the cool breeze of the morning tugging on my long hair. Gary and Evelyn are loading their suitcases into the bottom of the bus, but all I can focus on is Jaxon, standing by the bus entrance, smiling at and greeting his guests. Felicity pretends to stumble in her heels and grabs Jaxon by the shoulders to keep from falling and then paws at his chest. I shake my head over her moves and go to heft my suitcase into the bus when Jaxon runs over and takes it from my hands.

"Here." He reaches for my case. "Let me get that for you, Ms. Walker."

Ms. Walker? I hate how stiff and formal he's being—as if I hadn't been curled up in his arms, my body pressed against his.

"You don't need to do that." I keep my hand firmly on the handle. "I've got it."

"After everything that happened yesterday, I need to keep a

close eye on you." Then his face flushes red. "I mean, professionally, of course."

"Of course," I say just as formally as I relinquish my suitcase. "I appreciate your attention as our tour guide, Mr. Wolfe."

Look at us! We're so professional. Tour guide and tour guest. No heated glances or fingers brushing across the jawline. No lips a breath away from each other. This is just how it's supposed to be. I mean, the last thing I want is a repeat of what happened to my sister. With that solid resolve, I board the bus and slip into a seat beside Lilac.

Since I didn't sleep hardly at all last night after what happened with Trey, I just want to lean my head back and take a quick nap. But everyone on the bus wants to know the full story of why Jaxon had to go back to help Trey and me—and where Trey was now.

Thankfully, Jaxon makes a formal announcement, explaining Trey would not be joining us for the remainder of the trip and to respect my privacy. I shoot Jaxon a grateful smile. He keeps surprising me and I shouldn't like it.

As the bus pulls up to the Löwenburg Castle, it's like I've been whisked into a fantasy book. Thick trees surround the castle grounds while a tall tower overlooks the sprawling halls, battlements, and crumbling turrets. Dark stone and slitted windows give the castle an ominous mood, especially outlined against the shadows of a gloomy-gray sky.

"This place looks wicked scary." Lilac taps her fingers against each other with a devious grin. "I can't wait to see what Jaxon has planned for us."

Fog seeps out from the moat. "I bet he'll say it's haunted."

"Please let it be so," she says.

"Welcome to Löwenburg," Jaxon announces. "This Gothic revival-style structure was built to resemble medieval ruins, a hail to the heroes of the past."

We trail out of the bus to surround Jaxon in front of the imposing castle. Our group seems smaller than before, which is when I realize Rob isn't here either.

"Hey, where's Rob?" I ask Axel. "I don't see him."

"He had an emergency meeting with his producers," Axel explains. "He's planning on meeting us at Grimm World this afternoon."

I nod, hoping everything is okay with him, but my thoughts are interrupted when Jaxon speaks.

"For today's experience, you've been invited to be a part of the Enchanted Escape Room, which is an immersive, fairytale-inspired adventure."

We all cheer.

"An escape room in a castle?" I tell Lilac. "This is something I can get behind."

"If an escape room isn't your cup of tea," Jaxon continues, "you're welcome to tour the grounds and enjoy the sections of the castle open for guests. For the rest of you, I'd like to introduce Niles Schnieder, your Enchanted Escape Room host running the event."

We give another clap as a tall, thin balding man steps out from the shadows. His spectacles dangle from the tip of his nose. He's wearing a black-edged, evergreen jacket and black pants that look like they came out of the early 1900s.

"Greetings," he says solemnly. "If you would follow me."

He takes off across the drawbridge at a clipped pace, the tails of his jacket flying out behind him. Nearly everyone follows except for the three college girls—Natisha, Maxi, and Cara—who say that they want to get some Instagram photos, and Tom, who I have barely spoken to.

"This is just too exciting," Evelyn tells me. "I'm quite good at puzzles, I'll have you know. If we get divided into teams, be sure to be on mine."

Niles leads us through an arched doorway and into a large living room area. Old mahogany furniture is arranged by a large fireplace and thick tapestries of battles cling to the walls. The heavy brocade curtains are closed and the only lights in the room come from flickering candles that cast twisted fingers of light across the room. The place has the Gothic mood down to perfection.

"Long ago," Niles begins solemnly, "a princess lived happily in this castle until one day an evil sorcerer threw her and the entire castle into a deep and endless slumber. Unfortunately for you, the spell is still active. It is only a matter of time before you, too, will fall to this fateful curse."

Felicity makes a dramatic gasp. She pulls out an electric fan and holds it before her face.

"But not all is lost," he continues gravely. "You and your team must find the hidden relic before your time runs out. It has the power to break the curse. There are nine of you—ten if we include your tour guide, Jaxon—who are brave enough to try to uncover the relic."

"Is there a prize if we win?" Gary asks.

"But of course. A starry night dinner up on top of the turret above. Now gather yourself into three teams and we will begin."

Everyone cheers, and instantly, Lilac, Axel, and I form a group. Felicity teams up with her two other travel companions, Nancy and Cat, while Gary and Evelyn join up with Sara,

Tom's girlfriend. I haven't heard Sara speak hardly at all during the trip, but this time, I hope we win, at least for Lilac's sake.

"Mr. Wolfe," Felicity says, batting her lashes, "don't think you can just hide there in the corner. Niles did say you could compete. Come be a dear and join us. We could use a smart man on our team."

Jaxon visibly blanches. "I appreciate the offer but—"

"He's already agreed to be on our team," I interject. I bite my lip, hoping I didn't make things worse, but he did have a desperate look to him.

"I suppose I could." His shoulders relax. He steps to join us, and Lilac jumps up and down in excitement while Axel fist-bumps him.

Felicity pouts. "That's not fair. Scarlett already got to go on a picnic trip."

"Which didn't go as planned," Jaxon adds, his face darkening.

My face burns as everyone stares at me while Lilac makes a big O with her lips. Then she whispers, "I think our tour guide has the hots for you."

"I've no idea what you're talking about," I say loftily. But now my face isn't the only thing burning. Every part of my body is. Felicity's fan is looking tempting.

"Let's get started, shall we?" Niles asks. "Once inside your room, the door behind you will lock. You will have one hour before the curse takes hold of you. Good luck, valiant ones."

He escorts each team into three rooms. As Lilac, Axel, Jaxon, and I step through the thick oak doorway into our room, all I can think about is how I'll be locked in the same room with Jaxon for a whole hour. Staying professional is going to be harder than I thought.

Wolf Path: Want to take the escape room challenge? Continue with Chapter 32.

Movie Star Path: Hate escape rooms and forbidden love? Skip ahead to Chapter 33.

Wolf Path

THE ENCHANTED ESCAPE ROOM

Reader Note: You are continuing on the Wolf Path by daring to enter the escape room.

DARK OAK-PANELED walls enclose the room where we're beginning our escape room experience. Thick, red velvet curtains hang from floor-to-ceiling windows. An electric fireplace crackles in the hearth while tables are scattered among brocade couches. An assortment of skulls, a crystal ball, and potion bottles are set on a table. Cobwebs string from the chandelier above.

"Where do we begin?" Axel asks, looking at Jaxon. "I'm assuming you've participated in this game before."

Jaxon lumbers across the room, taking in the old paintings of very serious villains from various fairy tales. "Actually, this is a first. But you three go ahead. Don't let me get in your way of having fun."

"Don't be silly." I hit him lightly with a cushion. "You must help us. I insist."

"Do you always use violence to get your way?" Jaxon asks as he grins and points to the paintings. "I've heard that clues could be anywhere. Paintings, books, the walls."

"I've done three escape rooms," Lilac pipes up, practically skipping around the room. "Jaxon's right. There could be clues anywhere. Let's start with these books and pamphlets."

With only murky light pooling in through the windows, we rely on the electric candles around the room to read.

"It doesn't help that the candles are bolted to the tables," Axel mutters.

As we work, piecing together phrases and numbers, it's hard to focus. Every nerve in my body seems to be in tune with Jaxon. The way his hands gently touch the books or how he settles in to study something as if all his focus is undivided on that one object.

"Scarlett, help me out here," Jaxon says, breaking the stillness. "I think this is a two-person job."

I hurry to where he's wrestling with a drawer. His fingers are pressed on two levers.

"See if you can push or twist the other two knobs," he instructs.

I'm forced to squeeze in close to him and maneuver my arms so that his are stretched out on either side of my shoulders. I become intensely aware of his scent drifting over me. How the tendons in his forearms are stretched tight. The way his breath tickles the bare skin on my neck as I work the knobs. We're wedged in close, interlocked in perfect harmony.

I twist the two knobs and, *click*, the drawer pops open.

"You did it," Lilac says from where she's reading a pamphlet.

My throat is too tight to answer—or maybe I don't want to ruin this moment. Reluctantly, I extricate myself from his arms. His eyes are warm as thick molasses, pouring over me hungrily. My breath catches. I need to wrench my gaze free, but right now all I want to do is step closer to him. That would hardly be the professional stance we agreed to.

"What did you find?" Axel asks.

I pull out the map and the electric candle from inside the drawer.

"It's a map of the castle's interior," I say, grinding my voice steady.

"And it came with a candle," Jaxon adds, flicking on the switch on its base. "Perhaps it's an ultraviolet light."

He holds it up to the map as Lilac joins us.

"I bet it has a secret message," she says.

"It's hard to tell, but I think the light reveals one highlighted object in each room," I note and then look at the far side of the room we're in. "I believe the object highlighted is that mirror."

We rush to the fluted full-sized mirror, edged in golden designs.

"I don't see anything." Lilac's shoulders sag. "How much time do we have left?"

"Forty minutes," Axel says.

A flicker in the mirror's surface catches my eye. I hold out my hand to Jaxon. "Can I see that candle?"

I lift it to the glass, and sure enough, it reveals a message printed on the surface. Lilac squeals.

"Pull the lion's head," Jaxon reads.

Axel grabs the golden lion's head. The mirror pulls toward us, revealing a doorway into another room. We cheer, and I throw my arms around Jaxon's neck in a celebratory hug—

which is a very bad idea. His large hands wrap around my waist, his touch sending my nerves zinging. Realizing my mistake, I drop my arms, but my palms have a mind of their own, and instead of pulling away, they run down his firm chest. He doesn't move. Heat curls through my belly.

"Come on," Lilac interrupts, "we might actually win this."

She and Axel rush through the doorway, leaving Jaxon and me alone.

"Sorry," I say as I drag myself away from Jaxon, "I know we need to keep things professional."

"No need to apologize." He swallows, his whole body stiff as a board. "There's no rule against celebrating with your tour group in a game."

"Exactly." My head bounces up and down like a bobble-head. "Team effort!"

Ugh, I sound like an absolute idiot. I spin on my heels and dart through the doorway. I need to focus on escaping this damn game before I lose it with Jaxon and make a fool of myself again. He made it very clear he wants to keep things completely on the professional level, which is the right choice. But it's annoying how much he affects me. Why did I suggest for him to join us?!

This next room holds a harpsichord, a music stand with sheet music, a harp as tall as me, and mirrored walls that circle everything. Two tall candelabras illuminate the room in a pale glow, casting eerie shadows across the glimmering floor. Haunting music fills the room, completing the cursed atmosphere.

"Wouldn't it be so cool if we won?" Lilac says dreamily as Jaxon and I step inside. She's already busy at work using a magnifying glass to study sheet music. "How romantic would it be to have dinner under the stars?"

Axel moves to her side, grinning down at her. "I can't think of another person I'd like to share that moment with."

Jaxon clears his throat and moves to the far side of the room by the arched window as if their starry-eyed gazes might be contagious. He might be right.

"Sorry, man." Axel looks sheepishly at Jaxon. "Don't worry, we're keeping everything completely appropriate during the tour. PG only."

"I'm sure you're fine." Jaxon rakes a hand through his hair, looking more unsettled than ever.

"Oh, oh, oh!" Lilac says. "I think I found the next clue. It's a set of notes."

"According to the map, the next exit is in the center of this room," I say and frown at the floor where an oval carpet lies. I bend down and pull it back, revealing a trap door. "I think we just found it."

A keypad is in the center of the door. After a few tries, we realize the music notes are tied to the sounds of the keypad and enter the correct code. The trap door snaps open, revealing a staircase that plunges into the darkness.

"Oh, this looks super scary." Lilac grins. "I bet we're close. Come on!"

We scramble down the twisted stairwell. It spits us into a narrow stone passageway lit by flickering torches. We could turn either right or left.

"Which way should we go?" Lilac wrings her hands. "One wrong direction and we could get lost or lose time."

"We could split up," Axel suggests. "Lilac and I go left and Jaxon and Scarlett go right. The first one to find the right direction texts the others."

Being alone with Jaxon both terrifies and thrills me. "Are you sure we should split up?" I ask.

"I think it's a great idea!" Lilac tells Axel and then grabs his hand. "Hurry! We're running out of time."

The two take off running, leaving Jaxon and me behind. He seems to consume every inch of the air in the tunnel. The worst part is I don't mind one bit.

"Do you want to go first or should I?" Jaxon asks.

"I'll go first," I offer, not wanting to look at him more than I have to.

We take off down the twisted tunnel only to hit a dead end. I throw up my hands and turn to face him.

"Guess now we know which is the right way," I say.

I expect him to turn around and retrace our steps, but he doesn't move. Instead, his hand reaches up to my face. His thumb trails along my jawline, the heat of his gaze consuming every inch of my skin. I'm on fire—more alive than I've ever felt in my entire life. As if I'd been living in a cold shell, waiting for him to break me open and release me to a world of warmth and sunshine.

"I know we promised to keep things professional." His voice is husky, cavernous deep. "But I can't stop thinking about kissing you."

"No one would know," I whisper as if the world might hear us. "It could be our secret."

He leans down and his lips taste mine, tentatively as if they might be laced with poison. A shiver hurtles down my spine. With a groan, he steps even closer so his whole body encases me. His mouth fully presses against mine like he's found something he can't get enough of. My hands drag through his hair and down his neck, lost in the passion of the kiss.

Our phones ping, interrupting the enchantment. We jerk apart. I glance at my phone.

"Lilac texted," I say. "They found the exit, and if we hurry, we could win."

"Then I guess we should go," Jaxon replies, yet he makes no move to leave.

"We should let them have the starry night dinner alone. They seem like a perfect couple. Don't you think?"

"Sounds like a plan."

Reluctantly, we retrace our steps through the corridor until we exit and meet Niles, who is standing beside a beaming Lilac and Axel. They're holding up a wand, which must be the relic we were supposed to find.

"Congratulations," Niles says, "you four found the wand of the Fairy Godmother and successfully broke the curse."

We give each other high fives as the rest of our group joins us. Jaxon moves from my side, resuming his official tour guide demeanor. But my heart won't stop racing. It's as if his kiss woke my heart from a curse of my own making.

Wolf Path: Stay on this path by skipping ahead to Chapter 35.

Movie Star Path: Want to see what's happening in the Movie Star Path? Continue reading on with Chapter 33.

CHAPTER 33

Movie Star Path

WHEN THE FAIRY TALE BECOMES TOO REAL

eader Note: This is the Movie Star Path, starting when Scarlett kissed Rob on the turret and the paparazzi showed up.

I THROW myself on my bed. What had I been thinking? I knew kissing Robby Ricci was a bad, horrible, and wicked idea. But...

It was also an incredible, tingling, soul-aching idea. I've kissed a lot of boys, men, and wanna-be-men, but I've never felt like I did standing on the tower with Rob. It was like we had been whisked into a fairy tale of our own, a king and queen of a realm that only belonged to us.

But now that's been ruined. The paparazzi were vicious. I don't know what kind of photos they will post, but I'm sure they'll pick the ones that are the worst and most incriminating.

My brain rattles through the implications of the date. My boss will see those photos as well as Grams, my friends, and Hunter. He called three times today until I blocked him. I'm

206

trying to figure myself out, and I don't need a relationship from my past to interfere with a potential relationship in my future.

Am I really thinking of Rob as my future? That would be unrealistic. I mean, me dating a movie star? I do the only thing that feels right. I call Bella.

"You're lucky that I'm a night owl," she answers.

"Sorry to call so late." I groan, rubbing my face. "Something happened."

"What? Are you okay?"

"I kissed him."

"Who? The Wolfe guy or the movie star?"

I laugh. "You make it sound like I'm dating two guys at the same time."

"Sorry, it just feels like it from this perspective." She huffs. "Spill already! Who did you kiss?"

"Rob."

"The insanely hot movie star?"

"Yep, but that's not the worst thing. The paparazzi showed up and got photos of us. It would've been worse if Jaxon hadn't shown up with a car to rescue us."

She squeals, and I hear the pound of her feet like she's running. "This is exciting. I'm going online to see if I can find anything about it."

"Please don—"

"Oh, wow. Yeah, they got it. You're seriously kissing. But look at the positive, at least it's PG-rated."

"I can't believe this is happening. I didn't want any of this. I wanted to come here to help you."

Except the truth is, I'm getting sucked into this whole tour's fairytale vibe, dreaming I could have a happily-ever-after. Quickly, I switch the subject to her dreams of opening her own bookstore. When we finally hang up, she sounds excited about the ideas we brainstormed, but I find myself more confused.

~

THE NEXT MORNING, Lilac and I wearily drag our suitcases to the checkout counter. The man who usually attended the front desk has been replaced by an elderly woman with silvery hair tucked neatly in a bun. She's wearing a blue dress with lace edges, reminding me of the woman I met at the convention I spoke at.

I shake my head—because that would be impossible—and pass over my key. "Thanks for the wonderful stay," I say.

"You poor dear." She pats my hand. A spark tingles across my skin like she electrocuted me. "I heard about the paparazzi chasing you. Just dreadful."

"It's not your fault, but I appreciate your kind words."

"Here, take a gift." She holds out a bucket full of goodies. "I want you to have fond memories of our establishment."

"Don't mind if I do," Lilac says and pulls out a bar of handmade soap.

When I reach inside, I withdraw a black card dusted with sparkles. It says Cinematic Studios.

"This is strange." I hold it up. "I won this same gift card already. Wait a second. Have we met before?"

"I don't know what you speak of," she says, but there's an odd gleam to her eyes.

"Scarlett!" Lilac tugs on my arm. "Something is happening outside. Hurry."

I jam the card into my coat pocket and the two of us hurry outside to find a large crowd forming around the bus.

"What's going on?" Lilac asks. "Is this a protest or something?"

"No, they're here for Rob." I toss the hood of my red jacket over my hair and slide on my sunglasses.

"What are you doing?" Lilac eyes me skeptically. "Are you putting on a disguise?"

"Come on. Let's just get these suitcases loaded."

Lilac and I place them below the bus. Meanwhile, Jaxon is holding out his arms to protect Rob from the mob so he can get inside. One woman latches onto Rob's shirt, grasping it like she might die if she lets go. My heart stutters. Is she going to hurt him? I squeeze my way through the mob, and together Jaxon and I push back the crowd and help extricate Rob from the woman's clutches, but not before his shirt is torn.

"I got a piece!" she cries, waving a chunk of Rob's shirt.

"You can't be serious," I mutter.

"Get on the bus!" Jaxon orders.

I go to scramble up the stairs, but a guy grabs my arm and spins me around. His eyes widen, and he yells out something in German. The mob shifts to focus on me. Dread plummets into the pit of my stomach. Are they going to hurt me?

Jaxon pushes his large body between me and the man. He's like a wall, a fortress against the onslaught. His strong arms practically pick me up and set me onto the steps of the bus. As I clamber up the stairs, police car sirens fill the air.

Breathlessly, I stumble into the aisle where Rob is waiting. He draws me into his arms. They're a blanket, soothing my terror.

"You okay?" he asks. "I saw that man tried to grab you."

"I'm fine. Thanks to Jaxon." I turn and nod to our tour guide, who's coming up the bus's steps.

"It was nothing," Jaxon says, wiping the sweat from his

brow. "But we need to get moving. The police are going to help us get out of here. Go ahead and find a seat."

The rest of our tour group is quiet, staring out at the fanatics that are currently being dispersed by the police.

Rob and I settle into the plush seats. My hands shake as I take off my sunglasses and lower my hood. *Pull yourself together! You're not some silly damsel in distress.* Rob's hand encloses mine, and I let his warmth calm me. The bus hisses to life, and we take off, rumbling down the street.

"Gotta say," Trey leans out from his seat in front of us, "it looks like Fairy Tale Tours isn't keeping you very safe. You might want to consider suing them."

He winks at me as if he just gave me the best idea before turning back to face the front of the bus. I'd been thinking of doing that exact thing only days ago, but a lot has changed since then.

"I'm glad we're leaving all that behind." I attempt a brave smile at Rob.

His eyes darken. "I wish it were that simple. Maybe this tour wasn't a good idea."

"How did those people know you were staying at that hotel?" Axel asks from across the aisle.

"Someone must have followed us after Jaxon picked us up from the ruins last night," I offer.

"Maybe," Rob says, unconvinced. He wraps an arm around me. "I'm sorry you were treated like that."

"That's behind us now. Let's just have a good time." I lean my head against his chest, strangely feeling safe and protected by a guy who's one of the most famous public figures on the planet.

～

OUR BUS PULLS INTO LÖWENBURG, which according to Jaxon is translated as the Lion's Castle. It's something out of a dark fairy tale. The fortress-like sprawling structure is complete with pointed arches, ramparts, and towers. Above, gray skies darken the stone walls. A thick forest of trees surrounds the road and moat. They shift and sway in the breeze, giving the atmosphere a haunted vibe.

"This place looks creepy," Lilac says. "I almost feel like it could be the Evil Queen's home."

"This was the home of Wilhelm IX of Hesse-Kassel," Jaxon explains as the bus stops before the front of the long draw-bridge. "He had his architect design this castle to look intentionally ruined so it had the appearance of an ancient fortress."

"Such a shame to destroy a perfectly lovely palace." Felicity clucks her tongue in disapproval.

"Oh, I think it's kind of magical," Lilac says. "You know, in a sinister, scary sort of way."

We file out of the bus to gather around Jaxon when my phone pings. I check it to find a text from Bella.

Bella: This photo is trending on social media. Looks like you have a mole in your tour group.

I click on the link to discover a photo of Rob and me. My body chills. It's not just any photo. It's one of the two of us on the bus, wearing the exact clothes we're wearing now. Rob's arm is wrapped around me. Both of our eyes are closed, and my head is leaning against his chest.

The post comes from an account called Glam Gossiper.

Robby Ricci may have lost a part of his shirt in the mob outside his hotel. Not to worry! He's being consoled by his latest lover. Wonder what @TiannaUlci thinks about this.

I gasp and my eyes dart around to the group, but everyone

is paying close attention to Jaxon as he explains the rules to our next fairy tale experience, which apparently is an escape room.

I grab Rob's arm and haul him to the side. Felicity huffs, rolling her eyes, but otherwise, everyone is busy listening to Jaxon.

"What's wrong?" he asks. "You look like you saw a ghost. Which shouldn't surprise me considering the look of this place."

"There's someone on our tour taking pictures of us," I hiss, my eyes darting back to the group who just cheered with excitement over something Jaxon announced.

I show the photo to Rob. He runs his hands over his face and grimaces.

"Looks like my fairytale vacation is over," he mutters. "You should rejoin the group and have fun doing whatever escape room thing Jaxon has planned. I need to make some calls."

"I'm not going to ditch you to deal with this alone," I say. "I'll show this to Jaxon. Maybe he has some ideas."

"Not yet. He might be the mole. Right now we don't know who took the photo of us sleeping."

My heart sinks as I study our tour group. Who could it be?

CHAPTER 34

Movie Star Path

ENTRAPMENT 101

Reader Note: *You are reading the Movie Star Path when Scarlett and Rob discover someone on their tour has been posting pictures of them on Glam Gossiper.*

I CLENCH MY FISTS. It isn't right that someone on our tour is ruining Rob's reputation and invading his privacy. Could Rob be right? Is Jaxon selling pictures of us to make extra money? Or is the culprit someone else on our tour?

"I'm sorry to be rude," Rob points to his phone, "but I should take care of things."

"Wait." I touch his arm. "I have an idea. It's pretty wild, and a little risky, but I think it could draw out whoever is doing this and expose that person."

Rob grins. "Wild and risky? Sign me up."

I explain the details, and surprisingly, he agrees to my plan. He heads toward the castle while I rejoin the others by the gardens, pretending to listen to a guy named Niles explain how the escape room game will work.

"If you should wish not to join us," Niles says, finishing up his spiel, "you are free to explore the grounds."

Niles leads us toward the drawbridge only to be met with Rob standing in the middle, holding a bouquet of wildflowers —probably ones he picked right beforehand.

"Greetings, lords and ladies," Rob calls in a confident voice, showing off his acting skills. "If I could please speak to Princess Scarlett."

"Princess Scarlett?" Lilac asks. "Is this part of the escape room?"

"I've no idea what this is about." I plant a surprised expression on my face.

I squeeze through the group to stand before Rob on the drawbridge. He hands me the bouquet and then drops to one knee. Our whole group gasps in shock.

"My dearest Scarlett," Rob begins with grave sincerity. "As I stand before you here, it feels like we've entered our own fairy tale."

"You're really getting into this, aren't you?" I mutter under my breath.

His expression turns earnest as if the future of the world is dependent on my response. "Will you marry me, Scarlett? Will you be the queen of my heart, hold my hand through life's challenges, and battle against mortal enemies?"

His words touch me, but mortal enemies? A tad dramatic, but I guess that's what happens when you conspire with an actor.

Rob pulls out a ring, lifting it up. It's actually a vine he must have twisted into the shape of a ring, but the gasps and sighs tell me nobody cares.

"Yes," I exclaim, smiling down at Rob. "I'll be the queen of your heart."

Rob winks and slips the ring onto my finger. We turn and beam at the group as everyone cheers. Lilac's hands are clasped at her chest, and Evelyn has tears in her eyes. Then the two hurry to give me hugs. The proposal is merely a ruse to expose the person who's secretly been posting our photos, but somehow it feels real. Maybe even a little too real.

"This is the most ridiculous thing I've ever heard of," Felicity announces, arms crossed. "You two have only known each other for a week."

"Sometimes you know when you know," Rob says sagely, wrapping his arm around my waist.

"I couldn't agree more." I beam up at him, pretending I'm in love. Except it's not all that hard to pretend, which is a little terrifying because Felicity is right. We barely know each other.

"How about champagne all around to celebrate our engagement?" Rob asks the group. We get a round of approvals, and he asks Niles if the castle can meet his request.

"But of course," Niles says. "Come with me into the main room, and we will toast to your impending nuptials."

Niles hurries off, waving for us all to follow.

"Impending nuptials?" Rob whispers into my ear. "That sounds immensely serious."

"Are you getting cold feet already?" I cock my head and pretend to study my watch. "It's been less than five minutes."

"Hardly." Rob takes my hand in his and squeezes it. I expect him to let go, but he doesn't and my heart flutters in my chest. "In fact, I might like this too much and never want it to end."

I chuckle and continue along with the scheme as we head inside the castle, but deep down, I actually am starting to really like Rob. The tour guests ask to take our pictures with them, and Jaxon congratulates us. Things are starting to feel a little too real.

"You two are full of surprises," Jaxon says. "I certainly didn't see this coming."

"Yes." My smile feels strained. "I couldn't agree more."

Niles reenters the room with two servers carrying trays of champagne glasses.

"When are we going to tell them this isn't really happening?" I whisper to Rob. We've been engaged for less than five minutes, and I'm already growing too fond of the idea. This is highly concerning.

"This is your plan," he replies breezily. "I'm just a co-conspirator, remember?"

Thankfully, Axel hurries over to us and jerks his head to the hall. The three of us slip into the corridor, out of earshot.

"Please tell me you got evidence," I say.

"I think so. I just went off what you texted me." Axel holds up his phone and plays the video recording of our engagement. But instead of him videoing us, he's videoing the tour group. I study each tourist carefully until I spy Trey nonchalantly lifting up his phone just enough to get the right angle. He touches the screen and continues holding the phone so it's facing Rob and me.

"Look at Trey." I point him out. "I think he's recording it."

"And we have a winner," Rob says.

"What are you going to do?" Axel asks.

"Confront him, of course," I say, determined to get to the bottom of things.

"And there you have it." Rob nods emphatically. "My fiancée is a force to be reckoned with."

"That she is," Axel agrees, but he gives the two of us an odd look like he's seeing us in a new light.

"I'm going to make sure you feel safe during this tour—and everyone else here, too," I say. "I'm not ready for you to head back to your film shoot yet."

Then I stride back into the main room, before Rob can stop me.

"Can I have everyone's attention?" I call out. Everyone quiets. "This tour has been an amazing experience, but it has come to our attention that someone from our tour has been taking pictures of Rob and myself, and then posting them on social media as Glam Gossiper."

The group starts talking at once. Trey is the only one not looking around.

"I believe our culprit is Trey," I finish.

"What? That's bullshit. I don't know what you're talking about."

I step closer. Everyone ducks out of the way so I have a straight shot to march up to him.

"Then prove you're innocent," I challenge. "Open your phone and show me you have no pictures of Rob and me sleeping on the bus together and that there aren't any photos or videos of the marriage proposal."

"I don't need to prove anything to you," Trey sputters. "Besides, I bet a million bucks I'm not the only one who took pictures of you."

"And if you opened up the social media apps on your phone," I continue, "there would be no record of you posting those pictures."

"I just checked Glam Gossiper," Lilac says. "The video of the proposal is already online!"

Already? That was fast.

My body turns cold. *Great. Now the whole world thinks I'm engaged to Robby Ricci.* Maybe this wasn't such a good idea.

"Which means someone from this group took a video of it and posted it on their phone," Rob points out.

"I already made it clear that no one on this tour is allowed to take photos or footage of other guests," Jaxon's voice booms out, clearly annoyed. "I need everyone to open your phones and show me you did not break our rules or you are free to leave the tour."

"You can't make us show you our phones," Felicity says. "They are our personal possessions."

"I admit that I broke the rules," Axel announces. The room falls into silence. "I videoed all of you."

"What?" Trey asks.

"Why?" Felicity narrows her eyes.

"I did it during the proposal," Axel explains, and he turns on the video, muting the sound. "Instead of videoing the proposal, I was videoing the group to see who broke the rules. If you watch, you'll see that only one person was videoing the proposal. And it was Trey."

Chaos fills the room as everyone starts talking at once while Trey starts screaming that we can't prove it. Jaxon's face burns fiery red as he throws back his shoulders and steps up to Trey.

"You have two choices," Jaxon tells him in a low, commanding voice. "Either you prove your innocence by showing us your pictures and opening your social media apps right now, or you leave these premises this very instant."

Trey studies the group and starts to back away. "I didn't want to stay here anyway. Your company sucks. I can't wait to make sure everyone in the world knows about how you encourage the invasion of privacy and the half-ass tour you run."

He spins on his heels and marches out. The group cheers as he exits.

"I dare say it's time for more champagne to celebrate defeating the dragon that was in our midst," Rob says, and lifts his glass. "*Prost!*"

"*Prost!*"

As I take in our group, I realize how much I've changed this on this tour. A week ago, I'd never have been spontaneous enough to stand on a drawbridge and accept a pretend engagement from a movie star. I stare at my fake ring. After this is all over, I'm going to need to remind myself that yes, I can be brave and spontaneous.

Confronting the Real Big Bad Wolf

"Our final destination today," Jaxon calls out to the group as we board the bus once again, "is the Grimmwelt, also known as Grimm World. It's an interactive museum specializing in all things Grimm Brothers, including original manuscripts, reenactments, and a detailed explanation on how the brothers created the German dictionary."

My brain feels scattered with everything I have to deal with emotionally. I'd love to tour the Grimmwelt and actually take a vacation, but right now I need to focus on settling things between Bella and Karl as well as helping Sherly out as much as possible. I promised to help her, but so far, the day has been packed with touring and plenty of drama.

Once we arrive at the exhibit, Jaxon passes out tickets to each of us, but when he hands me mine, he says, "I'm meeting my brother at the café here. Would you like to join us and discuss your concerns directly with him?"

And just like that, Sherly's needs are thrown on the back burner. My sister comes first.

"Absolutely," I say.

"Excellent," Jaxon says in his stiff, Mr. Polite tone. "Go ahead inside and meet me at the Café Falada."

Nodding, I join the others in line.

"What's up with you and our tour guide?" Lilac hooks her arm in mine. "I can't figure out if you're hitting it off with Rob or having a secret love affair with Jaxon."

I gulp. *She's too close to the truth!* Today is not a good day to talk about love affairs.

"We're going to meet so I can give him some marketing advice for his company." Which is a lie, but I'd rather keep Bella's business her own.

"Once you're finished, text me," Lilac says. "Axel and I are going to wander around. And when Rob finishes up with the calls he has to make, he's planning on joining up with us, too."

I wave my friends goodbye and hurry down the hall, following the signs. The café is bright and modern with soft tan wood-paneled walls, crème-colored chairs, and bright sleek floors. It has a distinctive blend of a modern design with cozy, inviting touches. Large windows flood the space with natural light, creating a cheerful atmosphere.

Since we ate earlier, I only order a cappuccino. Soon, Jaxon Wolfe strides into the room, accompanied by the man that looks almost like the spitting image of him. Karl, the true Big Bad Wolf. The only difference between the two is Karl looks like he stepped out of a magazine with his hair slicked back, shiny black shoes, and impeccable black suit of which I can't imagine the cost. His skin is flawless. I would bet Grams's red velvet cake he gets weekly facials. Every hair on his eyebrows is perfectly sculpted. The closely trimmed beard is immaculate.

A fire burns inside me seeing him so composed and unflustered compared to how I left a bedraggled Bella at home.

"Scarlett," Jaxon greets as they stride up to me, "I'd like to introduce you to my brother, Karl Wolfe."

"It is a pleasure to make your acquaintance." Karl holds out his hand as if to shake mine, but I just glare at it.

"I can't say the same," I snap.

His eyebrows rise while Jaxon's lips quirk.

"Well." Karl smiles smoothly, tugging on the lapels of his jacket. "I do understand."

"Let's find ourselves a place where we can be more comfortable," Jaxon says. "I see you've already ordered."

We gather at a table by the large window overlooking the city. Jaxon shifts uncomfortably in his chair while Karl lounges in his as if he hasn't a worry in the world. My frown deepens.

"I brought you here, Karl," Jaxon begins, "because Scarlett has traveled all the way from America to get some closure for her sister, Bella."

"You're Bella's sister?" Karl sits up, startled. So, Jaxon *didn't* warn him. He eyes me like a beast preparing to devour its prey. "First off, I want you to know I never meant any harm to come to Bella."

"I don't believe you," I say, narrowing my eyes.

"Bella is a sweet young woman who—"

"She said you made it come across like you were in love with her. You slept with her and then disappeared before she even woke up."

Karl clears his throat. "I can explain."

"You left a single note. What did it say?" I tap the table, pretending to recall the memory. "Oh, that's right. 'You were really great, but I'm not looking for anything serious right now.'"

"I don't know if that's exactly what—"

I hold up the photo of the note. "Does this ring any bells? Recognize your handwriting?"

"Damn it, Karl." Jaxon blows out a long breath. "You're more of an ass than I thought."

"You're right," Karl finally admits, hanging his head. "I am, and I was then, too. It was stupid to get involved with her."

"Stupid? My sister is a gem. My grams and her are the most precious things in my whole life. You're lucky to even have met her. She deserves a prince. A gentleman. Not some gutter-wallower like you. *You* were the mistake, not her."

"You're right." He swallows and his face pales. I have no idea if he's just a good actor or if he really does feel bad. But I don't care. This guy needs to pay.

As if to verbalize my infuriated thoughts, Jaxon leans forward, jaw tight. "My brother is here to apologize and do whatever you and Bella need to make this right."

"An apology letter is a good start," I say. "And in that letter you need to tell her—are you taking notes?"

Karl's eyes widen and Jaxon whacks him on the arm saying, "Get out your phone and take notes."

"Yes, ma'am," Karl says.

"Tell her why you aren't good enough for her. That she can do better and you're the Devil's spawn who deserves to spend the rest of his days in a fiery furnace being tortured."

"Fiery furnace being tortured," Karl repeats, typing it on his phone.

But I'm not satisfied because he doesn't look upset enough. I lean forward, studying his perfect face.

"You think this is funny?" I press. "A game you can play? I know how you operate. I know all about your millions and how you're with a different girl every weekend."

Karl looks away, and his jaw ticks. "What else do you want me to do?" he asks.

"I want you to pay."

"Is that what this is about? Bribing me? You wouldn't be the first woman to do so."

"Shut your mouth and listen to what she has to say," Jaxon demands. Then he turns to me. "He will pay—and willingly."

"I don't want your money." I scrutinize him. "I want you to show me proof you mean what you say."

"What kind of proof?" Karl asks warily.

What does a guy like this value? I hardly know him other than he's a suave player who seduced my sister. But then it comes to me. He values his looks. That's what gives him the power to score girls month after month.

"Don't cut any hair on your body until I feel Bella has fully recovered," I announce.

"Are you serious?" Karl scoffs. "That's absurd. There's no way I'm doing that."

"He will do it," Jaxon says. "I'll set up a meeting with the lawyers to make sure he executes the agreement."

"You'll do no such thing," Karl says.

"Then I'll tell Father the truth about how you've been running his company, abusing your power with an innocent young woman, and also leak it to the papers so your board members see it," Jaxon says.

"You'll put Father in the grave." Karl glowers. "Is that what you want?"

"I want you to be a man and so does Father," Jaxon says. "You need to make this right. You've always relied on buying your way out of things instead of manning up to a situation. You smooth-talk people instead of apologizing. It's time you grew up."

I blink at Jaxon's outburst and take him in. Damn. That was pretty sexy.

"So what will it be?" I ask.

"I'll do it," Karl agrees grudgingly. There's anger in his eyes, a lion who's been cornered. "But I'm not going to wait around until I'm eighty-five for you to finally say she's fully recovered. What does that mean anyway? We need a time limit on this."

"Fine." I glare at him and take a sip of my coffee. "You have one year to make her happy and confident enough to go on a date again."

"And at the end of the year if she's not," Jaxon adds, "you pay her a million dollars."

"A million dollars?" Karl snorts.

Coffee spews out my mouth. A million dollars? Bella could do a lot with that sort of money. "I can agree to those terms."

I lift my chin and hold out my hand. Jaxon grins like he just scored a victory while Karl snarls at me. He reaches across and shakes my hand.

"I'll have my lawyers write up the contract and send it to you and Bella to review," he grumbles.

"Actually, just send it to me," I say. Bella would be horrified if she knew I made this deal. Sure, I feel a little guilty about manipulating the situation, but sometimes a sister has to do what she has to do. "She must never know that this contract, or even this discussion, took place."

CHAPTER 36

The Proposition

Karl storms off, leaving me and Jaxon alone at the table, and suddenly this feels really awkward.

"Thanks for backing me up," I say, finally breaking the silence. "I appreciated that."

"It's time for my brother to grow up and take responsibility for his actions."

We both stand and head outside into the museum area. We pass the displays of the Grimm Brothers' work and walls studded with giant-sized candy as if we were about to enter the tale of Hansel and Gretel.

"I admit I was surprised when you were so tough on him being twins and all. You two were close."

"We're close, which is why we don't put up with each other's shit. We might be tough on each other—probably comes from the German side—but we're also undeniably loyal."

A group of school children race past, heading to the theater. Their laughter and voices echo through the hall.

"You two look a lot alike," I say. "But one meeting with the two of you tells me you're both very different. No offense, but your brother is a complete asshole."

Jaxon laughs. It's full and rich like he forgot to be the professional tour guide. "He can be, but he's not that bad of a guy. He makes mistakes. No doubt about that. He got rich young and to be honest, maybe that was his downfall. Wealth can make you feel powerful and invincible. But he'd do anything in this world for me, even not cutting his hair."

"You think he agreed to my offer because of you?" I ask.

"Nah. He did it because you're a hell of a negotiator. It didn't hurt that I was your backup. What are you? A lawyer? Attorney?"

It's my turn to laugh. "Hardly. I'm a marketing manager. I provide my company with strategic planning when working with our clients."

"Fascinating. What types of planning do you offer?"

"I give companies a performance analysis and then offer brand alignment strategies to elevate their business."

"Fairy Tale Road could use someone like you. If only we could afford it."

"Considering your brother is a millionaire, I'm sure he could afford a company to help you all out."

"My father won't take a dime from him." Jaxon pauses to stare at a wall full of Ludwig Grimm's artwork. "It's a pride thing. That said, since I flew in from London to help out until he's recovered, I'm realizing we could use a fresh look. In your professional opinion, what changes would you recommend for us?"

"I've noticed a few things that could elevate your company. Except I don't know how I feel about helping out a company that hurt my sister."

"I'd argue it wasn't Fairy Tale Road that hurt your sister, it was my idiotic brother."

I tilt my head. "Maybe you're the one who should be a lawyer."

"I'll pass."

"Okay, I have noticed a few things. Like your logo is outdated, and the signage in your offices is faded and twenty-years old. You could freshen it up. Also, if the company is financially hurting, you should think about offering some higher-end packages on your tour. Like a Princess Tour or a Royal Tour where the guests are treated as if they truly are royalty. It'd be expensive, but there are people who would hand over their cash to be treated like a princess for a week."

"You have literally blown my mind. How would you feel about writing up a proposal for us? Unless you're planning on leaving now."

"What makes you say that?"

"Based on everything with your sister, I got the impression you hadn't taken this tour for pleasure."

"This is true." I settle on a bench and stare at the wall of old Grimm Brothers manuscripts. Jaxon slides in beside me, planting his elbows on his knees and his chin in his hands. "You bring up a good point. I've done what I came here to do. There's nothing else left for me here. Except, something is keeping me from jumping on that plane and returning to work. I'm not ready to leave yet."

"Even with that bonus offer waiting for you if you returned early?"

"Maybe I am crazy to stay. I have already gotten a week off."

"What's keeping you here then?"

My heart. Is it bad that I want to stay because I'm feeling emotions I've never felt before? In the last week, I've felt more alive than I have in my entire life. I've always told myself to never let go of a career for a man. But does my career truly give me satisfaction? Why am I so willing to leave everything I've worked so hard for behind?

"I really needed a vacation," I say, finally giving him the half-truth. "I've been working nonstop for years. Most weekends and even holidays. There's always something on fire or needs my undivided attention that Sherly is in panic over and needs my help with. Sure, my boss is dangling a bonus and a promotion before me like a carrot, but for the first time in my life, I wonder if there's something more for me than work."

"Your boss sounds intense."

"That would be an understatement."

"Have you thought about opening your own marketing business?"

"Actually, I have, but it's so expensive to start up a new company. I'd need credentials and a list of clients to start off with."

"But do you love your job? That's the question I've been asking myself since I've been on leave to take over my father's company. The answer I've come up with is no."

"Really? Does that mean you're going to leave your job in London?"

"I don't know, but being here has made me think about what I want out of life." He peeks over at me, his face open, defenses down. "I was serious about the contracting job. Think about it, will you?"

"Yeah. Okay."

His gaze shifts to stare at my lips and his body shifts closer so our legs and arms are touching, sending tingles up and down my spine. I should move, but somehow I can't seem to pull myself away. There's something about Jaxon that tears down my defenses one by one. It's like he sees me in ways no one else has ever before.

My phone rings, jerking me back to reality. I look at the ID. It's Hunter, now aptly named *DO NOT ANSWER!*

Jaxon chuckles as he stares at my phone. "You named someone Do Not Answer?"

"My ex." I sigh. "We broke up right before I went on this trip. He wants to get back together."

"What do you want?" Jaxon asks, brows dipped.

Before I can answer, someone calls my name. Even with the new blond wig, I recognize him right away. Rob is hurrying across the exhibit toward us, a smile on his face as if he can't wait to see me.

Behind him, a ghost from my past weaves through the crowd, waving at me and holding a bouquet of flowers.

Hunter, my ex-boyfriend. He's here in Germany.

CHAPTER 37

Three Men, Three Choices

I rise off the bench in shock, unable to believe my eyes. Hunter is here? How? Why?

I think about those missed calls. The texts I didn't read. Had he been trying to reach me because he wanted to tell me he was coming?

"Scarlett," Rob greets me first. "I'm so glad I found you in time."

Before I can ask him what he means by those words, Hunter rushes up to me. He's grinning like a kid running through a toy store with his parents' credit card.

"Scar," Hunter says, huffing. "Surprise!"

He throws his arms around me, drawing me into a hug. He smells nice, like the scent of wood. It's warm and familiar, reminding me of home. When he pulls back, his smile widens.

"These are for you." He presses the flowers into my hands.

"You got me flowers?" I ask. He never got me flowers while we dated. Is this a ruse to get me back or has he really made a change? "I thought you said flowers were impractical."

"Who's this bloke?" Rob interrupts, frowning as he looks Hunter up and down.

Jaxon moves beside me, his height looming over us all. "Do I need to call security or do you know this guy?" he asks.

Hunter's eyes finally take in Rob and Jaxon, and his face darkens. "I'm Scarlett's boyfriend. I came to see if she was okay. You weren't answering my calls. I wanted to surprise you to say I couldn't go another day without seeing you."

"Ex-boyfriend," I remedy. "I didn't answer your calls because we broke up. This trip was supposed to give me time to figure things out without interference from the past."

"Sorry, mate," Rob says. "Sounds like you came all this way for no reason."

"Except when you're in love with her," Hunter focuses back on me, "you'd do anything, even things that don't make sense, for the woman you love."

"That's sweet, Hunter," I say. "I can't believe you flew all the way over here for me. How were you able to afford it?"

"The question I have is how did you know where she'd be?" Jaxon asks gruffly. "As her tour guide, I find it alarming her location isn't private."

"To be honest," Hunter says, "I had a little help. Sherly, your boss, gave me the tour's itinerary and paid for my flight."

"She wanted you to convince me to come back home," I say, putting the pieces together.

"But we don't have to come home right away," he says. "Maybe I could join up with the tour. Based on your upcoming stops, it looks like you have some romantic locations planned." He looks at Jaxon. "You wouldn't mind if I crashed the tour, would you?"

"I would mind." Jaxon crosses his thick arms. "If you wish to tour with us, you'll have to book the next trip."

"I get it, man. No hard feelings," Hunter says, then he studies Rob. "Do I know you? You look really familiar."

"Trust me," Rob says, "you'd know if we'd met before."

I rub my forehead, completely thrown by Hunter's arrival. Then I remember Rob came to talk to me. I set my flowers on the bench and face him.

"You said you had something you wanted to tell me," I say.

Rob glances at Jaxon and Hunter and takes a deep breath. "As much as I want to stay, especially after meeting you during this trip, I need to get back to Fiji. I've been thinking about what you said. About facing my fears and not running away from the hard things. If I want to save my career, I need to go. So I'm going."

I reach out and squeeze his hands. "I'm proud of you. I know you're doing the right thing."

"We'll miss you on the tour," Jaxon says. "I'm sorry we weren't able to keep you safe from the paparazzi. But thanks to you and your feedback, I think we might be able to offer a more exclusive, private tour for celebrities in the future."

The two shake hands while Hunter mouths to me, "Who is this guy?"

"I know this isn't fair of me to ask this of you," Rob says as he turns to me. "But I'd love it if you came with me."

"Came with you?" I gasp. "To Fiji?"

"I know this sounds crazy," he says. "Sure, I'll be working on the set during the day, but it wouldn't be every day, and I'd be free most nights. I feel like we have something here. I'd like to explore that. Plus, after we finish filming, I need to seriously spend time marketing the movie. I'd like to hire you to run my marketing campaign."

"I don't know what to say."

"Who *are* you?" Hunter asks, eyes veiled.

"I'm Robby Ricci," Rob tells him, and then he hands me a black card that sparkles in the museum lights. It reads Cinematic Studios. My pulse thrums against my temples. It's the same card that strange lady with the basket gave me. "Here's my contact information. You don't have to come to be my marketing manager, but I'd like you to."

Hunter's eyes bug out. "Robby Ricci as in the famous movie star?"

"Scarlett," Jaxon interrupts, nodding to the two guys, "considering the circumstances, I think I should leave you with your ex."

"What? Why?" I ask, concern filling me. His heather-gray eyes are soft, with a vulnerability to him I've never seen before.

"I don't have a bonus waiting for you here in Germany," he says gently, and then his mouth flickers in mirth. "Nor am I a movie star. But I like you, Scarlett. A lot. I think we have something between us we could build off of. I'd love it if you stayed and finished out the tour. If by the end of the week, you don't feel the same way, you could head home to Florida or jet off to Fiji. What do you say?"

I stare at the three men, trying to see what my life would be like with each one.

I study Hunter with his rich brown eyes and smooth, dark skin. In so many ways, he represents comfort and familiarity. If I were to choose Hunter, I'd have the life I've been crafting since college. I could take that raise at work and be near Grams and Bella. Maybe I had been too harsh with Hunter. Maybe giving him a second chance is the right thing to do.

My gaze switches to Rob, whose bronze skin glows under the lights. His mischievous smile is contagious, and those dark eyes twinkle as if life is ready to be challenged. If I choose him, I'd be taking a big risk. To create a marketing campaign for a movie star launching a new film would mean I'd need to quit my job, or at least take a leave of absence. What if once we get to know each other we realize we're not compatible? What if he gets bored with me? I'm not some glamorous movie star like Tianna.

Except, being with him is exciting, and when have I ever really lived life to its fullest? Would I regret not taking this opportunity or at least seeing where it takes me?

Finally, I take in Jaxon's massive form, muscles hard as rock. His light skin is flushed as he studies me with those wolf-gray eyes. He has a point. If I choose to explore my relationship with him, I'd have time to see where this goes. After all, this is my vacation. The way we worked together, standing up to his brother, showed me how compatible we are.

I've only known him a short amount of time, but it feels like we're a team. He also opened my eyes to other possibilities with my talents. Working with him on his tour company would be a great way to start small and test the waters to see if I could run my own company. I could even offer my services to Sherly as a contract to get started. Except, if things worked out with him, could I live in Germany so far away from Grams and Bella?

These three guys are great choices but each one takes me down a different path. What do I want to do?

Wolf Path: It's obvious Jaxon Wolfe isn't the Big Bad Wolf she once thought. There's definitely potential here, and it's not worth throwing away. If you choose this path, keep reading to Chapter 38.

Hunter Path: Choose Hunter! He has proven his loyalty over the past year. Sure, he messed up, but we all make mistakes. If you choose this path, skip ahead to Chapter 48.

Movie Star Path: Hello? Fame, fortune, and love! This isn't even a choice. Choose Rob and live life to its fullest. If you choose this path, skip ahead to Chapter 53.

Wolf Path

THE MOST-OFTEN-KISSED GIRL IN THE WORLD

You have chosen for Scarlett to pick the Wolf Path.

As Jaxon leads our tour group down the cobblestone street in the town center of Göttingen, I'm glad I chose to stay.

I've been telling myself this whole trip has been about getting revenge, but as I take in the old churches and half-timbered buildings, I realize it's more than that. It's about figuring out who I am. I'd jumped on the work and dating-to-marriage path with the first guy who seemed compatible. I'd never thought there would be more to life than that.

But now, touring through these old towns a million miles from home, I see that there could be more out here for me. My eyes drift to Jaxon's muscular shoulders and the way his hair catches in the spring breeze as he points out different aspects of the city to our group. I'm not sure what it is about him, but there's no doubt in my mind I'm feeling things I've never felt with another person before.

Lilac and Axel are firmly together now after their date under the stars on the castle turret. Sure, joining them for dinner would've been lovely, but Jaxon and I ended up having so much fun wandering the streets of Kassel, talking about life, work, dreams, and hopes, that I realized it didn't matter where I was as long as I was with him.

Except when he tried to kiss me again, I couldn't.

"I'm not ready to take the next step," I told him. "I literally just got out of a relationship. You are amazing and wonderful, but for now, let's take it slowly."

"You're absolutely right," he said. "That's what we agreed to before, right?"

"Exactly!" I said.

Yesterday, while the rest of the tour group had a free day to rest or explore on their own, Jaxon and I met with the lawyers who drafted up the contract between Karl and myself. Karl made a brief, stormy appearance to sign the papers before growling at us and leaving.

The victory was sweet, and I called Bella to tell her I got everything worked out, omitting the whole contract and agreement we made, of course. Jaxon and I spent the rest of the day wandering around the sprawling Orangery Palace while I brainstormed marketing plans for Fairy Tale Tours. If I allowed my brain to leave work-related tasks, all I started thinking about was that kiss in the tunnel.

How it wasn't enough.

How I wanted to taste him again as I ran my hands over his firm body.

To feel the scruff of his facial hair under my palms as I cupped his face.

STOP IT ALREADY! I scream at myself.

I try to push aside the fun times with him at our last stop yesterday. Thankfully, Jaxon starts speaking to our group once again, jerking my mind away from my fantasy of kissing him firmly back to the cobblestone streets of Göttingen. My heart is beating too fast and my legs feel a little weak. I blink and force my mind to focus on what he's saying.

"From 1829 to 1837, Jacob and Wilhelm Grimm taught at the university here as well as worked as librarians while writing a number of publications," Jaxon explains, completely oblivious to my tormented thoughts. "Their time here is honored with this plaque."

He stops before a commemorative plaque in front of an old church made of red brick and stone. Its two rounded towers ringed with arched windows spear up toward the rain-threatening sky.

We continue our tour by heading to the old section of the city in front of the town hall. In the center of the market square, stands a statue of a girl with her goose. She's set over a fountain that bubbles at her feet. An arched wrought-iron canopy stretches over her head.

"This is the Gänseliesel—or in English, Little Goose Girl—statue," Jaxon points out as we all surround it. "She's considered the most-often-kissed girl in the world because there was a tradition at one point that when new doctorates from Göttingen University passed their exam, they kissed her bronze cheek."

We take pictures in front of the Goose Girl, but it takes all my effort to not edge closer to his sexy body. And there's the problem. I can't think of his body being sexy! Just a boring, snore-worthy tour guide. Except there's something about him that draws me to him, and my eyes can't get enough of the way his lips tip up when he smiles or the deep laugh that rumbles through his chest.

"Who's ready for your next fairytale competition?" Jaxon calls out. The group cheers and he rattles off the rules. "This challenge is called the Feather Hunt. It's inspired by the fairy tale, *Goose Girl*. You must wear one of these crowns."

He opens his backpack and withdraws a packet of plastic crowns.

"You'll visit the different shops in the market square that have the symbol of a goose on their door. Recite the line from the tale: "Falada, Falada, there thou hangest!" to the store attendant and they will give you a feather. After you've gathered nine feathers, bring them back to this statue. The first to do so wins."

"What do we win this time?" Felicity asks. "I haven't decided if I'm going to shop or play."

"An excellent question. The winner will earn a miniature replica of this lovely Goose Girl statue to remember your journey with us."

This seems to seal the deal for the group because right away, everyone takes a crown from Jaxon. When it's my turn, Jaxon doesn't hand one to me, but rather tucks it on my head, his eyes dark and stormy.

"I'm thinking fairy tales suit you quite well," he says, low enough for only me to hear.

"I suppose we're all full of surprises." I'm breathless, unable to get enough air.

His eyes drop to my lips and then abruptly jerk away as if it took all his effort. "Everyone all set, then?" he asks. "On your mark, get set, go!"

Our group squeals like school children let loose on the last day of school. But I can't move. It's like the force of his aura has locked me in place, and I'm his captive.

His eyebrows rise. "Not going to play, Red? I thought you'd be the first to leave with that competitive nature."

"Don't worry. I'm going."

I back up and turn, crossing the square with no destination in mind other than to get as far away before I pounce on him like I'm the wolf and he's the prey. But I just can't help myself. A glance over my shoulder tells me he hasn't moved. He's watching me like he's utterly entranced. I toss him a smile, because yes, I must pretend to be a good tourist even if I'm not.

Because I want more.

As if reading my dark thoughts, his long legs consume the space between us so quickly he reaches the narrow alley at the same time I do. Those strong hands grab my arms, pinning me to the stone wall. I gasp in shock and desire. His eyes are storm clouds once again, and I want to drown in their rainstorm.

"You torture me," he says gravely and deep with need. "I know we agreed we're friends, and I'm breaking my rules again, but I can't resist you."

My brain cells are screaming, *run away*, but my lips say, "Then don't."

My breath is shaky as he slips his tongue into my mouth. It's not the sweet kiss in the tunnels, but one with desire and aching desperation. I respond by sweeping my tongue against his. Thunder fills the air. A cold breeze cuts through the alley, but all my senses are in tune to his. He smells of earth and pine, like I've stepped into the deepest part of the forest. His arms wrap around me like he could protect me from any storm that should come our way.

The rain falls, drenching us in a deluge, yet our passion isn't dampened. We're creating our own tale, and I don't want this to be our ending. His lips drag down my neck, while his palms slip beneath my shirt to cup around my hips. My back arches and I groan from his touch.

In the distance, voices are calling out for Jaxon. "Mr. Wolfe! Where are you?"

Moaning, Jaxon pulls away, like releasing me is pure agony. Our clothes are soaked, clinging to us like second skin. His eyes drop to my chest, where my breath is coming out in heavy gasps.

A smile curls on his lips, and he leans in once again, whispering into my ear, "I do hope we can continue this in the future."

Then he steps away and leaves, rushing through the rainfall back to the statue. I stand immobile, my whole body tingling like I've been hit by lightning. As the water showers me, I realize I've never felt more alive than I do in this moment.

But where do I go from here?

CHAPTER 39

Wolf Path

RAPUNZEL, RAPUNZEL, LET DOWN YOUR GOLDEN HAIR!

"I have the first stage of your marketing plan laid out," I say, and pass the printed paper across the table to Jaxon. "I'm thinking Enchanted Journeys: Live Your Fairy Tale could be your tagline. Then I've laid out your brand positioning."

"My brand positioning?" He chuckles as he picks up the paper with one hand while rubbing the back of his neck with the other. "You know, I've no idea what any of this means."

This morning, he's wearing a dark evergreen polo that fits his broad shoulders and V-shaped figure perfectly. Morning light spills through the arched windows, threading his light brown hair with golden strands. I swallow hard, needing to get my mind off the way his lips dragged along my neck. We still haven't talked about our kiss in the rain, and it's one hundred percent my fault because I'm avoiding it like the plague.

Because then I'd have to ask hard questions like what is this really between us? Is it a fling? Or is this something bigger? Something more than a kiss in a rainstorm? And if it is, what does that mean for me? For my future?

Yep. Not going there.

"Basically it looks at your target audience and what your USP is," I say, pretending to be completely professional.

"USP?" His brows quirk as he sips his coffee. Is it weird that I'm jealous of his coffee mug? *Yes. Very.*

"Unique selling proposition," I say, explaining the abbreviation. "If you offered a set of tours at the higher end, it could help offset the costs for tours like this one. I need to do more research in your market, but I think it'd give you a greater profit margin."

He reads my words out loud. "Fairy Tale Tours offers an exclusive, bespoke experience on Germany's Fairy Tale Road with access to private events, luxury accommodations, and guided tours by experts in folklore and history. Each tour is personalized, ensuring a unique and unforgettable journey as you live out your fairy tale."

"What do you think?" I nibble on my roll. "How do you feel about the direction of this?"

"It's good." A smile creeps across his face, and he looks at me like he's seeing me in a whole new light. "I like it, but it will take time to put together a tour like this."

"And that's what you have me for." I crack open my hard boiled egg.

"I want you to enjoy this trip, not work yourself to death." He reaches over and touches my arm, but then glances around the breakfast room as if realizing we're eating in the atrium with the rest of our tour. He pulls away. "But I appreciate you doing this. You know you can do it after the tour, too."

"Of course. It's just being on the tour actually helps get my creative juices flowing."

The bigger problem is he's far more of a distraction than any tour could be. The more I'm with him, the more I want him. Except the tour ends in less than a week, and I'll have to fly back to Florida. Then what will I do?

OUR NEXT TOUR stop is Trendelburg, where according to our schedule, we will spend two days. I stare out the bus window, taking in the wide, rolling countryside of fields and crops lined with soothing green and brown pockets of forest. The hillsides are dotted with windmills that lazily spin on the sharp blue horizon.

"This castle is the one I've been looking forward to visiting the most," Lilac says, interrupting my thoughts. "But we're getting close to the end of our tour. I wish it wouldn't end."

"Will you see Axel after all of this?" I ask.

"I hope so." She fingers the edges of her planner. "It's just that he lives in Dallas while I'm in Chicago. I need to finish up school, and he's trying to get his perfume line sold. I don't know how to make it work."

"You don't have to make the decision now. You have plenty of time. Trust me on that. I dated a guy I thought I was going to marry only to find out we weren't actually right for each other. You never know where life will take you."

"That's good advice." She sighs and leans back in her seat. "I need to keep telling myself that."

It's advice I need to remind myself of about five million more times today. Or at least every time I see Jaxon.

We pull into a quaint town that looks like it has a population of one hundred. The road curves through two-story wooden houses, around a steepled church, and then shims along a line of trees until it reaches a walled castle with a tall stone tower peeking over the top. It could've been pulled out of a fairy tale and plopped in front of us, it's that charming.

Once the bus stops, we gather up our belongings after Jaxon explains we'll be staying at the castle.

"I've never stayed in a castle before," I tell Lilac. "This is incredible."

"See what I mean? We're not going to want to go back home after this."

Her words churn all the worries and emotions inside me as we roll our suitcases through the walled entrance. The thought of returning to Florida and work doesn't excite me. Sure, I miss Grams and Bella, but now that Hunter and I aren't together, it doesn't quite have that same pull. Plus, Jaxon has gotten me thinking a lot about my job and future. Could I really pull off creating my own business? Could I start my own marketing company?

Every night since Jaxon proposed for me to work for them at Grimm World, I've been staying up working, dreaming, hoping. Because to be my own boss is something I never considered, but now it's all I can think about. Then there's Jaxon. My biggest problem.

"If you're participating in our next fairytale game," Jaxon interrupts my worries, "keep your suitcases in the storeroom for now because the winner gets to stay two nights in the royal suite."

This brings a round of approval, but Felicity narrows her eyes.

"That's an awfully nice prize," she says. "What do we have to do to win is what I'm worried about. I got drenched in that last game of yours."

My cheeks burn at the memory of the rainstorm. How Jaxon

kissed me like he'd been waiting his whole life for it. As if reading my mind, Jaxon's eyes swivel to find mine. A wolfish smile plays across his features, lighting me up like a fireworks display.

"Yes, it was quite a memorable afternoon for all of us," he says. Then he clears his throat. "If you would follow me, I think it might be best if I show you what the challenge is."

Curious, we follow him into the castle's courtyard. The pebbled path is edged by low stone walls, holding beds of flowers, herbs, and bushes. The sweet scent of wildflowers mixed with wood smoke coats the air. Jaxon stands at the base of a massive tower, three yellow ropes trailing from its top. My heart dives. I'm not scared of many things, but I'm definitely scared of heights.

"Are you saying we need to climb this tower?" I ask, my voice shaking.

"You couldn't be more right, Ms. Walker," he says and turns to view our shocked faces. "Our hosts here at Trendelburg Castle have set up a climbing course for us. Your ascent to the top will be timed. The fastest to the top wins the royal suite."

As he explains this, some staff members join us with harnesses and climbing equipment.

"Uh-uh. I'm out." Felicity makes a cutting motion with her hand. "That's way too high."

"It is quite tall," Jaxon agrees. "This tower is often referred to as Rapunzel's Tower at one hundred and twenty-five feet tall. It dates back to the 13th century and was used for many years as a defensive structure, but over time it became more of a storage and living space. Ah, and speaking of Rapunzel, there she is now. Give her a wave, will you?"

A young woman with long blonde hair wearing a medieval

dress leans over the side and tosses a handful of petals over the edge as we wave to her.

"If this is something you'd like to do," Jaxon says, "grab a harness and get ready to climb. You're about to discover how far the prince in Rapunzel's fairy tale would go for love."

His eyes swivel to mine. Is he talking about us? He couldn't possibly be in love with me.

"Are you alright?" Lilac touches my arm. "You look like you might pass out."

"I'm afraid of heights."

"Ah, well you don't have to climb the tower. No one would think less of you. I mean, I'm not afraid of heights, and it scares me."

My first instinct is to say, "Nope, sitting this one out." Except that was the old me. The one too afraid to step off the path and experiment with the unknown. The thought of climbing that tower sends a cold chill through my body, but since I stepped off that plane, I've realized I can break old habits and try new things.

"I'm competing," I announce. "Got to have the full fairy-tale experience, right?"

"Let's do this!" she says, and we head over to grab a harness.

CHAPTER 40

Wolf Path

CLIMBING TO NEW HEIGHTS

My hands shake as I strap the buckle to my harness. At the rate it's taking my trembling fingers, I'm never going to be ready in time to even climb.

"Here," Jaxon says, coming to me, "let me help."

I should tell him no, that I'm perfectly fine fumbling with this strap all by myself. But I allow him to step closer. He gently clips the buckle into place and glides the straps on my hips so the harness settles on me correctly.

My eyes drift from his capable hands, up that toned torso, to his face. His eyes are comforting as a down blanket.

"You're all set now," he says. "Would you like me to belay you?"

"As in hold the rope so I don't fall and break every bone in my body?"

His lips twitch. "You're going to do no such thing. I'll make sure you get to the top."

A knot of fear clenches my stomach at the thought of reaching the top, but I nod mechanically and face the tower.

"You'll be next in line," one of the castle attendants tells me.

Yay, now I'll have extra time to think about how I'll crush every bone in my body.

Lilac, Axel, and Gary are all clipping into the ropes. Lilac is the first to attack the tower.

"Take a picture of me, will you?" she calls to me over her shoulder.

"Will do. You're going to be awesome!"

I snap some photos of her, happy to distract myself, when my phone rings with a FaceTime call from Bella. I answer.

"Hey," I say, staring at my sister's face. "It's great seeing you. How are you doing?"

"Where are you?" She frowns. "Are you at a castle?"

"Yes, we're about to climb Rapunzel's Tower. Did you climb it?" I hold up the phone to show her the three climbers scaling up the stone.

"We never visited that stop on our tour, but it looks cool." She's biting her lips like she's wanting to tell me something but isn't sure if she should.

"Everything okay?" I dare ask.

The phone shakes a little and then Grams's face appears before the screen. Her hair is in curlers and she's wearing the same faded blue robe I've seen her wear every night my entire life.

"No, it's not okay," she says. "This man. This Karl Wolfe. He's trouble. Why won't he just leave Bella alone?"

My heart slams against my ribcage. "What did he do now?"

"It's nothing," Bella says, trying to take the phone back. "I wanted to tell you he sent over the apology."

"Is this how young men these days end relationships?" Grams turns the phone around to show me the living room.

I gasp. The room is full of roses. Tons of arrangements. Hundreds of flowers.

"Back in my day, a man only sent roses to a young woman he was trying to woo," Grams huffs. "He's trouble and don't say I didn't warn you."

"I don't know what Karl is up to," I tell Grams. "But you're one hundred percent right. I'm going to get to the bottom of this. I promise."

"Ms. Walker," Jaxon interrupts. "It's your turn."

My body turns cold as I look up at the top to see Lilac waving down at me. "Already?"

"Don't worry," Jaxon says. "I'll help you along every step of the way."

"I've got to go now," I tell Grams and Bella.

"Who's helping you every step of the way?" Grams asks, her eyes glaring over the rims of her glasses. "I hope that's not another one of those wolf men."

"Love you." I blow them a kiss. "Bye." I hang up, feeling all fired up and annoyed as I step up to get clipped in the line. "By the way, you don't have to call me Ms. Walker. We're friends now."

"Are we?" His eyes twinkle as he snaps the carabiner to the ring in my harness so I'm attached to the rope. "Well, then, Red, you're all set."

He gives me a short lesson on how to hold onto the stones on the tower and then shows me how he can keep me from falling by holding the rope tight.

"Even if you let go of the castle," he explains, "you won't fall. You'll just hang mid-air."

"That sounds terrifying," I mumble. Right now I just want to get this over with.

I step up to the tower's base and gaze up for what feels like a million miles of stone.

"Grab hold of two chunks of stone just higher than your head," Jaxon begins, "and then find a low rock to step onto."

"But they're all so tiny," I say, wondering if my sneaker can actually fit on any of those stones.

Soon I find an edge of stone jutting out. I jam the side of my foot onto it and step up. I'm one foot off the ground, but the victory is real. I glance over my shoulder and grin at Jaxon.

"I'm off the ground!" I say triumphantly.

"You're doing brilliantly," he encourages, flashing me a melt-worthy smile.

Crap. I can't look at him because seeing him there makes me want to forget about this wall challenge and just run to him and throw my arms around those massive shoulders. I refocus on the tower.

"Now you're going to look for another stone to step on," Jaxon says calmly. "Your legs are the strongest muscles in your body. Use them to do the work while your arms balance you."

I inch up some more, but then I dare to glance at the ground. I'm only like three feet off the ground, but my legs start to wobble. When I step up onto the next rock, my foot slips and suddenly, my body falls off the tower.

A squeak escapes me and my heart tumbles, but instead of falling, I find myself swinging through the air like a pendulum.

"I got you," Jaxon says.

My breath comes out in long gasps. A peek below tells me that if I were to fall, I'd break some bones but I live. If I were to climb higher, that wouldn't be the case.

"You're doing great," Jaxon continues calmly as if climbing towers is something one does every day before breakfast.

"Focus back on the tower and grab onto it to bring you back to where you were."

"I don't know if I can do this," I say, hating that I'm giving up, but my heart is slamming so hard against my chest I'm sure it alone might throw me off balance.

"See that large stone sticking out to your right?" he asks, his hands holding firmly to my rope. "That looks promising."

I see what he means, and it's close enough for me to reach out and grab it. The rough stone scratches my fingers, but I manage to pull myself back to the tower. My foot finds a place to stand on. I'm back on track.

The quicker I get to the top, the faster this whole horrifying experience will be done.

I close my eyes and let the rest of the world fall away, focusing on his calming voice rather than the pounding of my pulse. Step by step, I follow his instructions. I don't look down even when I slip twice. Higher and higher, I climb. A breeze kicks up, tugging some of my hair out of my ponytail. But I don't waver. I just keep climbing, Jaxon's voice guiding me along the way.

Before I realize it, hands are reaching for me from above. I look up to find I'm at the top. The attendants help me slip over the edge and collapse on the ground.

"I did it!" I tell the two men as they unhook me from the rope.

"Well done," they say, grinning.

Once I've coerced my legs to work again, I scramble to my feet and lean over the edge, searching for Jaxon. But he's not there. I scan the full castle courtyard. The three college girls are being hooked up to the ropes while others are milling around in the gardens.

"You were absolutely brilliant," Jaxon's voice says behind me.

I turn to see him striding my way. Maybe it's the thrill of the climb or the adrenaline rush from seeing what I could accomplish, but I toss caution over the ledge and rush to him, winding my arms around his neck.

"I can't believe I did it," I say breathlessly. "I never thought of myself as someone who climbs towers."

He smiles. "Something tells me you could do anything you put your mind to."

"I couldn't have done it without you," I say.

"That isn't true, but I'm glad I got to be a part of that moment."

Suddenly our lips meet, and we're kissing again. All pretenses have fallen away. It's like we can't resist each other, completely captive to the other's essence. A voice in the back of my head tells me to stop, but I ignore it and focus on how wonderful his lips are crushed against mine.

Someone clears their throat. "I knew something was going on between you two." Lilac's voice cuts through the haze of Jaxon's scent. "I just didn't know it was this serious."

We break apart, but I'm sure I must look as hot and bothered as I feel. Lilac has this big grin on her face.

"Lilac," I say, trying to settle my spinning brain, "it was nothing."

Jaxon actually looks a little worried himself and rubs a hand over his eyes.

She smirks. "Didn't look like nothing to me."

"Maybe it is." I side-glance over at Jaxon. "We don't really know ourselves. But could you just keep this to yourself? We don't want to make a big deal about it."

"We don't know how the other guests would feel," Jaxon adds.

"Your secret is safe with me," she teases. "I won't tell a soul about how naughty you two are."

With our emotions going wild like they just were, she might be more accurate than I'd like to admit.

CHAPTER 41

Wolf Path

MAGICAL DINING

Our group gathers at the base of the tower and a man dressed up like someone from the medieval age complete with blue pants and a velvety tunic and cap stands before us. He holds up a piece of aged paper and says, "Each of your times was recorded on this parchment. Your winner—who has earned two nights in the royal suite—is Scarlett Walker."

I'm so shocked I'm not sure what to say. There's a tentative round of applause except for Axel and Lilac, who both give me woots and shouts. Jaxon encourages us to rest before the royal feast tonight and a castle attendant comes to my side, offering to escort me to my room. Felicity murmurs under her breath to her friends about favoritism as I pass by her, but I don't respond. After all, Jaxon wasn't keeping track of the times; it was the castle staff.

The moment I step through the arched entrance into the castle, it's like I've been transported in time. The hallways smell of aged wood and lost memories. Armored knights, spinning wheels, and statues are tucked into the hall corners while velvet-trimmed furniture clutters along the edges. Tapestries, swords, and wood-carved images hang on white walls illuminated by large lanterns and wrought-iron chandeliers. Wooden beams cross along a white ceiling.

I soak it all in as I trail after the attendant who leads me up a red carpet-lined staircase. He escorts me to a room far too big just for one person. The walls are painted royal blue except for the top quarter, which is white, and wood beams crisscross the ceiling. There's a sitting area and a king-size canopy bed draped with white linens.

"Here you are, Fräulein," the attendant announces and sets my suitcase on a chest at the end of the bed. "Enjoy your stay."

"Thank you."

Once he's gone, I kick off my shoes and wander the room, inspecting every aspect of this charming place. When I pass by the bed, I realize a blanket has been rolled into the shape of a heart with a swan created from twisted towels in its center. It's romantic and I swallow, trying not to think about Jaxon.

No good will come of that, that's for sure.

After a shower and arranging my clothes, I remember Bella's phone call. I'd gotten so wrapped up in climbing the tower I'd completely forgotten about talking to Jaxon about the situation with Karl. But the bed looks too cozy. I decide to lie down just for a moment and rest before dealing with that horrible beast of a man.

IT'S dark when I blink awake. My phone is ringing, which must have woken me. I fumble in the shadows until I find my phone and answer.

"Red," Jaxon greets me cheerily. "Are you joining us for dinner tonight?"

I rub my eyes, trying to process his words, but my stomach growls, reminding me that food sounds really good right now. "Yes, I fell asleep. I think that tower climbing took it out of me."

"Excellent. We're in the dungeon," he says.

"The dungeon?" I sputter. "Don't tell me we'll have to eat our meal chained up."

Considering all the wild adventures we've had so far, it wouldn't surprise me.

He chuckles. "I'll save you a place at the table. They're going to start serving dinner in about ten minutes. See you soon."

Quickly, I scramble to get dressed. The little black dress Bella threw in my suitcase just in case has yet to be worn. Considering my victory today, I think it's a fitting occasion to wear it.

Once I've slipped on the dress and applied some makeup, I grab my heels, hopping out of the room as I put them on. The castle is even more magical at night with the fires crackling in their hearths and lanterns casting a warm glow.

When I arrive at the dungeon, I find our whole tour group laughing and talking around a long rectangular table lit by candles. Horns for drinking are placed in front of each setting and baskets brimming with rolls are being passed around. An arched brick ceiling swoops overhead and various coats of arms are set along the brick walls, backlit so they appear as if they're glowing.

Jaxon catches my eye and waves me to a seat beside him. As I settle at the table, his gaze soaks me in like I'm a feast of its own.

"You look breathtaking," he says. Tonight his German accent is more pronounced. He rises from his seat and lifts up his horn, calling to the group, "A toast to Scarlett, the climber of the castle! *Prost!*"

Everyone heartedly drinks while I try to smile, feeling a little overwhelmed by the beauty of this dining room and everyone's kindness. Servers dressed up as ghosts enter and set down large platters full of roasted venison, poached salmon, and a vegetarian dish of peppers, eggplant, and zucchini layered on top of each other, aptly named Rapunzel's Tower.

Wine and beer are served, and I eat until I can't eat another bite. Our group laughs over Axel's poor German that got him kicked out of a store because he mistakenly said the wrong word. Gary admits how his pants ripped while chopping wood at the competition, which was why they really lost. Lilac shows off pictures of us all drenched, frowning, and cold as we waited in the rain for Tom and Sara to return from the Goose Girl Hunt.

Meanwhile, I lean back in my chair, sipping my wine, savoring this moment. The candlelit room is full and bright. Laughter fills the air and seeps into my pores. As for tonight, all is perfect with the world.

"What are you thinking?" Jaxon leans in closer, whispering in my ear. A shiver zips down my spine.

"That I don't want this moment to end," I say while Axel gets out of his seat to demonstrate some new German break-dance he learned in Kassel. "I don't normally do this sort of thing."

"Travel, eat in dungeons, or stay in castles?" Jaxon asks.

"Have fun, hang out with friends, and laugh about our adventures. I can't remember the last time I've done these things. Maybe ever."

Jaxon's finger runs along my arm lightly, like he's memorizing each freckle along the way. "That's no way to live."

"I've been thinking a lot about that. About living. I don't know if I've been doing that. My parents died when Bella and I were young. I hardly remember them, which sometimes makes me feel awful. But Grams took us in, and I guess I've always felt indebted to her because she gave up so much for us every day. She never had money but somehow we always had enough."

"So you felt like you had to work harder to show your worth?" he asks.

"Something like that." I take another sip of my wine as Natisha and Maxi get up and try to learn the dance moves from Axel. "But maybe I've been doing it all wrong. Maybe I need a change."

"Every choice and every step you've made during your life has made you into the woman you are," he says, studying me carefully. "And from what I see, it's made you into a talented, resilient, and brave woman. I don't think you should second-guess anything."

"That's a nice way of looking at things. Maybe you're right. Maybe all those choices led me here to this moment. With you."

His eyes darken at those words. They're scary words, and maybe it's the wine helping me say them, but they're true.

The ghosts bring in the dessert, which they call Snow White's Poison Apple. I fork the white chocolate apple filled with spiced compote and caramel mousse and take a bite.

"This," I point to my dessert with my fork, "I could really get used to."

"Maybe you should."

"Should what?" I smile. "There's no way I could recreate this back home. It would end up being a mushy soup."

He smiles at me but there's something in his eyes that warns me he means more than just having this dessert again.

CHAPTER 42

THE ROYAL SUITE

After dinner, I wish everyone a good night, but sleeping is the last thing on my mind. Sitting next to Jaxon has gotten me all twisted up inside so instead of going to my room, I duck out into the gardens. The air is crisp and sweet. Torches are set around the grounds, flickering off the shifting trees and casting shadows across the castle walls.

"Mind some company?" Jaxon's voice cuts through the darkness, drenching me like honey.

"I'd love that." He joins my side, and seeing me shiver, he shucks off his jacket and drapes it over my shoulders. It smells like him, and I just want to curl up in it.

I shake my head as we stroll down the path. These thoughts of mine lately are getting more and more dangerous. If I let things get out of control, I could see my heart getting broken. It's already way too open considering how short our relationship has been. Besides, where can this go with me leaving in a few days?

"You have a look about you," Jaxon interrupts our silence. "Did I upset you by kissing you earlier in the tower?"

"Hardly." I chuckle. "And let's be honest, I was the one who started the shenanigans."

"I will admit I was not opposed." He side-glances me and rubs his chin like he's thinking hard. "Tomorrow night we're going to do the fairy tale lantern walk. I think you'll really enjoy it."

"There hasn't been a thing that I haven't enjoyed. Well, other than Trey, but thankfully, he's gone."

"Yes, I apologize again for that."

"I know we only have a few days left. I think I'm going to miss this country."

"It will miss you, too." He takes my hand, circling his thumb over my palm. My skin feels like he's lit sparklers on it. "I'll miss you."

He leans down and his lips press against my forehead as if I'm the most precious thing on the planet. As if he means every word.

"I'm supposed to return to London after the next tour," he says. "My father says he should be able to get back to the touring business soon."

"You don't sound happy about that. Is that what you want?"

"We're adults now. Do we really get what we want?"

"If you could choose anything without something holding you back, what would you do?"

"I left Germany because of something that happened in my past." He looks down at our clasped hands. "I promised to never return."

"What happened?" I search his face, but it's shrouded in darkness.

"It's hard for me to talk about, but it changed me. How I see the world. How I react to the world."

"I don't know what you want out of life, but I will say that sitting there at dinner tonight, listening to everyone tell their stories and share their experiences, has shown me that these tours are so much more than merely entertaining people. Even me climbing that tower was empowering. I never thought I could ever do something like that, but you brought that out in me. You showed me a part of myself I didn't even know existed. You're bringing magic to everyone's lives through your tours. When I leave this trip, I won't be the same person. You've changed me."

He cups my face with his palms. "You have no idea how much your words mean to me."

And then he kisses me. I feel like Sleeping Beauty, woken by a kiss after sleeping her whole life. I'm truly alive, my heart beating in ways it's never done before.

Finally, we break apart and wordlessly head back toward the castle, holding hands until the last second when Felicity and her two friends spot us from where they're drinking on the patio.

"Giving out private tours now, huh, Mr. Wolfe?" Felicity asks, her words slightly slurred.

"Just making sure each of you makes it back to your rooms safely," Jaxon calls out. Once we're out of earshot, he whispers, "I don't trust that woman. It's not that I am embarrassed to be seen with you, but I don't want to jeopardize my father's company any more than it already has been. I don't need to add to the scandals."

"I could see her going to the press about how you're sleeping around with your guests." Then my eyes twinkle. "By the way, who do you plan on sleeping with tonight?"

I meant it to be teasing, but his eyes smolder like fire. "Don't tempt me."

"Jaxon!" Felicity calls out, and her two friends twitter with laughter. "We're ready for you to escort us to our rooms."

"I don't know if I have the patience to deal with them." He scrubs a hand over his face. "Or even want to."

"It's fine," I say. "Go be that amazing tour host you were meant to be."

I try to give him a relaxed smile so he doesn't know how much I want him to stay with me. How every cell in my body is calling for him to wrap his arms around me and kiss me all over again. We part ways, him heading outside to the patio area while I stop by the common room where a group is playing cards. After telling everyone goodnight, I trek upstairs, feeling very alone.

My thoughts go to Bella and I realize I still haven't dealt with Karl, but since it's after ten o'clock, Bella will be asleep, and I don't want to bother Jaxon about his brother. When I step into my room, I flick on the lights, but this place fit for a princess feels cold and empty.

And lonely.

Sighing, I kick off my shoes, wishing I had a good book to escape in, when there's a knock on the door. I crack it open to find Jaxon standing there, his body consuming every inch of the doorway. I'm so surprised to see him that I just stare up at that chiseled-cut jaw and into his stormy eyes.

His lips part as if he's about to say something, but then his eyes drop to my mouth. My skin feels like it has been electrocuted, and I'm holding my breath to see if I'll survive the moment or crumble to the floor. He bends down, those demanding lips crashing against mine. He is passionate, swallowing me whole. I'm encased in his arms and his taste. The sounds of the castle fade as we enter our own fairy tale.

His passion is unlike anything I've ever experienced. This

man loves with every fiber inside of him, I realize. And that's terrifying and wonderful all mixed into one. I know I need to stop this from happening, but I can't.

I grab his shirt and yank him inside my room, slamming the door shut behind us. He spins me around and pushes me up against the door, his arms pinning me in place while his lips devour me.

My eyes close as I focus on every touch. The way his hand trails along my shoulders, pulling the strap of my dress back. His lips follow and drag along my skin, leaving behind a trail of smoldering embers in his wake.

Heat pools in my belly, creating a need for him. Desperately, I rip off his shirt, the buttons popping off, clattering across the cold stone floor. He breathes heavily as I run my palms down his chest, feeling each ripple of hard muscle all the way down his stomach.

His hand slides up the back of my leg to my ass, cupping it tenderly. His eyes darken with heat.

"You're so beautiful," he whispers, fingers tracing my curves as if he is entranced. "I want this night between us to be perfect."

"It already is." I lift up on my toes, and my mouth skates over his collarbone. He groans as my breasts press against his chest.

"You need to know I haven't been with someone since..." He stops, and my eyes flick to his. His jaw flexes as if he wants to tell me something, but it's too hard.

"What is it?" I whisper.

He sucks in a shuddered breath. "It's been a long time since I last kissed a woman."

I hold him tighter, memorizing this moment. "I think this is the first time I've really kissed a man. We're good."

He grins, eyes sparkling. "Maybe together we're the best."

His lips find mine again, and my body liquifies under his touch. He's ruined me because any other man's kiss will never be enough.

CHAPTER 43

Wolf Path

BAKING A RAT INFESTATION

I never understood the expression, *walking on clouds*, until now. My body is feather-light, and there's a bounce to my steps as I join our group on the horseback riding trip through the forest. Jaxon and I pretend we're not a couple, but somehow he manages to pull me into a stable to kiss me passionately. Throughout the day, he shoots me smoldering looks that make me tingle all over when no one is watching.

During the fairy tale lantern walk, we steal away to make out in the shadows, and his hand keeps brushing against mine under the stars. But at night when no one on the tour sees us, all the barriers fall away, leaving me breathless and believing that this magic between us will never end.

Except when we arrive at Hamelin, reality does settle in. I only have two days left here in Germany. What does that mean for Jaxon's and my relationship? I haven't a clue.

"Welcome to Hamelin, famous for its origins of the Pied Piper fairy tale," Jaxon says as our bus pulls into a parking spot. "We've got a busy day ahead of us. Who here has a sweet tooth?"

A few of us raise our hands, including me, and he chuckles.

"Then you're in luck because we're starting our day at one of the most famous bakeries in Hamelin," he says.

We all scramble out of the bus and he leads us into a quaint shop with tall glass windows edged in aged wood, displaying cakes, pies, and cookies. Its entrance is a heavy wooden door with a large brass doorknob.

I'm greeted with the sweet scent of sugar and cinnamon and the aroma of freshly baked bread. Right away, my mouth waters. Glass cases full of more baked goods tease us and we gather around, eyeing the beautiful sweets.

"This bakery is one of my favorites," Jaxon tells us. "But I must warn you it's infested with rats."

Lilac squeaks.

"Rats?" I gasp.

"Disgusting!" Felicity exclaims.

"In fact," Jaxon continues, and from that curl on his lips, I can tell he's enjoying himself, "every bakery and restaurant in town is overrun with these rodents. Because everyone here makes rat-shaped cakes, bread, and other fun delicacies."

We all laugh while Evelyn shakes her head, saying, "Keep that up, and you'll put me in an early grave. I detest rats."

Felicity pulls out her fan. "Let's hope we don't find any live ones running around," she mumbles, eyeing the floor.

"Rest assured, the only rats you'll be seeing are the delicious ones," Jaxon assures. "To join in the theme of the town, we're going to help the bakers prepare their rat cookies. I'd like to introduce you to the head baker, Anton."

"A good day to you," Anton says, joining Jaxon's side. "I'm so pleased to welcome you to my *die Bäckerei*. Each of you will be baking cookies for the special showing of the Pied Piper show tonight at the Wedding House. The individual who bakes the most rat cookies gets to watch the show with a friend of their choice in a special viewing area, complete with drinks and appetizers. Afterward, they will be invited to meet the show's cast and receive a special basket of goodies. Who is ready to win?"

We give him a shout of approval and follow him into the kitchen, where we're instructed to find a baking station.

"I never thought I'd be so motivated to bake rat cookies," I tell Lilac as I head around the counter to find a workspace.

"Do you think they'll let us eat some afterward? Just stepping into this bakery is making me drool."

"I'm with you on that," I agree as I claim a station to the left of her.

Unfortunately, Felicity chooses to stand on my right side. As long as she keeps to herself, it should be fine. She's the last person on this tour I want to hang out with.

I focus on my workstation as everyone else finds a place to stand around the different counters in the kitchen. An apron is neatly rolled up in the center of my station along with a recipe card. A bowl, mixing spoon, and measuring cups are lined up like toy soldiers while a basket is packed with all the ingredients I'll need.

I slip on my apron and search the room until I find Jaxon. He's leaning against the far counter, chatting with one of the staff and drinking a coffee. His face is bright and smooth from that frown that used to pull at his face. In fact, he looks less like the grizzly wolfish guy I first met and more like a man who is very happy. As if sensing my gaze, his eyes swivel to meet mine. A smile bursts across his face and he lifts his eyebrows as if to say hello. My heart flutters in response.

"If you win this competition," Felicity says, "then I'll know for sure that it's rigged."

I drag my attention from Jaxon to find Felicity watching me and Jaxon with cunning eyes. I swallow, realizing I need to be very careful with this woman.

"The most important thing is to have fun," I tell her, needing to get her thoughts off the idea that Jaxon is giving me preferential treatment.

"I see everyone has their aprons on," Anton calls out. "You have forty-five minutes to infest this bakery with as many rats as you can. Go!"

I skim the recipe and begin arranging the ingredients in the order I'll need. If there's one thing I love, it's an organized and directional task. Follow the directions, execute each step precisely, get results.

Beside me, Lilac frantically dumps out her ingredients from her basket across her workstation. One of her eggs rolls off the counter and she screeches, trying to catch it. It falls on the ground, splattering egg everywhere.

"Damn it," she says. "There goes my chance at winning."

"Not necessarily," I tell her, dropping a stick of butter into my bowl. "You only need two eggs for the recipe. You should be fine."

"That's true. Thanks!"

"Everything okay over here?" Jaxon asks, coming up to inspect things.

"Just dropped an egg," Lilac says, pushing her loose strands of black hair behind her ears. "I'm afraid it only took me two seconds to make a mess."

"Not a worry," Jaxon says smoothly. "I think we can find a mop somewhere around here. And what is this?" He peers into my bowl and gives me a doubtful look. "Are you sure you followed the recipe correctly?"

"Who are you to judge? You're just sitting around drinking

coffee," I say, shooting a flirtatious glare at him. I pinch some flour and toss it at his face, causing him to laugh with shock.

"You are a vicious little baker, Red," he says.

"Now go away and let us get back to our rat infestation," I tease.

"As you wish," he says, and his words make my face burn. He grabs a mop and cleans up the egg. "I'll leave you all in Anton's capable hands. I can't wait to hear who the winner will be. I'm off to make sure everything is set up at the Wedding House for the show."

Then he gives a quick bow and exits the kitchen. Is it weird that I wish he'd stay? *Yes, it is.* I'm in a competition and having a blast creating cookies that look like an animal I normally run from screaming. I don't need him around to have fun.

As if sensing my inner war, Lilac winks at me with a knowing look. I roll my eyes back at her.

"You know, I saw Jaxon leaving your room the other day," Felicity says. My hands freeze from scooping sugar into the cup. "I couldn't but help wonder why our tour guide was with you so early in the morning. It's an odd time of day to be checking in on his guests, don't you think?"

"I had an issue with my shower," I quickly lie, trying to focus on the recipe card so she doesn't see the guilt plastered all over my face. "He came to check it out."

"Huh. How attentive," she says, but her lips are almost smiling, which tells me that she doesn't believe a lick of what I've said. "And here I thought he'd been sleeping around with his customers like his brother did. I'm not sure if you heard about Karl and that poor girl. It was in all the papers."

"No, I hadn't," I grind out. My hand clenches on my spoon, and I stir my mixture with fierce strokes. It angers me that she's just throwing out my sister's story as if it's something fun to gossip about. I need to change the subject before things get out of hand.

Felicity slides closer to me and lowers her voice. "Not that I'd mind so much if he slept with me. He's a catch for sure. But I'm not the kind of woman who breaks up a marriage."

Her words hit hard against my chest. I can't help but bite at her bait. "What are you talking about?"

"You didn't know?" Her eyes gleam with victory, and my heart sinks faster than stone. "Jaxon's married. I did some research on him before the trip. I like to know the kind of man who will be guiding me during my holiday."

I have no clue what she says next because a loud ringing fills my ears. She can't be right. Jaxon isn't married. She's just trying to get under my skin.

Unless that was the thing he didn't want to tell me.

My heart slips deeper and deeper into the sea, until it hits the bottom, anchoring me in its depths. Sand billows up, clouding my whole world into a murky darkness.

CHAPTER 44

Wolf Path

THE DEATHLY DIRGE OF THE PIED PIPER

I stare at my plate of burned rat cookies, not caring if I have one or two dozen. While Anton counts and inspects each of our plates to find the winner, I'm haunted by Felicity's announcement.

Jaxon married? Impossible! He never mentioned it nor did his mother. Even that scoundrel of a brother failed to ask him about his wife. Felicity must be wrong.

Anton interrupts my haunted thoughts by ringing a bell. "We have a winner!" he exclaims. "Let's give a round of applause for Natisha."

Natisha screams and jumps around with her two friends. I try to smile and celebrate with her, but my mind is not in a good place. Carefully, I untie my apron and methodically clean up my station because it's a simple task that makes sense. Lilac touches me lightly on the arm.

"Hey," she says, "you alright?"

"Yeah, just tired." But I feel as if I might tip over. I'm unbalanced, like one side of my body is heavier than the other.

"Something happened. You look like you just heard the Pied Piper's death dirge. What gives?"

I glance around the kitchen. Everyone is bringing their baskets to the bakers and dishes to the sink. Felicity is exiting into the main bakery with her two friends.

"Felicity knows about Jaxon and me," I confess.

"I wouldn't worry about it. It's not like it's illegal or anything." Lilac scoops up her basket of ingredients, and together we return them. "She was totally hitting on him earlier in the tour. She's probably jealous."

"Then she told me that Jaxon is married," I add.

"What?" Lilac spins to face me. "No."

"She said she looked him up and researched him before the tour."

"I don't buy it." She adjusts the cuffs of her stylish pink half-sleeved jacket. "Clearly, she's out to ruffle your feathers. The girl is jealous you won the suite stay *and* the wood-chopping competition. In fact, I might be a little, too."

"You think he rigged it so I could win?"

"I'm teasing, of course." She flicks her hand. "It's obvious he's in love with you. I wouldn't take Felicity's word on anything. Before you jump to conclusions, you should talk to Jaxon."

"Sure, no problem," I say sarcastically as we set our dishes at the washing station. "I'll just walk up to Jaxon and ask him if he's married. That won't be awkward at all."

Lilac chuckles. "You'll figure it out. Besides, Jaxon doesn't seem like a cheater."

That's what my sister thought about Karl, I think darkly.

We head into the main bakery area, where everyone is shaking Anton's hand, before heading outside to watch the

Pied Piper clock and listen to the chimes outside of the Wedding House.

"Thank you for such a lovely time," I tell Anton.

"It is my pleasure," he says.

"As much fun as I had," Lilac says, "I've learned that baking and I aren't compatible."

"That is why we are here. For you to enjoy baked goods without the fuss. It's why I look forward to the Fairy Tale Tours group every time they come through. It breaks the routine of our days."

"You've been doing this for a while, then?" I ask as a dangerous thought strikes me.

"Fifteen years. Time does fly."

"Then you've known Jaxon for a long time," I say, and then dare add, "Before he was married?"

"But of course." Anton's face bursts into a bright smile. "In fact, our bakery was chosen to bake his wedding cake four years ago. Such a lovely wedding."

My knees buckle and I reach for one of the chairs for support. Felicity was right? How is this possible?

"How special," Lilac says, quickly coming to my aid and hooking her arm through mine. "So he got married in Hamelin?"

"It was where his wife was from," Anton says. "In fact, since they were married in the Wedding House, you might find their wedding photo on the wall inside."

"Thank you," I say, desperately trying to keep my voice from shaking. "You've been very helpful."

Before Anton says another word, I practically race for the door. My feet can't take me away fast enough. Once I hit the street, I take off walking, not caring which way I'll go. My stomach aches as if I've been gutted. I want to throw up. I want to scream. I want to pretend what I just heard was a lie.

"Scarlett!" Lilac calls after me, running to catch up. "Where are you going?"

I stop to let her catch up. "I can't believe it. How could he lead me on like that when he's married?"

"I'm so sorry. This sucks." She reaches for my hand. "Why don't you come with the rest of us to the Wedding House to watch the clock? Jaxon said he's meeting up after the chimes ring to take us inside for the show. You should talk to him then. This sounds like something you two need to work out."

I nod vaguely as we walk down the street lined with half-timbered houses. We join up with our group gathered outside a Renaissance-style building. I stare numbly at the gables cut out of the peaked roof and the bells lined up along the edges as if ready to tell the tale of Hamelin's past. Normally, I'd be captivated by such a unique place, but all I can think about is the fact that Jaxon got married in this very building.

Who did he marry? Why didn't he tell me? How could I have been such an idiot for falling for someone like him? Maybe Bella and I aren't so different after all.

The others in our group eagerly gaze up to the top of the multi-storied structure, waiting for the moving figures to pop out of the top, but my eyes are on the entrance. Anton said there was a photo of Jaxon and his wife inside.

I need to see the proof of this supposed marriage with my own eyes. As soon as the bells start to play the Pied Piper song, I use the distraction to dart away and slip through an arched stone doorway. Once inside, I hurry through the musty corridors until I find a long hallway lined with photos of wedding couples. My heart hammers against my chest as I follow the dates to four years ago.

Maybe Anton was mistaken. He could have been talking about Karl or Jaxon's father or even a cousin. But then just ahead on my right, Jaxon's face fills every inch of my vision. I creep closer to the image. The world around me quiets as all my attention focuses on those gray eyes and the familiar square jawline.

He's wearing a sharp black tux and blue bow tie. A beautiful blonde woman stands at his side, gazing up at him in adoration, her wedding veil lifted as if caught in the wind.

I stare and stare at the photo, trying to understand this man before me. The one whose laugh is rich and whose smile electrifies every cell in my body. He made my world brighter, better.

But he also just broke my heart.

"I fell in love with you," I whisper to the photograph. "How could you do this to me?"

I think about that poor woman. I've participated in ruining her life. What have I done? How could I have been so stupid to have fallen for this horrible man?

My heart is ripping into pieces. A sob catches in my throat. I press my palm against my mouth to keep it from escaping, but the tears start coming and I can't stop them. I need to get out of here, far away from this photo.

No, far away from Germany.

From Jaxon.

I hurry back outside and search for our group. They're all standing before Jaxon, who is talking to them. My heart seizes seeing him there looking so beautiful and animated. I hate that my heart still wants him. That it's screaming to be with him.

This is why I need to leave—and fast. My heart is a fool, and I followed it blindly.

I pull out my phone and call the woman who has proven to always be there for me no matter what.

"Scarlett," Grams answers. "How are you doing, dear? I can't wait to see you in a few days."

"I changed my mind," I say, hurrying down the street. "I'm coming home early."

"Is everything okay?" Grams asks. "Did something happen?"

"The Big Bad Wolf is what happened," I snap, pushing my pain into anger because I need that anger to keep me walking, to take me far away from this place.

To escape the wolf.

Movie Star Path: If you think Scarlett should not go home, but go visit Rob instead, skip ahead to Chapter 53.

Wolf and Hunter Path: If you think Scarlett should go home, continue to the next chapter.

CHAPTER 45

Wolf Path

ESCAPING THE BIG BAD WOLF

The airport hums around me as people hustle to catch their flights. Meanwhile, I'm sitting in a hard plastic chair, staring at my phone and feeling like my insides have crystalized into cold stone. Jaxon tried to call twice, but I didn't answer. I'm afraid I'm not brave enough or strong enough right now to stand up to him. I can be fierce as a hurricane when fighting for my sister, but to fight for myself? Not so much.

Lilac sent a text, asking where I was. Meanwhile, Hunter messaged, saying he heard from Grams that I was flying back today.

> Hunter: If you change your mind about us, know I'm here. I'll always be here for you.

Tears spring to my eyes reading his words. He's seemed to have made an effort to change lately, and our history of being together makes his words feel that much stronger. A text from Rob pops in with a reminder I'm always welcome to join him.

Rob: I know you decided to finish the rest of the tour but feel free to hop over to visit me in Fiji when you're done. Just text me, and I'll arrange a flight for you.

I smile weakly. Rob always makes me feel happy and seen despite how rich and famous he is, except I don't feel as deeply about him as I once did about Jaxon and I don't think I can ever settle for less than what Jaxon and I had.

It's the last text that pops up on my phone that makes my skin shiver as if I've dived into a cold river.

Jaxon: Where are you? The bus driver said you took your luggage. Can we please talk?

Finally, I respond:

Stop pretending you're someone you're not. I know you're married. I'm headed home. Don't contact me.

I block him and turn off my phone as more tears trickle down my cheeks. I need to get back to Grams's house and start over with my life. These last two weeks I deviated too far off the path I set up for myself. Now I'm paying the price. This is what happens when you dream too big and love too much. You risk falling far and hard and break everything in the process.

"YOU WEREN'T KIDDING about the roses," I say as I roll my suitcase through the front door, gaping at the hundreds of roses filling every crook and cranny. "It's like I've entered a rose garden."

"Scarlett!" Grams bustles across the room, wearing a shiny bright-yellow top and khaki pants. "You made it back already. I was going to meet you at the airport, but you never called with your arrival time."

"I just wanted time to process everything," I say, giving her a hug. "It's good to be home."

"You poor dear." Grams clucks her tongue, patting my cheeks like she used to when I was in elementary school. "You've been through far too much. Both of my girls have. Now, go get yourself settled, and I'll whip up your favorite dinner. Does Bella know you're back?"

"Not yet. I'll text her."

"I already told her everything. These Wolfe men are pure trouble. And look at this place." She waves her hands around, gesturing at the roses. "You think you've gotten rid of them, but nope. They still keep coming back."

I grimace. "This is my fault. I told Karl to properly apologize, but he obviously got the wrong idea of what I meant."

"Nothing about this is your fault, only those horrible beasts of men. Now go take a nice long bath while I make dinner."

It feels strange stepping into my bedroom. As I take in my green wrinkle-free bedspread, my organizational wall packed with my whiteboard, corkboard, three calendars, and my white desk that overlooks the pond, I hardly feel like the same person I was before my trip. I park my suitcase in the middle of the room and wander to the window. While in Germany, my future seemed to open up to me with so many possibilities, but now the world feels gray and pointless.

I suppose this is how it feels to have your heart broken.

The long bath is soothing, but my thoughts are constantly plagued by memories of my time on the Fairy Tale Road. Of drinks by candlelight, clasped hands while strolling medieval streets, stolen kisses in castle corridors.

These thoughts are going to torture me.

I need to do something other than think about Jaxon. Quickly, I get dressed and head to the kitchen to help Grams cook up pasta fettuccine, Caesar salad, and fresh rolls. We chat about her garden and book club, anything other than the trip and my heartbreak. I'm grateful for that. Grams has always known best how to help me through tough times. When Bella finally arrives home from her class, we hug like we haven't seen each other in years. It sure feels that way.

"Grams told me." She squeezes me tight. "I'm so sorry. You went there to help me and got hurt yourself."

I shake my head. "I just want to put it all behind me and start fresh. In fact, one part of the trip made me realize I want to do something more than work for Sherly. I want to start up my own marketing business."

"Really?" Bella asks. "That sounds incredible!"

We settle at the table and I share my ideas for starting up my own company. How Axel wants me to help market his perfume company and maybe even help with Rob's movie promo. I decide not to tell them about my rebranding work for Fairy Tale Tours. That certainly isn't happening anymore.

"This is incredible, sis," Bella says. "I think it's a great new direction for you. But do you think you'll have time to work on this while working for Sherly?"

"I don't know, but I'm going to try until I can get my business running."

"Good heavens," Grams exclaims. "I say quit your job. Then you'll have extra time to build your business. You've got free rent and food while living here."

"Grams," I take her hand in mine, "I can't live off of your kindness forever."

"Butter my biscuits, of course you can. I insist."

The doorbell rings, startling me as I nearly fall out of my seat. Damn, I've been so jumpy since I left Germany.

"You girls expecting anyone?" Grams asks.

We shake our heads and I rise, saying, "It's probably a solicitor or delivery. I'll get it."

I throw open the door to find Jaxon standing before me.

CHAPTER 46

Wolf Path

TO GRAMS'S HOUSE WE GO

Seeing Jaxon on my doorstep sends my stomach dropping faster than riding a rollercoaster. His hair sticks up on its ends, he's got a five-o-clock shadow, and his clothing is wrinkled. In fact, I think they're the same clothes he was wearing when I last saw him in Hamelin.

"Scarlett," he says, "I wanted to—"

I slam the door shut and press my back against it. "He's here!" I squeak.

"The Big Bad Wolf?" Grams asks, rising to her feet, eyes wide beneath her spectacles.

"Yup."

Bella runs up to the peephole and looks through it. "Oh, you're right. Should I call the police?"

"Forget the police," Grams snaps. "I'll take care of things."

She marches down the hall while Bella wrings her hands. "He came all the way from Germany? Did you know he was coming?"

I rub my forehead. "I blocked him from my phone."

"I'd offer to hold him down while you punch him, but the dude is massive."

"I'm going to talk to him," I say, my heart beating like I've just run ten miles. "He's traveled far to get here. He deserves closure."

"Good luck." Bella runs over to the lamp and grabs it, clutching it like a weapon. "I'll be your backup."

Dizziness washes over me. "Okay, great," I say, but I feel anything but great.

As I slowly open the door, my stomach churns, a washing machine on full spin. I step outside and stare into the face I kissed. The one that blinded me from the truth. An ache cuts deep into my gut. I feel hollowed.

"How did you find my house and why are you here?" I demand in the coldest tone I can muster. "I told you it was over between us."

He eyes me and then my sister.

"You heard my sister." Bella creeps to my side, holding up her lamp like she's ready to whack him with it. "You aren't welcome here."

Grams bursts out of the house, pointing a shotgun at him.

"Don't you think about messing with my girls," she shouts, her white curls bouncing around. "Or I'll take matters into my own hands, you can be sure of that."

"Woah!" Jaxon backs up, holding up his hands. "I don't mean any harm. I promise."

"Grams!" Bella and I shout.

"Where did you get that thing?" I ask, gaping at the old wooden weapon she's holding.

"It was your grandpa's," she says breezily. "Used to pop a few rounds into the air to scare the old coyotes back at our farm. Don't mind if I scare this wolf with it, too."

"You can't do that, Grams," Bella whispers.

"Don't ya worry." Grams winks. "It's not loaded. Hasn't worked in years."

Leave it to Grams to keep us safe, I think as I go along with Grams's charade and face Jaxon, crossing my arms. "You heard our Grams," I tell him. "She's not messing around."

"I know this looks bad, Scarlett." Jaxon's face is pained with worry. "But you gave the company your address for emergency purposes when you registered for the tour. I'd like to think of this as an emergency. Please, at least hear me out."

Damn it, he's good. "Grams, I don't think we need the gun. You'll behave, right, Jaxon?"

At his nod, she lowers it, and Jaxon lets out a long breath. "Fine, but don't you dare try anything fishy, young man, or I won't hesitate to use Betty on you."

She pats her gun, which apparently is named Betty, and moves behind me.

"What's your emergency?" I cross my arms.

"In your text, you said you left because I was married." At my nod, he continues, "When I explained things, you didn't respond so I figured you blocked me or turned off your phone. I couldn't live with the fact that you didn't know the truth."

"You should've told me the truth when you had a chance. You had plenty of opportunities."

"You're right, I should've. I'd been in denial, and I was so happy, the happiest I've maybe ever been, so I didn't want things from my past to sour our relationship."

"How did that turn out for you?" I ask.

"Not so great," he says soberly.

"You came a long way for no reason. I don't mess with married men. Period. So goodbye and don't come back."

I turn to head inside when he calls to my back, "I guess it's a good thing I'm not married."

"What?" I spin around. "But Felicity said you were."

"You believed Felicity?"

"And Anton. He said he baked a cake for your wedding. Plus, I saw your wedding photo in the Wedding House."

"They were correct." He grimaces. "Except my wife, Adele, died in a car crash two years ago."

My head feels like he just threw a ton of bricks at it. I'm speechless.

"You poor dear," Grams says. "Such a tragedy."

"I'm sorry to hear that," I say softly. "I didn't realize…"

"It's not something I like to talk about," Jaxon admits, his eyes clouding. "Ever."

"That must have been really hard for you," Bella adds. Then she turns to Grams. "Maybe we should head inside."

Once the two of them leave, I focus back on Jaxon. "Why couldn't you tell me?"

"It's why I left for England," he explains. "I couldn't stay in Germany. Everything about that place reminded me of her. We'd only been married a little over a year, but it felt like a perfect marriage. I thought I'd never find anyone better than her."

My heart whirls with a million emotions. "I wish you'd told me."

"I was planning on it before Hamelin. I mean, we were going to be in the same venue as the one Adele and I got married in. I'd been nervous about telling you because I didn't want to dredge up those old memories. Now I realize I should've told you earlier. It was a mistake on my part."

A mail truck barrels to a stop in front of our house, interrupting us. The mail carrier leaps out, but instead of slipping the letter into the mailbox, she strides down the sidewalk with brisk purpose toward us.

"Excuse me," she says. "I have a special delivery for Ms. Scarlett Walker."

CHAPTER 47

Wolf Path

THE BEGINNING OF A FAIRY TALE ENDING

"That's me," I tell the mail carrier, who's holding out a letter. "I'm Scarlett."

"You most certainly are," she says, a twinkle in her eyes.

I reach for the envelope but pause as I study the lady who looks far too old to be leaping out of trucks, delivering mail. With the uniform and dark-brimmed hat, I almost didn't recognize her, but it's the same woman that keeps appearing in my life. Shocking silver-white hair, sparkling eyes, and lace trim peeking out from beneath her uniform.

"Wait a minute," I say, completely bewildered. "I know you."

"Your mail carrier called in sick," she says with a flick of her hand. "I offered to take his place."

"But...we've met before," I stammer. "I know it sounds impossible, but aren't you the one who gave me the basket at the convention center? And I'm sure I saw you in Germany."

"Trust me." She pushes the envelope into my hands. "This is worth a read."

It sparkles like it's been dusted in sugar. I blink to study it closer only to find the envelope is just plain white with my name on it. Maybe I imagined it.

"Have a magical day!" the mail carrier says with a wink. She hurries away, jumping into her truck and disappearing before I can process what just happened.

"Did you see her?" I ask Jaxon. "Am I losing it?"

He chuckles. "You have very attentive mail carriers here in America. Quite friendly."

"Look." I point to the return address. "This is from your brother."

Jaxon frowns. "Why is Karl sending you letters?"

I rip it open and read.

Scarlett,

It has come to my attention you have left Fairy Tale Tours quite suddenly under the assumption my brother was cheating on his wife with you. I am here to assure you that while I may be a bit of an asshole from time to time, my brother is not. He's the most trustworthy, honorable, and integrity-driven man you will ever encounter.

Unfortunately, life has not been kind to him with the passing of his late wife. When I saw the two of you together, conspiring against me like two conniving rascals, I realized perhaps his luck has turned and he has found love once again.

When you see my idiotic brother—and I hope you do—give him a chance. You won't regret it.
Karl
(Or as you so kindly referred to me as, The Beast. I have excellent hearing.)

"Your brother has a way of words," I say, unable to stop my smile. Sure, Karl is a scoundrel, but I can also sense the truth in his words. I let Jaxon read it.

"I'd like to say he's the true idiot, but then I wouldn't want to refute anything else he mentioned in that letter. It is odd how quickly that got here, though."

"It is strange." I stare down the street as if waiting for that strange lady to reappear. "But the important thing is you're not married."

"I'm not," he says.

A zing of hope shoots through me like lightning. It's dangerous and wondrous all mixed together. "And you're here now because you care about me?"

He inches closer. "I'm here because when I got your text saying you were leaving the country, I knew I couldn't survive another broken heart. I know this sounds too fast, but I think there's something here between us. I want to do whatever I can to explore what we have."

"I don't know how to process this," I say. "I'd been so sure you were cheating on your wife."

"Adele was a good person and I will always love what we had," Jaxon says. There's sadness in his tone, yet it's like he's come to terms with what happened. "But being with you has shown me I can find love again. That I still could have a happily-ever-after. Will you give us a chance?"

Tentatively, he reaches for my hand. My pulse hammers against my veins. My breathing hitches, but I take his hand. It's warm and large, and it feels so right in mine.

"Yes," I say. "I don't know what all this means yet, but yes."

"What this means is we need to celebrate," Grams says, peeking her head out of the doorway just as Jaxon leans down to kiss me. "I baked up a nice-sized red velvet cake earlier when she called saying she was coming home. It's Scarlett's favorite. Come on inside, and let's party. Good gracious, I could use a little sugar right now."

"We will, Grams," I say. "Thank you."

"You have no idea how relieved I am right now," Jaxon says, pulling me into his arms. It feels like home, warm and comfortable.

"By the way," I say. "How did you get to Florida so fast?"

"When I couldn't reach you, I jumped in a cab and raced to the airport. I missed your flight by a few minutes so I took the next flight out."

"What about your tour group?"

"I put Gary in charge." Jaxon pushes my hair back, studying my face like he never wants to let me go.

Before I can ask if it's a good idea to put Gary in charge, Jaxon is kissing me. The moment his lips touch mine, it's like I'm breathing once again. I twine my arms around his neck, deciding I'm never going to let him go again. I don't know what our future holds, but this sure is a good start to what feels like the perfect fairytale ending.

"You two get yourselves in here!" Grams calls out. "Otherwise, I'm going to eat your cake for you."

We break apart, chuckling, and Jaxon takes my hand, kissing it as he flashes me that wolfish smile. "I could get used to living this life with you, Ms. Walker. Also, your grandma is pretty awesome."

"Come on." I pull him inside the house, laughing. "You're going to love her cooking."

Congratulations! Your journey along the Wolf Path where Scarlett gets her happily ever after with Jaxon has ended. But it doesn't have to end here—there are two more paths that you can take.

Plus, look for Book 2, Fairy Tale Bookshop, where you can choose Bella's happily ever after and see moments of Scarlett and Jaxon living out their love story.

Finally, grab the bonus scene where Jaxon proposes to Scarlett! Go to ChristinaFarley.com/romantic-adventures.

Hunter Path: Want to see what would happen if Scarlett chose Hunter in Chapter 37? Read the next chapter to find out how their relationship blooms into something special.

Movie Star Path: Want to see what would happen if Scarlett chose Rob in Chapter 37? Skip ahead to Chapter 53 for plenty of drama and starstruck fun.

CHAPTER 48
Hunter Path
WARM PRETZELS AND WALKING TOURS

R*eader Note: This is the beginning of Hunter's Path if you choose this path after Chapter 37.*

IT FELT strange telling everyone on the tour goodbye, but when I hugged Lilac, it was like I was losing a good friend.

"You'll keep in touch, right?" I ask her. "I want to get updates on how things go with you and Axel."

"Absolutely," she says, grinning. "It's so romantic Hunter flew across the world for you. A guy like that you don't let get away."

"I think this breakup has been good for both of us. We were able to take time and really think about what we want from life and our relationship."

I take a good look at the group, glad everyone met up here to send me off.

"It was great meeting you all," I tell them. "I hope you have a blast during the last week of your trip."

Everyone waves and wishes Hunter and me good luck. Jaxon steps closer, and in a low voice meant for only the two of us, says, "Tomorrow I'm meeting with Karl to sign off on the legal documents with the lawyers to make sure he follows through with making things right with your sister. I'll make sure everything is sent to you for an electronic signature."

"I appreciate that. Thank you for helping me with my sister."

He nods and steps back, his face stoic. He's back to his old brooding self. I hope he'll be okay. Once I've gathered my luggage from the bus, Hunter and I find a cute café to grab lunch at.

"I'm so excited to be here with you," Hunter says. "This city is incredible, but being with you is even more so."

I place my hand on top of his. "I'm glad you came back. This trip was great, but I kept missing you, wondering if I'd made a mistake breaking up with you."

"I'm glad you did." He squeezes my hand. "We needed to reevaluate our lives. I needed a little kick in the butt to get me back into the action of wooing you once again. I got lazy."

"Me, too. As much as it hurt, I realized I also got into a rut, and I needed to prioritize our relationship. Sherly wants to give me a promotion and raise if I go back, but if I take the promotion, I want to make sure it's our relationship that has priority."

"That means a lot to me." He nods to my phone. "So, are you going to call her?"

"Maybe later. Right now I want this moment to be about us."

We book our flight back to Florida, and since it's a night flight, we spend the rest of the day wandering the streets of

Kassel. Hunter, a lover of all things art, discovers they have a street art tour.

"We can see Stephen Hawking's *Goldfisch of Jakules*," he says. "It's my favorite photo in that coffee table book you gave me last Christmas. I've always wanted to visit it."

"Really?" I giggle at his enthusiasm. "Then we have to go!"

I can't remember a time when we had so much fun. We hunt down as many of the street art paintings we can find on the walking tour. Some are tucked away on the sides of shops, others displayed on the sidewalks and some painted proudly across an entire apartment building. We take selfies, eat warm pretzels, and guess at each painting's true interpretation. Somewhere along the tour, we start holding hands again.

I glance at our clasped palms and smile. "This feels natural," I say. "I know we had a huge fight that unfortunately everyone at the Path to Success conference got to also experience." We both laugh. "But here we are, finding each other again and making things work. It's been a long time since we had this much fun together."

"It's been a long time since we allowed ourselves the time to do it," he points out. "We both got lost in our careers. I love that you've always supported me in my house hunting, but you made me see I need to focus more on you. Which reminds me, I wanted to tell you about this new app I got."

"An app?" I lift my eyebrows skeptically.

"Yup. I'm hoping it will help me with our relationship." He pulls out his phone and shows me. "It sends me reminders of when your birthday is and our anniversary. Then it gives ideas of ways to celebrate like gifts and dates. I realized the idea of a special event stressed me out because it was just one more thing. But I realized I'd been looking at it all wrong."

"How is that?"

"This app took away the stress of forgetting events and trying to be creative with my gifts. It lets me now just focus on having fun and celebrating."

"That's awesome. So, what does the app say we should do next?" I'm teasing him now, but he goes with it.

"Let's look, shall we?" He taps a button and a suggestion pops up.

Don't forget to kiss and tell her you love her today!

"Appears as if I'm supposed to kiss you," he says, but then his face turns serious. "I don't ever want to lose you again. Those weeks without you were more than too many for me. I don't need an app to remind me how I feel about you. I love you, Scarlett. More than anything."

He kisses me. It's sweet and gentle, and my heart soars like a kite taking off in the wind. I latch onto him and kiss him back because this is true love. It stays with you no matter how hard or difficult a relationship is. You fight with the one you love through the hard times and then come out on the other side victorious.

CHAPTER 49

Hunter Path

CHARTING MY PATH

The hum of the airport buzzes around me as I clutch my boarding pass in one hand and grip my carry-on bag in the other.

"You ready?" Hunter kisses my forehead. "Back to the real world."

"Absolutely." I grin and pull out my phone. "I'm going to text Grams and Bella. They'll be so excited."

"I hope so." Hunter's face pulls into worry. "Your grams and sister weren't so happy to see me last time."

"Not to worry." I pass my boarding pass to the attendant. "I'll explain everything."

We head down the jetway as I wait for my phone to turn back on. I'd shut it off earlier, deciding to enjoy my last few hours in Germany with Hunter without distractions. I promised him he'd come first in my life and I wanted to start us off on the right path.

But as my phone blinks back to life, a long text message from my boss pops on the screen.

I stop abruptly to read Sherly's words, pressing my lips together.

> Sherly: You've gone silent on me. I'm assuming this means you aren't taking this job. I'm going to give the promotion to Larson. He's been working nonstop and will be presenting his proposal to the board first thing in the morning.

"What is it?" Hunter asks. "Everything okay?"

"I got a tough email from my boss," I say, sucking in a deep breath as we board. Once we find our seats, I explain what's been going on with work to Hunter. "I shouldn't be shocked. She's being true to form. Tough as nails and hardcore to the bone. I've always loved that about her. Her passion for her agency has driven me to be the very best I could be all these years."

"What has changed that?" Hunter asks.

"Germany." I stare out the window at the tarmac. The small trucks and luggage carriers zip past as if they're late to their destinations. "It changed my whole view on life."

The truth is, this time, her words rub against my nerves like nails scratching a chalkboard. I read her text to Hunter.

"You sure you don't want to call her?" Hunter asks.

I tap my fingers on my armrests and check out flight details. We land at 8 a.m. "Do you have your laptop?"

"How did you guess?"

"You never go anywhere without it."

"Guilty as charged." He digs through his carry-on, logs in, and passes it to me. "I'm assuming you want to borrow it."

"I've got an idea," I say, unable to stop the devious curve of my lips. "If I can pull it off, it's going to make a huge difference in how our agency deals with first-party data, measurement, and marketing technology."

"You sure you shouldn't call her?" Hunter asks as the plane's engines roar.

"It's been too long since Sherly's had a proper surprise."

Using the airplane internet, I get to work. I log into the agency's network and assess the problems they're facing. Based on Larson's initial reports, it appears as if he has some Band-Aid fixes put into place, but the reality is they aren't going to solve their problems long term. For the rest of the flight, I hash out immediate action steps to solve her issues along with a full PowerPoint proposal on future ideas for the agency. This will either be a complete disaster or launch me to get that promotion I deserve.

Hunter works beside me on his phone, researching a new contractor he wants to hire for his latest fixer-upper. We only take a quick break for dinner and a short nap before the plane begins its descent into Orlando.

"Once we land," I tell Hunter, "I'm going to go directly to the office. But this weekend is ours with no work. How does that sound?"

"I love it." He beams. "Besides, I have something I want to show you."

My nerves are tangled strands of yarn inside my chest as I kiss Hunter goodbye and we enter separate taxis. It pains me to leave him, but this is the right choice. I uploaded my files and PowerPoint presentation online so I could pull them up on my personal computer.

When the taxi pulls into my agency's headquarters and I

step out onto the sidewalk, the heat slams into me like a tidal wave. I'm sweating all over the place. If only I had time for a quick shower and a second cup of coffee.

My suitcase rolls behind me as I stride through the glass front doors. Thankfully, I packed a pantsuit for the trip and changed into it at the airport. I'd brought it to intimidate the Big Bad Wolf, but ironically, it's becoming quite useful now.

"Scarlett." Nadia, one of my coworkers, stops mid-stride in the hallway as I pass by her, nearly spilling the coffee in her mug. "Why are you back from your trip so early? I thought you had another week in Germany."

"I did. But when I heard about all the issues you were having with the new Google algorithm, I decided to come back and help sort things out."

"Oh." Her face pales and she leans closer to me, whispering, "Did you not hear? She put Larson in charge of the whole project. He's presenting to Sherly and the board right now."

"Is he?" I grin. "Fantastic. Are they in the boardroom?"

She nods. "But Sherly's in the worst mood. I wouldn't go in there if I were you."

"Thanks for the warning. You're the best."

I take off down the hall, stopping briefly at my office to park my suitcase and snatch my laptop. Next, I head for the break room to snag a cup of bland coffee—briefly missing Germany's cappuccinos—and march into the board room.

When I reach the glassed-in conference room, I pause outside the door. Larson's standing at the front of the room, pointing to his PowerPoint displaying a graph that tells me he's in way over his head.

The board members lounge around the large rectangular table, looking grim and quite frankly unenthused. Meanwhile,

Sherly sits shock-straight at the front, fidgeting with her pen, a sign she's annoyed.

I take a swig of my coffee, grimace at its flavor, and shove open the glass door.

It's time to take control of my future.

CHAPTER 50

Hunter Path

DESIGNING MY FUTURE

Everyone in the boardroom startles as I stride along the edge of the room toward the front. It takes every fiber of willpower to keep my chin up and a smile plastered to my face. I can't let them see an ounce of the fear swirling in my stomach.

What if I am making a mistake by barging in like this? Things could flip and everything could go wrong. Sherly can be volatile like that. One moment you've got a promotion, and the next, you're packing up your office.

"Scarlett?" Sherly says, her dark brows jerking up. With her hair drawn tightly into a twisted bun at the nape of her neck and those thin red lips, she looks knife-sharp. Like she could slice me in half with one sentence. "You're supposed to be in Germany."

"I couldn't stay away," I explain as I settle into an empty chair at the front of the room.

Larson shoots me a dark look, running a hand along his poorly cut hair. "This is a private presentation," he says. "It would be best if you waited outside until we're finished."

My pulse drives at my temples as a part of me screams, "*Flee!*" But I don't miss how he reaches for his collar to loosen it, like he can't get enough air in his lungs. *He's even more nervous than I am.*

"But I came across the ocean to be here," I counter. "I heard things turned bad quickly at the company so I packed my bags and came home."

Mostly true.

"Hunter changed your mind, then," Sherly said, not beating around the bush.

True, but I'm not going to bring him into this. "After you're finished presenting, Larson, I have a few ideas I'd also like to share with the team." I flash the board members a smile. "If you don't mind."

"I think they do," Larson says through gritted teeth.

"Not at all," Sonia, the senior board member, overrides. "We're here because we're eager to explore and find solutions."

Larson clears his now very splotchy throat and turns stiffly back to his presentation, finishing off his findings. The board members ask him a few pointed questions about the privacy delivery of each campaign, to which he responds with, "We haven't gotten quite that far, but we hope to tackle that step next." Which, as I expected, brought about a round of sighs and frustrated whispers around the room.

Sherly's laser-focused brown eyes turn to me. "Ms. Walker, do you have anything you wish to add to the conversation? Considering you flew all the way back from Germany, I hope it was worth the risk of barging into a board meeting unannounced."

And there it is. She's pissed I didn't warn her. Sherly doesn't like surprises. She likes to be on top of things and in the know. The fact that she has no idea what I'm about to say has her unnerved and unsettled. Which means I'm about to get a promotion or be fired.

It's a risk I have to take. I didn't want to hand over my ideas to her privately in case she decided to claim them for herself or give them to Larson. I needed everyone to know this is my idea and mine alone.

Here goes nothing.

"I have some ideas on how to solve the Google privacy issue." I rise to my feet and cast my computer to the large screen. "I think we could go beyond just patching up this problem. We need to look at using it to our advantage."

"I'm intrigued," Tania says as my PowerPoint presentation pops onto the screen.

"I think a starting place would be to leverage advanced predictive models," I begin and point to some starter models. "I developed a few to start us off. As you can see, I've built audiences based on modeled and predictive data. The key here is to make sure their privacy is maintained and not rely on one-to-one user targeting."

I explain how using this type of approach allows us to deliver successful campaigns. As I go through each component of the plan, the board members perk up. Their faces soften. Some take notes. I even get a few nods.

"This is innovative," Sonia says. "I'm quite impressed."

Hearing that from our head board member gives me the boost I need.

"This plan is all about using data in a whole new way to market to our customers," I finish. "I believe it will solve the issues we are facing and take our company to the next level."

One of the board members starts clapping and then a few others join in, saying we need to follow through with my plan. I smile, feeling a bloom of strength flood through my body even though I haven't slept in far too long. Larson is scowling at me from the back of the room, but we never really got along anyway, so it's no surprise. Sherly is the one person I'm worried about.

But she's grinning and shaking her head at me like she can't believe it.

"This is good work, Scarlett," she says. "And proof of why we can't lose you."

"Which is why I have some requests before I go forward with implementing this plan," I say.

I swallow. *Here it goes.* While in Germany, I realized not only do I know what I'm doing, but I'm good at what I do. I've been grinding away on this one path, so focused on the ground beneath my feet, that I haven't taken the time to look up and see the shining castles in front of me.

Those days are gone. It's time to take control of my life and my career. To earn my worth and get paid for my potential.

"I'd like to request a raise and a promotion with staff under me to start working on this new system," I say.

"You're putting us in a tough position," Sonia says. "The company is on a downward spike with the issues we're facing."

"I might be a risk," I say, "but I also might be exactly what this company needs to not just get us out of the hole but take us to the next level."

"I already offered you the bonus," Sherly says. "It expired when Larson started taking over the project."

"I'm going to be blunt," I say. "I've put in the hours and time into this company. Don't you want to keep me and use this plan that only I can execute? Do you really think Larson can take what I just showed you and run with it?"

"Can you give us a moment?" Sonia asks. "We'll need to discuss this."

"Of course." I close my computer and head for the door.

"You too, Larson," Sonia adds.

Larson and I step out of the glass room. My nerves zing around me like I've stuck my finger on a hot wire. He turns on me, his face a storm of anger.

"You think you can just waltz in here with all the answers?" he asks.

"Actually, yes. Not only have I worked here longer than you, but I've worked my butt off."

"But to demand a raise *and* promotion?" he barrels on. Seething, he points at the board members through the glass. "That promotion belongs to me. You weren't here when everything fell apart. But I was."

"I was on vacation." I cross my arms. "My first since I started working here, which is a problem in itself. But I don't regret it. It made me reevaluate my life and see the world with a new perspective. In fact, I don't know if I'd have found a way to solve our company's issue if I hadn't stepped away from work."

A person clears their throat. It's Sherly, standing at the opened door to the conference room, a slight smirk on her face. I gulp. How long had she been listening?

"We're ready for both of you," she says.

Larson walks inside with a slight jerking motion as if it's taking all his strength to keep his anger bottled up. I follow. Once we're both standing back at the front of the room, Tania rises from her seat, clasping her hands before her.

"We have discussed both of your plans at length," she says, "and took your request, Ms. Walker, into consideration."

I hold my breath, praying for a yes.

"We've decided to give you the promotion," she continues,

"and the raise you deserve as well as a team of two individuals who will help you execute this new data systems creation."

Yes! I want to scream and dance around the room, but somehow I maintain a mostly dignified disposition, only bouncing on my toes. "Thank you very much. It's an honor to continue working with you."

Larson grumbles something under his breath and stalks out of the room. Meanwhile, I shake the board members' hands and float my way back to my desk.

I text Grams and Bella: *I got a promotion and a raise!*

> Bella: I can't believe you went straight from the airport to work.

> Grams: It's party time tonight! I'll get cooking.

I grin, reading their texts. Then I call Hunter. He answers on the first ring. *Well, that's new.*

"Hey, babe," I say, and tell him everything that happened.

"I'm so proud of you. We need to celebrate."

"I promised dinner tonight with Grams and Bella, but this weekend is still ours, right?"

I know we've made a commitment to put each other first, but I'd be lying to myself to not believe how easy it would be to slip back into our old habits.

"Absolutely," he says. "In fact, I've got a full Saturday planned."

"Really? Now I'm curious."

"It's a surprise. I'll pick you up at ten on Saturday morning."

CHAPTER 51

Hunter Path

CREATING MAGIC

"Grams!" I call out as I step inside the house. "Bella! I'm home."

I roll my suitcase through the doorway but stop short at the sight before me. What in the world?

There are roses everywhere. Pink ones stuffed into glass jars on the shelf. Yellow ones overflowing out of baskets on the floor. Long-stemmed ruby-red roses in crystal vases on the coffee table. Grams's living room smells like a rose garden—sweet and heady.

It's beautiful. And also kind of creepy.

"Is that my Scarlett?" Grams voice calls from her bedroom. She hurries out, wearing her crafting apron. Silver curls frame her face, and her eyes widen with joy at seeing me. "You're back safely. I was so worried."

"Yes, I'm back." I hug her thin frame. She smells like lilac and sugar, reminding me of home. "Why were you worried?"

"It's what grandmas do, right? I just couldn't get it out of my mind that you'd get hurt by that big, bad wolf guy. His brother sure did a number on your sister, that's what."

"I love you, you know that? But don't worry about the Wolfe brothers. They're on the other side of the ocean. Besides, I have a feeling we won't have to worry about Karl anymore. I took care of that situation."

"Really?" She fists her hips. "Then what is all this about?"

She looks meaningfully at the rose garden that now fills her living room. I frown, but before I can answer, Bella rushes into the room. Her long brown hair hangs wet over her shoulders, and she's wearing a robe.

"Hey, sis!" She beams and throws her arms around me. "I got out of the shower and I thought I heard your voice. So, tell us everything. Did you really come back early with Hunter? How did things go at work? I'm dying to hear everything."

Grams shoos us into the kitchen, demanding every little detail. She puts the kettle on and sets out the teacups while I relay how Hunter flew all the way to Germany to tell me he loved me.

"How romantic," Bella says with a sigh.

"We decided to come back right away," I explain as I help Grams slice pumpkin bread. "There really wasn't a need for me to stay in Germany anymore. Especially when I had a chance to talk to Karl and make sure he apologized properly to you, which by the way, did he?"

Bella snorts. "If you mean by sending me a thousand roses, then yes?"

"That's why there are all those roses in the living room?" I ask.

"He wrote her a card." Grams passes us our teacups with steam curling out of them. "Said he was a thousand times sorry and each rose symbolized that."

"Wow." I cup the warm drink with my palms. Maybe seeking Karl out wasn't such a good idea. Him sending her roses only reminds her once again that he exists. I focus on Bella. "When I talked to him, I never expected him to intrude back into your life."

"Or have him take over my living room," Grams grumbles.

"It's fine." She waves her hand as if a thousand roses are no big deal. "I'm over him. One hundred percent. He's nothing. A distant, bad memory. That's all."

"Right." I sip my tea. "I'm glad."

She obviously isn't over him. Did I make things worse?

"But you haven't told us about work." Bella switches the subject smoothly. "You were so cryptic in your text. Tell us everything."

We finish off the pumpkin bread and drink a second cup of tea as I explain how I not only impressed the board but landed myself a promotion and pay raise.

"I'm proud of you." Grams pats my cheek. "You were always such a smart girl."

"You are bada...ashtrays," Bella says, quickly amending her word choice for Grams.

"Ashtrays?" Grams frowns. "I never understand the words you young ones say these days. I just figured out chill means to relax rather than something cold."

Bella and I giggle. I've got the best family.

I ask Grams about her garden and book club. Afterward, Bella shares about her classes and her assignments. It feels great sitting with the two of them, catching up on life.

"Now that you're here," Bella says, "you can help us throw out the roses. I need to get rid of the reminder of Karl."

"And I need my living room back," Grams adds. "I can hardly watch my Golden Girls show without sneezing. Still, it pains me to throw all of those beautiful flowers away."

"I have an idea of what you can do with all of those roses,"

I say. "Right now these flowers aren't bringing anyone joy, but there's a place full of people who I think would enjoy them."

So we load up the flowers into the back of Grams's pickup truck and drive over to the elderly home down the street. When I step up to the receptionist's desk, I'm startled to find the very same lady who gave me the basket I won at the conference. Her white hair is still pulled into a bun and she's still wearing the same blue dress.

"Oh, hello there," I say. "We've met before. You gave me that winning basket at the conference."

"Did I?" She shuffles through her stack of papers. "I might have. I have so many clients I take care of these days."

"But you know what the strangest thing is?" I lean against the counter. "I thought for sure I saw you a number of times while I was in Germany. Isn't that funny?"

A mischievous smile curves on her face. "Life is rather unexpected, isn't it? You never know who you will meet or which path you might take."

That was an odd response, but Grams and Bella are already coming inside with armfuls of flowers.

"We brought roses for the residents," I explain. "Would it be okay if we passed some of these bouquets out?"

"How can I say no to someone who wants to add a little magic to another person's day?" the receptionist says. "There's a cart just over there for you to use. And here is a map of the residents you can deliver flowers to."

She shuffles through her papers again. It might be just me but I could've sworn one of them had the header on it, "League of Fairy Godmothers."

"Here you are." She hands me a piece of paper. It sparkles under the fluorescent lights. "Have a magical day."

"Thanks. You, too," I say, a bit warily. There's something

about that saying. Was that what she told me when she handed me that raffle winner basket?

I turn around and grab the cart by the wall. The three of us spend the rest of the evening delivering flowers to the residents.

"That was the best idea," Bella tells me once we're finished. "Those flowers made me so upset, but today changed all of that after seeing the glow on everyone's faces after we gave them the flowers."

"It was truly magical," I say.

The receptionist was right. We were creating magic.

CHAPTER 52

Hunter's Path

HUNTER'S SURPRISE

It's silly, but for some reason as I get ready for my date with Hunter, my hands can't stop shaking. I have to call for Bella to help with getting into my sundress.

"This is a cute dress," Bella says, zipping the tight bodice into place. "Blue always looks great with your blue eyes. What's the occasion?"

"Actually, I don't know." I swipe on some lipstick. "Hunter's taking me out on a date. It's a surprise."

"Sounds cryptic. Maybe it's something about your future?"

My heart skips. "He's probably just showing me a new home he's getting ready to flip or taking me out for lunch."

"Based on everything you told me yesterday, it sounds like you and Hunter are finally getting serious about your relationship."

My mouth dries up. She's right. Things have gotten serious. Both of us were off course before. Are we on the right path now? I want to believe we are.

315

I slide my feet into a pair of strappy sandals just as the door-bell rings.

"That's him," I say and grab my sister's hand, my heart oddly thumping.

"You look freaked out." Her brow dips in worry. "Wait, do you think he's taking you skydiving? Or what if the date is that new swimming with the sharks experience?" She shudders. "If so, call me. I can pick you up right away."

"I'll be fine." I laugh lightly to brush away my sudden terror. What if she's right?

When I open the front door, Hunter is there beaming at me, looking sexy in his tight white shirt and khaki shorts. He smells fresh like the sea, and he's holding a bouquet of flowers.

"These are for you," he says.

Bella peeks her head around the corner and groans. "Not more flowers."

Hunter's eyebrows rise. "Did I do something wrong?"

"Not at all." I take the flowers and push them into Bella's hands. "They're perfect."

"I'll put them in water," Bella concedes. "At least they're wildflowers and not roses."

I wave goodbye and jump in the car with Hunter. He shoots me that charming smile that makes my heart flip a few times as he backs out of Grams's driveway. As we drive away, I decide that being with him feels right. Like we were always meant for each other. Germany was exactly what I needed—time to get away and set my priorities straight. This is the life I want, the right path for me.

"So, what's the big surprise?" I ask.

"We're going to Daytona," he announces, turning on the music.

"Daytona? Why? Oh..." I remember that picture he

showed me of the cute house by the sea. "We're going to see the fixer-upper you found the day of our breakup, aren't we?"

"The very one."

"It didn't sell? I thought you said it was so promising it'd go fast. That's why you had to leave right away."

"It did sell," he says, tapping his palm against the steering wheel to the beat of the music.

"I'm confused."

"I brought us a picnic lunch, too. With all of your favorite snacks. It's been too long since we've had a picnic on the beach. We've been too busy with work, but that's all changing now with our new commitment."

I lean back in my seat. "That does sound lovely. Much better than skydiving or shark swimming."

"Shark swimming?"

"Bella thought maybe that's what we were doing. She has an overactive imagination from all the books she reads."

The hour-long drive to Daytona goes by faster than I expected. Soon, we're driving through the beach town, crossing the intercoastal, and heading down A-1 to a more remote section. I roll down the window, letting the sea air fill the car and blow against my skin. The warmth soaks into my body, soothing me.

When we pull into an old beat-up cottage, I sit straight in my seat. A SOLD sign hangs in front of the property. He parks in front of the sagging porch.

"Are you sure the owners are okay with us being here?" I ask.

"I got permission to come for the day, so don't worry."

"This is kind of a strange place to have a picnic, don't you think? Maybe we should go to a park. We passed by one on our way here."

"This place will give us a little more privacy."

I climb out of the car while Hunter grabs the picnic basket and blanket. Sand pools into my sandals and sunshine beams on my shoulders as we work our way to the cottage. The steps are storm-worn and the wooden structure is whitewashed.

"The house is cute," I say, "but clearly neglected. It's kind of sad to see a place fall to ruin like this."

"I think that's my favorite part about house hunting and fixing up places," he says, staring at the old building. "I can bring back a house's old glory or give her a new purpose."

"Wow." I stare at him appreciatively. "That's a wonderful way to think about what you do."

"Let's head to the beach and eat some food. I'm starving."

He leads me around the house, fighting through wild palms and Florida scrub to get to the back. Finally, we step out into an overgrown yard that slopes down to the beach and eventually the ocean.

I suck in a deep breath of sea air, tasting salt on my lips. The roar of the waves crashing against the sand fills my ears, and the breeze snaps my red hair like a kite. I dig into my pocket for a tie and twist my hair into place.

"It's so beautiful," I say. "Just a few moments here and I'm already feeling less tense."

"The ocean will do that to you."

He opens up the blanket and lays it on a sandy patch in front of the house. Once we settle onto it, he pulls out containers with an assortment of cheese, crackers, breads, berries, sliced meats, and seltzer water.

"This is so thoughtful," I say, popping a blueberry into my mouth. "Also, why does food always taste better outside?"

"It's the air. It brings out the flavor in everything." He

holds up his seltzer water. "I'd like to make a toast. To us and new beginnings."

"Cheers to that." I clink my bottle against his.

We spend the next hour eating and talking, dreaming and hoping. Conversation with Hunter is always so easy, but unlike the past where he'd always be checking his phone or taking calls in the middle of our date, I don't see his phone anywhere.

"Where's your phone?" I ask. "I'm not used to seeing you without it."

"I left it in the car. I needed to have some time where it wasn't accessible. That way my whole focus was on you. People lived for ten thousand years without a phone. I'm working on living without it for a few hours."

"I'm impressed."

"I'm a work in progress. A true fixer-upper."

I lean over and kiss him. "You're far more than a fixer-upper. You're an incredible guy, and I'm glad we found each other."

"You have no idea how glad I am, too." He takes my hand. "There's something I want to show you inside the house."

"Won't the owners be upset with us trespassing?"

He pulls me along with him, up a set of rickety stairs. "Watch that third step," he warns. "It's rotted out."

At the door, he fits a key into the lock and opens the door.

"Some of the walls have holes in them and the glass on the window overlooking the ocean is cracked," he explains. "But like I first thought when I saw this place pop up for sale, its bones are good."

"It's adorable." I take in the small kitchen and the rounded-walled dining nook with the cracked bay window. "And the view is fantastic."

He tugs on my hand and leads me through a doorway into

a living area that looks out at the ocean, but my eyes are riveted to the rose petals placed on the dusty floor in the shape of a heart. My head spins.

"What's that?" I ask.

He draws me over to the heart and gets down on one knee in its center.

"Oh!" I suck in a shocked breath. He's proposing?

"Scarlett." He holds up a glittering diamond ring.

I gasp. He's proposing!

"I know we've had our ups and downs. But I wouldn't want to go through the highs and lows of life with anyone else. I'm madly in love with you and want to spend my life with you. Will you marry me?"

Tears well up in my eyes and spill down my cheeks. "Yes. Yes, I'll marry you. I love you, too."

He slips on the ring and rises, kissing me soundly on the lips. "You've just made me so happy, Scarlett. I can't wait to spend the rest of my life making you happy as well. Also, I have a confession to make."

I lift my eyebrows. "What kind of confession?"

"I'm actually the owner of this house." He grins. "It was too good of a price to let pass, so I bought it. I figured if things didn't work out for us, I could fix it up and sell it. But I was secretly hoping I could convince you to be with me and this could become our home."

"This is amazing. I absolutely love it, but it's so far from Grams and Bella and work."

"I thought about that, too." He squeezes my hand. "This could also be our weekend home or even vacation getaway that we could rent out when we're not using it. It could be anything we want it to be. I don't care as long as we're together."

"As long as we're together, we can choose whatever we want," I agree.

I wrap my arms around his neck, kissing him once again. That's when I realize our paths finally have merged, and we're beginning a whole new journey together.

CONGRATULATIONS! You've reached the end of Hunter's Path! You can either:

Movie Star Path: Experience the drama when Scarlett chooses the dashing movie star and jets off to the film set with him by reading on in Chapter 53.

Wolf Path: Did you skip the Wolf Path? If so, go back and read the Wolf Path starting at Chapter 38.

Movie Star Path

A JET PLANE TO FIJI

Reader Note: This is the beginning of the Movie Star Path if you choose this path after Chapter 37.

"You're engaged?" Bella asks, her voice half-screeching on the phone. I'm not sure if it's from panic or excitement. Probably a little of both. "Because I'm watching you get proposed to on YouTube by Robby Ricci. Tell me I'm seeing things."

"That was just an act," I say, tossing the last of my clothes into my suitcase. "A ploy to help dig out the mole on our tour. It's a complete sham."

"It sure doesn't look like a sham. It looks like a romcom movie. I mean, a proposal in front of a castle?"

"It was actually a lot of fun."

"I'm so confused. So, are you two dating?"

"Not exactly." I snap my suitcase closed and assess my hotel room in Kassel one last time. "He asked me to go with him to Fiji and I said yes, but I'm going to miss Germany."

"What? You're going to Fiji *now*? With a stranger. A guy you hardly know. Just up and leaving your amazing tour? This is not a good idea. Why can't you two just fall in love in Germany on your tour?"

My decision to go with Rob wavers, but his words in the museum earlier call back to me like a fairy tale.

I feel like we have something here. I'd like to explore that.

"When you say it like that," I tell her, "it does sound weird. But he has to return to his movie set in Fiji, so it's not just a fun holiday." I slip on the red jacket Grams got me and tote my suitcase out of the room. "I think there's a spark between us and I want to explore that. Besides, he says he wants to hire me to run his movie marketing campaign. So going there will give me the chance to get all the footage and information I need."

"This is risky. You don't really know him."

"That's what I'm counting on you for. You love to read all the latest juicy gossip, right?"

"No, I read novels, not *Glam Gossiper* or *Celebrity Unchecked*. There's a difference."

"I know, I know. But will you do some research on him for me? It might help..." I'm about to say 'ease my mind from running off with some guy I hardly know,' but instead, I say, "Acclimate to his life."

"Botox, loss of privacy, scandals, and obsessive dieting await that sort of life. Are you sure this is what you want?"

"You're making a bigger deal over this than it is. I'm just having a little fun and potentially branching out in my career. You told me to do both of those things, remember?"

"You're right." She sighs. "Go have fun, but call me if anything goes sour, okay?"

Promising her I would, I hang up and step out of the elevator, pausing at the front door of the hotel. Rob is waiting for me by the car, wearing sunglasses minus the wig. He looks different today. His hair is gelled back, and he's wearing khaki pants and a nice button-down shirt that probably cost more than my entire wardrobe.

Do I really want to do this with him? Is Bella right and I'm getting in too deep? I have no idea what the life of those in Hollywood is like. I'm just a workaholic who is finally taking her first real vacation.

But then I think about the way my toes tingle when he looks at me and how I melt like butter under his touch. What do I have to lose, right?

I take a deep breath and step outside, my suitcase bouncing along behind me.

"There she is," Rob says, his smile showing off his million-dollar dimple. As I stroll up, he kisses me lightly on the forehead like I'm the most precious thing in his life. Like he doesn't have a million other things to worry about besides me. He smells fresh like citrus and fresh-cut grass. "Your chariot awaits."

Butterflies take flight in my stomach. *See, I made the right choice. Rob is perfect for me.*

I take in the limo, sleek and shiny black. "Fancy."

The hotel attendant opens the door for us, and we slip inside. As we ride to the airport, my insides tumble in excitement and anticipation. This is the first time I've ever ridden in a limo and it takes all my self-control not to touch every button. While Rob answers emails on his phone, I work very hard to be cool and relaxed as if riding in a limo is perfectly normal and I take this same sort of transportation to work every day.

When we pull up to the airport, I expect the driver to drop us off at the arrivals section, but instead, we drive around to a different area until we park right by a small jet. Rob acts as if this is no big deal, but as I climb out of the car, my head is spinning. My mouth gapes open, unable to hide my shock.

"Is this the plane we're taking?" I ask. My stomach feels a little queasy, like I ate too much ice cream.

"You like it?" Rob asks, smiling at me as if he's clearly having a blast watching my expression. "I bought it a few years ago when I just couldn't take all the dreadful stares and endless autograph requests on regular flights."

"Right." I shrug. "As one does when feeling inundated with the world."

He chuckles and takes my hand. I'm glad because I'm a little dizzy as we head across the tarmac and up the stairs into the plane. *What have I gotten myself into?* The interior is plush with soft white cushioned seats, dark carpeting, and calm music playing on the speakers. An attendant takes my luggage and Rob helps me out of my jacket. He plops into one of the large chairs and waves for me to sit in the one beside him.

"Sit down and relax. I imagine you must be hungry since there wasn't time to grab food after we left Kassel. I ordered lunch for you. I hope you don't mind."

My stomach growls as if in response, and I laugh. "No, that sounds perfect."

The attendant glides over and hands us a glass of champagne as the captain tells us over the intercom we're about to take off.

"Cheers to this new adventure we're about to have," Rob says.

"Cheers." I clink my glass against his. We sip our drinks as the plane begins rolling down the runway. "Thank you for inviting me."

"Hardly. I couldn't bear the idea of going back to the

madness I'm about to face without you." He takes a deep breath. "You have no idea how grateful I am to you."

The engines roar and the plane hurtles off down the runway until it lifts into the air. The moment we're airborne, I peek over Rob to stare at the German countryside below us.

"Goodbye, Germany," I say. Rob's forehead bunches as if he's worried. "When I was packing, I realized all I had were warmer clothes for the cold weather. I might have to do some shopping when we arrive."

"Absolutely. Anything you want."

"You don't have to buy me anything. I have my own money."

"It will be my treat." When I go to refuse, he holds up a finger. "There's something I want to ask of you. A favor. You are completely welcome to say no, but it would mean a great deal to me if you said yes."

My heart stutters and a million bad, horrible things flash through my mind of what he wants. "What is it?" I ask breathlessly.

"First off, I do want to hire you as my marketing expert for the promotion of the movie. But there's something else. As you may have remembered, we got engaged in front of the castle."

"How could I forget?" I nod in understanding. "You don't have to worry. I totally understand it was a fake engagement, a ruse, and I had fun acting out the whole thing with you."

"Right." He grimaces and sets down his glass. "I was wondering if you'd be willing to carry on the ruse for a little longer."

"What do you mean?"

"The thing is Tia, as you know, will be there."

"In Fiji."

He tugs on the collar of his shirt. "I've been told she

watched the video of our engagement."

"Our fake engagement."

"Right. Yes. And apparently, she's quite upset over it all. She told the press she's destroyed and gutted to the core, which I admit is rather vindicating."

"So you want to do a fake breakup?"

"Absolutely not!" He takes my left hand and stares at the finger where the vine he had twisted into the shape of a ring once was. "I want to continue our engagement. I want Tia to loathe the fact we're engaged. I want her to see me with—gorgeous, stunning—you."

"You do know Tianna Ulci is a model and one of the most beautiful movie stars on screen. And I am not."

"Nonsense. You are superior to her in every way. It will be glorious. What do you say?"

"I don't know." I pull my hand away, feeling uncertain about this whole thing. "It's risky, and I don't want anything to come between us, especially when we're just beginning whatever this is."

"There is no one in the world that I trust more than you."

"You hardly know me."

He shakes his head slowly, his eyes soaking me in like I'm a work of art. "Sometimes the heart knows more than the mind, and my heart tells me we can do this."

This is a bad idea. I can think of a million things that could go wrong. What if someone finds out? What if one of us gets hurt? But then I glance over at his face, begging me to say yes. I take a swig of my drink and set down the glass.

"Okay," I say. "Let's do this engagement thing!"

"Brilliant!"

We make another toast. I'm sure I'm overanalyzing everything. What could go wrong?

CHAPTER 54
Movie Star Path
WHEN CELEBRITIES COLLIDE

Heat washes over me as I step out of the taxi. We've arrived at the Villas of Fiji. The air smells of flowers and brine, scattering my nerves over this fake engagement. *Everything will be fine*, I tell myself. *Think of this as a relaxing extension of my vacation with a very hot movie star, no less.*

"You good?" Rob asks me, wrapping his hand around mine.

I startle, realizing I'd been staring at the revolving lobby door like it was about to chew me up and spit me out. "Yes. Great."

"Don't worry about a thing," he says as he pulls me inside the lobby. "I'm not about to take you away from your fairytale vacation for a week of drudgery."

"I'm sure it will be fabulous." I smile. "How can Fiji not be?"

He kisses my forehead. "I'm going to check us in. You relax and enjoy that view of the ocean."

Large arched windows overlook a breathtaking cerulean

sea. I wander to a sleek couch with a perfect view. The moment I sit, an attendant hurries to me with a juice topped with a hibiscus flower.

"I could get used to this," I say, and happily sip at the mango and strawberry drink, already planning a day of swimming and sunning by the pool.

I'm mid-daydream when I hear a woman squeal behind me. I glance over my shoulder. The woman is stunning with long flowing black hair, wearing a tight-fitting white dress that barely covers her ass. She's crossing the lobby dramatically holding her hands out to Rob like he's her long-lost love.

My heart drops. This is Tianna Ulci, his co-star and ex. One glance at her and you'd know she was a cover model, while I sit here all rumpled and haggard like the leftovers from a bad in-flight meal.

"Robby!" She screeches and throws her arms around him even as it appears he's pushing her away. "You're here. I knew you'd come back. That's why I told the producers you just needed a little time away."

"If it isn't the Tiaster." Rob untangles himself from her. "What are you doing here?"

"I switched hotel locations," she explains, waving a glittering hand ringed with gems breezily. "The last place had dreadful service."

"Cancel my reservations," Rob tells the attendant checking us in. "I need to find a place as far from this woman as possible."

"Don't be so dramatic." Tia titters. "This is a huge resort. We won't even see each other. I'm so relieved you came to your senses and returned. There were all sorts of rumors flying around that you got engaged to some nobody on your tour.

One look at those photos and I knew it was all lies. You'd never stoop that low."

And that's my cue. I stalk over to join them, my rage and embarrassment bubbling inside me like a dangerous concoction. If I'm not careful, I might "accidentally" spill my drink all over her pretty white dress.

"Hello," I greet Tia. Rob instantly relaxes when I tuck my arm through his. A reminder that Tia may have raised my hackles, but if I'm going to help Rob get through this situation so he can finish his movie, I need to stay in control of my emotions. "You must be Tia. I've heard all about you."

Her face drops for an instant before she flashes that movie-star smile of hers. "And who is this, Rob?"

"This is Scarlett Walker." Rob slips his arm around my waist. "My fiancée."

Hearing him call me that out loud to someone outside of our small tour group makes our ruse feel very real—and very volatile. What if she finds out the truth?

As if to confirm my suspicions, her eyes flicker to the hand holding my juice. My left hand without an engagement ring. Her mouth tips up just enough to tell me she's not buying our announcement. Crap.

"How sweet," she says. "You two didn't waste any time, did you? But then life is too short to wait. Well, I'm off to sit by the pool and read over my lines before our filming tonight."

I frown and turn to Rob. "You're filming tonight?"

"Oh!" Tia says. "He didn't tell you? We have only two weeks to shoot all the scenes we're in together, so it's going to be intense. At least tonight we hardly have any lines. Mainly just kissing and making out."

A sickness swirls in my stomach. They're going to be kissing tonight? While I'm here all alone?

"*Au revoir!*" Tia blows us a kiss and sashays away, moving her hips a little too exaggeratedly for my taste.

I take a deep breath and try to not let my mind go to the places it wants to, imagining the two of them passionately kissing on a beach—or maybe on a bed.

Yep. This is bad.

"I can't do this," I say suddenly, setting my drink on one of the tables. "I know it's acting, but she's awful."

Rob's face is stretched thin, full of pain. "Now do you see why I didn't want to come back? But you know what?" He takes my hands in his, staring into my eyes. "To hell with all of this. Let's just go. Refuel the plane and get as far away from the witch as possible."

I take a deep breath and close my eyes, reminding myself why I'm here. To build a relationship with Rob and see where this can go. If I can't survive a minor bump with him, how can I expect to endure the mountains we will face in the future?

"No," I say. "I want to do this. She doesn't get to ruin your life anymore. We're not going to give her that power. Instead, we're going to stay here. You're going to make an incredible film, and we're going to have a blast."

"You sure?"

"Absolutely. And the first break you get, we're going to get me a ring." I hold up my empty finger, scrunching up my nose. "I think she noticed."

"You're going to get anything you want." He kisses me right there in the lobby with the staff and guests watching us. It's so soft that I allow myself to sink into him.

When we finally untangle ourselves, Rob turns back to the check-in counter. The front desk agent is an elderly woman who looks very familiar. There's something strange about her, and it's not just because she doesn't look like any of the locals with her pale skin and long white hair hanging around her shoulders. Maybe it's the pink flower pinned in her hair. Or maybe it's that sparkle in her eyes as she checks us in.

"Engaged, are you?" she says. "How lovely."

"Do I know you?" I ask. "Because you look really familiar."

"Have you been to Fiji before?" I shake my head, unable to place her. "You two lovebirds are in for a treat. I'm putting you in our honeymoon suite. The best room on the island."

"That sounds great," Rob says, beaming at me like he really is on his honeymoon. "Appreciate that."

Once we're checked in, we follow our bellhop outside and down a narrow path lined with flowers and palms waving in the sea breeze. We cross over a wooden bridge that leads us to a thatched villa perched over the water like it's its own romantic island. Our butler unlocks the door, and I step into the cool air conditioning. It's a large room with a peaked wooden ceiling and a glass wall overlooking the ocean. A king-sized bed piled with pillows is set on one side of the room while an electric fireplace and TV fill the opposite wall. There's even a cute little kitchenette area.

"The view of the sunset will take your breath away," our butler says, parking our suitcases by the wall. "Do you need anything else before I leave?"

"Please have some appetizers and drinks sent over," Rob says, taking off his sunglasses and giving the man a tip.

"Of course." The butler bows his head and goes to leave.

"Just one more thing," I call after him as I open the different doors in the room. "Where is the second bedroom? I only see a bathroom and a closet."

"This is the honeymoon suite, the best room on property," he explains. "There is no second bedroom. Enjoy your stay."

The door shuts, leaving us to stare at the one bed in the room.

"Well." I clear my throat. "This is a little awkward."

"I'm sorry." He grimaces. "I didn't know. I'll call the front desk right away and see if the agent can get us a different room."

Relieved, I let out a long breath. "That would be great."

But when he makes the call, he only frowns and says, "I see. Right. Of course." When he hangs up, his forehead bunches up.

"What's wrong?" I ask.

"It appears as if this is the only room left."

Which means I'm sharing a bed. With a movie star.

CHAPTER 55

Movie Star Path

EAVESDROPPING 101: HOW TO HEAR WHAT YOU SHOULDN'T

Rob shoots me an I'm-sorry look. "First thing tomorrow, we'll find a different hotel. Well, after we get you a ring. I'll sleep in the chair tonight."

"You're not sleeping in the chair." I roll my eyes. "Not when you have filming tonight on top of everything. I'll just sleep on one side of the bed and you can sleep on the other. We're adults, right?"

I can totally resist those flutters every time I smell his intoxicating scent begging me to move closer to him. I will not think about how his lips pressed against mine, drowning me in a whirlwind of passion. Nor will I wonder what it would be like to press my body against his as my limbs tangle around him.

Nope, I shake my head, needing to get my brain on straight. *Do not let your mind go there, Scarlett!*

The doorbell rings, breaking the awkward moment between us. It's room service, bringing in our evening hors d'oeuvres. We pile up plates of food.

"To my pretend fiancée and our impending non-nuptials," he says, holding up a cracker with cheese.

As we eat, my eyes covertly glance at the bed. What have I gotten myself into? This was a bad, bad idea! But I'm here, and I need to make the best of things.

No! Inwardly, I groan. *Do not make the best of things.* What I must do is resist all temptations.

~

WHILE ROB IS off kissing and making out with his ex-girlfriend—I mean shooting their make-out scenes for the film—I spend the evening exploring the beautiful resort. The pools are lit with pale blue lights, and tiki torches flicker along the pathways. I take in all the romantic places and stare out at the moonlit ocean, but walking through this resort would be so much more fun with Rob.

When 1 a.m. comes around and Rob still hasn't shown up, I decide to climb into the enormous king-sized bed, perching myself at the very edge. I can't sleep. All I can think about is him kissing Tia with those full red lips and breasts spilling out of her dress.

I must have fallen asleep eventually because when I wake up again, sunlight is pouring through the cracks in the blinds. I roll over, stretching, only for my face to land on a large bicep.

I squeak and jerk up.

Rob blinks his eyes awake, staring at me blearily. His gaze latches onto mine and my heart swoops as I take in his bare chest, smooth-cut pecs, and bronze skin that's begging for my hands to run over it.

"You're not wearing a shirt," I say. My voice is still high-pitched as if I've seen a ghost. Oh, crap. What if he's not wearing anything under those covers? My face burns at the thought.

"Morning." He smiles, which is bad. That crooked smile has made him millions of dollars, and right now I think it's worth every penny. "Sorry. I forgot to put a shirt on. I always sleep only in boxers."

Do not think about his boxers or other parts. I swallow and push aside my hair that has fallen in my face. Which reminds me that I must look like a disaster. My hair is all over the place, I've got on no makeup, and my pajamas are simple shorts and a tank. Not even close to the sexy fiancée of a superstar.

"I didn't mean to roll on top of you," I say and wave to that well-cut arm. "It was purely accidental."

"You can roll on top of me anytime you want, princess." He lifts a brow as if inviting me to do just that.

Heat flows through my body. He has no idea how tempting that is. Quickly, I scramble out of the bed, feeling super confused. I mean, we kissed and it was great, fabulous even. But the only non-pretend one was back at the castle in Germany. Since then, everything has felt a bit off between the secretly not-actually-being engaged, meeting his ex who he apparently was kissing last night, and sleeping in the same bed.

"How was last night?" I ask, unable to stop my curiosity. Okay, that made me sound desperately jealous so I add, "Did the shoot go well?"

Rob rubs his eyes and sits up. His hair is disheveled, which only makes him look sexier. I want to run my hands through it.

"It went as well as can be expected with Tiaster," he says and walks over to me. "I gargled with mouthwash after the kissing scene. It brought back so many bad memories."

Now I feel bad for being jealous. "I'm sorry you had to go through that."

He rests his hands around my waist, staring at me with those deep brown eyes. "Everything is better with you here.

Let's get some breakfast and then go get that ring. How does that sound?"

"Perfect."

He kisses me on the forehead and then goes to take a shower. I stand there for a moment, realizing we haven't kissed —like really *kissed*—since we got on the plane. Is that good or bad? Is that my fault or his? I don't even know anymore.

Once we've showered and changed, we head into the dining room where a gorgeous buffet is laid out with everything I could imagine eating—stacks of delicate pastries, meats roasting over a wood fire, egg dishes, exotic fruit, and platters stacked with cheese and vegetables.

"I think we just entered Heaven," I tell Rob as we settle at a table overlooking the ocean.

"Good," he beams, "you deserve it."

As the server pours us fresh coffee, Rob shares a little about his schedule for the film shoot and how he envisions his character playing out. We pile our plates full of food and he tells me about the future projects he would like to do. Listening to him talk, I realize how little we really know about each other, and yet, how natural it is to be with him.

"I need to take notes on all of this," I tell him and pull out my phone. "This is a great starting point for your marketing campaign."

We're interrupted when his producer calls, so I decide this is the perfect time to get seconds on food. I'm piling my plate high with every pastry they offer when a familiar voice drifts from the other side of the massive flower arrangement. Tianna Ulci! I freeze, unable to resist eavesdropping.

"Last night was divine," she is telling someone. I peek through the foliage to spot her sitting at a table with another woman. "I think it really got us on the right track."

Last night? My heart flips. She must be talking about Rob and her kissing scene.

"Are you sure you want to get back together with him?" the woman asks. "You were so determined to never speak to him again."

"Everyone loves us together." Tianna sips from her teacup and sets it down. "When I saw him yesterday in the lobby, I realized what a terrible mistake it was to leave him."

My heart stills. Tianna wants him back! I knew she was up to something. I keep piling croissants onto my plate so no one gets suspicious of me not moving.

"But doesn't he hate you? I mean, you did burn his most prized possessions."

Tianna waves her hand. "Love overcomes all. Besides, I know him better than anyone. I just need a little bit of time with him and he'll be begging for me to come back. After that kiss last night, I know he wants me, too."

"But didn't *Celebrity Unchecked* say he's engaged?"

"That was a fling." Tianna titters as if that's the funniest bit of news she's ever seen. I bristle, glaring through the flowers. "I don't know why he stooped to that level, but he'll come to his senses soon. Men always do."

I fume. It takes all my effort not to hurl my now very large pile of pastries at her. I need to walk away. Tianna is not good for my mental state, so I stiffly head back across the restaurant and settle across from Rob, trying to get the actress's words out of my head.

And after that kiss last night, I know he wants me, too.

This is bad. Like really bad. How can Rob resist a beautiful ex like her? She's definitely a ten while I'm a five on a good day.

"Wow," Rob says, eyeing my horde, "you really love those pastries, don't you?"

I stare at my overflowing plate and set it in the center of the table. "I got them for both of us. Maybe they'll let us box some up for a midnight snack."

Every part of me wants to tell him what I overheard, but that would only make me seem like a paranoid girlfriend who goes around listening to people's private conversations. I can't have him think that about me.

Even if it's true.

Ugh. How have I become that person?

"Boxing those up sounds like a great idea." Rob tosses his napkin onto the table. "Because it's time for us to go ring shopping!"

CHAPTER 56

Movie Star Path

DIAMONDS AND DAYDREAMS

S parkling sapphires, gilded bracelets, and glittering gems are propped up on midnight-black pillows to showcase the depths of their colors. This store displays jewelry that are more works of art than just a set of earrings to wear as an accessory.

Rob's hand securely wraps around mine as we stroll along the cases, but I still feel like a fraud. I'm living the movie star life—I should be enjoying myself—but all I can think about is when it will come crashing down on me.

Tianna's words hit a little too close to home. Especially when she said, "I don't know why he stooped to that level, but he'll come to his senses soon. Men always do."

I need to stop thinking so negatively and enjoy myself. This is my vacation, after all. Thankfully, Sherly stopped messaging me. Apparently, Larson did some damage control and even got a promotion to boot. The old me would be on the first plane back to try to win my way to the top spot at the company, but this new me is looking at other possibilities.

"Which style are you most interested in?" Rob asks. His

eyes are shining as bright as the diamonds spread out in front of us. I think he might actually be enjoying himself. "I never knew there were so many different kinds of diamonds. Princess cut, square cut, round."

"You're right," I agree, peering at the glittering gems. "They are all so stunning."

The shopkeeper hurries over to greet us, clearly recognizing Rob right away. But I'll give it to the guy. He's discreet and doesn't make a big deal about us being here other than offering us a private place to sit so he can bring out his very best rings.

"We're fine," I say, not wanting this to be a big deal. I mean, it's not like we're actually getting engaged. I don't want Rob spending thousands of dollars on our little farce. "I want something very simple."

"I think she needs only the best," Rob says, winking at the shopkeeper.

He leans over and kisses me on the temple of my forehead. I remind myself it's not a real kiss, but my heart patters in my chest as if screaming for him to pull me closer to him and kiss me soundly.

"Of course she must have the best," the shopkeeper agrees and snaps his fingers.

Rob and I are brought into a back room and escorted to a plush white couch in front of a glass table. A lady hurries in with tall flutes of bubbly champagne.

"We don't really need all of this," I tell Rob. "The vine ring worked great. I don't want you to waste your money on me."

"Cheers." Rob hands me a glass and clinks his against mine. "To our engagement and my beautiful fiancée."

His eyes take me in like he really believes what he said, and my face burns like I'm a teenager who's never been complimented.

"Thank you." I sip the liquid, trying to relax.

The shopkeeper returns with two women carrying trays laden with rings and sets them in front of us. My jaw literally drops open. I'm stunned by their sheer magnificence. One by one, I try them on, twisting my hand to capture each gem's light. Our host explains the depth of the color and clarity of each ring. I try to listen but my eyes keep darting to Rob, sitting there beside me, eagerly listening and nodding as if this is the most important decision.

Sure, the guy is gorgeous, but what I'm finding is he's also kind and thoughtful. He always listens to what I have to say as if he really cares about me. And he genuinely seems interested in my pitifully boring life.

My heart twists. What if this were real? What if we really were in love and sitting here planning our future? If I'm honest with myself, my heart yearns for that. Could I fall in love with Rob? The answer is too scary to think about right now.

"Would you like to try on this princess cut?" the shopkeeper asks, startling me back to the rings.

"Actually, I'd like to try that one." I point to the oval-cut ring set on a band of twisted vines. "This reminds me of the one you made for me in front of the castle."

Rob wraps his arm around me so we're pressed against each other. Warmth pools through me at his touch. I want to pour this moment into a locket and wear it around my neck so I can remember it forever.

"This is so beautiful," I say, staring at the massive rock. "It glitters like a star. How much does a ring like this cost?"

When he tells us, I choke on my champagne, nearly spitting it across the table. I slap my hand over my mouth just in time.

"I think that's a little too much." I quickly slip the ring off and set it back onto its velvet mound. "Maybe I need something smaller or even a simple gold band."

Rob's eyes dart to mine, and then he says to the shopkeeper, "Can you give us a minute?" Once we're alone, Rob takes my hand. "Are you okay with this? You seem worried."

"I am!" I check the doorway to make sure no one can overhear us. "But this isn't a real engagement. I can't have you spend that kind of money. It just isn't right."

Wrinkles form across his forehead, and his eyes shift, suddenly sad. "I might have gotten a little carried away. How about we get a nice enough ring to satisfy the media but not too nice for the real deal? Would that make you happy?"

"I like that plan."

Rob calls back the staff and I end up with a ring that's still too pricey and too pretty, but at least it's not as expensive as the one I had tried on. It's a round two-carat ring, classic and simple. But as they carry away the trays, I can't help but gaze at that oval ring with the twisted vines. It's the what-if and what-could-be ring.

I must not think about that one.

Once the ring is paid for, Rob insists on slipping it on my finger. He leans in and kisses me lightly on the lips as if to prove to the staff that yes, we truly are engaged, not pretending. But it's not enough for me. I want to feel those lips press hard against mine, to run my hands through his hair, to nip at the edge of his ear as I whisper I want more of him.

His eyes are dreamy as he stares down at me. I should move away, but I don't. Then we're kissing again, passion rippling between us like electricity. My skin prickles with delight and the world fades as his hands run up and down my back, pulling me closer as if he doesn't want to lose me.

Finally, we pull apart, leaving me feeling breathless and unsteady.

"That was," I swallow, "wow."

"We're going to finish off that kiss later." Rob grins mischievously. "When no one else is around."

"I'm not complaining." My heart sings at that thought.

We take a selfie with me showing off my ring to the camera while he kisses my temple. The photo makes my heart ache as I post it onto social media because suddenly I want this to be real.

I want *us* to be real.

We wave goodbye to the staff and head outside. We don't even make it a foot before the paparazzi mobs us. Cameras start snapping and mics are thrust into my face.

"Is it true you two really are engaged?" one reporter asks.

"Sources tell us this engagement is a ruse to help with ratings," another says.

"Aren't you still engaged to Tianna Ulci?"

I gape at the cameras, unsure how to respond.

"Welcome to my life," Rob whispers into my ear. "There's no turning back now."

He flashes me that wry smile as the world captures us on camera.

Movie Star Path
ON-SET SHENANIGANS

"It is true," Rob tells the reporters, hungrily waiting outside the jewelry store. "I proposed to Scarlett Walker on our fairy tale tour in Germany. Today, I got her an official ring to signify our love."

He lifts up my left hand, showing off the diamond. Cameras flash and the crowd peppers us with even more questions. They are a swarm of sharks on a feeding frenzy. But Rob effortlessly maneuvers me to the limo and we slip inside without another word.

The limo takes off and I lean against Rob's shoulder in relief.

"That went rather well, I think," Rob says.

"Now the whole world knows we really are engaged," I add.

My emotions are all over the place. A part of me finds it thrilling—the glamorous hotel, the glitzy jeweler, the limo. But another part is terrified because I think I'm really falling for Rob. After that last kiss, I didn't want it to stop.

Rob's arm tucks warmly around me. "You alright?" he asks.

"I'm still in shock over that big announcement with the reporters. You did a great job with the paparazzi. You're a pro."

"It's called years of practice."

"I'll miss you today while you're on set."

"I was thinking about that. You're only here for one more week before you have to get back home to that job of yours. Since I can't stand the thought of letting you out of my sight, how about you come to the movie set with me?"

"Won't I be in the way?"

"Hardly. You will be my inspiration."

"You are a charmer." I roll my eyes. "But it is a good opportunity for me to get some photos and video footage of you in action to promote the film. We could even get some small clips of you talking with some of your fellow cast members."

"See? You're brilliant. I'm not going to want to let you go back to work for that Sherly lady."

Then he's kissing me again and I find myself leaning into his soft lips. His tongue slips into my mouth as his hands roam up and down along my back. A groan escapes me and an ache to be even closer to him consumes me. Rob pushes a button and the privacy window between us and the driver slides into place. He tugs me closer, and unable to resist him, I crawl onto his lap.

His mouth trails along my neck, sending flares of heat down to my navel. His hands slide along my waist and then up to cup my breast. Another moan escapes me, while Rob's breath is ragged and his eyes are heavy as if he's intoxicated.

A thrill shoots through me and I kiss him passionately once again. Blood rages through my veins, hot as fire. The world is a breathless blur as if all our pent-up emotions are flooding out of us like a tide unleashed.

"We're here at the studio, Mr. Rob," the limo driver's voice says over the intercom, breaking through the haze of passion.

I pull away and slip off his lap. My face is flushed, my whole body in flames.

"You keep kissing me like that," I tell him, still catching my breath, "and I'm going to jump you while on set."

"And that would be a bad thing?" He flashes me one of his wicked smiles. "Perhaps later we can finish this properly."

"I think that could be arranged."

Walking into the studio is a little daunting. Rob's hand securely tucks into mine and he introduces me to the crew, the director, and one of the producers who looks severely frazzled. While Rob heads off to hair and makeup, I decide to grab a coffee while I wait.

A full spread of food is laid out for the crew, and the production manager waves for me to help myself. I grab a granola bar and then fill a cup of medium roast coffee, letting its scent relax me.

"So it's really true," Tia says, strolling up, looking like she stepped out of a magazine. Her makeup is perfect and her long black hair trails in a rope down her back, bound by silver bands. The tight black jumpsuit she's wearing accents every curve of her body. "At first I thought your engagement was a ruse for attention. Guess I was wrong."

My stomach squirms. She's too close to the truth. But now that she says it like that, I wish our engagement *was* real. Not some sham where we break up and I never see him again.

"We can't always be right," I say, sipping my coffee.

"We should have lunch sometime and talk." She picks up a grape from the spread and pops it into her mouth. Her eyes flicker over me from head to toe, and from the lift of her brow, I know she finds me lacking. "You know Rob and I were once a thing. I have plenty of juicy gossip on him."

She literally makes me want to throw things at her. No wonder Rob hates her so much But I plant a smile on my face regardless.

"I'm pretty busy between helping Rob promote the movie and planning the wedding."

Why did you say planning the wedding? I scream inwardly. *There is no wedding! There will be no planning!*

"Wedding?" Tia gasps, and my evil heart is thrilled. "You two sure are moving things along quickly."

Run away quickly before you say anything else stupid. "We both figured, why wait? I mean, when you're in love, you just *know.*"

"Right." Tianna's face is stone. "So you have a date then?"

"We're waiting to officially announce that to the world. See you around."

I don't wait for her to say anything else and book it back to Rob. Thankfully, he just finished getting his hair and makeup done. I should tell him what I told Tianna but I can't bring myself to admit how stupid I was. Still, the surge of victory at seeing Tianna's face so upset is racing through my veins.

"How about we do a video clip of you walking us through parts of the studio?" I suggest. "You can share what you are most excited about for this film."

The rest of the afternoon flies between shooting small clips of him talking or acting out scenes while I write up text to go along with the videos. I also use the opportunity to do some research on what other celebrities are doing for their movie promotions and make a list of ideas for Rob.

Once he finishes up for the day and has changed out of his

costume, he hurries to join me where I'm blocking out a full action plan for him.

"You must have been dreadfully bored all day," he says, taking my hands to pull me to my feet. He kisses me and my heart swoons like a silly teenage girl.

"Actually, it was amazing. I loved learning about what you do. Plus, I got a good start on your promotion campaign. Honestly, I had a blast."

"Then you must come every day."

"Maybe I will, except now I wish I brought my computer with me on this trip. It'd make my work so much easier."

"Then we must buy you one."

I fist my hips, shaking my head as I laugh. "You just can't buy me random things."

"It's for my business, remember? How am I supposed to properly promote this movie if my staff doesn't have the tools? Think of it as a business expense."

"Fine. You win." I take his shirt in my hands and lean in close to kiss him.

"I like winning," he says, grinning.

Before my lips touch his, Tianna's voice cuts through our moment. "I do hope I'll get an invitation to the wedding," she says.

Rob stiffens and draws back from me. His whole face darkens. "I thought I made it clear that we only talk when necessary."

"I just wanted to congratulate you on your engagement and upcoming wedding," she says, her lips forming a plump pout. "Although I admit I was surprised when Scarlett told me she was planning the wedding already. You two sure are in a hurry."

Rob's eyes swivel to mine. There's a moment of surprise

and panic in them and my heart sinks. I shouldn't have mentioned a wedding or plans or dates. *I'm an idiot!*

"Tianna offered to have lunch with me to talk about our engagement," I quickly explain. "I told her I was very busy planning the wedding."

Rob's eyes soften and he refocuses on his ex. "That's what people do when they get engaged and are committed. They plan a wedding and a future together." Then he turns back to me. "That's what this is all about, isn't it, baby?"

Rob wraps his arm around my waist, looking down at me with those movie star eyes of his. I'm a bit breathless to respond. He just called me "baby." It's the first time he's used a term of endearment with me and I want to swim in the perfectness of it all.

Except it's not perfect. Tianna is right. I hate that.

"I hope we won't see you around the hotel, Tia," Rob says with his arm still around my waist. Then to me, "I just remembered I forgot my script in my dressing room. I'll meet you in the limo, okay?"

He kisses my forehead and takes off in a light jog down the hall. Stiffly, I smile at Tianna and turn to leave, but she grabs my arm.

"I'm not an idiot," she says tightly. "I know this whole engagement is fake. He'd never in a million years fall for a girl like you. I don't know what he's offering you to pretend to be engaged to him, but I'll offer double if you break it off tonight."

"I can't believe you're trying to bribe me," I snap. "Now I get why he despises you so much."

I yank my arm free of her and hurry away. I can't get inside the limo fast enough. The moment the door is closed and I'm safely out of Tianna's sight, I let the tears come. Because the reality is, she's right. This engagement *is* fake, and I'm not the glamorous girl Rob falls for.

The worst part is he's definitely the kind of guy I'd fall in love with.

Maybe I already am.

CHAPTER 58

Movie Star Path

LIES AND SPIES

I'd been hoping for a romantic dinner with Rob and then a quiet evening with just the two of us. But when we arrive at the hotel, Rob's old college buddy, Terrance, is waiting for him in the lobby. Apparently, Rob had called him to talk about hiring him to be his new manager, so Terrance flew in right away to talk one-on-one with him.

Which is why dinner became a work session with Terrance instead of a romantic time between Rob and me. Still, dinner ends up being more fun than I expect. Terrance is easygoing, and as he lays out ideas for Rob's future, I don't get the impression he's pressuring Rob in any way like the manager Rob fired. We laugh over stories from when Terrance and Rob snuck into an exclusive golf club and played soccer tennis on the lawn for a few holes until security showed up.

"We ran out of that place so fast." Rob chuckles at the memory. He's leaning back in his chair, rubbing his chin, a ghost of a smile on his face. "I thought for sure they'd catch us."

"But we were fast, man," Terrance points out, his dark eyes twinkling. "Nobody could catch us."

"More like they didn't want to bother with the marshes that we trudged through to escape," Rob notes.

"I thought we agreed to not talk about the marshes." Terrance wags his finger at Rob, which causes Rob to choke on the water he's drinking.

"Oh," I say, buttering my roll, "now I need to know about the marshes."

"There were leeches in the water," Rob explains.

"Enough!" Terrance warns, palming his face as if the memory is still too painful.

"And they seemed to like Terrance more than me." Rob clears his throat. "They stuck to some of his more private parts, shall we say."

"That's terrible!" I exclaim, shuddering. "You poor thing."

Terrance groans inwardly. "I thought we agreed this story was never to be repeated to another individual!"

"Scarlett is different," Rob says. "We can trust her."

"I'm happy for you two," Terrance says. "And for the record, Scarlett, I haven't ever heard him say such a thing about another woman. I get why you two are meant to be with each other."

The grin on my face dies. I'm a fraud sitting here, laughing with these two and listening in on their inner secrets. I duck my head and focus on cutting my chicken. Rob clears his throat and shifts in his seat uneasily.

"I think it's safe to say," Rob says, quickly changing the subject, "that I'd like to hire you to be my manager. Go ahead and draft up the paperwork and send it my way."

We finish up dinner, with Rob and Terrance hashing out the final details. As much fun as I had meeting Terrance, I'm eager to have some alone time with Rob. We say goodbye to Terrance and are heading out of the hotel restaurant when Rob's phone rings. After a quick conversation, he hangs up, a frown pulling on his face.

"Unfortunately, I have bad news," he tells me. "They need me back in the studio right now. It's supposed to rain tomorrow night so they're moving up our night scene shots to tonight. And thanks to my little trip to Germany, we're on a tight deadline."

Disappointment floods my chest, but I press on a smile. "I totally understand. We both knew this was a work trip for you."

"You're the best," he says and kisses me softly.

But it's too fast of a kiss and before I know it, he's hurrying out the hotel lobby door and into his limo. I wave goodbye and trudge out into the hotel's gardens to walk them alone again. I find myself standing by the pool, watching the dark waters shimmer under the full moon. Unlike the daytime where the pool is packed with sunbathers and swimmers, tonight this area is quiet and calm other than the soft music playing over the speakers and a breeze shifting through the palms. A sliver of loneliness slices through me.

Shaking off my depressed mood, I decide to call Bella. I always feel better after I talk to her, plus I owe her an update other than the few texts I've sent her.

"Scarlett!" Bella exclaims. "How is the life of a movie star?"

I laugh and sink onto one of the empty lounge chairs ringing the pool. Already my heart warms hearing her voice.

"I'm not a movie star," I say. "I'm just helping Rob out with his movie. But I will say this hotel is pretty classy. I mean, it even passes the toilet paper test."

"That's nice and all, but why are you talking to me about

toilet paper when I'm looking at a photo of a giant diamond ring on your hand?"

"Wow, that went live quickly. I should've called to warn you."

"No kidding!" She huffs. "I walk into work this morning and everyone is talking about it and asking me for details, but I don't have any. Shame on you."

"It was very romantic." I twist my ring around my finger, staring at its glittery shine, and then tell her how I chose the ring and each detail.

"What a dream," she says.

"More like a fairy tale that belongs on the fantasy shelf of your bookstore." I groan. "I know this engagement is fake. I mean, we had a deal. He offers me work to launch my own business while I pretend to be his fiancée to get back at his ex. But after today, pretending is becoming so hard. I don't know if I can keep up the lying and acting."

Except, I'm not lying or acting. I'm falling for him, which puts me in dangerous territory.

"I'm sorry." She sighs. "That sucks. How much longer are you two going to keep this engagement going?"

"I don't know. We haven't talked about when we're ending it." I lean against the back of the lounge chair and stare up at the moon. "He's gone most of the time and I'm now wondering why I'm even here, you know? I love working for him and this is a great opportunity to launch my own business, but it's all starting to feel weird."

"Is he gone now?"

"He's at the studio doing some night shots."

"You sound like you want to be with him."

"I do."

"Then what are you doing sitting there at the hotel? Get your tush over there, girl!"

I sit up. "You know what? Maybe I will."

"Good. Now go have fun while I gossip about you to my coworkers. Love you."

"Love you, too."

I hang up and as I do, the bushes rustle behind me. I jump to my feet and look around, but I don't see anyone. Frantically, I review what I'd been talking about. Did someone overhear me telling Bella about how Rob's and my relationship was fake? A chill slides down my spine. I ease closer to the bushes and stare into the thick overgrowth, searching for any sign of someone hiding there. But nothing moves and all is quiet.

It must have been one of those large lizards or some sort of wildlife. My shoulders relax and I let out a long breath. I'm really starting to get paranoid.

CHAPTER 59

Movie Star Path

SHE'S A MOVIE STAR!

I change into a fresh pair of jeans and a bright green shirt that accents my red hair. A swipe of lipstick and a brush through my hair and then I'm off to the front desk. Thankfully, the front desk attendant is that same lady who checked us in.

"Can you order me a taxi?" I ask. "I'd like to surprise Rob at the studio tonight."

"That's very sweet of you," she says, picking up her phone. It looks like one of those old-fashioned kinds from the 1800s. But apparently, it works because she orders me a car. "Your limo is pulling up right now. It will get you into the studio with no problem."

"Thank you," I say. "But I can't afford a limo."

"It's all part of Rob's package here," she explains smoothly. "Have a lovely night."

I wave her goodbye and hurry inside the posh limo. The leather seat is comfortable and calm music plays over the speaker, yet it's just not the same without Rob. He always makes everything brighter and richer.

Thankfully, the limo takes me straight through the security checkpoint and drops me off at the front of the studio. My nerves jangle through me like a percussion band as I head inside. Will Rob be happy that I've surprised him? Or maybe I've read this whole situation wrong and he'll be annoyed and upset.

A crowd of camera crew, extras, and assistants swarm the perimeter of the set. An explosion of fire blooms in the center of the stage and Rob's voice cries out, "I won't rest until you're avenged!"

"Cut!" the director calls out over a speaker. "We need another take on that. The lighting is off. Charlie, why can't you get the damn lighting correct?"

Things seem pretty tense based on the expressions of the crew. I slip to the edge of the set, searching for Rob. He's standing on a tall rock up above, wearing khakis and a rugged shirt that's half unbuttoned, exposing his chest. A brimmed hat in the style of Indiana Jones is tucked low over his eyes, shrouding his face. Basically, he looks sexy as hell.

I want to grab him by his shirt and haul him off to his dressing room and kiss him passionately, except a quick glance at the frazzled director—whose hair is sticking up on end and clothes look like he's been wearing them for a week—warns me that I'll just have to stand on the sidelines until they're finished filming.

"Ready, and...action!" a voice calls, sending the actors into motion once again.

The extras at the bottom of the cliff cry out and jerk around like they've been shot. Rob grabs onto a rope and swoops down the cliffside, landing with that dramatic flair that I always loved in his past movies. He whips out some sort of explosive device and tosses it, sending the stage into flames.

Next, he reaches out to catch a woman who's pretending to faint, except she straightens and sneezes. Not just once but three times.

Rob shrugs as if to tell the director that he can't catch a woman who is refusing to faint, but then his eyes drift to land on me. He grins and lifts his eyebrows suggestively, making my face burn hot. I give a little wave, my heart swooping. I made the right decision to come.

"Cut!" the director says and throws his clipboard to the ground, letting loose a long stream of swearing. "If we don't get this scene worked out we're going to be here all night, folks. You need to get it together."

"I can't kiss her," Rob says, pointing to the woman pulling out a wad of tissues from her pocket. "She's sick."

The director rolls his eyes but seems to agree with Rob since he calls for a break. The extras rise off the stage and wander off, chatting as if they hadn't just suffered a horrible death. The lights dim to normal and the flames that licked across the stage area have vanished. I remain rooted to my spot, unable to stop the smile that seems to spread all the way to my toes—because Rob is striding over to me with a swagger that makes my knees weak.

"Hey, you." He takes my hand while pulling his hat off. "This is a fun surprise."

"I thought I'd come to support you. You know, as your marketing expert. I can take pictures or can get some videos of you in action. You did look pretty hot swinging down from that cliff."

"I've got a better idea." And that mischievous twinkle in his eye is back. "Follow me."

Before I know it, Rob has enlisted me as one of the extras. I'm quickly signing waivers, throwing on some ragged clothes that barely cover my body, and the hair and makeup teams are swarming me with brushes and yanking at my hair.

"Are you sure this is a good idea?" I ask Rob when he returns to check in on me. I cringe as the one woman tugs at my hair to braid it. "I don't know anything about acting."

"It's simple really." He shrugs and takes a swig of water. "You scream and fall to the ground. Piece of cake."

"Maybe for you. The closest thing to acting I've ever done is pretend I was a reporter for a newspaper to get back at our tour guide."

"See?" He points at me. "You're innovative and creative to boot. You'll be perfect. You sure look perfect."

He trots off while I swallow the lump that's formed in my throat and turn to stare at myself in the mirror. I hardly recognize myself. My long hair has been assembled in a series of small braids that trail down my back. The makeup is a mix of bruises and blood and dirt. Combined with my torn brown tank top and ragged pants, I look like I just stepped out of a science fiction war zone.

"Find your places!" the set coordinator yells out. "Extras, don't lag behind!"

I join the other rag-torn groupies to the stage, the floor cold against my bare feet. A couple of them introduce themselves and say hi, but all I hear is buzzing.

Why did I agree to do this? Why can't I say no to Rob? This is a terrible, horrible idea!

I huddle with the others under the cliff while the extra coordinator explains my role.

"When you hear the aliens shoot at you," she says, "you scream, look terrified, and shake like you've been shot. Then drop to the ground and die. Got it?"

"Scream, shake, and die," I say with a nod. "Got it."

Except, I really don't. Actually, I might have the terrified look down perfectly. The set springs to action as the lights dim and my group of extras start acting. It's impressive, really. Between their screams and faces looking around in terror, I have to give it to them—they really are professional.

I join in with the screaming, covering my head as if the whole sky might fall on top of me. Gunshots ricochet through the air and I join my fellow extras in shaking. I'm about to fall when I spy Rob swooping down from above. He's the hero of my dreams—confident, strong, and brave. Seeing him in action, I'm in awe of the natural way he owns the stage. It's impressive, and I get why millions will hand over their hard-earned money at the theaters to watch him in action.

I need to fall down, but all I can do is gape at him.

Fall to the ground already! I scream at myself.

I press a hand dramatically to my side as if to explain why I haven't died yet and then sag to the ground.

Except my body never falls. Rob's arms are swooping around me, encasing me close to his body. I blink up at him.

What are you doing? I'm asking with my eyes. He's supposed to catch the woman to my right.

"I'm too late," he says, his voice choked. "I failed you."

I know I'm supposed to close my eyes and die, but the way his expression is so intense and earnest, I find myself slipping into this imaginary world we're standing in. Words spill from my lips before I can stop them.

"You came. That's all I wanted."

Then he's pulling me closer to him. His lips are on mine, hot and hungry. The set, the actors, and the lights all fall away as I reach a hand for his face, desperate for every inch of him. An explosion booms, yanking me out of my fantasy and reminding me I am supposed to die, not be here kissing him passionately. I drop my hand and let my head fall back, closing my eyes. Rob gently eases me to the ground.

"I will avenge you," he says fiercely. "Your name will be on my lips as I destroy those who did this to you."

My heart stutters. The words are so dramatic and sincere that I almost feel they are meant for me. But I force my body to stay still and keep my eyes closed.

"Cut!" the director says.

The lights blink to life and everyone is moving. Rob helps me to my feet.

"That was hot," he whispers into my ear. "You were hot."

"You weren't supposed to speak," the extra coordinator snaps at me and then turns to the director. "I'm sorry. Rob recommended that extra. I didn't know she was going to say anything."

"It's fine." The director waves his hand. "It worked. We're going to keep it."

"You're lucky," one of the extras tells me. "I've never gotten a speaking part in a movie and I've been acting for fifteen years."

"Extras, get off the stage," the coordinator says, glaring at me. "You are done for the day."

I turn to Rob. "I'm sorry. I guess I shouldn't have said anything. I just got a little carried away with you looking at me like that."

"I loved it," Rob says. "It was perfect. You were perfect. I have one more scene to shoot. Will you wait for me?"

"Absolutely."

CHAPTER 60

Movie Star Path

SCRIPTED HEARTS

During the entire limo ride back, Rob and I laugh over our scene along with the expression on the stage manager's face when the director chose to keep the take with me speaking.

"She was so ticked off that I said that line," I say, smiling at the memory. "I thought she was going to lose it."

"I'm glad you said something. It always sounded stilted and odd before when the girl whom I was supposed to be in love with and inspired my vengeance for the rest of the movie didn't have a single line."

"I still feel odd about improvising, but it did feel like the moment needed it. Like why wouldn't she say something to the man she's in love with before she dies?"

"Exactly! Plus, if that line survives the edit and makes it into the movie, you'll get a movie credit."

"Really?" I lean against the seat, staring up at the ceiling. "That's so cool. I never would've thought of myself as an actress, but it was fun. I can't wait to see the final product on the big screen. It's going to be epic. Maybe not the part with me in it, but definitely all the parts with you."

"I could connect you with some people if you'd be interested in doing more acting."

"More acting? No way. Well, unless of course, I get to be in your arms again. I'll sign up for that every time."

Rob leans closer so it almost feels like I'm pinned against the seat. "Really? Every time?"

I get the feeling we're not talking about movies anymore. I stare into his dark, rich eyes and nod.

"Yeah, every time." And I mean those words. I don't want this relationship to just be a vacation fling. I want it to last.

His hand cups my face and his thumb rubs my cheek tenderly. "After Tia hurt me, I never thought I could have feelings this deep ever again. But you changed all of that."

When the limo pulls up to our hotel it's nearly four in the morning, but I'm still on a high from our time together.

"Tia is going to flip out when she finds out about you being in that scene," Rob says, unlocking the door to our villa. "I wish I could see her face when she hears about it."

My insides chill a little, and it's not just from the cool AC in the room. What if our relationship really isn't about us? What if it's still about Rob and his vengeance?

"Once this is all over," I say, biting my lip because I'm scared to ask the question on the tip of my tongue. But I need to know the answer. "What will happen to us?"

Rob steps closer to me, not bothering to turn the lights on. "You know what I want to happen?" he asks, his voice whispering in my ear, sending a chill down my spine.

"What?" I whisper back because this feels like a moment meant for only the two of us to hear. A secret that even the walls shouldn't know.

"I don't want us to end. I want to wake up every morning, day after day, to your beautiful face. To kiss you," his lips trail across mine like a ghost at midnight, "the moment you open your eyes and then again as you close them. To hold you and never let go."

Heat sears through my veins, fire bursting through me. I surrender to his kisses, letting his lips trail down my neck and along my shoulders.

"Yes," I say in a breathless gasp. "That is what I want, too."

His hands glide down my waist, and he pulls me closer so our bodies are pressed together like they were meant to be. My heart thrums like the wings of a hummingbird, beating with passion. This is the kind of love I've been seeking. This is what I've been searching for all my life.

"Do you want me to stop?" he finally asks, pulling away to take in my expression. "Because we don't have to do this. I can sleep on the floor."

"Who said we're going to be sleeping?" I tease.

"Or the bathtub," he continues, nodding to the massive bathroom down the hallway. "It's large enough. I measured it."

I lightly punch him. He pretends to be wounded.

"You can't get away with acting like you're hurt. I know what you do for a living."

"Were you impressed?" He gives me a cheeky smile. "Because if you were impressed with that, wait until I show you what else I can do."

Now my face is in flames. "Wow. How can I say no to that? But in all seriousness, yes, I do want this. I know a lot of our relationship has been about pretending, but for me it was more real than anything I've ever done. I want us."

"I was hoping that was your answer. Because come to find out, bathtub surfaces are rather cold and hard."

I laugh and he kisses my hand, sending another wave of tingles through me.

He guides me out onto the private balcony that hangs over the ocean's edge. Stars glitter above us as he kisses me once again, this time softer and yet also deeper. Like he wants to drag out time so it becomes ours to do what we wish with it.

My fears wash away as I sink into his embrace and let love unfold between us.

CHAPTER 61

Movie Star Path

THE PRICE OF FAME

The next morning comes all too soon. We only got a few hours of sleep before it was time for Rob to head back to the set. Thankfully, Rob ordered room service, allowing us a few extra minutes to relax.

"After all this is over," Rob says, pouring himself a coffee to go, "I'm taking you far away from everyone and we're going to spend quality time together, just the two of us. No media. No cameras. And definitely no Tiasters."

I laugh and kiss him. He groans. "You make it so difficult to go to work," he tells me, grabbing at the hem of my shirt while I'm trying to pull on my jeans. "You're coming with me."

"Absolutely, but you've got to let me wear my pants or the media won't leave us alone."

"Fine, fine, put on some pants if you must."

As much as I don't want Rob to work, when we step out of the hotel, I'm still on a high from last night. A large mob of paparazzi is outside, waiting for us, but like a pro, I slip on my sunglasses and prepare to barrel my way to the limo waiting for us.

"I'm dreadfully sorry about the crowds," the car service attendant apologizes to us. "I've called the police. They should be here any moment to deal with the situation."

A woman who was sitting off to the side, filing her nails, leaps to her feet, whipping out a microphone from her purse. "Excuse me, Scarlett Walker."

"Well, that was a tricky move I've yet to see," Rob says, but he grabs my hand and makes to leave.

Except the woman follows us. "When were you planning on breaking off your fake engagement with Robby Ricci?"

This stops me in my tracks. "What?" I know I need to keep walking, but my heart is starting to thump against my chest.

"The deal you made with Rob," she continues, and now it's Rob's turn to freeze and slowly turn around. "Where he offers you work and you pretend to be his fiancée."

A lump forms in my throat, my mouth stuffed with cotton. I don't know what to say. The crowd has swarmed to circle us, vultures picking apart their prey.

"Where did you hear that lie?" Rob asks gruffly.

"From your fiancée." The nail filer beams like she's delivering the news of the century.

"I could sue you for slander," Rob says.

"Is it true that Scarlett got a speaking part in the movie because she's offering you favors?" another reporter asks, leaping into the fray.

Dizziness washes over me. Camera lights are flashing. Microphones are being jammed in my face.

"That's another lie," Rob says. "One of the extras got sick and Scarlett took her place."

"These aren't lies," Nail Filer says. She holds up her phone and starts playing a blurry night clip. "It's all over social media where she admits that pretending to be your lover is starting to get too hard."

"And you believe everything you see on social media?" Rob asks. "Scarlett and I are loyal to each other."

But my eyes laser on Nail Filer's phone. There's something familiar about what she's showing me. And then it hits me—it's a recording of me at the pool last night talking to Bella! Sure, it's a little blurry and dark, but I recognize the setting right away.

Terror streaks through me. I need to get out of here away from the paparazzi and cameras. I need to see what is being posted and what damning words I said. There's only one option for me—flee.

So I take off back into the safety of the hotel, but when I step inside the lobby, I'm met with another group of people who were apparently hopeful I'd do exactly what I did.

"Scarlett Walker, why did you make that deal with Robby Ricci?"

"Is the ring you're wearing fake, too?"

"Do you think Tianna Ulci and Rob will get back together now?"

I dart through the crowd just as security arrives, which gives me the chance to break away and slip outside to our room.

"Scarlett!" Rob's voice calls after me, but I run the rest of the way back.

The moment I'm back in the seclusion of our room, my fingers tap nervously on my phone. A quick search and I find the video Nail File was talking about. Actually, one of many. The internet is drowning in various forms of the video.

Heart pounding, I press play just as Rob comes into the room. But I can't look at him, my eyes are riveted to the screen as I watch myself talking on the phone telling Bella how Rob's and my engagement is fake and it was all a deal.

But I cringe when I hear myself saying, *Pretending is becoming so hard. I don't know if I can keep up the lying and acting.*

"What is this?" Rob asks. "Is that you in the video?"

It's obviously me. Whoever filmed this video was clearly hiding in the bushes. I suck in a deep breath, clamping a hand over my forehead. "I remember hearing something in the bushes. I thought it was an animal."

"Wait," Rob says. "That *is* you?"

I hear myself saying on the video, "It's all starting to feel weird."

"It feels weird?" Rob's face twists. "I thought... I guess I thought... Damn... I don't know what to think."

"Rob," I say quickly. "It's not how this looks. I was talking to my sister. I was second-guessing things because I didn't know where you stood with the two of us."

Rob points to the timestamp on the video. "This was recorded last night."

"That was before I went to the studio." I cover my face, shock and anger and resentment raging through me. "I can't believe someone filmed me."

"Of course someone filmed you! That's the way things are. Everything you do, I do. The world is always watching. Damn it, Scarlett. Why did you say that at the pool? Why did you say that at all?"

His face is twisted with anger, jaw tight as if holding in a myriad of emotions. But it's the pain in his eyes that kills me. He thinks I really was only here for the fake relationship.

"You have to believe me that I don't feel that way now," I

say. "I was just going through a tough time, worrying if I could deal with everything."

"Obviously you didn't deal with it well." He throws his hands in the air. "Now Tia can rub it all in my face. Plus, they're going to think I got you that speaking line because you slept with me."

"That's the thing. All you can keep talking about is Tia this and what will Tia think about that. It's because of her I'm worried about our relationship. We haven't known each other that long when you think about it. How do I know that you're not using me to get her jealous and win her back?"

"You think I want Tia back?" He laughs, a bit hysterically. "Hardly."

"You're right, I shouldn't have told my sister those things by the pool. I thought I was alone, but I was obviously an idiot to think that. But this has also shown me what's between us isn't strong enough to weather the storms ahead of us."

I bite my lip, waiting for him to respond. He runs a palm over his face and takes a deep breath before walking over to the balcony and staring out at the sea.

"I trusted you." He hangs his head. "I don't know how to deal with this."

"Don't worry." I grab my suitcase and fill it with my clothes. "I'm going to leave so your problem can disappear. You can tell the press whatever you want. I'm not going to cause you any problems."

"Don't leave," he says in a low voice, but he doesn't move from the window.

"It's for the best." I snap my suitcase closed. "We both know that. It was fun while it lasted."

No, it wasn't fun. He had become my everything. My beginning and what I hoped to be my future.

"I'll email you the details of your movie launch campaign," I say. "I think it's best we communicate solely by email from now on."

He nods, but his whole body is still stiff as a board. I turn and practically run out of the room before I burst into tears. I find a secluded place to book my flight out of Fiji and then duck out of the staff entrance rather than the front doors of the hotel.

When the taxi comes to pick me up, I order myself to not look back. I cry the whole way to the airport.

CHAPTER 62

Movie Star Path

THE PREMIERE OF SHADOW HUNTER

6 Months Later

It all still feels like a dream. The romantic escape to Fiji. Acting in a movie. A magical engagement.

But it was all one big, fat lie.

I take another swig of coffee and settle in to finish up the last promo reel for Rob. Despite our sour breakup and the cruel messages that poured onto my social media, causing me to switch my accounts to private, working with Rob on his promotional tour for the movie has been a dream. It's a job I realize I'm very good at. Plus, I enjoy showcasing the person behind a project.

The biggest negative is I have to watch and stare at Rob's face, listening to his voice all day long. If there was something awful about him, it would make all of this a whole lot easier. For the past six months, we've been in this weird and awkward

373

relationship where we're business partners, professional and polite.

Except, all I can think about is how much I love his endearing accent, how he listens to me and believes in me like no one else has ever done before, and the kindness he always shows me. I miss his winks and those passionate kisses trailing down my neck. I miss curling up beside him and chatting with him, not just about my deepest insecurities but also about trivial things like whether or not I should get a dog or a cat.

STOP THINKING ABOUT HIM! I scream at myself, and yet, my hand instinctively goes to my ring finger that once held the engagement ring I sent back to him.

The worst part is that tonight's the premiere of his movie, *Shadow Hunter*. Maybe after it's over and my work with Rob is finished, I'll finally be able to move on from him. My mind drifts, wondering what he'll be doing tonight. Who will he be walking the red carpet with? How will he be celebrating afterward? The producers were asking him to be pictured with Tianna and he agreed purely to fulfill his contract obligations. It makes perfect sense, but deep down the whole situation makes me feel like throwing up. Actually, ever since I left Fiji, I've felt awful. Like I left behind a part of me and now my heart feels empty and achy.

Bella rushes into the room, her eyes wide. "There's a man here at the door. He says he has a message for you."

"Can you pretend you're me?" I ask. "I really need to finish this last piece and get it off to Rob. It's the last thing I have for him and then I won't have to look at his beautiful face anymore."

"I think you're going to want to come to the door," Bella says, wringing her hands.

Curious, I send off the last press document and head out

into Grams's living room to the front door. Standing there is a man dressed in a black uniform with white gloves. He's holding a letter on a pillow. Behind him, a limo waits in the street.

"Are you Scarlett Walker?" the man asks.

"Yes," I say tentatively.

"Then this is for you." He holds out the pillow to me.

I rip open the envelope and read the letter.

Scarlett,

I've been thinking a lot about how I ended things with you. I was stupid and an idiot and I want to officially apologize. Every day apart from you is worse than the last. You and I were the best thing ever and I ruined that by putting the blame on you for my idea to do the fake relationship.

Please let me make it up to you. I want you to come to the movie premiere. You had a speaking part that actually made it into the movie and with all the extra hours you've put into this promotional project, you deserve to have fun. Don't do it for me, do it for you.

Always yours,
Rob

"Oh my gosh!" Bella exclaims. I turn to find she was reading the letter over my shoulder. "You totally have to go!"

"I can't go." I bite my lip, staring at the words *always yours*. "I mean, I don't have anything to wear and it starts in a few hours."

"It's in LA," Bella reminds me. "They're three hours behind us."

"Rob said if you hesitated," the gloved man adds and pulls another letter from his pocket, "I should give you this."

THE LIMO IS TAKING you to a plane. When you land, you'll be chauffeured to a boutique where you can pick any dress you want.

No excuses.
Rob

"ANY DRESS YOU WANT!" Bella squeals. "Go do this. Have your fairytale moment. You certainly deserve it."

"You know what?" I clutch the letter to my chest. "I think I will."

"Good!" Bella hugs me. "Now go have some fun and enjoy yourself."

I grab my purse and sweater and then hug Bella. "Tell Grams goodbye for me, okay?" And then before I know it, I'm on my way to the premiere of *Shadow Hunter*.

The private airplane ride still feels a bit surreal as I take the trip, except this time I'm riding alone. It's a great experience but without Rob, it's missing all the magic. When I arrive at Hollywood Fashion Boutique, I'm greeted by a hostess who hands me a refreshing glass of juice and escorts me to a velvet chair. She showcases different dresses, a stunning mix of sequins, chiffon, and tight black leather. I pick a few I like and then try them on, finally landing on a sequined emerald dress since it accents my hair. While they make the alterations, I'm brought over to have my hair and makeup done.

By the time they're finished with me, I hardly recognize myself. I look like a girl who stepped out of a fashion magazine rather than a marketing expert with frazzled hair and wrinkled clothes.

"You look magnificent," the owner of the shop tells me after I thank the staff for the transformation. "A car is waiting for you outside to take you to the premiere. Have an incredible time!"

When I slip inside the car, I feel like a princess. In fact, everything is perfect except I'm missing the one thing I really want.

Rob.

It's then I realize I'm always going to feel a little empty without him in my life. Planes, beautiful dresses, and fancy cars will never be able to come close to filling the void inside of me.

The car rolls up to a private building and the driver opens the door for me. I step outside, looking around. "Is this the entrance to the premiere?" I ask.

Rob stands a few feet in front of me. He looks immaculate in his tuxedo and hair styled to perfection. A wave of dizziness washes over me, and I suck in a breath, startled at how much my body yearns for him. How much I've missed him. All our work together these last six months has been virtual.

"Hey," I say.

"I'm so glad you came." In three strides, he's in front of me, taking my hands. "You look stunning. Then again, you could look stunning in a burlap tunic."

"A burlap tunic?" I laugh despite myself.

"I wanted to apologize in person. It was wrong of me to place the blame of our fake engagement on you. You had no idea some creeper would be stalking you in the bushes and videoing you on vacation. You have every right to tell your sister whatever you want. I completely overacted."

"I appreciate you saying that. I wish I could go back and undo what I said. I made it a mess for us."

"No, you reminded me once again I need to stop letting my insecurities dictate my life. I need to open the door to my heart and my life and let you in." He lets out a big breath. "I wanted to tell you all of this in person, not over the phone. Now that we're both here in the same country and I'm done filming and promoting the movie, I've had time to think about what a jerk I've been. I did it all wrong and believed a lie."

"I thought I could just leave and pick up my life where I left it, except it's been so hard. Everything is hard without you. I've missed you."

"I'm so glad to hear that because I've found it impossible to live life without you. Also, I did a little investigating of my own. Turns out it was Tia who was videoing you in the bushes. I had the resort staff pull up their security footage and they sent me a copy."

He pulls out his phone and plays a video of her sneaking around the pool area and the bushes in a black suit. It would've been impossible to see her face except she decided to climb over a wall that was lit up with video footage.

"I'm shocked," I say. "I always thought she was so refined. I never thought she'd stoop so low."

"We totally caught her in the act," Rob says, chuckling.

"You're not going to leak that, are you?"

"As much as I want to, I'm going to be the better man in this situation. Instead, I want to focus on you tonight. The reason why I brought you here wasn't just so you could watch the premiere, but I was wondering if you'd be my date."

"Your real date or your fake date?" I can't help but tease.

"Real all the way."

And then we're kissing each other as if we never stopped

being in love. Deep down, I know we're going to be okay. In fact, I think we're going to be more than okay.

Rob escorts me back to the car I was riding in and the driver takes off just as the sun dips below the horizon. The streets light up, glitzy and bright as if they're celebrating our reunion. Finally, we pull up to a theater where a long crimson carpet is rolled out before us, lined with photographers and videographers.

"Are you ready for this?" he asks.

"As long as we're in this together."

He kisses me again. "Always." Then he opens the door, and holding my hand, we walk down the red carpet.

Lights are flashing and microphones are thrust into our faces as reporters ask their shocked questions.

"Are you two back together?"

"Is this a fake relationship again or the real thing?"

"We saw some video footage that Tianna Ulci was the one who filmed you," another says. "Did you have anything to do with that?"

Rob stops before *Shadow Hunter*'s big screen where the others before us posed for photos for the media. But instead of posing, Rob looks out at the group.

"To answer some of your questions," he begins. "Yes, we are here together. No, it's not fake. In fact, it really never was fake. I don't have any comments to share about my co-star or her bizarre antics, but I do have something very important to do."

He gets on his knee and holds my hand. My breath escapes and my eyes widen.

"What are you doing?" I ask.

He grins a wicked smile and pulls out a velvet box from his

pocket. He opens it, revealing the most beautiful ring—the oval cut ring set on a band of twisted vines. My favorite.

"Scarlett," he says, loud enough for all the cameras to hear, "I messed up our first engagement, but that's okay because I had a thing or two to learn about true love. Will you give me a second chance? I'm madly in love with you, and I want to spend the rest of my life showing you how much I love you. You make my life complete in ways I never knew was possible. Will you marry me?"

I stare down at him, my heart full of love for him. "Yes. The answer is definitely yes."

He slips the ring on my finger and then kisses me soundly.

I've found my happily ever after.

~

IF YOU ENJOYED THIS STORY, I'd appreciate it if you'd leave a review. Tell me what your favorite path was!

~

WOULD you like to read the bonus scene showing Jaxon's proposal to Scarlett? *Go to ChristinaFarley.com/romantic-adventures*

~

DON'T WANT the fun to end? Take the journey of love with Bella in FAIRY TALE BOOKSHOP, a modern retelling of Beauty and the Beast. Note: This story uses the Wolf Path as Scarlett's happily ever after.

Book Club Questions

1. Which path was your favorite and why?
2. If you were Scarlett, which character would you choose? Why?
3. What is your favorite fairy tale mentioned in the book?
4. If you traveled the Fairy Tale Road in real life, what stops would you take?
5. How did Scarlett's choices affect her future? Which one did you relate to the most?
6. Did your opinion of the three paths change as you read each one?

Visit ChristinaFarley.com/romantic-adventures *for the complete Fairytale Book Club Kit.*

<h1 style="text-align:center">Your Next Adventure</h1>

The Immortal Bound Series: A contemporary romantasy full of supernatural thrills and mystery.

The Dreamscape Series: A thrilling near-future adventure where your dreams are no longer safe.

The Gilded Series: A contemporary fantasy set in Korea.

Choose Your Happily Ever After Series: You get to choose your fairy tale ending in each book in this romantic comedy series.

About the Author

CHRISTINA FARLEY writes romantic fantasy and thrilling adventures inspired by her travels. When not wandering the world or creating imaginary ones, she spends time with her family in Florida where they are busy preparing for the next World Cup, baking cheesecakes, and raising a pet dragon in disguise as a very furry cat.

Visit her online:
ChristinaFarley.com
Instagram: @ChristinaLFarley
Facebook: @ChristinaFarleyAuthor
YouTube: @ChristinaFarley
TikTok: @ChristinaFarleyAuthor

Join Christina's Newsletter, the Travelogue: Exclusive access to videos, book updates, giveaways:
https://tinyurl.com/ypb9pm9a

Stay In Touch

I hope you'll stay in touch by joining my newsletter group, The Travelogue, or Keepers of the Realms so we can continue to take more adventures together. If you sign up, you'll receive a free book as my way of saying you're awesome.

Christina's Newsletter, The Travelogue: Reader news, writing tips, giveaways, and book updates: www.ChristinaFarley.com

Christina's Keepers of the Realms: Join Christina's VIP Reader Club called the Keepers of the Realm. This community is designed for passionate readers like you to not only dive deeper into my stories but also help spread the magic of my books. Gain exclusive content, have a say in my worlds, and join the monthly giveaway! https://dashboard.mailerlite.com/forms/1319551/147882278724306162/share

Acknowledgments

The idea for this book started long ago when we took a family trip to Germany. While there, I heard about the Fairy Tale Road and how the different cities celebrated the Grimm fairy tales. I was so inspired by the castles, customs, fairy tales, and foods that I knew a book would be born from that trip.

Fast forward to a date night when my husband and I were watching *Choose Love*. I'd already brainstormed the characters, locations and concepts for *Fairy Tale Road* so when my husband told me that I needed to write a book in that same choose-your-own-ending style, I couldn't resist. And I did it! This story was be so much fun to write in that format. I loved being able to let go and not take anything too seriously. Sometimes we need things in our lives like that!

A special thanks goes out to my Keeper of the Realm Group: Laura P, Mila C, Beth G, Andrea M, Ava M, Kendra P, Laziz T, Ana B, Amanda F, Jennifer A, Aziza E, Marisela Z, Eva M, Jenny H, Christina V, Amber J, Shana D, Kelli J, Bert B, Dianna B, Tez M, Bri L, Candi M, Julianne J, Amy P, Kris D, Sheree W, Jamie G, Jan W, Stephanie B, Ells, Heath W, Willa Z, Jerry N, Kate H, Joyce K, Tiffany L, Vivi B, Alison R, Callie T, Sarah W, Sunny B, Finely T, Margaret T, Billy F, Jocelyn M, Laziza T, Merry M, Megan B, Susan L, Emily I, Yvonne V, JB, Theresa L, Adalyn B, Jamie, Christy S, Jennifer J, Susan L, Megan L, Jasmine B, Lolly G, Theresa L, Bonnie M, Maria V,

Monica, Kristian B, Michael E, Ashley S, Megan B, Misty P, Kat M, Ella H, and Lolly G. You all are the best!

Thank you to Books and Moods for the adorable cover. You captured the essence of the story so well.

Thank you to my copyeditor, Sarah Ward. This manuscript was a tricky one with so many storylines and alternative endings.

Thank you to Amy Parker and Vivi Barnes for encouraging me to write this story. I was so nervous about writing a book in this format and you both were like, "You can do this!" I guess you can now say you were right.

I'm incredibly grateful to my crit partners, Janice Hardy and Sarah McGuire, for your brainstorming sessions and edits. They were invaluable! It's always so fun developing stories with you.

To Kadance and Kayleigh: Thank you for all of your support and brainstorming ideas with me. You are both the best!

To my boys, Caleb and Luke. I will never forget drinking hot chocolate and pastries with you while we explored castles in Germany. Here's to more adventures!

To my husband, Doug, my ultimate book boyfriend. I'd choose your path in every universe.